ALSO BY AURORA STEINHART

Checked and Balanced

Book One in

"The Lady and The Stag"

A hockey romance experiment

where we meet Tiana and Gunnar

for the first time.

Check or Treat

Book Two in

"The Lady and The Stag"

A fall-inspired hockey romance sequel

following Gunnar and Tiana as they navigate

life together.

Elevated Ambitions

Book One in

The "Up in the Air" Series

A contemporary billionaire romance

where SHE is the billionaire.

Hunted By Fate

Book One in

"A Gown of Leather and Bone"

A dark, romantic fantasy ft. a succubus general and a human hunter
on a mission to save their world from the terrors outside of their
wards.

Merry Checkmas

Aurora Steinhart

Page edge design by Painted Wings Publishing

First edition: 2025

Print ISBN 13: 979-8-9914855-7-9

 Formatted with Vellum

MERRY CHECKMAS

AURORA STEINHART

PLAYLIST

I LISTEN TO SO MUCH DAMN MUSIC WHEN I
WRITE. UNFORTUNATELY, I'M NOT ABLE TO
CATALOGUE IT ALL HERE. IT WOULD JUST BE
SO MANY PAGES. SO NOW I HAVE RESORTED TO
QR CODES FOR SUCH THINGS.
ANYWAY.
ENJOY THIS HORRIFICALLY CHAOTIC PLAYLIST
FOR MERRY CHECKMAS. IT'S A MESS. JUST
LIKE ME AND JUST LIKE THIS BOOK.
BUT I THINK WE KNOW BY NOW THAT AURORA
DOESN'T DO ORGANIZED. IT'S ALWAYS A MESS
OVER HERE AND THAT'S HOW WE LIKE IT.
DON'T WE, GIRLS? 😉

PLAY BY PLAY
THE SPICY CHAPTER LIST

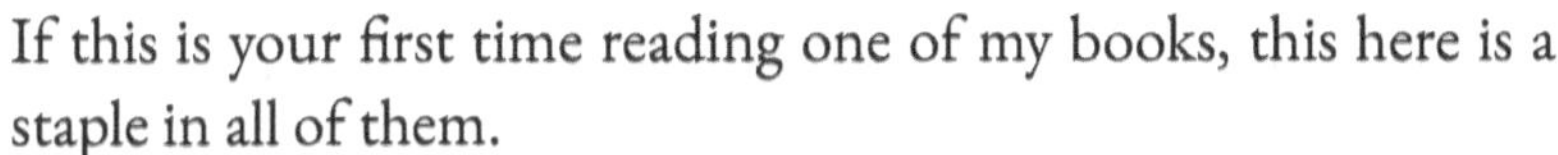

If this is your first time reading one of my books, this here is a staple in all of them.

They go by different names.

<u>"Table of Cuntents"</u> in **Elevated Ambitions**
<u>"Cock Docket"</u> in **Hunted by Fate**
<u>"Play by Play"</u> in **CAB and COT**
(shameless self-rec, this is my book I can do those things here)

It's a little list of all the spicy chapters in this book. That way you can either go read them, because you're a horny degenerate like me.

Or you can skip them.

But I reckon if you're picking up this book, I doubt you're here to skip the spicy scenes.

So without further ado, here are all the smutty little scenes your heart desires in one neat little package.

- Chapter Two
- Chapter Five
- Chapter Seven
- Chapter Thirteen
- Chapter Eighteen
- Chapter Nineteen
- Chapter Twenty-One
- Chapter Twenty-Four
- Chapter Twenty-Seven
- Chapter Twenty-Nine
- Chapter Thirty-Four
- Chapter Thirty-Eight

Sad. Alright.

We're getting fucking *sad*, because we're approaching territory that hits a little too close to home for me and a little close to some others as well.

And if this book is some outlet of healing for me, then so be it.

For those of you who were unaware, once upon a time, romance, love, all of those things, they didn't entice me.

Never cared for romance movies, didn't care for romance in general because I've been hurt. To me... love was a waste of time.

I know we all have been hurt. But I still carry some of those wounds with me. Some of them haven't healed.

Some I don't think ever will.

But, when you have been in a compromised emotional position, through formative years of your life, with pattern recognition, and the reactionary tendencies of a dog.

You tend to... cower, in the face of perceived threats.

Tiana is strong. We know that. We love her for it.

But now that Tiana is realizing things, there are insecurities and fears that have begun to surface, when she faces the threat of emotional damage (in her eyes).

You think irrationally, you act irrationally, you try to preserve happiness by avoiding the pain.

For individuals like Tiana, (and me), you could tell us one thing, but if we pick up on another. Sometimes, you could do everything right. But if there is one small pattern... one thing out of place that signals in our brains something is amiss.

We will react.

We will get scared, we will ruminate and it will eat at us until we can't handle it. We will cower, because the idea of a pain like that is much worse than the reality of the situation. What's the term? Snowballing?

Spiraling?

Regardless,

pattern recognition, it surely is a fickle beast.

And unfortunately, it happens to be most effective, in the most heartbreaking ways.

That being said, Tiana may panic over some things, see the way things happen and react... differently.

But unlike you, or me... Tiana gets the... response, that sometimes I wish I could have had.

A reassurance that sometimes I've dreamed of.

Tiana is an undiagnosed autistic. Low supports needs. If you needed me to tell you this, then you haven't read any of the other books.

She processes differently. She picks up on different things. She works differently.

Your response, is not Tiana's. And Tiana's response, is not yours.

Most people would think, "Why would she do that?"

Because **Tiana. Works. Differently.**

That's the whole point of the story.

So please.

Give Tiana some grace. Her entire life she's been burned, and Gunnar is trying to put out the fire.

And a blaze like that takes time and care to douse completely.

Healing is not linear. And neither is love.

Another warning I have is that if you have struggled with infertility, this one may sting a little. While what Tiana goes through doesn't technically qualify as infertility, her eagerness to get pregnant and the doubts that accompany it can bring about the same emotions.

Tiana finds the disappointment of getting her period draining, and she wants to give Gunnar this thing he wants. Which leaves her feeling inadequate. Even if Gunnar tells her she is everything he's ever needed, she still feels those things.

And so I need to remind you, the reader, that if you have faced these same circumstances, that you are not less than. It has never been your fault, and you are more worthy than anything you could imagine.

Take care of yourself, and if it becomes too much, **_please put yourself first._**

ALLLLLLRIGHTY, SO IF YOU'RE HERE TO THE END, AND YOU AREN'T SOBBING, LET ME SWITCH GEARS.

At the time of writing this specific part of this disclaimer, I'm currently at Chapter 26 of the first draft.

Anyway, I realized there was a whole lotta fawkin' goin' on, so I decided to get some of the spicy chapters written down in the play-by-play.... Uhhhhh as of right now, 50% into the first draft, we're lookin' at...

8 Spicy Chapters... and there will surely be more.

SO. UH. I suppose now is a good time to warn you that uh, just a whole lotta sex, is happening here.

They are trying to have a baby, so like, come on, that makes sense, give me a break, I like writing their scenes, they're both just so hot, I can't. ANYWAYYYYYYYYYY.

There's a whole bunch of fuckin' so, I don't know. BUT... but... but but... some of them are important to part of their... what's the word?

...Situation??

Healing??? Relationship?? I don't fucking know, okay?

But there are things that happen, during which, that lead to other things and so on and so forth.

So as always, you are more than welcome to skip the spicy scenes, it's your life, not mine. Just know that some things are... said–or better yet, not said–that lead to other things later in the story, that is somewhat integral to the growth of this couple.

ANNNYYYWAAAYYYYY.

Without further adeiu, let's jump back into Tiana and Gunnar, and make our way one book closer to Gunnar's daddy era.

ENJOY THE RIDE DEGENS.

CHAPTER ONE
TIANA

The wind ripping through my hair is the greatest thing I've felt in a *while*, especially when it's combined with the knowledge that I'm running through land that belongs to *us*.

I could barely believe what I read on the paper. With a small map at the bottom of the page, highlighting what's ours.

Well, technically, it's Gunnar's land, since we aren't married. But he bought it for *us*.

I don't know why I've run off the edge of the ridge and straight into the woods.

Right now, it feels like the only thing I can do to express the way I feel. The excitement feels like so much to experience that all I want to do is *run*.

Because for once, my excitement isn't coming with fear. It comes with elation, it comes without questions, and it comes without "what-ifs."

That in and of itself is a reason for celebration.

Once I've run across the field, past the lake and into the

trees, I dip and dive through the low branches, pushing deeper into the forest.

My feet pound harder, and I'm sincerely thankful Charlotte lent me her cowboy boots as I bound over logs and the underbrush that covers the forest floor. My breath heaves in and out of me in puffs of white steam as I push myself faster. The trees whiz past my line of sight until I can see the creek up ahead that rests inside the woods.

Twigs and branches snap behind me as Gunnar closes in, along with his heavy breaths and grunts as I slide to a stop right at the creek's edge.

With more heaving breaths, my gaze roams over the crystal-clear water of the creek for only a moment before I jump it, running farther. An excited smile pulls at my lips when I know I'm getting closer to the stump; with the anticipation damn near choking me.

Soon, my legs ache and my chest burns from the influx of cool, damp forest air, and I halt in the middle of the woods, right before the stump.

The air in this part of the woods is so fresh and crisp, especially because of fall. And the vibrant sound of the birds chirping, with the dappled sunlight that filters through the leaves, only pushes my happiness higher.

My arms fling out at my sides as I inhale a deep breath and spin in place, relishing this part of the forest.

It's absolutely beautiful in here. Secluded, quiet... *breathtaking.*

This land is ours. This *space* is ours.

It's away from the city, away from eyes, away from the ones that don't matter.

And Charlotte... is just right *there.*

I stop my turn, landing on the sight of Gunnar in the trees, who has an exhausted smile plastered on his face as he stops his pursuit to admire me and my happiness.

He braces a hand against a tree as he gulps air, his other hand on his hip as he watches me in warm exasperation.

A soft sheen of sweat is laid on his brow, with a drip running down the side of his face. Soon, his tongue darts out to swipe his lower lip as he watches me.

"You have an advantage in the woods, you know?" he says with a worn-out chuckle.

He maneuvers himself over the logs blocking this area of the wood, stepping over them and ducking under low branches.

"Oh yeah? Why's that?" I ask through a breathless smile.

"Well, you're smaller. You don't have to duck and dive as much as I do," he says as he comes up beside me.

My gaze roams around the forest, up at the tree canopy, before it floats back down to the forest floor, only to land on Gunnar and the way he watches me.

Gunnar leans over to press his lips softly to my forehead before he moves behind me. Wrapping his arms around my shoulders, he rests his chin on the top of my head as he rocks us from side to side.

I can't even decipher the warmth filling me.

Land, right beside my sister, closer to my parents. And all *ours*. Where the stars will shine bright above us. All this land is for him, Tucker and me.

All because he knew that there would be no house I'd settle for.

I turn around in his arms, his face blurring against the happy tears filling my eyes as I look up at him.

"It's ours," I murmur softly.

He nods. "All for us, sugar," he says with a smile and a tilt of his head. His hand comes up to caress my cheek.

"You... are far too good for me, Gunnar Hayze," I respond with a deep, steeling breath.

"I don't think I'll ever be good enough for you, Tiana Dawn," he whispers as he presses a lock of hair behind my ear.

"When do we get to start?" I ask as my happy tears run dry and my mood shifts to excitement.

I... I get to build a fucking *house*. I get to *plan* building a house!

This is even better than planning a wedding.

My heart beats harder at the realization of it all. The rush of planning zooms through me so fast that I feel it through all my fingers and all my toes, like a live wire almost.

The external parts of the house, the layouts, the rooms, the crown moldings! I get to design a kitchen, and an office and my library! It'll be everything I've ever dreamed of and m-

He laughs softly, pulling me from my reverie. "Hold your horses there, sweet pea. There's a lot that has to be done before we can hire contractors. There are a lot of trees that have to be cleared out. We have to get the foundation poured. And *you* have to make sure you're staying on top of your health, as well as your job. So don't go too crazy," he says with a small tap to my nose.

I groan. "Gunnar!"

"Nope. Don't give me that. You know the deal; you know the priorities. *You* are the priority right now. You can create as many Pinterest boards as you would like. But you can't plan shit until the other things are squared away. The only thing you can plan and create is where you would like to have the house placed. Then, Banks and I will take care of the trees and foundation," he says.

My eyes narrow at him as my arms cross against my chest. "This is rude, you know," I murmur.

"I'm aware. But I'm not letting you pull out the whiteboard just yet. You'll have your time. It's not now, though," he says with a small smile as he presses a kiss to my forehead.

I fight the smile that tries to tug at the corner of my mouth as I glare playfully at him and turn back around to the land, surveying it to get *some* kind of idea on where I want to set up the house.

"I don't want all the trees taken down. I want the house hidden in the forest. And you don't touch the creek," I say as I press a finger into his chest.

"10-4, sugar," he says with a warm grin.

I turn around to lean my back against his chest, taking a deep breath as I look up at the tree-covered sky. Because I am still trying to grasp the fact that... holy shit, we're going to have a house here.

Something that he and I created together, not just his or mine. It's something we share.

With the apartments, there is still an area of separation. His apartment, my apartment, even if we sleep in one or the other.

"It's our space," I whisper as I tilt my head back against his chest with a smile.

His head tilts as he looks down at me, almost confused. "Yes? It is," he says.

"No, it's *ours*. Not just my place, or yours. It's *ours*. Something that we make together, *build* together," I say as I turn around to grasp his hands.

He smiles as his eyes move to our hands, before his tighten around my own.

"It is, sugar," he says softly. His smile melts, dripping with love and adoration as he gazes at me.

"What made you do this?" I ask.

He watches me for a moment, admiring my happiness before his eyes track around the forest. His gaze moves around the trees, lingering on the stump and surrounding logs before moving up toward the sun in the leaves.

"I had to. There wasn't another option that would be good enough for you," he says with a small shrug as he looks back down at me.

I smile at that, at him.

At the brightness in the trees, and at the brightness in the future that lies ahead.

Eventually, we make it back to the ranch house, where Charlotte and Adrian are in the paddock with the horses.

Waffle and Tucker are curled around one another on the porch. Granted, Tucker is basically a circle of black fur wrapped around Waffle with his head tucked in her neck.

The sight is sweet as it is strange, considering how excited Tucker gets when he knows we're coming out here.

Parking the ATV by the stables, Gunnar hops off the back and removes his helmet before he offers a hand out to help me off. I take my helmet off and together we walk to the stables to put them back on their hooks, where he looks at me with a warm smile as he throws an arm over my shoulders and we walk back out to the wooden fence.

Charlotte stands on one of the lower rails, watching Adrian ride Chauncey inside the fence, but as she hears us approach, she squirms and titters with excitement.

"Congratulations, Ti!" she says with a grin as she throws her arms around me in a hug.

A small smile ghosts across my face, and I pat her back softly.

"Thanks. I'm kind of excited that I get to live so close to you," I say.

She pulls away and tilts her head lovingly at me. "When Gunnar asked, I told him he just had to! It's not far, and I know how much you love the stars," she says.

My smile widens, and I nod in agreement before I come to stand on the wooden fence rail beside her.

Gunnar comes beside me, but because he's so tall, he just places his arms over the top railing, flicking his foot behind him to steady himself.

"Didn't realize you were such an amazing rider!" Gunnar calls out to Adrian, but he has a smug grin on his face.

"Shut your trap, Hayze," Adrian calls back before Chauncey trots past us. As he does, Adrian brings a hand down to swipe at Gunnar's head. The loud *thwack* echoes through the valley, and I can't help the giggle that forces out of me as Gunnar rubs his head.

"Ow," he grumbles.

It's hard to believe that this will be a place we'll be frequenting more often. It's... *exciting*. A new chapter, a new page, one with a multitude of promises.

Gunnar moves behind me, wrapping his arms around my waist, adding some stability to where I stand on the fence. I relieve some of my weight, leaning back into him a bit, and his hands come up to rub softly on my stomach.

I look down at where his large hands cover my belly, placing my hand on top of his and sighing.

After last month, I'm hoping all our efforts before now and anything coming up will be *it*.

I didn't think it'd be so discouraging. But there's also the feeling that I'm being a bit more dramatic than I need to be. We've really only been *actually* trying to make a baby for a month, and I've had one period.

That really isn't enough time for things to happen, especially after having a hormonal IUD for so long.

But it still sucks... mostly because of the visions and the daydreams that constantly rock through my skull. And when he rubs my tummy, it makes me feel like he's rubbing where our child *should* be.

I know he does it out of habit, that it's just something he dreams about too.

Still.

I lean more of my weight into him before he grasps harder around my waist. Soon, he tilts me back, shifting my weight so that he can hook an arm under my knees and carry me off.

I rest my head on his chest, smiling at him as he brings me inside the ranch house.

CHAPTER TWO

GUNNAR

I don't think I could have paid for a better reaction from Tiana when it came to showing her the land. I also don't know if I will ever see her run that fast again.

I'm just glad I got to see her reaction in real time.

There was the most incredible feeling that welled in my chest to watch her live out this sense of childlike wonder. To run through the forest—a place where we would build our home.

And now I can't wait. I can't wait to see what the future will look like for us. I've learned that I have to be careful when it comes to telling Tiana things and what our plans are. Only because her mind runs so fast. If I plant a seed, that thing will take off and take *over*. I can't have that for her; not when she really needs to focus on herself. I know that planning makes her happy, and I know that building the house will make her even happier. But I also know how her mind moves. So, treading with caution is my best play here.

Those thoughts keep me company as I carry her into the ranch house and toward the back guest room.

When we enter the room, I softly lay her on the bed, making sure she's comfy before I shed my hoodie and toss it to the side. I take a deep breath as I let the cool house air whisk the heat off my skin.

In general, I run pretty hot. Which helps, especially on the ice, so I rarely ever really get cold. And it feels as if Banks may be the same way with how cold he keeps his house.

But he's from Montana, so... I reckon that's just his default.

Running my hands over my face, I take a deep breath before I place my hands on my hips and look down at Tiana with a smile.

When I placed her on the bed, I had put her head at the foot of the bed and her on her back. But now, she turns over onto her stomach, looking up at me as she places her hands under her chin. She looks up at me with loving doe eyes as her feet kick behind her, but soon her eyes drift around my body. Though I can definitely tell her mind is elsewhere.

"Penny for your thoughts, Big Mama?" I ask with a tilt of my head before I move some of the haywire clothes back to the duffle bag that are strewn about the floor.

"How long is your lease?" she asks.

I glance at her, only to find her watching me as I put the clothes away.

My head tilts, trying to remember. "I think it's about a year. I signed it in August, so probably until next August."

She humphs in thought, her feet kicking mindlessly behind her. "I re-signed for a year in May... so I'll have to move out my things to not renew my lease," she murmurs; almost to herself.

"Sugar. No," I say sternly as I stand from where I'm putting clothes into our duffle.

Her mind is running; I can see it in her eyes. If she boards a train of thought that doesn't need to arrive at the station for a few more months, she'll drive herself insane. I can't have her losing her mind over something that isn't happening immediately.

"But Gunnar," she groans as she flips onto her back. Her eyes lock onto the ceiling, but *my* eyes lock onto the way her tits move against her chest. Like slow waves, the weight of them moves so... fluidly. She does have a larger than average chest, and a rather nice ass to go with it.

But I've always loved playing with her tits. They're just so fucking nice.

My cock twitches in my jeans, and with a small cough, I adjust it as it hardens.

"No buts. We square away the land first; we'll take care of the logistics later," I say.

She makes another groan of defiance. Part of me would really like to focus on her annoyance, butttt I'm a little preoccupied with a different vision.

The way her jersey tightens around her body catches my attention. She'll still wear my jersey sometimes, the massive one that covers her like a poncho, usually to bed. But right now she wears *her* jersey, the one made specifically for her, and also highlights her curves and tits.

I can't help the way I gaze over her; with my eyes sliding over her body, which causes a grin to rise on my face. A thought comes to mind as I remember that Charlotte and Banks are outside.

Plus, there's just *something* about solidifying things with sex.

"You're being a brat, sugar," I say lowly.

Her head tilts back against the bed, and she looks at me, though upside down, and her face contorts in what I imagine is curiosity. Her eyes roam over my body, taking in the rigid mound in my jeans, and I watch as her throat bobs in a gulp.

I unzip and unbutton my pants, pressing them and my boxers to the floor before stepping out of them.

Taking hold of my cock, I stroke it slowly. As she watches me, her eyes widen and her lips part in awe.

"I really like watching you do that," she murmurs softly before she bites down on her lip. Her eyes volley between my face and the grip I have on my cock.

My brow quirks in intrigue, and a grin lifts at my lips.

"Like watching me do what, sugar?" I ask.

My hand moves slowly, gripping tight before the other one stacks on top of it, twisting and moving up and down along my length. My head tosses back with a groan, tempting her more before my head drops to lock my gaze onto hers with a devilish grin.

Of course I know what she means, but I always love hearing her say it.

"I..." she stops. Her cheeks flush before she takes a breath. "I love watching you stroke your cock," she says quietly as her gaze pins to mine in a heady submission.

A pulse of arousal rocks through me; the sound of her voice when she says those things is always one of the best things about sex with Tiana. It's why I make her respond to me.

My cock hardens more, causing pre-cum to pool and leak from the tip.

She flips over onto her stomach, watching me, and I shake my head.

"Turn back over. Pants off," I tell her. My tongue slides against my lower lip as I nod to her leggings.

Slowly, she turns over onto her back, her head tilted back, watching me. However... her head is *right* fucking there, almost at the edge of the bed, and I think about fucking her throat before I get distracted. The slow and sensual way her hands move down her body, making their way to the band of her leggings and pushing them off her hips, makes me salivate. She moves them down further and further until she rubs her legs together to get them off her lower legs and feet.

When she does, she throws them to the side and her legs fall open.

My hands continue moving faster, almost without thought, as I watch her strip.

"Fuck," I growl as I admire every fucking bit of her.

Tiana almost never wears underwear anymore. And I love it, especially in moments like these. With her knees bent, and her legs splayed open for me, I can see the way her pussy glistens.

My head tosses back, a pant leaking from my throat as I think about getting to fucking taste her.

"Scoot back," I pant as my head tilts back down to look at her.

She moves closer to me, her head hanging off the edge of the bed.

"Mouth open, tongue out," I tell her gruffly as I take a tight hold at the base of my cock.

Her jaw drops, with her eyes pinned to mine as her perfectly pink tongue comes out of her mouth.

I slap my cock against it, groaning when I feel the warm wetness against me.

With her head tilted back like this, I wonder how deep into her throat I can go.

The wicked thought runs through my mind as I look over her.

"Obedient little slut," I say with a wolfish grin. "So fucking eager to taste me," I pant.

Right now, I am so glad I have the advantage of my height, because as I slowly press my cock into her mouth, I lean over her, reaching for her pussy and running my fingers through it.

My eyes roll as her mouth tightens around me, with another rough groan filling the room as I press myself further into her throat. I feel one of her hands wrapping around my cock, while the other cups my balls. It doesn't help my composure either when she squeezes and tugs them as she pumps her hand up and down my length.

"Goddamnit," I damn near growl. My head drops, breaths heaving in and out of me as I look down at her between my legs. I can see the slight bulge in her throat when I press deeper, and my eyes roll. Losing myself in the sight and sensation, I take a deep breath as my hand pauses against her clit. My fingers flex as I try to regain my bearings and focus on this thing I want to do. But the way her tongue swirls, the way it coats me, has my hips rocking softly in and out, trying to work myself deeper.

A muffled moan vibrates my cock as her hips buck into my hand, urging me toward her clit. I slide my fingers up and down her pussy, lingering when I reach her clit and circling it with deliberate pressure. Her muffled moans turn to whimpers, but her noises only pleasure me more with the way they shiver down my shaft.

I grunt, focusing on all the things happening before I slip two fingers inside of her, grinding the heel of my palm against her clit as I work them in and out of her. More of her moans work along my length, and I advance just a little more into her throat. But holy fuck, I don't think I've ever been so deep before.

My eyes move back to her neck, and my mind blanks as another groan leaves me at the sight of my cock stretching out her throat. I wrap my other hand around her delicate neck, and slowly press in and out. My grip tightens when I feel myself expand in her throat.

Holy shit, I can feel the squeeze of my hand on my dick.

Leaning up, I get a better view of her spread out in front of me with my cock in her throat, wrapping a tight hand around her neck.

"Pretty whore. You were made to choke on my fucking cock," I growl as I slowly press in and out.

The sound of her sucking me rings through the room with slurps and gags. And I can't help the groan that works out of me as she swallows me so perfectly.

Then, all at once, it becomes too much. I pull out of her mouth, panting as I watch the spit web from her puffy, swollen lips and she takes a deep breath.

Her wanton eyes water and drip with tears, but the obedience in them... the *submission.*

It's enough to drive a man wild.

My brow rises as I pant, a grin forming on my lips as I bring my fingers up to suck them clean.

"Christ, you're a tasty little thing," I say as I keep my eyes on her. Splitting my fingers against my tongue, I show her how I taste every bit of her that I can.

A feral grin twists my face at the way her heady musk coats my tongue, and I reach down to the hem of her jersey to tug it off of her before tossing it to the ground.

"All fours, let's go," I tell her as I fist my cock and nod toward the bed.

She nods with a submissive little smile and flips onto her stomach, turning around so that her ass is right there in front of me. Though she moves further up the bed to leave room for me.

I send a low whistle into the air as I take in all of her. Her big, thick ass and thighs, and the way her pussy glistens between them. She looks over her shoulder at me as she leans down, arching her back just the way I like.

Christ, she's the sexiest fucking thing on this planet.

Getting on my knees behind her, I press myself into her entrance and rock the head in slowly. She tries to tamp her moans down. They're muffled behind what I know is a bit lip, and I lay a slap across her ass before squeezing the cheek.

She makes a small yelp, and I lean over her. Gripping the

back of her neck and planting a foot into the bed beside her hip to gain leverage, I nip at her earlobe.

"They're outside, baby. You're going to give me *all* those fucking moans," I tell her.

I press halfway in, and her noises get louder. Moans and whimpers as she arches her back more, letting me hit deeper.

"You're such a pretty little slut. So fucking pretty, huh, baby? God, you were made to take all of me, weren't you?" I say with a gruff chuckle.

In one solid stroke, I punch forward. Filling her to the hilt, her moans echo through the empty house, and she whimpers as I settle inside of her, letting her relax around my length.

"Yeah, you fuckin' were," I growl as I pull out to the tip before ramming every bit back into her.

She cries out with each solid thrust, and I see the way her hands grip tight at the sheets as she rocks back to take me.

"Thatta girl. I don't give a shit if they hear you. I want every single one of those sexy noises you make. I wanna hear how well I'm stretching this fucking pussy," I pant.

My hips piston in and out of her, and every bit of her grips and tightens around my cock, causing me to release a low groan of approval.

I love the submissive Tiana. I love being able to be this personality for her in the bedroom. It's really one of the few times I've been this dominant before. And I love it, especially considering the way she controls me outside of the bedroom.

"My perfect cock-sleeve. My pretty slut, always eagerly swallowing my cock and letting me fuck her like the whore she is," I pant as I kiss at her shoulder. With each thrust, my balls hit her wet clit, sending shock waves of pleasure through me every fucking time.

"I'm your whore, fuck, yes. I'm your pretty little whore," she pants.

"Ohhh, there she is. There's my good girl," I groan as I move my grip from the back of her neck to a handful of hair. I tilt her head, gazing into her eyes as I keep up the rhythm of my thrusts.

"Fuck, you're so deep… so fucking deep," she whimpers before she bites her lip. Her eyes heavy with desire, she's lost in a daze of pleasure as she searches mine.

"Look at you, *fuck*, look at you. My obedient, needy girl," I growl as I meet her gaze with a lustful one of my own.

All mine, her brain is lost to the pleasure I've given her, and that look in her eyes will never fail to satisfy me.

Sloppily kissing over her lips, I grip tighter at her hair as I thrust, before I send one hard pound into her, specifically to knock her onto her stomach.

As she lands, her elbows catch her, and I release her hair, leaving her to throw it over her shoulder as she looks back at me. Locking her legs between mine, I press my thumbs into the dimples on the small of her back, gripping tight on her hips and forcing her to arch for me.

I move in and out of her slowly, watching the way her pussy covers me in its wetness.

"Goddammit, you know how to make a mess of my cock," I groan with a small chuckle.

My head tosses back, getting lost in the way it feels to thrust in and out of her. When I come back to the present, I look down, watching the way her ass ripples with each thrust and the way her pussy stretches around me.

I lean over her, wrapping a hand around her throat to press her head back. Gazing into her eyes, I see they've gone misty, lost to pleasure.

"Such a pretty girl when your slate's been wiped clean," I say with a grin.

"All yours. Fuck, Gunnar, it's all yours, take it," she pleas in a breathless whimper.

"I know it is, baby. That's why I'm using you like the slut you are," I pant as I latch onto her lips, kissing her deeply.

"B-breed.... f-fu-" Her mouth moves against my lips, attempting to get the words out, but she can't fucking think. Her eyes roll as she lets me do what I want with her.

I don't even know if she knows her own name right now; she's so far gone.

"Words, baby, focus. I wanna hear you. Use your fucking words," I growl as I slow down just enough for her to regain some semblance of composure.

"Breed me. Put a fucking baby in me, please... pleasepleaseplease..." she whimpers. And when she begs in that desperate, breathy plea, I speed up. My hand tightens around her throat, compressing those pulse points just enough to heighten her senses, my hips pounding recklessly into her.

Those magic fucking words will always get me.

"You want me to fill you, sugar? Want me to drip out of that cunt?"

She bites her lip, nodding as her eyes roll back.

"Ah ah, eyes open. I want your fucking eyes on me when I fuck this baby into you," I growl.

Slowly, her eyes flutter open, her jaw dropping and her gaze locking onto mine.

So far gone to the other side, I feel her pussy tighten around me, her body begging for release, and I slam deeper into her, reaching that spot I know makes her crumble.

"You're right there, sugar. Come for me, show me how you take this cock," I pant.

Her pupils blow, her eyes rolling into her head as she cries out, and her pussy moves in waves against me as her body shudders under me.

I come with her, spilling in rigid waves as she locks me in place.

My hand releases her throat, with a groan leaving me as I brace my hands against the bed, forcing my hips deeper in, letting her take every fucking drop from me.

Her body continues to shudder, her hips grinding back against me as I stroke a hand down her side with hard groans.

"That's it, sugar. Ride it out. You've got more in you," I grit as my head drops onto her back, looking down at where I'm stuffed to the hilt inside of her.

My own eyes continue to roll, feeling her pulse and flutter around me for what feels like forever until it slows and she's left in a heap of melted bones under me.

I don't think I've ever had a woman who not only orgasms this long but also makes me orgasm just as long.

After a few heavy breaths and feeling her out, I test her tension with a few test strokes before I take a deep breath, slowly pulling out.

My cock is shiny with her slick and my cum, causing a grin to twist my lips. I grip one of her ass cheeks in my hand, leaning down to press a kiss to her cheek, and she grins up at me before her head falls onto the bed.

I stroke her side, panting with her and waiting for her to recuperate before she slowly turns over. Her tongue slides across her lower lip as she glances at me with satisfied eyes.

"You did so fucking good, baby. You're my perfect girl," I croon as I lean in, cupping her cheek and kissing her softly on her lips.

Her hands come up, wrapping around my face with a giggle before she tosses her arms around my neck.

I lean into her, letting her take me, before falling onto the bed beside her, wrapping myself around her body. My leg slings over hers as she cradles my head in her arms.

I wrap my arms around her body, nuzzling into her breasts with small kisses as I pull her close. Slowly our breaths even out, and I rest against her as I feel her nails slide through my hair, scratching at my scalp, and the calm, stillness of it all closes in around us.

CHAPTER THREE
TIANA

"Dinner!" A loud knock awakens me, causing me to jolt out of my sleep.

My heart pounds in my chest from the scare and I take heaving breaths as I look around the room.

It's pitch black, according to the window on the wall across from us, and I groan as I bring a hand up to wipe across my face.

Gunnar is tucked tight against me, gripping my body with all of his.

I let the panic subside before I wrap an arm around his shoulders, kissing softly at his head.

"Dinnertime," I whisper, trying to get him to wake.

He groans as he buries his face deeper in my breasts. "No food. Only sleep," he groans before softly kissing at them.

I give a small laugh. "Gunnar Hayze, are you denying a meal?"

"Noooooo," he groans again.

I roll my eyes in faux disbelief before I nudge him, and he makes a noise of annoyance as he rolls onto his back.

I watch as his eyes sleepily blink at the ceiling.

"How long have we been out?" he groans in that deep, sleepy voice as he reaches around for his phone.

"I have no idea," I say.

I get up, turning on the overhead light before I look around the floor for the leggings and jersey I had earlier and tug them on.

Gunnar turns over onto his stomach, clutching the pillow and huffing in annoyance.

"These mid-days are dangerous, sugar," he murmurs against the pillow.

I shake my head as I find his hoodie, jeans, and boxers and toss them at him.

"You're the one that said I needed to eat, so let's go," I say as I place my hands on my hips.

He makes another groan of annoyance before he sits up on the bed. "Fine," he grumbles as he tugs his hoodie on.

He slowly presses a leg off the bed, running his hands over his face before he sighs and stands. Taking a wide stretch, some of his joints and bones pop as he pulls his boxers and jeans on. He comes around the bed, to me, where he buries his heavy head into the crook of my neck with another sleepy groan before he presses a small kiss to the skin and inhales a deep gust of my scent.

"You're lucky you're pretty," he grumbles as he wraps his arms tight around me and kisses at my neck more.

"Rude," I scoff as I press his head off my shoulder and open the door.

I tug out of his arms, leading the way to the kitchen and I hear his heavy steps follow behind.

"Sugar, noooo, that's not what I meant!" he groans.

"Shush, it's time for food," I say as I reach the kitchen.

Charlotte is taking some baked potatoes out of the oven as

Adrian comes in from outside with some large, cooked steaks. I imagine fresh off the grill.

"You guys are too nice to us," I say with a small smile as I sit at the dining room table.

"You're just lucky Charlotte told me how much you love steak and potatoes. I'm the same way, Miss Tiana," Adrian says as he places the plate of steaks on the counter. He rummages through the cabinets, procuring some plates before he goes through the drawers to look for steak knives and forks.

"You can't beat steak and potatoes," I say with a smile.

Gunnar comes to sit in the chair beside me, his head tilted all the way back as his legs spread, and he rests a hand on one of his thighs.

It's sinful the way he sits sometimes. Mostly because I can almost always imagine the way it would look for him to be naked and for me to be in his lap.

His other hand lazily digs his chain from the inside of his hoodie, bringing it to his mouth to chew on before he crosses his arms over his chest. His foot bouncing against the floor like he always has some level of energy pent up in him.

"Tired there, Hayze?" Adrian asks.

"Tiana likes naps, and I think I may be falling prey to the she-witch's tricks," he murmurs.

I can see the way his jaw ticks and moves as his tongue plays with his chain.

"She-witch's tricks is gratuitous, considering how comfy you get to rest on me," I say as I kick playfully at his foot.

"I am but a man, sugar. You empty my balls and smell like the beach and expect me not to fall asleep real deep. That's trickery if I've ever seen it," he says with a shrug.

The entire time, his head stays tilted back, and I roll my eyes.

"You guys had sex while we were outside?" Charlotte asks with glee.

Glee? The fuck for?

I groan as I wipe a hand over my face. "Yes," I grumble.

"Isn't that... what you're supposed to be doing?" she asks.

"Charlotte!?" I groan.

"What?! That's how making a baby works, right?"

My eyes float to the top of my head in disbelief. "Do you think we come out here just to fuck?" I ask.

"I mean obviously not, but he said you emptied his balls," Charlotte says with a shrug.

"So out of all the shit he said, that's the thing you focus on?"

"I want to be AN AUNTIE, TIANA! MAKE HASTE, DAMN YOU!" she shouts as she throws a bread roll at my head.

It bonks me on the forehead, and I look at her in confusion.

"What has gotten into you?" I ask.

"She won't stop yapping about all the things she plans to do with your baby," Adrian says with a shrug.

"Have your own!?" I say with a scoff as I throw my arms out.

"Ew, no. I don't want to be pregnant," Charlotte says as she waves her hand toward me in dismissal.

"That makes one of us," Adrian grumbles.

"What was that?" Charlotte asks as she points a pair of tongs at his chest.

"I ain't said nothin' Miss Lotty," Adrian says as he puts his hands up in surrender.

"That's what I thought," she grumbles.

He lays a soft slap on her ass, and she yelps as her cheeks tint a pink color.

I roll my eyes when Adrian comes to set the plates on the table in front of us.

"So are you happy with the land, Miss Tiana?" he asks.

My mind goes back to earlier in the day, when Gunnar took me out to see where we'd build our house, and I nod with a sweet smile.

"I do. Gunnar said you have guys lined up to get the trees squared away, and the foundation situated?" I ask.

"Yes ma'am. I know he has a rough idea of where he wants the road to lead in and out. But as far as where the house needs to be, that's up to you two," he says as he brings the plate of steaks over to the table next.

I look over them, my mouth watering with a grin as I squeal in excitement. My hands flap and tighten as I think about the way medium-rare steak feels in my mouth. As well as the combination of potatoes with it. One of the best sensations as far as eating goes.

"Could we possibly go out there tomorrow and make some plans? I would like to get the process going," I say.

"Of course, if that's what y'all would like to do," Adrian says.

I nod in excitement. But my mind works, trying to figure out how all of this is going to work. The apartments, the baby... getting married.

"Did I tell you guys we're pushing out the wedding?" I say mindlessly.

There is a halt in all the noise, and my brow arches as I look over at Adrian and Charlotte.

Charlotte's brows scrunch, and her head tilts in question. Adrian merely glances at Charlotte to gauge her reaction. If Adrian knew this already, I have no idea. There's no telling what Gunnar tells him.

"What?" Charlotte asks.

"We're just going to do the legalities so we can make things easier on us, and then push the wedding out," I say.

"I want the baby to be a ring bearer or flower girl," Gunnar says as he holds a hand up. Though his head stays reclined back against the chair.

I smirk with a roll of my eyes.

"So it won't be for a while?" Charlotte asks.

"No, probably not. It helps, because I think it'll be fun to build our house in the meantime," I say with a shrug.

Gunnar nudges me with a foot. "No planning," he says, and I groan in response. I huff as I cross my arms over my chest with a pout.

"He's right, Tiana. House isn't the priority right now," Charlotte says as she points at me.

"Since when were all of you against me?" I groan.

"We weren't! I literally bought you a whiteboard!" Gunnar says as he brings his head up.

"Yeah, but now I can't even use it," I grumble.

"You can use it for all your baby planning now," he says with a shrug and a smug smile.

I fight the smile that threatens to rise on my face. "You need to know less about me," I grumble playfully.

"I don't think I know enough about you, Big Mama," he says with a sly grin against his chain.

"It's your baby too, you know. Except!" I scoff in annoyance. "Wait! I'm not even pregnant!" I say as I throw my hands out.

"One, of course it is. Two, we don't know if you're pregnant yet. You could be growing my baby as we speak," he says with a shrug.

"Can we eat, please?" Adrian groans.

Charlotte brings the plate of baked potatoes over to the table, sets them down, and soon the conversation is forgotten as we dig in.

The next morning, after Charlotte makes us some pancakes and bacon, we all suit up to head out to the lake.

Of course the dogs come with, running through the woods with the happiest looks I've ever seen, at least from Tucker, and Adrian riding Chauncey.

However, when we get to the ridge that rests above the lake, the three of us abandon our ATVs, while Adrian rides Chauncey down the broken ridge face.

The dogs make it easily down to the small field, but I ask Gunnar for a piggyback ride. He complies with a serene smile, and I adjust on his back, wrapping my arms around his shoulders as he reaches his hands back to grip my ass. When I'm situated, he slides sideways down the rocky face before he hits the bottom, levels out, and readjusts me.

As he walks through the field, I look around, off toward the west side of the lake, before I track my gaze to the north, where the woods are.

"Whatcha thinkin', Big Mama?" Gunnar asks.

I look around for a little while longer. "Go past the tree line, toward the stump that's past the creek," I tell him with a point into the woods.

"10-4, sugar," he says.

Adrian climbs off of Chauncey, whistling for Waffle. Soon, an orange ball of fur zooms toward us, stopping in front of him with excited barks.

There's a ghost of a smile on Adrian's face, and even though I know he would have rather had a Border Collie or Australian Shepherd, I can tell he really loves Waffle.

He kneels down in front of her. "Be a good girl and keep Chauncey here, would ya?" he asks as he scratches her head.

She barks in response, and he pulls a piece of beef jerky from his pocket that she greedily chomps down.

Adrian stuffs his hands in his pockets as he stands to come up beside Charlotte and walks with us, while Gunnar leads the way into the woods.

He ducks, bobs, and steps over the branches and logs that get in our way until we reach the creek that hides further past the tree line.

"Okay, stop here," I say.

He stops, letting me jump down, and I take another look around.

Adrian comes to rest his foot on a downed log on the forest floor, looking around the area with me. Though, I can tell it's with a different eye than what I'm using. Charlotte takes steps through the creek, almost like a child playing in a puddle.

"I don't want the creek destroyed, but I also don't want to be stacked right up to the lake," I think out loud to myself.

Adrian and Gunnar both seem to nod. Charlotte is still in her own world.

"How is it getting in and out of here?" I ask.

"Not too hard. I told Hayze here that once you plan how you want the road to come in and out, I'll have Lotty and I do some preliminary tamp downs for ease of access until we can get some loggers out here," he says.

I hum in thought, looking around again.

"I still want woods surrounding some of the house," I murmur. "How far away is the nearest grocery store?" I ask.

"'Bout fifteen to twenty minutes," Adrian says.

Definitely a stretch from what I'm used to, but that's fine. If I have to drive an hour into work every day, I can just figure that out later.

It's hard to believe that this is actually where we'll be

living... where we have set down our roots and will enjoy the rest of our lives.

"When do you guys think you're going to get the legal marriage stuff out of the way?" Charlotte asks.

I turn to look at Gunnar, and he shrugs.

"Soon," he says with a smile.

My cheeks heat, and the idea of becoming a wife is genuinely terrifying. Only because I am still processing the fact that I'll be a wife. But, I also enjoy the idea of becoming Mrs. Hayze... A contradicting conundrum if I've ever experienced one.

"We'll workshop it," I murmur.

"You're a lawyer. I'm sure it'll be easier for you to get legally married than you think," Charlotte says.

I freeze where I stand, looking at her.

Holy shit.

There's a saying in the medical field.

Something to the tune of, if you hear hooves, you don't think of zebras. You're supposed to think of horses... I think? I don't know.

Either way.

I *am* a fucking lawyer.

I *should* know how easy this is.

Hell, if I really wanted to, I could just ask my damn mother.

I shake my head as I come back to the present.

"Thanks for that, Charlotte," I say with a grin.

She tilts her head at me. "Were...? Did you forget you could do that?"

My cheeks heat even more as I try to distract them with a cough. "No, of course I remember. Who said I didn't? That's weird. Anyway, we need to get back to the house. I have some stuff I need to research," I say quickly as I look to Gunnar.

He gives me a strange look, tilting his head as he looks down at me.

"Turn around, goon," I whisper as I spin my finger around in front of him.

His brow quirks and he does. I pat his shoulder, standing on my tippy toes because, of course, I can't fucking reach him.

"Crouch. Piggy-back time," I say.

He crouches and I jump up, wrapping my arms around his neck. He wraps his arms around my legs, shifting me more comfortably on his back.

"So, this is where you want it?" Adrian asks.

Gunnar turns around so we can face them, where he has his foot propped up on a log, looking at the space that I've picked.

"Yes, I think here should be good," I say. "Gunnar and I are going to go back up to the house."

"That's fine. Make sure Waffle is still watching Chauncey," Adrian says.

"What are you guys about to do?" Charlotte asks.

"I have to do a bit more research on the legalities of everything so I can get that done and out of the way and focus on the rest of life," I tell her.

"Oh, well, the Wi-Fi password is inside the drawer beside the kitchen sink," she responds.

I nod before I have Gunnar turn back around.

Slowly, he moves through the foliage and the trees, taking us back to the open area where the rest of our ATV's are.

When we make it out of the tree line, Tucker and Waffle are running around the open field, and Chauncey merely stands by the lake, taking a drink of water.

"So... are you happy with this place?" Gunnar asks as he trudges up the hill to the flat space of the ridge with our ATVs.

I smile as I look behind me, gazing at the lake one last time.

The sun shines ethereally on it. Secluded, peaceful.

All of it is perfect.

"I don't think I could love a place more," I murmur happily in response.

CHAPTER FOUR

TIANA

The weekend at Adrian and Charlotte's was well-needed. Especially because I now know all the things I need to be focusing on for the rest of the year.

With the course of action I have laid ahead of me, I am renewed with a sense of *vigor*. One where I'm not on a deadline, and it helps me as Gunnar and I go into work on Monday.

I find myself able to focus on my job and my work. But with the holidays closing in, this time of year slows down for me. There isn't much to do, and I get a majority of my work done, which leaves me leisure time to look through floor plans and baby things...

All of it gives me a sense of joy.

With the wedding, there was a sense of urgency. I felt like I was on a strict deadline, even if I wasn't. There was no set date. Maybe the one Gunnar had said, but it was a throwaway date if anything, considering I never got to make any solid plans.

But this... *this* gives me the chance to window shop, to look at things and learn things, and the world runs around me instead of me running around the world.

I spend almost all of my time running on *my* deadlines. And I like it that way because it is my every day, it gives me a sense of security and self.

The wedding was an event. A thing to look forward to.

And while a lot of my excitement from the wedding came from the planning of it all. I really was not looking forward to the interactions involved. It was a notion I merely threw to the wayside at the moment because the idea of planning the wedding was so much better than the actual idea of the day.

But with the world moving around me, it almost feels like a walk through the park versus a sprint across the Golden Gate Bridge.

Even now, I'm busy looking at car seats when Gunnar comes in at the end of the day. I finished pretty much all of my work for the day hours ago, and I've been researching all kinds of things. It's been one of the greatest days I've had here in what feels like ages.

When his piney scent wafts into my office, a wide grin spreads across my face.

He returns my smile as he ducks into my office door. "That's a happy girl," he says with a soft chuckle.

"I've been looking at house and baby stuff all day," I say with a grin.

I know he may be upset I'm not doing the stuff I need to, but I did it all, so he can kick rocks.

He has a small frown as his head tilts. "Sugar, what did I say about-"

I hold up a hand, stopping him. "Bap bap. I finished all my work hours ago. Don't worry," I say with a smile as I stand.

His smile returns, and he comes close to my desk. Rounding it, I meet him half-way to throw my arms around his shoulders.

"Well, as long as you got your work done. Do whatever

your little heart pleases," he says as his powerful hands grip tight at my hips.

He pulls me against his hard body before he leans down to press a kiss to my lips softly.

"How was practice?" I ask softly in between his pecks.

"Very good. But I doooooo have some news," he says nervously as he pulls away.

I pull away as my brow furrows, because that tone is terrifying. "What news?" I murmur.

He gives me a shy smile as he rubs the back of his neck. "We've got some away games in Toronto," he says softly.

My jaw drops as I look at him. "Toronto? I can't go. My passport isn't updated," I groan.

"You're a lawyer. Shouldn't that be like... I don't know, a priority?" he asks.

"Shush. Don't tell me how to do my job," I grumble as I shoo him away with a hand.

"We'll be there... for a week," he says with a nervous twist to his face. It's like he's expecting me to hit him.

"What the fuck am I going to do for an entire week?!" I groan as I push out of his arms.

I don't think I've gone a day without Gunnar since we were apart when we first started dating. Other than that, we have spent every single day together.

Part of me is nervous, the other is confused.

Confused because I have never been nervous. Old Tiana would have cheered to the heavens to have her space back and her routine to herself.

But Gunnar *is* part of my routine now.

Even though there are times I just don't want to speak or interact much, I do like being in his presence. I like knowing he's there, watching hockey games or doing his own thing.

But as I fall deeper into my thoughts, his voice brings me out.

"Charlotte can't go. The Canadians have all the equipment stuff handled and Russel is back, so she's staying behind. At least you'll have her with you," Gunnar says with a smile.

I take the smallest breath of relief, because there is *some* ease in those words.

At least I'll have Charlotte.

"Do you think she'd want to stay with me in the apartment?" I ask as I look to him.

He shrugs. "Your sister, babe. I reckon you'd have to ask her," he says.

I groan before I slap at his chest. "Thanks for the help," I murmur.

"No problem!" he says with a grin. "Anyway, we leave on Friday, so these next few days we kind of have off to prepare for it."

I barely notice the way his scent has enveloped me as I lose myself in my thoughts. I think about all the things I could do while he's gone. It'll suck for him to be away. But I think Charlotte and I can do a lot of planning. There's a part of me that feels like I could relive my childhood with her for at least a few moments.

Being twins, Charlotte and I were incredibly close growing up. As we grew older and stepped into ourselves, we didn't spend as much time together. Especially when I was in college and working at the big firm.

But I look back on those times of us together with fondness, and while I will miss Gunnar, I am excited to have those moments again with Charlotte.

If not to talk about the property and house things, at least to experience that small bit of nostalgia I had with her.

I look up at Gunnar with a grin, though his is heated desire as he clasps his lip in his teeth.

He looks me up and down like I'm some kind of meal and my brow rises as I look up at him.

I don't even realize he's been stroking my ass until I bring my awareness back to where he touches me.

"You okay?" I ask.

"Oh, sugar, I don't think I could be any better," he murmurs mindlessly. His hand comes up to wrap around my jaw, pulling me in as he leans down to press a deep and heated kiss to my lips.

I let a soft moan bleed through it as my hands press to his chest, where I feel his heart drumming violently under my fingertips.

"I'm going to fuck the shit out of you before I leave," he rasps into our kiss.

Lust pulses straight through my body, directly into my pussy. I inhale a deep breath at the jolt of pleasure from the sound of his voice and the tone of his words.

"Jesus," I whisper into his lips.

"That surely won't be who you'll call for when I'm stretching that pussy," he pants.

He pulls me tight into his body; the hand on my jaw slowly slides down my throat, my chest and side to clasp tight on my hip. As he does, I feel his hardened length against me, and he moves his kisses down my jaw, to my neck, where he sucks my skin into his teeth and inhales my scent.

"I'm going to fuck you, nice and slow, take my time with you. I wanna hear those moans for hours, baby."

I gulp. His words... God, always so fucking sexy. I can't with the sound of his voice and the way he's always begging for me.

"Nice and slow? I didn't think you were capable of that," I whisper as I tilt my head back, exposing more of my throat to him. My hands reach up, threading through his hair and tightening as the heat begins to devour me.

His fingers splay wide on my hips, with his pinkies stroking over the crest of my ass as he grinds slowly into me. He presses further into my body, bending me back against the grip he has on my spine and hip. Leaving me feeling like I'm at the whim of him and everything he is.

"I'm capable of many things, Mama. But when it comes to you, I have to be as deep as I can. I can't let any part of you go unfilled... fuck... un-*stretched*..." His words trail off, his breath cool against the wet spots he's laid on my neck.

"Your pussy stretches so nicely around me. Takes me... so well," he groans as he grinds his hips again for emphasis.

I come back to the present, slowly pressing him back. "Let's get home first, yeah?" I say with a soft pant as I try to get sight of his eyes.

He shakes his head as if he's come out of a trance, and his gaze connects with mine.

"Fuck, I'm so sorry. I get into these visions of you and I lose myself," he says as he stands to his full height to run a hand through his hair.

I take a soft bite of my lip as I look at the tent he's pitched in his sweatpants and my eyebrows raise.

"You were about to fuck me right here, weren't you?" I ask with a grin as I look back up at him.

He glances at it before he presses his cock down with his wrist, shaking out his leg.

"I was so close, you have no idea," he says with a shameless grin.

I shake my head with a small smile before I reach for my things, handing them to him, and he leans down to kiss me as he takes them.

As I walk to the door, his free hand comes to my waist, tugging me back against him in the doorway.

"Give me a minute," he murmurs.

His cock is still hard as stone at my back, and my cheeks heat as players pass us to leave the arena.

"Better hope there's no traffic on the way home," I say as I lean my head back against his chest to look up at him.

He glances down at me with a small smirk, and soon he softens enough for us to leave the arena hand in hand.

CHAPTER FIVE
GUNNAR

The drive home was able to distract me enough from jumping on Tiana because my mind went on thinking about all the stuff I needed to pack.

There was something my mother always taught me growing up. Especially since she was a mother to three massive hockey players.

"Pack your own shit."

Because we were all different ages, playing different leagues of hockey, we were separated pretty often for away tournaments. That meant I usually got Grandpa, and Gretz and Brooks would get my parents.

Either way, my mother couldn't be bothered to pack hockey gear for all three boys. Not only that, it was one thing she taught us not to place on our partners.

And even though it's Monday, I know there is stuff that needs to be washed. I know there's shit I gotta collect between the two apartments and there's stuff at the arena.

All of it, I think about. What bags I need to pack, and when I need to have everything packed by.

But I also think about what it'll be like to be in Canada without Tiana.

I wish she could come with me. I'd love to take her to a Timmy's or have her try some poutine. But in all honesty, with some of the stuff I've seen her eat, I doubt she would like poutine. I would still enjoy it for her.

By the time we get to the apartment, I have my arm slung around her shoulders, as I usually do, and lean against her as we make our way through the elevators. Though my mind is still rifling through all the things I need to pack. In the next few days I have off, I'll still go into the arena with Tiana.

If only to make sure her schedule is normal while I'm still here.

But I plan on bugging her the whole time. Hell, I could make sure she fucking eats while I have the chance to watch her. At least after I gather all the shit I need to. I could also pack while I'm in her office — a two birds, one stone type of situation because I reckon that'll be-

"Gunnar?" Tiana's voice cuts through the haze in my brain, and I look down at her.

My chain has been in my teeth, my tongue running along the underside as I've retreated into my thoughts.

"What's up?" I murmur as we continue walking to her apartment.

"Are you okay?" she asks as she unlocks the door and pushes it open for us.

I sigh, removing my hand from her shoulder to run a hand through my hair. "Yeah, sorry. I was thinking about all the stuff I have to do before I leave," I say quietly.

"Well, I could help you," she says. I look down at her with a small smile. Her gaze is soft and genuine, which only makes my smile grow more.

I shake my head softly as I walk to the kitchen island, placing her tote on it. "I appreciate it, sugar, but my mom always taught me to pack my own shit," I say with a sweet smile.

Her eyebrow quirks. "Oh?"

I give a light chuckle and watch as she takes her suit jacket off and tosses it on the counter next to her tote.

As she does, I notice the way her tits strain against her blouse, with her nipples hardened against the thin fabric.

Which only makes me remember the way I was about to make her scream back in her office.

My teeth grit tight on the chain, and I lean a hip against the island as I cross my arms against my chest.

Looking her up and down, I try to speak... but *fuck*...

"Yeah... she uh..." I get lost in the sight of her as she moves to the door, bracing a hand against the wall. It's like she knows I want her because of the way she brings her foot up to remove her heel... so delicate, slow. She does the same to the other foot before she places her shoes by the door.

With a sigh of relief, she takes a few pins from her hair, shaking some pieces she pinned back free before she smiles at me.

"She what?" Tiana asks innocently.

"Can I, uh..." I pause, looking over her again. "Can I help you get out of... your work clothes?" I ask in a low murmur.

My blood runs hot, straight to my cock as I take in the way her skirt tightens at her waist. It accentuates every bit of her perfectly sculpted frame, and it only makes my hunger for her heighten.

Fuck *me*, this is going to be my wife.

"If you'd like," she responds. Her cheeks heat, highlighting the freckles spattered across her nose and cheeks as she nips her bottom lip, smiling submissively up at me.

Pressing away from the kitchen island, I take a few steps toward her, and her hands move to clasp behind her back.

Her eyelids lower, beckoning me with a lustful gaze as I

bring a hand up to her chin. My thumb and forefinger grasp it gently, pressing her head up toward me before I run my thumb over her lower lip. Dropping the chain in my teeth, I grin at the submission she gives me so freely.

"Such an obedient little thing, aren't you, sugar?" I whisper.

She nods, and I press my thumb between her lips, where her tongue swirls around it. Her eyes lock onto me, watching my reaction.

"Good girl... that's a good girl," I whisper with a steeling as I admire the way her tongue feels against me... as I remember how tongue feels on my cock.

As she continues on my thumb, my other hand comes up to tug her blouse from her skirt.

She stands utterly still, letting me do what I please with her.

When I get the hem of her blouse free, I get each button open from the bottom, working my way up as I look in her eyes.

She tries to shy away as she keeps swirling her tongue around my thumb. I know she's not a fan of eye contact, but I enjoy making her nervous. I enjoy making her *sweat*.

"How do you want it?" I whisper as I slide my thumb from her mouth, dragging it down over her lower lip.

I want her every way but fucking loose, but I want her to tell me.

As I reach the top button, I glide the back of my fingers across her chest, her collarbone, pressing the fabric from her shoulder.

Her arm loosens from behind her, allowing the fabric to fall.

"Make me yours," she whispers.

My brow quirks and my lips tighten in a grin.

"She's submissive today, is she?" I whisper.

She nods, her eyes bright with desire and anticipation as she leans into me.

"That's a good girl, baby," I say.

I lean down, pressing soft and tender kisses into the pocket of space in her collarbone. She inhales the smallest gasp, and I use my free hand to press the fabric from her other shoulder.

"I wanna feel every bit of your skin against mine," I whisper into her beach-scented skin. Like sea salt, flowers and coconut mixed into one. My lips graze her neck as I roam up, pressing a kiss to her pulse point beside her throat. Soon, her blouse falls to the ground behind her, and I use the hand to slide down her back, pulling her tight to my body.

My lips linger against her neck, letting her pulse thrum against them.

"Thumpthumpthumpthumpthump," I whisper in time with her heartbeat. "Fast."

"It's always like that when you touch me," she breathes.

My brow arches at that, and as my hand falls to the small of her back, I find the zipper of her skirt to drag it down. When it reaches the bottom, I pull more, taking the skirt with it.

Soon, she's in nothing but a bra in the middle of the entryway.

"Shoulders," I whisper.

She complies, throwing her arms around my neck, and I scoop her up to wrap her thick legs around my waist.

My cock damn near throbs in my fucking sweatpants. I'm still wound up from the office, and now that I remember the way it felt to be in her presence then, I'm raring to go.

I suck and nibble on the skin at her neck as I take her to the bedroom. The entire way there, my hands squeeze tight on her ass.

When I make it to her room, I flick the door shut behind me with my foot and bring her to the bed. Placing her gently on it, I lean down, kissing her deeply as my hands move to pull my sweatpants and boxers down.

I step out of them, leaning up to pull my shirt off.

Her eyes move slowly around my body, lingering on my cock, my abs... *me.* Her hands do the same, running over the hardened lines of my stomach before grazing her nails over my skin. A shiver of pleasure rocks through me at the way her soft hands feel teasing me like this.

I lean down, taking her hand and wrapping it around my cock as I kiss her.

"Stroke me," I rasp.

Almost greedily, she does. Both of her hands come up, one over the other, pumping my length with a delicious grip.

I groan into her lips, and my hands come up to her tits. I squeeze the mounds, pinching at her tight nipples through her bra, and she moans into me.

"I'm going to miss this," she whispers into our kiss.

"God sugar, you have no idea the trouble I'm going to have," I say with a chuckle.

Sliding my hands down her body, her skin causes my pulse to race even faster, my urgency heightening the longer I go without her stretched around me. I reach that patch of skin above her core, gliding my fingers through her wetness before slipping two fingers into her.

She makes a small gasp before she hums in satisfaction and rolls her hips against my hand.

Seeking her clit, I pull my fingers out to shift my approach and circle against it, changing in pressure as she writhes. Moving farther down, I press those two fingers back into her, slowly pumping them in and out as my thumb slides back and forth against her clit.

Her small gasps and moans leak into our deep, slow kiss.

"There she is; there's my girl," I whisper.

"Fuck...!" she whimpers the longer I work her up.

"So wet. Every time I'm about to fuck this pussy. You're so fucking incredible," I whisper into her lips before I kiss down her jaw.

I move my kisses down her throat, her neck, her collarbone.

Soon, her touch abandons my cock as I move my kisses down her chest, over the soft flesh of her breast before I linger at her nipple. Pulling the fabric of her lace bra down, I bare the tight, hardened peak. Sucking it into my mouth, my fingers keep pace on her core. Her body tenses and writhes, while her hips buck under my touch. All the while, my tongue swirls and laps at her nipple before I nip softly at it.

"There you go. Fall baby, I've got you," I pant against her tit.

Soon, I move lower. I remove my fingers, capturing the back of her knees in my hands and pressing her legs up.

A grin pulls at my lips as I look at the way she opens for me... how she *drips* for me.

"Fuck," I groan as I stuff my face between her legs.

She moans out, her hands scrambling for purchase against my scalp, tugging me in deeper.

I lap the wetness from her entrance to her clit, flattening my tongue against all of her before flicking it against her clit. She gasps and moans, her hips moving in time with the way I lick her.

Before long, her moans pitch, and her body tenses as I feel her pussy flutter against my mouth as she climbs that summit. I pull away, edging the fuck out of her, to come up from her core with a devilish grin.

Tiana groans in protest. "Gunnar, what the fuck?" she pants as she looks at me.

"Sorry, baby, I wanna feel you come around my cock," I say with a shrug before I hook my arms under her knees. I lean over her, and she wraps her arms around my neck before I lift her and move us onto the bed.

I climb on, moving to the head of the bed before I sit. With my cock between us, she sits on my thighs, and her hands come to wrap around my length, stroking me up and down with a perfect grip. Then, her legs slide down my thighs, giving her room to lean in and take my cock into her mouth.

"God... fucking... dammit," I grit as my head falls back, hitting the headboard with a *thunk*.

Her tongue roams over all of me, sucking more and more of me into her throat.

My hand comes to grip her hip, using it as some kind of tether to this world as she sucks more of me into her mouth.

Soon, she bobs her head up and down on my cock, slurping and sucking my cock like a woman starved. My groans turn to huffs and growls as she makes me approach that edge, just as I made her.

"Fuck... fuckfuckfuck," I growl. My hips roll, trying to stave off the orgasm, and as if she can feel it, she releases me. Her mouth comes off my cock, leaving it sore and harder than ever.

My eyes roll with the lack of her hot, wet mouth, and I heave breaths as I look down at her. One of my hands comes to grip around the bottom of her neck.

"Such a naughty girl, sugar," I say with a panting grin.

Soon, I press her back onto the bed until I'm hovering above her, and her eyes change to mock fear.

"Dangerous games, sugar? You know better than to play those with me," I growl lowly as I lean down.

"I-I'm sorry, I wanted t-" she whimpers.

I stop her, nipping at her earlobe as I grip my cock at the base to slap it against her clit.

She jolts and makes small squeaks of pleasure as I do.

I run it through her wetness, up and down, teasing her entrance before I slide it up to rub against her clit.

She makes another noise of frustration as her head tilts back.

"In... please! I want it in!" she groans. Her eyes connect with mine, dripping with the plea to fuck her.

"*I'm* in charge, Tiana. You asked for this. You *teased* me... naughty girl thinking she can just suck my cock and get away with not letting me come," I growl in her ear.

I tsk my tongue, tightening my grip on her neck as I slowly press the head into her. I take shallow presses, teasing her more. Letting go of the base of my cock, I press a hand hard into her lower stomach, compressing the space I thrust into.

"You don't get to tease me and not face the consequences. You're *my* fucktoy... *my* perfect cock-sleeve to do whatever the fuck I want with, remember? You do what *I* say. Are we clear, Tiana?"

I thrust just enough to have the head move in and out of her.

"Gunnar... Gunnar please, more, I need *more*," she whimpers again.

"Not the response I asked for, Tiana. I said," I pull out entirely. "Are... we... clear?"

She groans and writhes against the grip I have on her neck, her hips swirling to seek my cock.

"Clear! Crystal! Please, in!" she groans with a desperate huff.

"Now... what is it you did to me? Why am I punishing you?" I ask as I shift my grip from her throat to her jaw.

"Gunnar, please, I just want it in. I want you to stretch me," she pleads as she looks desperately up at me with obedient eyes. She hitches herself just right to get the head of me into her.

I groan as I feel her, her pussy tightening around the head from her efforts, and I let a tortured laugh go in response. She's good at distracting me. But she's my brat right now, so I need to treat her like one.

Shifting my grip one last time, I pull her up just enough by her neck and pull my hips back to keep her from getting me deeper.

"Nah, ah, ah. You're a slippery one, aren't you? You just... can't..." I release her neck and the pressure I've kept on her lower stomach. I bring my hands to her hips, twisting her hard enough to flip her to her stomach. Gathering her wrists, I clasp them behind her back. My hands are big enough that I can hold both of hers with just one, and with my other hand, I lead my cock right back into her entrance.

"Can't seem to listen, can you?" I say as I lean down. Biting her shoulder, I thrust into her before pulling out. I move torturously slow, because I know exactly what she wants. Hard, fast, deep.

But I'm about to go a week without her pussy wrapped around me, I'm going to use every bit of her that I can.

"Now tell me, what is it you did wrong?" I whisper as I thrust just a little bit more into her before pausing.

I hate to admit this slow teasing is doing as much to her as it is to me. She got me right to the edge, and having to go slow is making everything so much more intense. I'm struggling to focus on my game as I move.

"I-I..." she groans, shifting her hips for more of me, and I tilt back, not letting her take more.

"Nope. Words, Tiana. What'd you do?" I growl. I nudge her head with my chin, tilting it to the side so I can see her eyes.

She looks up at me, a glimmer of excitement shining in her gaze amidst the painful teasing.

"I-I edged you. I didn't let you come..." she pants softly.

"There's a good girl," I say as I kiss her lips. My hips rock slowly, but I still don't give it all to her. I grip tighter on the hold I have of her wrists as I brace my other hand against the bed.

My hips rock just enough, still half of my cock outside of her, and I watch her pussy swallow it. Soon, I pull her ass cheeks apart to watch more of her pussy take me.

"Fuuuuuuck," I growl. And soon, I *snap*.

With a tight grip on her wrists, I punch forward, shoving every solid inch into her. She moans out a half-cry as I fill her, and I pause, letting her adjust.

"Tight fucking cunt," I grit as I look down at where I've buried myself into her. "So fucking pretty, too," I add.

I release her hands for only a moment, fixing them above her head, where I pin them into the mattress. Using them to brace myself as my other hand comes to her hip. Holding her in place, I thrust in and out of her. I lose myself in the feeling of her pussy wrapped around me, in the feel of her taking me deep and hard.

"So pretty, baby. Fuck, you were made for me. My perfect fucking wife. You stretch like a goddess around me," I pant into her ear.

"Fuck yes, yes. Your perfect wife, your perfect cock-sleeve," she whimpers in between her moans. I watch the way her hands tighten above her head, her fingers flexing in and out as her body tenses under me.

Nipping at her neck, I fall into the taste of her skin. Licking and kissing the bite as I slow down, I rock deep into her. Every thrust into her results in a loud, pleasured moan.

"This is what you wanted, right? My thick cock stretching this cunt? Stuffing you so full you can barely fucking breathe?" I ask.

"Gods, yes. Everything," she responds.

Soon, I stop, using the moment to pull out, flip her onto her back and shove myself back in.

Her eyes are hazy and lost, her pleasure devouring her whole as I lean up, gripping under her knees.

I sit back on my knees, thrusting in and out of her, watching as her hands come to pinch and work her nipples.

"Thatta girl, baby. Work those fucking tits," I growl as I release one of her legs.

I grip one of her hands, pulling it down to wrap around the length of my cock not inside her. She gasps as she feels me, her wetness soaking me, and I move my hand to her clit, rubbing quickly over it.

Her moans turn to whimpers and gasps as her head tilts back.

"Look at that... look at *you*. Feel how fucking wet you are for me?" I growl.

Her body tightens, her pussy spasms, and I feel her grip tighten around my cock, both hand and pussy as she climbs.

"That's it. There she is. Come for me. I want you screaming when I pump this fucking womb full of my spend. Let the neighbors hear who's putting a fucking baby in you," I say as I lean down. My thrusts speed up at the same time my fingers do against her clit.

"Fuck, I'm gonna come, I'm gonna fucking come, fuck, fuck, fuck," she whimpers desperately.

"Come for me, lock me inside of you, I *want* it. Come for me," I grit, and with those last words, she does.

She unravels below me at the same time stars blast my field of vision. The pleasure rocks through my spine, my brain, consuming my vision as I growl deep, feeling her orgasm tighten around me.

Her pussy pulses and throbs at the same time her screams echo through the bedroom, leaving me locked inside her.

I grit, breathing through the tightness of her as I keep filling her with my spend. I hunch over her, burying my head in her shoulder as I scratch a hand down her side, groaning as her muscles work my entire length. All the while I press soft and spent kisses into her skin, waiting for the orgasm to fade so I can catch my breath.

Her body writhes, and she pants and moans under me until her orgasm is wrung out. Before long, she relaxes against the bed in a heap of skin and bones.

I chuckle breathlessly as I brace my hands against the bed and take a test piston to feel the resistance.

I keep myself in just a little longer as I hold myself above her, two hands on either side of her head as I gaze down at her.

She's flung her arm over her eyes, and her skin gleams with a light layer of sweat and pink flush against her honey-tinted skin.

I lean down further, coming to press soft kisses onto her sternum. Her heart pounds against my lips and I grin as I feel it.

"Was I too aggressive?" I ask softly.

I'm not sure how some of these different personas come out of me. But she makes me play with different parts of myself.

To an extent, it makes me feel safe. I get to indulge in whatever my mind pulls me toward, and she takes it.

Even though she can be rather rigid elsewhere, she's incredibly pliant in bed, and I love that about her.

"No, no," she pants as she waves me off in dismissal. "That was amazing," she says with a soft grin as she looks up at me.

She runs her tongue along her lower lip as she presses her arms above her head, opening her chest for more air.

"Are you sure? I thought I was too much at one point, but I couldn't stop myself," I say as I come to put some of my body weight on her. My elbows brace against the bed, with my hands coming up to stroke through her hair softly as I kiss her neck.

"I like that you explore yourself with me. It's something I got to do with you, and I'm glad that... I can give that to you," she says. Her hand strokes through my hair slowly, sometimes stopping to curl a lock around her finger.

I lean against her body, keeping half of myself on her as I relax.

Instinctively, my hand comes to her stomach, rubbing softly.

Her head leans on top of mine, stroking my hair as she presses small kisses into my forehead.

I do this with her all the time. It's a small token of affection that I find does the trick of showing her how precious she is to me.

I didn't realize how safe and comforting it felt to have it done to me. Not that I need safety or protection, I'm plenty big enough.

But it feels more like if someone tried to come at me sideways, she'd take care of them, because she's taking care of me.

And... I've never had that feeling before.

I also never want it to end.

With that, and the feeling of our skin, sticky and damp, as well as the bliss from finishing, slowly I fall asleep against her.

CHAPTER SIX

TIANA

Maybe I should kick Gunnar out of my office. He leaves in only a few days, so I *should want* to spend that time with him.

Technically, I do.

But he has taken to using my damn office and the hallway *outside* of it as a place to pack all of his shit.

There are so many shirts, pants, and jerseys EVERYWHERE.

I try to ignore it while I work, but every time I look over, I feel like he's not packing stuff right.

There's no fucking packing cubes! He's just *folding* the damn things, with no rhyme or reason.

It's stressing me out, and soon I stand, slamming my hands on the desk.

Gunnar looks up from his phone, where he's watching a video as he takes a break from packing. He sits on the floor, surrounded by a ton of his shit, including his massive hockey duffle bag, which takes up most of the office, with all his pads and skates. Not to mention, it smells like fucking hockey gear.

It's not the nastiest gear I've smelled, but it's still HOCKEY GEAR.

"Gunnar... dear..." I say softly with a fake smile.

"What's up, sugar?" he asks with an oblivious smile as he looks up at me. His chain hangs on his bottom teeth because, of course, he's chewing on it.

"Is there a reason... you pack like a fucking caveman?" I ask through a gritted smile.

He looks around his things before he shrugs. "This is just how I do it."

"Mmm, mhm..." I murmur with a quick nod of my head, trying to keep my cool. "You ever heard of... a packing cube?" I ask with a slow breath out.

"Nope. Seems dumb," he says with a shrug before he looks back at his phone.

I run my hands over my face, groaning loudly before I come around my desk. Because there is shit everywhere–including four different pairs of skates–it is hard as fuck to maneuver around this man's mess.

Clumsily, I hike my legs up and over his things, trying not to step on them.

When I get to a small area of space untouched by hockey gear, I look at everything, and all at once I am not only over-whelmed, I'm vastly overstimulated and need to not be HERE. Along with the fact that he's packing. All. Fucking. *WRONG.*

It's only noon, but I can't take this anymore.

"Let's go," I growl as I reach for my jacket on the wall beside the door.

Climbing over even more shit, I make for the door, groaning when I see *more* of his shit lined up against the wall.

My heels tap aggressively against the cement, and soon I hear the bounding footsteps of Gunnar as he follows behind me.

"Whoa, where are we going? Lunch? I could do with some lunch," he says.

I love him. I do; he's terrific.

He's also a fucking *man*. I legitimately cannot handle this.

"Yes, Gunnar. We're going to get some lunch," I murmur.

It's not entirely a lie. We can go get lunch after I get these items that I need for my sanity.

"Sweet, I wan-"

"Nah ah. Nope. I pick, you shut your face," I say with a series of points to him and me.

"Copy that, Big Mama," he says.

I lead him out of the arena, straight to the truck. Which we took today because he stuffed the bed full of shit to bring with him to pack.

He said this morning that he's just going to take care of all of his packing in my office.

Fine, if he'll get to hang out with me for these few days before he leaves, *fine.* Cool, I love that.

But. *MY.* OFFICE.

When we get to the truck, I get in the driver's seat. Gunnar doesn't question it, merely getting in the passenger seat. And when he buckles up, I throw the truck into gear.

There are cheers and whistles coming from his phone as he watches whatever it is. I imagine it's hockey highlights. That seems to be the only thing he watches.

I know that packing cubes may not always be the easiest thing to find, but I know I'll find some at a department store. And there are tons in downtown Seattle.

Considering we aren't too far, I get us to one of the parking structures for a nearby mall and park, taking a deep breath before getting out.

Gunnar continues to follow. Sometimes he's capable of just being a massive dog, so he won't really ask questions in these "dog modes" of his. He usually just comes along for the ride.

I take us into the mall, heading straight for a map to find the largest department store.

Gunnar is so wrapped up in his video that he doesn't even realize where I'm taking him.

Finding the department store on the other side of this building, I tug his hand and speed walk through the mall with him in tow. It's a long walk, which is a bitch to do in heels, but if it gets his stuff neater; I don't care.

We take a few escalators until we reach the area of the department store where the travel stuff should be. However, on our way there, we pass the baby section, and I pause.

Gunnar bumps into me from behind, damn near barreling over me. But he grips tight on my shoulder, stopping us both from tumbling before he looks around at where we are.

"Baby stuff?" he asks in confusion.

My heart drums nervously in my chest. It really shouldn't. But I caught sight of the cute onesies and I walk up to them. Pinks and blues — they're just so tiny, and I grab the bottom of one of them, looking at the size.

Newborn.

Oh my God, *it's so little.*

"I thought we were getting lunch," I hear Gunnar say from behind me.

I pull the hanger off the rack, turning around to show him the stacked onesies.

"Look at how tiny," I say with a pouty lip and big doe eyes.

He smiles as he catches sight of it, locking his phone and shoving it into his pocket.

"Very tiny," he says with a smile.

I place it back on the rack, delving deeper into the space.

Since it's so close to Thanksgiving and Christmas, there are tons of themed onesies.

Turkeys, elves, Santa-type things, reindeer.

There's a onesie that says, "I'm just here for the milk." And I can't help but giggle.

Some things are so absurd, but it makes my heart ache.

Mostly because I've had a period, and we've been trying so far. It causes some of my doubts and fears to surface, deepening my already irritated mood.

"Do you think we're ready for this?" I ask softly as I continue walking through the racks.

He takes a second to respond, and I look back to find him looking over some onesies.

"I don't know, sugar. Does anyone ever truly think they're ready?" Gunnar asks as he turns to me, shoving his hands back in his pockets. He's looped his chain over his lower jaw, his tongue sliding against it as he follows me.

My lips quirk to the side in thought as I turn back to the clothes.

Little boy pants and shirts with a little bow tie.

"Do you think the universe is telling us we aren't ready since it hasn't happened yet?" I ask as I stop in front of a rack of little girl clothes.

Gunnar comes around the rack I'm looking at, leaning over it. His arms fold over the top, and he places his chin on top of them, tilting his head as he watches me.

As I look up, he gives me an amused smile, and one of his hands folds out to press his fingers under my chin, forcing my head up slowly.

My brow furrows at him, his smile still amused, though considering, with his eyes half-lidded in thought.

"I need you to understand something, sugar," he says. His words are slow. Serious, but gentle. "Your worth and my love for you, is not defined by your ability to get pregnant."

"But w-"

He stops me, placing a finger over my lips. "Let me finish," he says.

My eyes narrow, and I cross my arms over my chest, while his fingers come back down to press under my chin.

"I think it's my fault. Maybe I've made you feel as if there is pressure behind you getting pregnant so quickly. But," he says with a soft sigh. His grip changes, shifting his hand to hold my cheek and stroke his thumb across it. "Part of it is just the game, sugar. Us, in the moment, it's part of it. But in real life, the idea, and the reality we want... I will never, ever fault you, nor look at you differently just because you didn't get pregnant right away, or ever," he says.

A small frown pulls at my lips as I look up at him, my eyes drifting away as I sigh. "I know," I murmur.

"These things take time, too, baby. I know it's frustrating," he says.

"I just... getting my period is disappointing," I say with a sigh.

"I can't imagine the feeling. But I'm sorry I've put weight on you that makes it a disappointment. That was never my intention," he says quietly.

"I-... You didn't-"

He stops me again with a shake of his head. "I did. And that's not okay. I would never force you into anything or an idea that you didn't want. But I got ahead of myself. You are more than enough for me, every single day. You will *always* be enough for me, Tiana Dawn. You always *have* been," he says.

I fight back the tears in my eyes as I lock onto his eyes.

He's sincere in his apology, even if I feel like he doesn't need to give me one. But I appreciate that he's taken some sort of self-reflection. I've never really thought of it that way. Maybe it is. But I also have my own ideas and feelings about everything.

I think every woman does. We're taught this one thing for our entire lives, conditioned, in a way. I never thought about it all until I found a man worth all of it.

And Gunnar *is* worth all of it to me.

Still, part of me can't help but feel upset. Even if I know I shouldn't. These things take time. And of course... I just can't stop thinking about it.

Another fucking hyper-fixation attempting to ruin my life.

"I just want to enjoy my time with you. Baby-making doesn't have to result in it right away. I'm more than happy to make a baby with you for the rest of my life. Even if it never results in one," he says with a feral grin.

I roll my eyes playfully, pushing away some of the tears and sadness. "Okay," I say softly, sniffling.

His playful smile melts away into one of genuine affection and love. "What can I do to help?" he whispers as he continues to stroke my cheek.

I look around, and wouldn't you know on a rack a few feet behind him...

I smile at him, pulling away from his grasp to grab the thing I spotted from across the baby clothes. Turning around, I hold it out to him. He turns around from the rack to look at me, and his head tilts with a smile as he presses his hands into his pockets.

"You sure?" he asks with a tilt of his head, and a raise of his brows.

It's a Seattle Stags merchandised jersey onesie.

I nod as I come back to him, holding it to my chest as I gaze convincingly at him.

It may feel counterintuitive to buy a onesie when I'm so down about the circumstance.

But I think it'll be a small bit of hope for me during this process.

"Alright, if you really want it," he says as he wraps an arm around my shoulder. Leaning over to press a kiss to my forehead, he leads us out of the baby area.

Gunnar was surprised to find out I had actually brought him to the department store for packing cubes.

It took me forever to find them, but I knew they had them there. When I purchased far too many for any normal human, the cashier looked at me strangely. And of course, just because Gunnar was such a good sport, I took him up to the food court to get him some food. He deserved that at the very least.

Eventually, we came back to the arena, and now here I sit, with the baby onesie sitting over my keyboard as I look over it.

My heart beats a little brighter. That our little one will wear this one day...

I shake my head as I look over at Gunnar.

He has unwrapped all the packing cubes, and holds one completely open, looking between his things and the cube.

Standing from my desk, I maneuver around his things before I come to kneel in front of him. "Need help?" I ask with a smile.

He looks up at me before looking at his stuff. "What is the point of these things again?" he murmurs.

I shake my head with a soft sigh and pull out a stool that sits in the corner of my office.

I bring it over to his mess of things, and one by one, I go through all his things, helping him pack everything just the right way.

It takes the rest of our workday to get most of it squared away. But it's organized enough for me to not lose my mind.

By the end, I smile at him and the fact that the mess is much more contained.

Gunnar merely looks around at all the cubes that now

neatly hold most of his things. "My mom is going to be so mad at me," he murmurs.

I laugh as I wrap a hand around his cheek, pulling his gaze to mine. Rubbing a thumb over his cheek, I give him a sweet smile. "Gunnar, if I had to sit here and watch you pack these bags any longer, I was going to lose it. This is fine," I say. But he can hear the threat in my tone. I can see it in his eyes.

His eyes widen, and he nods hastily in agreement. "Yep, got it, noted," he says nervously.

"Good boy," I whisper with a small pat to his cheek.

A blush creeps across his nose. "Can you call me that later, please?" he whispers as he leans closer to me, looking up at me like a lovesick puppy.

"If you really want it," I say with a grin.

"Fuck, I really, really do," he whispers as a soft hand grips at my hip.

I laugh and lean in to press a kiss to his forehead.

"I'll miss you, you big goon," I say.

His smile turns from nervous and begging to sweet and sincere. "I'll miss *you*, sugar," he responds.

CHAPTER SEVEN

GUNNAR

There's a bone-deep feeling of sadness that runs through me as I throw my hockey duffle down against the wall. There're dozens staged here as we get ready to board the bus for the airport. But I can't be bothered to get excited about it.

Normally, Canadian tournaments are fun. They always have been in the past with good cellies, good drinks and some solid fucking games.

But this will be my first time away from Tiana for an extended amount of time, and I'm not gonna lie, it's eating me up. Hell, it's my first time actually having a serious relationship and being away for a tournament.

Tiana is more than capable of taking care of herself. She's done it for a long time. So technically I shouldn't be worried. But I am an integral part of her routine now, and I wonder how different that will be for her.

What I've heard from Charlotte and her mom is that she gets kind of screwy when her routine is off. And I don't want my absence to throw her off so much that she can't care for herself.

I have to incorporate myself into her day somehow while I'm gone, so she knows she'll be fine if her schedule changes. Is there a chance that I'm being a tad overbearing for a full-grown woman? I think most people would say yes. But the reason I live and breathe now is for Tiana, and there will never be a moment where I don't worry about her and her every day.

Even now, I try to think of parts of our daily routine I can incorporate myself into from afar. At least to give her the impression that I'm still here with her. I may be gone physically, but I need her to know she'll always have my heart.

As my mind works, I retrieve my phone from my pocket as I lean against the wall, propping one of my feet up on it before I pull my chain from my hoodie. Taking a deep breath, I loop it around my tongue as I tuck my hand under my elbow to support my arm while I scroll through my apps.

I pass by a few of them before my head tilts with a thought on how I can make myself useful to her.

Coffee.

I look for her favorite coffee shop, and when I find it, I see if they have some sort of scheduling option available. Scrolling through a few of the options, my eyes roam around the screen, hoping they do these sorts of things.

Lucky for me. They *do.*

I take a few moments setting it up, making sure it's the right order, at the right time, exactly when she needs it. And as I finish, I feel a little less nervous about Tiana as I pay, stuff my phone in my pocket and lean back with a smile.

Hopefully that will help her out some.

Soon, Banks knocks into my shoulder as he throws his duffle down beside mine.

"Toronto," he says as he leans against the wall with me.

He's in his cowboy getup today. Even the cowboy hat.

Wrangler jeans, a flannel and his cowboy boots. I should have heard him approach because the heels on those things are loud as shit against the finished cement.

I lean my head back with a sigh. "Toronto," I respond solemnly.

"What's the matter? You love Toronto." He stuffs his hands in his pockets as he props his foot against the wall and tilts his head toward me.

"I worry about Tiana," I say as I bring a hand up to rake my fingers through my hair. I may have done my little idea, but that's barely even a band-aid for her day to day.

"Ah, she'll be fine. Strong girl, that one. She's always done things on her own," Banks says with a shrug.

"Yeah, yeah, I know. But I'm part of her day to day now. You ever seen her off her schedule?" I ask as I tilt my head toward him.

Banks rolls his head back to look up at the big overhead lights, where he's quiet for a moment.

"I haven't. But I know Stamen has. Know Miss Lotty has as well. I reckon asking them would be a good start," he finally says.

"Mmm..." I hum in thought as I pin my gaze back up at the ceiling. "I also haven't gone that long without fuckin' her either," I add.

"I reckon you made it your whole life up to this point without her," Banks returns.

"Hardy har, smart ass. Obviously. But now I've had her. You're telling me you're not gonna struggle without Charlotte?" I ask.

"I'll be fine. I'm not a horny fuck-nut," he says.

"Fair point," I grumble before I take a deep sigh.

Shouts come from the door beside the exit, and I watch as Bubbles comes out of it, yelling at some of the lingering players to start loading up the duffles onto the bus.

Stamen holds the exit doors open for Leroy and Crowder as they pick up some bags and take them outside.

"She's been upset as well. About the whole… baby-making thing," I say with a groan of disappointment as I bring a hand up to the middle of my eyebrows, pinching softly.

"I reckon that's your fault," he says.

"Wow, you are *not* helpful at all today, are you?" I ask as I stare dumbfounded at him.

"You know me. I'll never tell you what you wanna hear, dozer," he says with another shrug.

I roll my eyes with a sigh. "I just don't want her to think it's a deal-breaker for me. I told her, but you know how Tiana is," I say.

"Well, maybe lay off the talk for a bit. Focus on somethin' else. Like the house. If you just keep her mind preoccupied with the house, I reckon she'll be too into house planning to think about a baby."

I look at him with a furrowed brow. "How the fuck do you know so much about Tiana?" I ask.

"Aside from the fact that she's always been my lawyer? And I'm dating her sister? Don't take much if you pay attention."

I scoff.

"She's always been real serious about her job and making sure people get what they deserve. She's got a real knack for getting sucked into things," he says.

"Well, pay less attention, she's mine," I grumble.

Banks slaps me on the back of the head, knocking my chain out of my mouth.

"Ow!? The fuck was that for?!" I say as I rub the spot. Man has a heavy hand, Christ.

"For being stupid. I don't want your woman, fool," he says as he folds his arms across his chest.

I grumble in annoyance as I grab my chain, hooking it back on my teeth. "How much longer until we set off?"

"Reckon a few more hours. You say bye to Tiana?" he asks.

"Not yet. She had some stuff to get done this morning, so I'mma head down to her office in a few. Charlotte told me she's gonna stay out with Tiana, since she knows the first day is the hardest for her," I respond.

"I don't want Lotty out at the ranch house all on her own either, so I reckon that's a good idea," he says.

"What about the horses and chores?"

"Ah, I got a rodeo buddy that will come and chore for em. Decided to give Miss Lotty the week off. She's not the biggest fan of chorin' but she helps anyway because that's just her default."

"Right," I murmur.

Another sigh racks through me, and I look around, trying to see if I can spot Charlotte. I find her going over some things with Bubbles on a clipboard.

"Be right back," I murmur as I push off the wall.

I send a whistle through the air, where a few people look over at me, Charlotte being one of them. Pointing at her, I rock my head to the side to signal for her to come to me, and her brow furrows in response.

Charlotte says something to her dad before she presses the clipboard into his hands and pats him on the shoulder. I watch as he scoffs and rolls his eyes and she skips to me.

"What's up?" she asks with a big smile.

"Everything going alright?" I ask as I nod to the commotion behind her.

Her hands clasp behind her back, and as she turns around to look, she seems to bounce up and down on her toes. Almost as if she can't contain her excitement.

"Yeah! There's always a lot to do for these big away tournaments, so I have to be on my A-game," she says with a smile as she turns back to me.

"I reckon so, eh," I murmur. Taking a deep breath, I try to find the words to tell Charlotte what's on my mind.

"I am worried about Tiana though," I say quietly.

Her brow furrows. "She'll be fine. What are you worried about?" she asks.

"Well, I know her thing is all about routine, and I don't want my absence to mess up her whole..." I gesture around the arena. "Ya know."

Charlotte nods in understanding. "Ahhhhh yes, gotcha," she says, though her voice trails off at the same time her gaze does. She seems to drift away in thought, and my brow arches as I watch her.

"So... hm..." Charlotte says as she brings her hand up to her chin. "The first few days she may be more... inward, I think. She can handle her schedule being messed up, but she becomes just a bit meaner. More of an edge-type situation. I think her breakdowns only really happen when it's just kind of all too much at once. But it's the holidays, and there's not much going on. So, she should be okay. Maybe a tad worried, but she'll be fine," she says with a confident nod.

"You're staying with her?" I ask.

She nods with a big grin. "Yup. Me and Waffle."

"Good. I reckon Tucker will be happy about that," I murmur. "Alright, well I just wanted to make sure. I don't want her to... fall apart, I guess," I sigh.

Charlotte tilts her head as she looks at me. "You're really that worried about her, aren't you?"

"Of course. Why wouldn't I be?" I ask with a furrow of my brow.

She smiles with admiration, clapping a hand on my shoulder. "It's nice. I like that you worry," she says.

"Go finish getting the bus loaded. I'll see you when we leave," I say with a small smile.

She nods before she shoves me and dashes away.

I can't help the small chuckle that leaves me as I head toward Tiana's office. Charlotte being with Tiana helps my nerves immensely. Because at least she won't be alone.

As I approach Tiana's office, the door is already open. When I peek in, she's busy with something at her computer.

She looks up as I crouch in; and she smiles. But it doesn't reach her eyes the way it usually would when I come into her office. There's a sadness there, and I can tell. There's no scrunch at the corner of her eyes, or the breath of relief she usually takes when she sees me.

I sigh in return, and hold my arms out for her. She stands slowly, coming around her desk to walk toward me. As she reaches me, she falls into my chest before she wraps her arms around my waist. I feel her back expand and the heat of her breath through my hoodie as she takes a sad, deep inhale.

I wrap my arms around her, leaning down to kiss the top of her head before I lean my head against it and stroke up and down her back softly.

"It's only a week, sugar. It'll go by fast," I say quietly.

"I know. I'm just so used to you being here. Who is going to warm me up at night?" she asks as she tilts her head back. She rests her chin against my chest, a playful frown pulling at her lips as she looks up at me with her sad puppy-dog eyes.

I look down at her, bringing a hand up to curl a lock of her hair around my finger as I admire her. All the while, I offer a small but reassuring smile.

"I reckon Charlotte has the capabilities," I say as my smile widens.

She rolls her eyes before she shifts her head again, resting her cheek against me.

"I don't like sleeping with Charlotte. She's like an octopus. Her limbs just fucking go everywhere. She knows she'll be in the guest room," she murmurs.

"I'll call whenever I can. We have a day or two of nothing

before the tourney, but I'll call when I'm free, I promise," I say as I bring a hand up to the back of her head. I stroke her hair softly, sighing as I rock us back and forth.

"It's okay. Charlotte and I have already decided we're going to get the Christmas gifts out of the way while you guys are gone," she says.

"Oh, you'll be more than fine then," I say with a laugh.

She tilts her head up to glare at me. "Not funny," she grumbles.

"You have plenty to plan. Imagine all the things you'll get to plan for the house. And you have to get the paperwork stuff ready for us to get married when I get back," I say with a grin.

Her eyes widen, a heated blush tinting her cheeks. "When... when you get back?" she murmurs softly.

I nod. "I'd like to get it done. One less thing to worry about. Plus, I just wanna be able to call you my wife," I say. Bringing a hand up to her cheek, I stroke a thumb over it with a grin. "Don't you wanna hear me call you Mrs. Hayze when you're riding my cock?" I ask in a low whisper.

I watch her pupils blow, her throat working in a gulp as she nods sheepishly. "Yes, please," she whispers.

"I knew you would, sugar," I respond as I lean down. Shifting my grip from her cheek to her chin, I press it up, leaning down to kiss her slowly, deeply. My other hand comes to grip her hip, pulling her tight to my body.

Fuck, I'm going to miss her so much. What *am* I going to do without her beachy scent? Just the feel of her body against mine. I won't be waking up to her or going to sleep with her at night.

The thought sends a pang of hurt through my chest, and I pull away from the kiss to admire her face again.

But her eyes bounce around my face, and I tilt my head in question.

"What's up?"

"Do... do you want one last hurrah before you go?" she asks softly.

My brows rise, and I look behind me, making sure no one is nearby.

"Here? Now?" I whisper.

"Or the cars. The showers. Doesn't matter where. I just want to know if you want it before you go?" she asks with a shy grin. Her lip catches in her teeth, and her blush deepens.

"Fuck... if you're offering," I whisper with a grin. My pulse rages as I think about taking her here. My cock hardens in damn near an instant, and I move to her door to peek my head out.

I look both ways, scoping out the terrain. No one gives a single fuck about us right now, so I close the door and lock it.

I take one big step toward her, wrapping my hands around her face to bring her in for a deep kiss. I groan at the taste of her. It's usually her coffee, which is always sweet and caramel-y.

Her hands grip tight on the band of my sweatpants at my hips, and she pulls her body tight against mine. The pang of lust that runs through me is enough to make me weak in the knees, and I pull away for just a moment to see what can be done in here.

I move my hands to her hips, twisting her around and moving her to her desk. She braces her hands against it, looking over her shoulder at me as she lowers her torso to the surface. Her back arches, leaving her ass taut and round before me, covered in her black pencil skirt.

"Fucking hell," I growl as I come up behind it.

My cock throbs with a fervency as I press it against the crease in her skirt, and she grinds back against me. The pressure of her movements is intoxicating, along with the fluid way she swirls her hips. Placing my hands on her ass, I rub over it softly, watching as she flicks her hips.

Her ass jumps, moving like water against my cock as she shakes it against me.

"Holy fuck, Tiana. Where were you hiding this?" I ask with a heavy breath as I watch the way her ass moves against me.

"I went to college, Gunnar," she says with a giggle as she looks back at me.

Leaning down, I press kisses into the small of her back as I glide my fingers along the backs of her thighs. Her skin shivers under my touch, and she makes a small moan of approval as I continue gliding my fingers up. When I reach the hem of her skirt, I drag it up to her hips, baring her ass for me.

She shakes her ass again, where the cheeks ripple like waves, and I lay a hard swat against one of them in satisfaction.

"Do that shit again," I murmur as I get lost in the sight of her.

She flicks her hips again, up and down, back and forth. I'm so damn near mesmerized at the way she moves against me I forget that I'm supposed to be *inside* her right now.

Tugging the band of my sweatpants down, I let my hard cock free with a groan and grip tight at the base. I slap it against her ass, watching the way she moves against it.

It's one of the sexiest things I think I've ever seen her do, and I can't believe she's never done it before. Hell, even reverse cowgirl. I'd bust in a second if she did. But I come back into focus, shifting my hips to run the head of my cock through her core.

My eyes roll, and my head falls back with a deep breath as I try to keep my composure.

"Christ Almighty," I groan as I feel her.

Hot, wet, and so *fucking* perfect.

She whimpers, trying to keep her noises low as I press the head to her entrance.

Her pussy tightens as I press in more, gripping me as she

adjusts to my size. There is something about her at this angle. Something fucking deadly if I wasn't a man trying to knock his girl up.

Her hips swirl back and forth, moving her ass as I press deeper into her.

"Keep doing that, fuck," I pant as I bring my head back down to watch her.

Is this what the girls call twerking? I didn't know Tiana could do this, but holy fuck, I'm so mad she didn't show me she could do this earlier.

Soon I can't take it anymore and I punch forward, shoving all of me into her to the hilt.

I know my girl though. Before she has a chance to even make a noise, I cage her body into mine as I lean forward and wrap a hand around her mouth.

"Quiet baby. You know you have to be quiet here," I pant as I grip her hip with my other hand.

I thrust in and out of her, looking down her spine to see the way my cock comes out shiny and covered in her slick.

"God fucking dammit, you're a messy thing," I say with a growling chuckle as I find a rhythm.

While she may be quiet from my hand, there's no way to stop the sound of her ass slapping back against me.

I try to slow down, moving in more calculated thrusts to make sure the boys don't hear me fucking the brains out of her.

But her pussy... fuck *me*, is just too fucking *good*.

I speed up, growling as my head buries into the side of her neck and I take heavy breaths into her skin. Every inhale sends her scent through me in bursts of desire. It's like getting high on a human, and I wish I could drown in it.

"My perfect girl. Fuck, your pussy is so good to me. I'm gonna miss burying myself inside of you," I pant.

My eyes clench, my mind losing itself to her pussy tightening and clenching around my cock.

Her tongue lathes against my palm as a grounding point, and the press of her skin against my lips with the scent of her thick against my senses forces me in faster. Soon, I throw caution to the wind and fuck her the way she deserves. The noises I'm making be damned.

"*My* good girl, fuck you're such a good girl baby," I growl. My pleasure climbs, tightening around my spine, and my pace picks up. Her moans grow behind my hand, and I press her head back enough to see into her eyes.

There's always this look of obedience to her, one where she knows I'm making her take all of me. One where she's giving in so deep to her submissive side she'd do anything I asked. There's even a sparkle in her eyes as they connect with mine.

"Fuck, there she is. There's my beautiful girl," I pant as I lean over her. My thrusts are punishing, with my balls slapping into her wet clit as I thrust hard and fast.

The emerald green is misty with pleasure, and it's almost as if her eyes beg for more, to keep giving her everything.

"You gonna keep your eyes here as you come, baby? You gonna show me what I'm doing to you?" I ask breathlessly.

She nods desperately against my palm, her hips rocking back, challenging my thrusts as I feel her pussy tighten and throb around me.

"There it is. Come for me. You're so close, come for me. You're doing so good for me, sugar, you're almost there," I pant desperately in response.

Her eyes half-lidded, staying right on me as I watch her climb, more and more, I feel her pussy tighten and flutter. And I climb that summit with her, until all at once, we explode.

Her pupils blow, her moans vibrate hard against my hand as she comes, and her eyes roll into her skull. Her body tightens, along with her pussy as we orgasm together. Her pussy locks me in, holding tight to me as my cock pumps hot, rigid spurts of cum into her.

I pull my hand from her mouth, bracing it against the desk as the other comes to grip her hip. I groan low with pleasure as my head drops onto her shoulder, sinking deeper into the way she takes every bit of my release for herself. And, fuck me, she's the only woman I would ever let suck me dry like this.

"Keep going, baby. You're almost done; there's more in you," I pant as I press kisses into her neck. Her pussy spasms around me, her hips grinding back as she takes everything. I let her use me until she's wrung herself out, my chest heaving as I brace my hands against the desk. Her body collapses against the surface as breaths beat in and out of her, her head tilting against it to look up at me with a grin.

"Fucking beautiful," I say with a breathless smile as I lean down to press soft kisses into her lips.

I stroke her hair gently, pressing my hips in and out of her so... *so* slowly.

She moans into our kiss, and I grip tighter on her hair.

"I'm going to miss you so fucking much," I whisper against her lips.

She grinds back against me, and I hiss from the sensitivity of it all. And that I can feel how much I've filled her.

"I'll miss you more," she says with a grin.

"I didn't know you could twerk. Why the fuck were you hiding that from me?" I ask.

"I don't know... maybe I thought I wasn't good at it," she says with a shrug.

"Lying ass," I say with a teasing grin as I kiss her again. My hand comes to her ass, rubbing over it softly before I pat it and lean up.

I slowly pull out, stuffing my cock back into my sweatpants before I pull her skirt down over her ass, adjusting it so no one can tell the things that I just did to her in her office.

Slowly, she leans up from the desk and turns around to face me as she takes a deep, satisfied breath.

I grip her hips, lifting her onto the desk and pressing in between her legs.

Her smile turns sad for a moment, and I bring a hand up to grip her chin to press her head up.

"Just a week, sugar. I'll text every day, I promise," I whisper.

"I know. Just sucks," she says softly as she leans into me. Her arms wrap around my back, and I return her embrace.

"I know, baby," I whisper as I rub my hands up and down her back.

I wish I could bring her to Canada... I wish I didn't have to leave her.

When we return and get married, I'm making her fix her passport, because I don't want this to happen again. I don't want to have last-minute quickies just because I won't get to for a week. I want to always give her the love she deserves. Alongside that, I really just want to see the world with her.

I want my woman by my side, *always.*

I feel like having Tiana with me to explore these places would be a dream come true.

And I think one day, I'll get to have that.

For now, I have to leave her here. And that hurts, because I had no idea how much love I could feel for a woman.

Not until Tiana.

CHAPTER EIGHT

TIANA

After Gunnar and I finished, I sat in his lap as he sat in my office chair until someone came to look for us. Charlotte specifically had knocked on the door.

I only know because I recognized the sound of her knock.

It was then my stomach dropped, and a wave of nausea swept over me.

It's such a strange feeling worrying about my... almost husband leaving. I've never worried about men leaving for some kind of business something or other in the past.

But fuck, I'm going to miss Gunnar. *Real* badly.

He gives me a reassuring smile, stroking a thumb over my cheek before he leans in to press a kiss to my forehead.

"It's just a week, sugar," he says again.

I nod, with a tight-lipped smile attempting to break through as I climb out of his lap.

He grabs me by the shoulders, giving me another once-over before tugging my skirt down again. Then, he leans over to grab his backpack, tossing it onto his back.

"You've got your passport?" I ask.

He nods with a smile as he adjusts the weight of his pack.

"Headphones? Phone charger? Laptop? Laptop charger?" I ask.

He gives me a soft chuckle before he wraps a hand around the back of my head to bring to his lips for another forehead kiss. Though he lingers there for a moment, pressing tiny pecks into it before he pulls away and runs a hand down the back of my head.

"Yes, sugar. I've got it all, don't worry. This isn't my first Canada trip," he says.

I take a deep breath as we open the door, and Charlotte gives me a slightly sad smile.

"You guys ready?" she asks.

Gunnar nods before he exits the office, with me following behind.

He offers his hand, and I grip it tight, wrapping myself around his arm as we walk down the hall. My dad is already speaking, and the team has gathered by the exit doors to listen.

"Alright. We're taking the bus to Sea-Tac. From there, we're on our way to Canada. You guys better hope you're on your fucking A-game because the last game here in our barn against Edmonton was close. We're in their fuckin' barn this time. And we've got 'em on our roster again. So whatever stick is up your ass, work on getting it out on our way there. We've had a solid season so far, but it's go-time," my dad says.

Gunnar appears to be focused on my dad's speech, but I zone out as I lean into him, gazing at the floor.

My mind goes to what I can do to keep myself busy. It's just one week. I don't even know what Charlotte is going to do if she's not taking care of the team. She usually does social media, but I guess they have someone in Toronto for that as well.

To be fair, I feel like Charlotte needs a break. She works a lot harder than I do. Not to mention, she's always choring and taking care of Adrian's animals now that she lives out there with him, and I know that's a struggle.

Eventually, I hear men moving, and I come back to the present to see them all heading toward the door after they grab whatever smaller duffle bags they brought.

Adrian approaches Charlotte, considering he was in the front with Russel and my dad, and grips her hips to pull her into him to slowly kiss her.

Part of it makes me sad because I know she'll miss him. I just know she won't struggle as hard with it as I will.

Gunnar turns to me, wrapping his arms tight around my shoulders, resting his head on top of mine as he twists his hips back and forth.

I return his grip, wrapping my arms around his back and burying my face into his hoodie to absorb as much of his scent as I can.

He pulls away, smiling before he reaches down, pulling the hem of his hoodie up and off over him.

He tugs his shirt down as it comes up with his hoodie before he offers it to me.

My brow furrows as I look over it.

"Take it. I made sure to get my smell on it for you," he says with a sincere smile.

"Are you going to be cold on the plane?" I say as I slowly take it from his hands. I can't help bringing it to my face to inhale a deep gust of it. It calms me almost immediately, and a smile tugs at my lips as I bring it to my chest and gaze up at him.

He merely smiles as he wraps his hand around my cheek. "I'm a furnace, sugar. I'll be fine. I have other hoodies with me," he says.

I look down at the bundle of black fabric before I press myself against him again for one last feel of his hard body.

He hugs me back, rubbing my back before he backs up,

and leans down to kiss me. His kiss is slow and deep, trying to taste all of me.

I kiss back, with one of my hands coming to wrap around his jaw, gripping just enough to hold him there for another moment longer before he pulls away.

Soon my dad whistles, and Gunnar looks over at him with a nod.

"I've gotta go, sugar. I love you," he whispers.

I sigh, nodding. "I love you, Gunnar Hayze," I whisper back.

He smiles lovingly at me, his thumb moving against my cheek. "I love you more, Tiana Dawn."

Then, he pulls away, meeting halfway with Adrian, and the two go in front of my dad and Russel, leading them out. Charlotte and I look at each other with small smiles before we follow the rest of them.

The boys continue walking to the bus as Charlotte and I pause on the curb, watching them load the bus.

The heaviness in my chest is immense, and I lean against Charlotte as I watch.

I watch the windows, seeing where Gunnar may sit, and of course it seems as if Gunnar and Adrian sit together.

When he sits down, he presses his face against the bus glass, blowing against it before he presses his tongue out. His cheeks expand, showing all of his teeth as his tongue lies against the glass and his eyes cross.

I can't help laughing and rolling my eyes as I pinch the bridge of my nose.

"That fucking man," I say with a sigh.

Charlotte's arm comes around me, and after a few minutes, the bus hisses as it shifts out of park, and moves away.

Gunnar finally comes off the window, wiping his saliva away before he breathes on the glass. His finger traces a quick heart in the steam he made, and he waves goodbye, long enough for me to no longer see the window.

My smile from his antics slowly fades away, and I take a heavy sigh as I watch the bus leave the parking lot.

It's silent for a while as I lean against Charlotte. But the feeling of her rubbing my shoulder helps ground me just enough.

"You have any more work to do?" Charlotte asks.

"Sort of. But I want to go home and rot..." I say quietly.

"We can do that. Can you do any of the work at home if you feel up for it?" she asks.

"I can, but we'll see what happens." I stare at the space where the bus was for a long moment before I lean away from Charlotte with a groan.

"We're going to have so much fun, Ti. I promise. It's going to be a great time!" Charlotte says enthusiastically.

I glance at her with a small smirk I try to fight.

"I have ideas," I return. "What do you need to do now?" I ask.

"Well. I have to take Adrian's truck back to the ranch house, and then I need to grab my stuff and Waffle. I have to make sure the instructions are set up for Adrian's rodeo buddy, and then I'll head out to your place," she says with a reassuring nod and smile.

"Alright... that's fine. I think I need to go let out Tucker and wallow in my sadness enough to feel like I can interact like a normal human with you," I respond as I take another sad, deep breath.

"Sounds good. So you're going home now?" she asks.

My mind works, because I need to go home, but I also wanna talk to my mom about all of this... she knows how these things go.

"Think I might go see Mom first," I murmur.

She nods. "Alright, well... I'll see you at your apartment then?"

I nod. "Yeah. Just bring me some food on your way home if you could," I say.

"Will do. Text me what you want," she says before she gives me a tight hug.

I return it, and we turn to the arena doors. Charlotte moves toward her office on the right side of the arena, while I take the normal left back toward my office.

It is eerily quiet walking right now, without the sound of the workers that are usually here and of course the rink and players. But even worse, walking down this hall without Gunnar, even if he just left, fucking sucks.

I almost never walk down these halls without him. Or without his even being on the property.

It's a weird thought. And part of me feels... empty. *Missing.*

He's almost the other half of my brain now. And I miss his jokes or just some of the outrageous things he would say. It causes my sadness to seep in deeper as I enter my office with a sigh.

I look at the bundle of cloth in my arms, burying my face in it and huffing a deep gust of his scent again before I pull it on me.

It's absolutely massive, with the sleeves extending way past my hands. It's damn near a dress on me with the length of it.

But I love it. I love that it smells so much like him; it feels like he's giving me a big hug.

Lingering in the entry of my office for a moment longer, I finally come back to the present. I move to my desk to pack my stuff up for the day.

If I'm going to go see my mom, I need to meet her at the firm before she leaves for the day. Mostly because if she has left, I don't want to drive all the way out to Tacoma to see her.

When I pack my stuff, I leave my office, locking the door behind me before walking down the hall. I hold the sleeves up to my face to continue smelling him as I walk to the BMW. When I get in, I take one more deep breath as I grip the steering wheel, pressing my forehead against it before starting my car and shifting into gear.

As I park at the firm, I try to keep my eyes open for my mom's Suburban.

Luckily for me, I see it at the front of the building, and I park in the empty spot beside her.

Most people are going home, with several walking out the front doors with joyous faces, since it is Friday. But my mom is usually here later than most.

I dig through my tote for my keys before I get out of the car to head into the building, passing by a few familiar faces. Though most people know to leave me alone.

As I walk in, I'm hit with the familiar scent of the beginning of my career. Lingering coffee, paper, floor wax. There's also a strange mix of body scents that just mingle together at all hours of the day.

But all of it is nostalgic.

This was the first place I worked. My mom wanted me to work at the firm to make sure I progressed exactly the way she wanted me to. And in all fairness, I would have rather worked here for my first firm than anywhere else. So at least I could ask for help when I needed it.

As I walk through the lobby to the elevators, I'm reminded of the route I used to take every day. I needed to say "Hi" to the security guards and needed to put on a cheerful face for all the people in the building.

I didn't enjoy having to partake in small talk. I hated having to pretend that I cared about what people were doing or how their lives were.

In general, I just... hate small talk. If they were friends or people I worked closely with, sure I'd love to talk to them then, finding out how their lives are.

But for the people I didn't see every day... interacting was a chore.

Which is why when the position opened up at the arena, I dove for it. Along with Charlotte telling me I should go for it.

But this place will always hold a small space in my heart. This is where it all began for me. And at the end of the day, there has to be a place in my heart for this time in my life. Otherwise, I wouldn't be who I am today.

The elevator takes forever to go up because my mom's office is on the very top floor. With people leaving for the day, the elevator stops every so often for people to get on. But when the elevator opens to the waiting room, where my mom's assistant Renee sits, I give her a small smile.

Though her brow furrows seeing me in Gunnar's massive hoodie.

"Hi, Tiana. What can I do for you?" she asks.

"Is my mom free?" I ask as I approach her desk.

Renee turns to the computer, typing a few things before she looks over my mom's calendar.

"Yeah, you should be good; all her appointments are done for the day, and I think she's just finishing up," she says.

"Mrs. Dawn? Your daughter is here," Renee says as she leans over to press the button for her phone.

"Send her in," my mom responds through the line.

Renee looks at me with a smile before gesturing to the door, and I nod in thanks before I walk toward it.

I knock once before I open it and lean my head in. "Hey Mom," I say as I enter.

I give her a nervous smile, and my mom looks from her computer to me, smiling.

"Tiana, good to see you, sweetie," she says.

I enter, closing the door behind me before I go to sit in one of the chairs in front of her desk.

My mom's office is rather intimate. It always has been.

Her large oak desk sits in the center, with a massive window that looks straight down into the lobby. You can see the people coming in and out of the entry doors. When I've looked up at it from below, it looks like a giant panel of a mirror.

There are large bookcases on either wall that are lined with books on law and the inner workings of different sports, including rules and regulations.

She also never uses the overhead lights. It's the perfect brightness every time because all the light she gets comes from the window behind her.

My mom types into her computer for a few more seconds before she finally turns her attention to me with a smile.

"What can I do for you?" she asks as she clasps her hands on her desk.

I sigh as I settle into the seat, flapping the large sleeves of Gunnar's hoodie back and forth. I watch them for a second, trying to find the words I need to express the way I feel.

But...

"I don't know what to do," I admit.

"About Gunnar leaving?" She adds.

I sigh with a nod.

This was the reason I came here. My mom has dealt with my dad leaving constantly for years. She's used to this.

Right now, she's the only one who would really have the best advice for me.

"It gets easier. But if you're going to be a hockey wife, this is just how it is. Why didn't you go with?" she asks.

I groan as I throw my head back. "My passport is expired," I grumble as I glance shamefully away.

"Ah, probably would be a good idea to get that updated, don't you think?" she asks.

I glance at her with a glare before I huff. "Yeah, yeah, I know," I say with another sigh. "What am I supposed to do for a week? I've never given a single shit about a man leaving for work in the past. This is all unfamiliar territory for me. I don't think I've actually ever 'missed' a partner before."

She gives me a smile, a thoughtful one, as her head tilts. "The first few days are the hardest part. Just moving into a new routine without them. But life keeps moving, you get to talk to them and get updates. And I know it's hard, but you're a big girl. I know you'll be okay," she says.

I groan in annoyance. "You seem pretty sure about that," I say as I finally level my gaze on her.

"Tiana, do you remember how you would get when your dad would leave?" She asks.

My brow furrows.

I do. It sucked. Dad having to leave always messed with my routines because he was the one who got Charlotte and me ready in the mornings. He would take us to school because Mom had to be at work earlier.

I remember being upset for a few days... and then once I got into the routine of Mom taking us. It eased off.

But part of me feels like this is different. This isn't my parents.

My safety net and routine anchor is essentially gone. Not only do I not know how to deal with that, I'm annoyed that I'm in a position where I am dealing with it. I don't like feeling helpless or co-dependent.

But fuck, Gunnar has given me the space to do that, and now I'm dealing with it all.

A double-edged sword.

"I do," I murmur.

"And do you remember how you'd be fine afterwards?" She asks.

I roll my eyes. "Mom, this is different. This is my almost-husband, *leaving*," I remind her. "We do everything together. All of my routines have him in them. I don't even know if Tucker is going to be okay with Gunnar leaving," I say with a sigh.

"Tiana, I'm sure you have a bunch of things that can be done while he's gone. You know how to keep busy. You always have. Take some time to yourself, just like you used to do. I'm more surprised you aren't chomping at the bit to spend time by yourself," she says.

"Well, Charlotte is staying with me. Adrian didn't want her out at the ranch house by herself."

"Mmm, probably a good idea. She's strong, but there's nothing out there for miles," my mom murmurs as she turns to her computer again.

"What are you going to do while Dad is gone?" I ask.

"Tiana, this is not my first, nor my last rodeo. This is just another Friday for me," she says with a shrug.

"Well. Do you want to meet up with us at some point to get the gift for Dad out of the way while he's gone? Charlotte and I planned on doing some shopping while the men were gone, so at least we can get their Christmases out of the way."

"Yeah, we can do that. Maybe this weekend, I don't have anything going on," my mom responds mindlessly as she sinks deeper into whatever it is she's working on.

"Is there anything for me at work? With the players gone, I'm really just on call in case any of them need a damn lawyer while they're in Canada. But you know how they are in Toronto," I say as I cross my arms over my chest.

"No, go take a break. Enjoy some time by yourself, like you used to. I'll take over anything that may come up. I like to stay busy," my mom says as she waves a hand toward me dismissively.

I groan. "I do too!"

"Well, go stay busy with Charlotte. You know she'll be bored out of her mind without hockey."

I huff. "Fine. Text us when you want to do this shopping situation," I grumble as I stand.

"Mmm hmm," my mom hums in response.

"Love you," I murmur as I go to the door.

"Love you too, Tiana," she responds.

I leave her office with a sigh. But on my way out, I stop at Renee's desk.

"Can you do me a favor?" I ask.

She looks up at me with a smile. "Yes, of course, what do you need?"

"Put on her calendar sometime in the next week that she needs to go Christmas gift shopping with Charlotte and me, if you can? I know she'll forget," I say.

"Of course! I can do that," she says.

"Thanks, Renee," I respond, and she nods before I make my way to the elevator.

I press the button, leaning back against the wall with a deep breath.

Soon, the thought of Gunnar not being home when I get there seeps into me, and there's a level of... gloom that accompanies it.

It's foreign in a sense.

I've... I've never missed someone like this.

The idea of going home to someone I want to see and they're not there. Taking out his dog at night without him, waking up without him. And now that my mom says I don't even have to go into work, it feels like my entire routine is thrown completely out and off.

I can't even text him right now because my phone is in my car.

And with the thought of that, I pound on the button for the lobby, trying to get the elevator to move a lot faster so I can get to my car.

When it finally gets to the lobby, I damn near sprint from it. As much as I can in my heels, at least.

My little feet tip-tapping hurriedly across the floor has some people coming in and out of the building looking at me funny. But I don't care. I want to see if Gunnar has texted me.

I make my way to the car as fast as I can, opening the door and climbing in to rifle through my tote for my phone.

When I find it, there's no message.

Part of my heart sinks. I was hoping to get something from him.

But as my head tilts back against my headrest and I place my phone in my lap to grip the steering wheel, it vibrates.

I look down, with a smile tugging at my cheeks as I see who it's from.

HUSBAND 🖤

I'll miss you, sugar. It'll go by fast, I promise. Take care of TuckTuck for me :)

CHAPTER NINE

GUNNAR

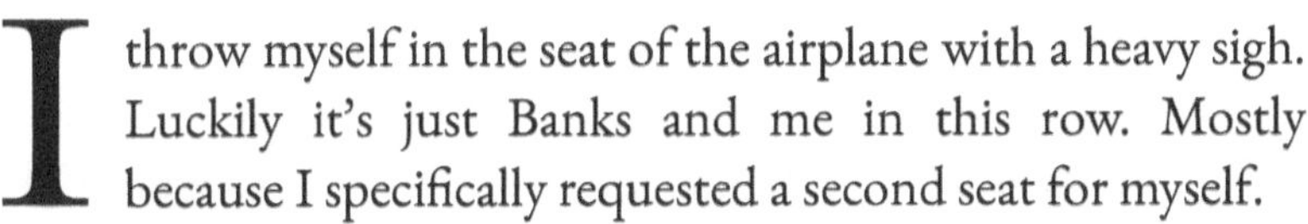

I throw myself in the seat of the airplane with a heavy sigh. Luckily it's just Banks and me in this row. Mostly because I specifically requested a second seat for myself.

Being as big as I am, it's absolute hell traveling on flights where I have to squish myself into one seat.

I've learned that it's just better to get two seats. And Banks does not enjoy looking out the window on planes, so he takes the aisle seat. I found this out when we were in college and we had to get on a plane to play some cross-country games.

Kinda funny, I feel like, considering the man has no problems wrangling cattle or riding Mach speed on horses. But the window seat on the plane is where he draws the line.

I relax against my headrest, watching as the people on the ground load the bags into the plane.

"You ready for Toronto?" Banks asks as he stuffs his backpack under the seat in front of him.

"Not entirely. You know how the Canadians can get in their barn," I say.

"Sure do," he responds as he leans back.

"I'm still worried about Tiana," I admit. I pull my chain from the inside of my hoodie, bringing it to my mouth and hanging it on my bottom teeth.

I was able to pull a spare hoodie from my duffle before we checked them.

My legs spread, and my hands rest on my thighs, but my leg bounces with nerves.

I should be excited. Sure, playing the Canadians is always terrifying. But there was usually some level of excitement getting to go full-tilt on them.

Right now, all I really worry about is Tiana. Her routine is completely disrupted with me gone, doing all of her daily life without me.

Alongside that... I realize that I've never had to worry about this before. And soon, it won't just be Tiana I have to worry about.

It'll be Tiana *and* the baby. I won't be able to keep them safe if they can't come with. And I know Tiana can handle herself. She's a big girl.

But I'm going to worry about her. That's just how I'm programmed.

Hell, I'm going to have a wife. I'm going to have to fight off whatever puck bunnies try to chirp at me overseas, and that's annoying as hell.

"Miss Lotty is real good at handling Miss Tiana. They are sisters, ya know," he says.

I glance at him before I rake a hand through my hair.

"This is all different for me," I murmur.

"I know it is, hoss. But Miss Lotty and Miss Tiana were right as rain before us. I reckon the storm won't bother them now," he responds.

"Why aren't you worried about it?" I ask.

"Well, Miss Lotty don't mess around when it comes to Miss Tiana. She'll always protect her sister, even if she knows she's good."

My gaze stays stuck on the ground, watching the ramp guys throw the suitcases and bags into the airplane.

"It's going to be even harder when we have a baby... how am I supposed to leave them here?" I ask.

"Well, I reckon it's not time to worry about that right now when your little lady isn't pregnant," he says.

"Yeah, you're right... I just can't help it. Life is all..." I let out a sigh.

"Just focus on the game right now. Miss Tiana's gonna be just fine with Miss Lotty," Banks says in a low reassurance.

With a groan, and a rub of my hands over my face, I take another deep breath before the flight attendant starts the pre-flight process.

Quickly, I check my phone one last time.

SUGAR

I'll miss you more.):

I just took him out and he's happy now. I told him Waffle is coming and he seemed to remember the name lol

I smile at my phone as I text back.

ME

Boarded the flight, ready for takeoff

Txt you when we get to Ro Town

Love you

SUGAR

Love you big daddy

I shake my head with a chuckle and shift in my seat as my cock jumps.

Not here, bastard. She's not even here.

Soon, I put my phone on airplane mode, relax in my seat, and wait for the plane to take off.

The next thing I know, Banks is nudging me, and I groan back in annoyance.

I peek through the window from where I've curled myself against it, and notice we're on the ground. It is also pitch black, save for the lights that line the taxiway.

The window is frigid where I lay against it, and the plane is slowly taxiing its way to our gate. Trying to take a wide stretch, I groan, because of course I can't; this area is too small. But I try to open up my chest as much as I can before I relax back in my seat.

I notice Banks has said nothing else since his nudge, and I tilt my body into the corner to look at him. He sits eerily rigid with his hands on his thighs as he looks toward the front of the plane.

"There a reason you look like some kind of fuckin' robot right now?" I ask with a sleepy furrow of my brow.

"You know how I feel about planes," he mumbles.

"Ah yeah. Turbulence?" I ask with a small grin.

He merely glares at me from the corner of his eye before he looks ahead again.

"I figured you would have grown out of that by now," I say as I press my face against the back of the seat in front of me. I reach my hands down, rifling through my backpack for my phone.

When I find it, I take it off airplane mode and place it back in my lap as I look toward the front of the plane. The people in the front have unbuckled their seatbelts and are rising to grab their stuff from the overhead bins. All the while, my phone is going crazy with buzzing in my lap.

My heart races for a moment as I look down, hoping at least one of them is Tiana.

Of course, my social media is going crazy. That's nothing new.

I scroll through some of the texts from my parents, looking for anything from Tiana.

There's nothing.

I can't help but feel a bit sad over it all.

But it is nighttime, and if she hasn't texted, then she's more than likely sleeping. Which is more than fine for me.

She's a few hours behind me by this point, but Tiana is pretty strict as far as her bedtime goes.

I sigh, typing a message anyway.

ME

Hey sugar. I hope you're cozy in bed and sleeping

Just landed in Ro Town

Txt me when you wake up

I love you

I watch my phone for a few more minutes, before I check the time again.

I sigh, shoving my phone in my pocket as I wait to exit the plane.

As the line finally gets to us, I stay sitting until I'm able to really move. Because one thing about airplanes and massive hockey men is that it's fucking impossible to maneuver in here.

Thank fuck I'm not claustrophobic.

Soon, everyone can move, with Banks standing to pull out one of his personal duffles from the overhead bin.

I take to merely bringing a backpack with me and just packing all my shit in my hockey duffles.

So I yank my bag from under the seat in front of me and turn against the chairs so I can throw it on my back.

I wait for him to move enough before I can get into the aisle, and we make our way down the ramp toward the gate.

And when the lot of us file out into the airport, Bubbles and Stamen are taking inventory of the people coming off, making sure we're all here.

I merely stand, stretching and yawning before shoving my hands in my pockets as I watch.

Bubbles is counting and taking a head count as Stamen marks everyone off on his little clipboard.

"Alright, boys, bags are at claim three. We're going to grab our stuff, hope it all made it here and get to the hotel. I know it's late, so don't stay awake doing dumb stuff. We're going to the arena early tomorrow morning because we've got a game tomorrow night," he says.

There are some groans, some sighs. But Bubbles and Stamen lead us off to the baggage claim. As we follow, I throw an arm over Banks' shoulder.

"You think we'll be rooming together?" I ask with a grin.

He glares at me from the corner of his eye as we walk.

"Sure fuckin' hope not," he grumbles.

"Aw, you don't wanna have a good cuddle? I reckon Charlotte will like that I kept you nice and warm," I say with a grin.

"I reckon I don't wanna hear you crank your fuckin' hog in the middle of the night."

I give him a laugh. "Ahhh the good ol' days, huh?"

"If you wanna call 'em that," he says with a sigh.

We go down a few escalators, moving our way through the airport. And boy howdy, it's always a sight to behold an entire group of hockey players moving as a unit.

I surely wouldn't wanna take any of us in a fight.

There's something missing as I take in on the Canadian merchandise. How there are some signs in French and the overall feeling of being somewhere new without Tiana, and it tamps down my mood with a sigh.

I miss my sugar…

It takes so much longer to get to the hotel than it should have.

But at least I get to room with Banks.

When we finally get to our room, I drop my massive bags at the foot of my bed, crashing onto it with a groan of relaxation.

I lay there against it for a second, resisting the urge to pass the fuck out, because I have to shower.

It's something like two in the morning, but I've been traveling all day, and we've got an early morning.

I press off the bed and quickly get into the shower, using whatever soap is in there to wash my body off and get out.

I dry off and tug on a new pair of boxers I pull from my backpack before laying back down on the bed. When I do, I curl under the blankets and take a deep breath of relaxation before I stare up at the ceiling.

Banks goes into the bathroom to shower and comes out a few minutes later, sans any fucking clothes and I get a gooood look at his dick.

"Is there a reason you're butt ass naked?" I groan as I cover my face with a pillow.

"What? I thought we were enjoying the good ol' days. We forget I sleep naked?"

I hear the blankets on the other bed move and the sound of a body contorting mattress springs before Banks says anything.

"You're good, Hayze," Banks says and I take a deep breath as I peek out of the pillow.

Banks is fully under the blankets and laying on the pillows.

"Thank fuck. I like to think I got rid of the memory of you sleeping naked in college," I grumble.

Banks doesn't respond, and I take the moment to grab my phone and look through it.

Of course, no messages from Tiana, but at least I know she's asleep.

I send one last message.

ME

At the hotel, got a game tomorrow. Hopefully I'll have a message from u when u wake up

But Im glad ur asleep

Love you sugar

I plug my phone in, placing it on the night stand and cuddling under the blankets with a sigh.

This is one of my first nights sleeping without Tiana in a while.

And I think it's one of the worst things I've experienced... in a while.

Is that dramatic? Probably.

But is Tiana also the glue to my day?

Yes.

I grab one of the free pillows I'm not using, wrapping my arms tightly around it and clutching it as I turn over and eventually fall asleep.

CHAPTER TEN

TIANA

The first weekend without Gunnar... and I think I hate this.

Usually, Gunnar wakes up before me, takes out Tucker and comes back to cuddle with me depending on who played the night before. If it's a team he follows, he wakes up early to watch their game.

But now... I not only wake up to a cold-ass bed, I wake up without Gunnar, AND I have to take Tucker out.

Not to mention, I slept like shit last night.

I tossed and turned for what felt like hours and was just frustrated over everything. Missing him, the paradox of being annoyed that I miss him, and then being frustrated with being annoyed over missing him... all of it is STUPID. I hate my brain and the way it moves thoughts and emotions around in a hurricane of pure bullshit.

Gunnar would not only get me off the damn roller coaster, he'd make me laugh the whole time.

My complex emotions are only further deepened when I wake up to see all the messages I missed in my sleep.

HUSBAND 🖤

Hey sugar. I hope you're cozy in bed
and sleeping

Just landed in Ro Town

Txt me when you wake up I love you

HUSBAND 🖤

At the hotel, got a game tomorrow.
Hopefully I'll have a message from u
when u wake up

But Im glad ur asleep

Love you sugar

At least he got there safely. Part of me feels bad that I wasn't awake to answer these messages, but he knows my schedule so well that he knew I was asleep, and there's a soft sense of security in that.

I groan as I throw my feet over the side of the bed and take a deep breath. Ripping off my bonnet, I throw it onto the bed before I ruffle my fingers through my scalp to release some of the deeper curls. I run my hands over my face, mulling through the things I have to do in my head without Gunnar.

Tucker. Coffee. Whatever Charlotte wants to do. Tucker. Coffee. Charlotte.

The mantra rolls through my brain on repeat as I go to the bathroom to brush my teeth and fix my hair for the day. I decide to go with Gunnar's hoodie and some flared black yoga pants. Fall is in full force, which means outside is definitely colder, but the smell of Gunnar's hoodie sets everything right. At least right now, it does.

When I leave the room, I hear Waffle scratching at the guest bedroom door that Charlotte is staying in. As I get down the hall to get a better look, I see Tucker whimpering in front of it as he paws at the carpet under the door. A sideways smile paints my face as I shake my head and he turns around to bark at me.

"Alright, alright. I know you wanna see Waffle, but Charlotte is a heavy sleeper," I whisper as I gesture for him. "Come here," I add.

He trots up to me with a panting smile, and I kneel to scratch his ears.

To be honest, I'm not much of a dog person. I have nothing against them. They just have a lot of energy. I'd rather have a cat. But I don't mind Tucker. He is a very good boy, and he listens well. He seems to like me too. And to be completely fair, he has always seemed to like me.

I give him a few more scratches before I move to his food container in the kitchen to fill his bowl. He attacks it greedily after I fill it, and then I quietly make my way to the room Charlotte is staying in.

Her corridor is directly across the hallway from my room hallway.

So it goes; my hallway is on the right when you enter the apartment. Dead ahead; the living room. Directly to the left; the kitchen. The hallway beside the kitchen, and to the left of the living room; guest rooms hallway.

Either way, when I get to the door, I knock quietly before opening it. I don't wait for her to respond because that girl is not awake and my knock is not going to wake her up.

Waffle, apparently, is a master escape artist because when I open the door, she bolts straight through my legs to find Tucker. As I bounce back and forth between my feet so as not to step on her, I watch her run off to find Tucker.

Tucker has pulled away from his food, with his tail wagging excitedly as Waffle runs up to him.

I shake my head with a small scoff before I look into the room.

Charlotte is sprawled out over the bed, her arms and legs

tangled in different directions with her head tilted as far back as possible. She looks like someone dropped her from an insane height directly into bed, and she just landed like that.

"Charlotte!" I whisper into the room.

She does not budge.

I groan in frustration as I walk in further, looking over her with a roll of my eyes before I nudge her shoulder a few times.

She groans as she rolls over, hiding her face under the pillows.

"What tiiiiime is it?" she mumbles.

I lean over the headboard, throwing open the curtains behind it and letting the light shine through the windows.

"Morning time. So much for chorin' life," I say with a scoff as I rest my hands on my hips.

"Hey, I chore because I'm *asked* to. I'm not asked to chore here, gimme a break," she grumbles.

I roll my eyes. "We still have to let the dogs out," I remind her.

"Better than taking Priscilla for turnout in the mornings."

With a grip at the corner of the sheets, I toss the blankets from her body, only to find that she's buck naked.

"In my sheets, dude?" I sigh.

"Fuck off!" she groans as she tugs the blankets back over her.

"You're lucky Tucker is keeping Waffle busy. She was scratching at your door," I grumble in annoyance as I walk back toward the door.

"She's an early riser," Charlotte grumbles as she wraps the blankets tight around herself and turns over.

I sigh, going back to the kitchen and leaving the door wide open. Realizing that Charlotte isn't going to be up and moving soon, I decide I'm going to take the dogs myself.

Waffle and Tucker seem to share their food as they get close to each other, smacking loudly from Tucker's bowl. While they eat, I look for their leashes.

Apparently, they are more hidden than I thought they were. Tucker's is hanging in the closet, and I end up digging through Charlotte's stuff to find Waffle's leash.

When I find them, I whistle for the dogs, and they quickly leave the bowl to run up to me, barking in excitement.

A small laugh works out of me, and I shake my head. Leaning down, I attach the leashes, wrangle them just well enough to keep them from tangling around each other and head out of the apartment.

I thought they would be more unruly. But they're both relatively well-behaved as we walk down the hall. Tucker is on my side, prancing like a little show-pony with his eyes on me, while Waffle merely does a quick little run to keep up with us, considering her legs are so small.

Of course, the thought that I'm taking the dogs out without Gunnar is sad...

I can't remember the last time I actually took Tucker out without him.

Especially since nighttime dog trips are part of our routine, I had to do it with Charlotte last night. It wasn't bad, I guess. But it wasn't the same.

Because I was so upset about everything, I didn't really say anything. I just let Charlotte talk and yap for as long as she wanted as we sat on the bench. Though I had stared up at the stars as she spoke.

I guess it's not supposed to be the same. But that doesn't make it feel any better.

As we enter the elevator to make our way down to the lobby, the dogs sit nicely on either side of me, their eyes intent on the door as they wait for it to open. I, however, lean back against the railing on the back wall and tilt my head against the mirror. Taking a deep breath, I cross my arms over my chest as I bundle the leashes in one hand.

I just have to stay busy is the conclusion I've come to. It's just a week. I've been through tons of these things; this shouldn't be any different, should it?

I would like to believe that it's not that different.

But it *is*.

With everything happening so quickly, and *all* the time, I feel like a weight presses down on me.

Getting married, the house, making a baby. I'm a hockey fiancée; there's a fucking dog in my life. Hell, my *sister* has a boyfriend and a dog. Gunnar and I are going to move at some point.

Fuck, and my job. How am I supposed to handle all this shit while also doing my job?

The longer the thoughts run, the thinner my breath feels, and the nerves of being stuck in this elevator close in around me.

Luckily, the door dings and opens, giving me space to get the hell out of there with the dogs in tow. Now with pure fear and anxiety fueling my steps, I book it through the lobby and directly outside to the dog park.

Some of my nerves wane away as the cool fall air hits my face. Like a shock to the system, I feel like I can finally take a deep breath.

Dashing for the dog park, I let the dogs into the fence to run. I close the gate behind me and lean down to unclip the leashes from the dogs before they take off toward the other end of the field.

All the while, the pressure of everything—life, love, just every day—weighs so heavily on my shoulders I feel like my body will cave in on itself.

The thoughts come again, with even more things I hadn't thought of the first time around.

I have to plan the court stuff for our wedding legality things. The baby-making. Work on top of Thanksgiving planning, Christmas gifts, Christmas planning.

Hockey games. Life. The house we have to plan. I have to work; there are contracts to sign.

My breaths come in a little quicker, and my hands flap at my chest as I pace back and forth in a small spot. But the flapping isn't helping right now.

My arms cross against my chest, with my fingers scratching into the fabric at the pits of my elbows as a method to ground myself. But that also doesn't work because all the things in my head scream louder. They get *faster*. And my heart feels as if it's going to explode out of my chest. My eyes burn from holding back tears.

How the fuck am I going to get through all of this? How am I going to do all the things I need to and keep my head above water?

I pace a little more, my teeth worrying the inside of my lip as a small tear escapes. The emotions running through me are plentiful. Fear, sadness, worry, even excitement and anticipation for him to come home.

But they are all *overwhelming*, and I. Can't. Take it.

Life is too much and too fast all at once. And the only person who can take the weight off isn't here.

But it's stupid to feel like this.

I'm strong, I'm independent, I *can* handle all of this, because I always *have*. But now I fall apart on the first day he's gone? This isn't me, and the frustration of that only adds to the weight of it all.

I'd always done it on my own. I always carried the weight, and I was okay–mostly–but now another player has entered the game, and he carries most of the weight.

He carries the safety to let me be comfortable with myself and who I am.

But I let him carry so much of it that now, without him... it's so *fucking* heavy.

These thoughts course through me over and over, with different sounds, volumes, tones. Over and over and I can't make the screaming stop. Until, without looking, I crash into a body that quickly grips my shoulders.

I jump some, looking up into the eyes of the person, only to see Charlotte looking at me.

Her eyes dart back and forth between mine, appraising me before she tilts her head with a sigh. She wraps her arms around me, holding me close as the dam breaks and sobs beat through me. Wrapping my arms around her, I bury my face in her shoulder, letting it all go.

"It's so dumb... this is so dumb, I don't understand," I murmur into her heavy coat.

Charlotte doesn't respond; she merely strokes my back as I continue crying.

"I'm not supposed to fall apart like this! This is so stupid!" I cry into her jacket. "But I miss him so much," I murmur.

I cry until the nerves slowly wane away and my mind isn't a tornado of bullshit. When I feel calm enough, I slowly back up, sniffling some before wiping my hands over my face to get rid of my tears.

"Ti," Charlotte says softly as she grips my shoulders.

I take a few deep breaths, settling myself before I look up at her. Small gasps and sniffles still work through me as I wait for her to speak.

She gives me a gentle smile, with her head tilting sympathetically before she takes a deep breath.

"You love Gunnar. He's a big part of your day. Your night. Your life. This is all a big change for you," she starts.

"I know. But there's no reason I should be crying. It hasn't even been twenty-four hours!"

"How much of your day is spent with Gunnar? Legitimately," she asks.

My eyes drift to the ground, sighing. "Most of it."

"And how many times have you had to deal with something like this? Where someone has meant so much to you and they've had to leave?"

I take a deep breath. "What is your point, Charlotte?"

"You are a fiancée now, Tiana. You don't have to keep pretending that life is done on your own," she says.

My eyes connect with hers, and she gives me a smile.

"I..." I pause, sighing. "I know..."

I watch her for a moment longer before I move to the bench, sitting down on it. Pulling my knees into my chest, my heels anchor into the slats of the bench before I wrap my arms around my legs and rest my chin on top of them.

My gaze goes fuzzy against the grass, and I feel the bench creak as Charlotte sits down next to me.

"I don't know how to let go of that," I whisper.

Leaves flitter in the blades of grass as the cool breeze moves through the field. It wiggles the leaves, and I use that as a focal point for my gaze.

"It's hard. I know it can be. There're times I struggle with letting Adrian help me out. But we're grown. We have been doing this for years. I know Gunnar brings you happiness. And I know he helps with some of your internal struggles. But just because he's not here, doesn't mean he's not *here*, Tiana. He's not leaving. Someone else isn't going to come in and replace him. He's not going to stop being there for you," she says.

And part of that is something I know, but my brain is wired into the idea that all of this is a weird phase. That one day he'll be sick of me and walk away.

But he's here forever and I know that... I really just need to *believe* that and unwire the bullshit. He's gone for a week, and when he comes back, everything will go back to normal.

I look at Charlotte with a small smile before I nod. "You're right," I say with a sigh.

"I usually am," she says with a smile.

Rolling my eyes, I shove her in the shoulder, but she merely hugs me, pressing her face against mine with a heavy sigh of content.

"I know this is different. I know it's weird. But you're stuck with Gunnar, so you better get used to him being here," she teases.

I smile, though. Because she's right... I am stuck with Gunnar, and I wouldn't ask for anything else.

Eventually, Charlotte and I head back upstairs, but when we get to my door, there's a man waiting there. I don't recognize him, but he's holding a cup of coffee.

My brow furrows as I approach. "Can I help you?" I ask.

I hand Tucker's leash to Charlotte, and she goes inside the apartment with the dogs while I deal with the man.

"Are you Tiana?" he asks.

My brow arches as I look him up and down. He's unassuming, only a few inches shorter than Gunnar if I were to guess.

"Who's asking?"

He sighs. "I have a coffee order for a..." He pauses, looking at the label on the cup. "Tiana Hayze?"

Hayze?

Confusion tugs at my forehead, because I surely didn't order coffee.

"Is there a note or anything that was on the order?" I ask.

The man looks at his phone, scrolling for a second. "Says

'Coffee is for my fiancée, may have to knock hard because she's hard to wake up'," he says as his gaze boringly comes back to me.

My heart beats a little lovesick song in my chest, and a smile rises on my face, softening as I look at the cup in his hand.

"Is the name of the purchaser 'Gunnar Hayze' by chance?" I ask softly.

The man looks at his phone again before he nods in confirmation.

Offering my hand, he gives me the cup with a nod of thanks before he turns around and leaves. I hold the cup by its lid and bottom, turning it to see what the label says.

Good morning, sugar.
Have a good day. (-:

My heart melts... the words Charlotte told me at the dog park really hitting their mark as I take a sip of my coffee.

And it's perfectly made, just how I like it, and for just a small moment, it really feels like he's here.

I quickly find my phone, remembering I didn't respond to Gunnar this morning and text him back.

ME

Just got your coffee

Sorry for the late response, was taking the dogs out

I love you thank you so much (: 🖤

CHAPTER ELEVEN

GUNNAR

The fuckin' Canadians, man. Especially in their barn. We're so fucked.

I think the only reason we won a few weeks ago was because we were on our ice. But fuck, these guys look different in their arena.

We all took glances of them this morning when they were warming up, since we pass the rink on our way to the locker room. Fuckin' Edmonton.

But when there was a lull, and people were getting in the zone for warm-up, Leroy, Crowder and I snuck off to the stands... and now we stand here watching them with gaped jaws.

Talk about some fuckin' sharks in the water. They've got bull-balls in their arena.

"How in the hell," Crowder murmurs from beside me.

"Does Bubbles know?" Leroy asks.

"I'm sure he does. He's seen them play for years," I say through my chain as my arms tighten where they cross against my chest.

"They didn't play like this back in Seattle," Crowder adds.

"They sure as shit didn't," I say before turning around and heading down the arena stairs. I hear the scuffled foot movements of Leroy and Crowder as they follow me, and we make our way back to the arena. We're getting closer to our warm-up time. And to be honest, I should be locking in. But I needed to see what they were up to.

Fuckery, I reckon is what they're up to.

"Your mustaches are comin' in nice for No Nut November, boys. Wish I could participate as far as not nutting goes, but I got a lady to knock up. I'll keep the mustache in though," I say with a grin as I look over at Leroy and Crowder and rub a hand over my mouth.

Them boys can grow a caterpillar, that's for damn sure. The team talked about it before we left Seattle, and I've only been shaving my jaw. My mustache always takes a bit more time to come in, but Bubbles and Stamen have been so busy planning our demise that I don't even think they've noticed that half the team has mustaches now.

"The fuck you mean you got a lady to knock up?" Leroy groans.

"Tryna get Tiana pregnant. Requires nutting, I reckon," I say with a shrug.

"Tiana agreed to that? The fuck kind of magic do you have to talk her into that shit already?" Crowder asks.

"I'm nice to her. And I have an enormous dick," I say with a wolfish grin as I look to the two of them.

They shove me in annoyance, and I can't help snickering before they turn around to walk out of the stands. I shake my head as I follow them.

When the three of us return to the locker room, it's not the full team. Some are getting dressed, sure. But I think another number of them are roaming around the arena. But as far as I know, they haven't gone to watch the Canadians move.

The thought of the game tonight comes to the forefront of my mind. Which immediately dampens my mood, so with a loud groan and a run of my hands through my hair, I sit in front of my cubby. My tongue slides back and forth against my chain as I try to remember the words and plays Coach has told us as far as Edmonton goes.

Toronto? Fine, simple game.

Edmonton? Who fuckin' knows at this point. That's who was on the ice, and thinking about Coach's words about how to play them doesn't match up to the shit we saw out there.

Danglers from Hell, I reckon.

"They're fucking rabid, Bubbles," Crowder says with a sigh as he crashes in front of his cubby.

I reach up to the shelf above my head for my phone, letting the rest of the conversation fall away as I notice I have a text from Tiana.

A wide grin tugs at my lips, with my heart pounding in my chest as I open her message.

SUGAR

Just got your coffee

Sorry for the late response, was taking the dogs out

I love you thank you so much (: ♥

Oh shit, I totally forgot I ordered her coffee to be delivered while I was gone. I'm glad she got it.

ME

I hope they made it right

Did you sleep good?? I miss you

I put my phone beside me as I start pulling my gear on,

with my mind remembering how it was like to wake up without her this morning.

Hell, to even wake up in a different bed.

I've gotten so used to Tiana's bed that my body was on fire this morning. I think I've gotten spoiled because she's got a real nice mattress and sheets.

Aside from it missing the weight of my lady, it was just not the best sleep overall, and I woke up with a boner from hell and no Tiana to remedy it. I didn't fucking enjoy getting rid of that monstrosity this morning.

My gripes from this morning are forgotten as my phone vibrates beside me and I look down to see the message.

SUGAR 😊

> They did! I was so surprised when I saw the guy at the door lmao

> It helped my morning so much

> How is Canada?

ME

> Canada is fine. Cold, but the Timmy's this morning did the trick

> They're fuckin' nutso in their house

> Crowder, Leroy and I were watching them and Edmonton is going to beat our asses lol

I'm glad she got her coffee, and that it helped her some. I meant to text her this morning, but it was a quick-paced wake up.

I always get her coffee in the morning, so I wonder if she was going to make it after she took the dogs out.

But these thoughts somewhat awaken an... awareness of sorts. All of this is strange — this kind of... domestic life.

In a sense, at least.

This is my first real far away game, and I have a *fiancée*. The last time I was in Canada I was a single bachelor.

Granted, I didn't really do much of anything as far as women. Maybe flirted or had some drinks. But at the time I had the NHL's eyes on me. I couldn't be too wild. I had to keep my image squeaky clean.

But I have a lady now... The idea of everything I can do here changes some. I've gotta get something when I get the chance. I'd like to have a little collection of things I can give her over time.

I reckon she'd like a little trinket.

My phone vibrates again as I finish pulling on my long socks and skates.

SUGAR

Ouch. That sucks

My dad never likes going to Canada for that exact reason

Always stresses him out lol

ME

Yeah I can see why

It was already a hard game back home

SUGAR

I don't think Tucker even knows ur gone

He was too focused on Waffle this morning

ME

Well at least he's got his girlfriend

I miss mine

SUGAR

): I miss you too

It was tough this morning ngl

ME

Aw what happened?

SUGAR

Just sad

Brain doing brain things lol

But the coffee helped a lot

ME

Anything I can do to help??

SUGAR

Come home maybe???? Lmao

ME

One home, coming right up (:

SUGAR

Omg lmao go play hockey please

Charlotte and I are going out later so I'll text you later

I love you and win for me plz

I know you guys can do it (:

ME

Love you baby

I'll win extra hard just for you

I shake my head with a grin as I put my phone back on the top of my cubby and finish getting ready.

"Hayze! Dick out of your hand, the fuck is your problem?!" Bubbles' yells as I tug my chest protector on.

My eyes widen as I pause. "Shit, my bad, what's up?"

Bubbles' groans. "Russell, please deal with him before my fuckin' head explodes," he says as he gestures a rogue hand toward me.

"What'd you guys see up there?" Russell asks as he crosses his arms over his chest and stares intently at me.

"Canadians doin' what Canadians do best. But like... much more bester," I say with a shrug.

"Hayze, I'm going to beat your ass. You're so fucking lucky you can play, because I can't believe you're marrying my daughter," Bubbles grits as he grips the meat between his brows.

"First off, rude. I like to think your daughter likes me a whole lot. But listen, we've got this in the bag. We beat them on our ice, so we beat them again; it's no biggie," I say with a shrug.

I pull my chain up to my mouth, looping it around my tongue before I reach back, pulling my jersey from the cubby and tugging it on.

"Banks," Bubbles' groans.

"I reckon Gunnar is right, Coach. Fake it till you make it, or whatever the fuck it is y'all say when you're about to get thrown off the bull," he says as he leans back against his cubby with his arms across his chest.

"Real inspirational, Captain," I murmur.

"I've played them in their barn. They know how to rodeo," Banks says with another shrug. "Best advice is fakin' it till we make it."

"We have warm-up, then all of you fuckers get out there, and show them what the fuck they're playing with. You're not leaving here without a solid win. So get your fuckin' big-girl panties on, hike 'em up to your armpits and kick some ass," Bubbles says through a grit in his teeth.

Gotta admit. Man's got a way with words because I swear I just got a little tingle in my britches. I actually feel like I could kick Edmonton's ass today.

The group of us stand and walk our way out to the ice. Luckily it seems like there's not a single one of their players in sight.

So for the rest of my time on the ice, I lock the fuck in.

I tried to leave it all out on the ice. At least as much as I could.

By the end of our warm up–that could have been a full-on fucking game–I was sweating and depleted.

But with bigger games like this, Bubbles and Stamen push the shit out of us. Yeah, I may be good, but I'm still a rookie. I'm not on the same level as Banks or Crawshack. Those are some big boys that know how to rock and roll.

We trudge back into the locker room, and collapse with collective groans against the cubbies.

I take my warm up jersey off and reach for my game jersey, holding it in my lap as I tilt my head back.

I bring my chain from inside my chest protector, not even giving a shit if it's sweaty, and loop it on my tongue before folding my arms against my chest.

Bubbles goes from player to player, telling them their strengths and weaknesses. He also reminds them about some players on the Edmonton team he knows, and how our boys can handle them.

I try to listen to him, because right now I need to, but part of me wishes I'd be walking out of this damn locker room to see my girl.

I wanna reach up and check my phone, but I know I can't, I need to listen.

It's strange being here without Tiana. I wish we could go

out after all of this and see Toronto together. When I get home, I'm making her update her damn passport so she can come with me next time. I'm not trying to leave her back again.

Eventually, Bubbles ends his little speech, and the group of us talk amongst ourselves. We trade info about some players we've collided with on the ice, and how to deal with them.

The longer we talk and trade information, the better I feel about this first game.

At least enough to walk out onto that ice confidently.

We'll see though.

CHAPTER TWELVE

TIANA

It's been a while since I heard from Gunnar.

Which right now is fine, considering I've been knee-deep in research all morning as far as getting legally married goes.

I never thought this would be my path. Getting legally married without a wedding, having a baby and building a house all at once.

But to be fair, Gunnar was right. If there is so much going on with all things planning, I would much rather plan the house and baby things than a wedding.

Sure, I loved planning the wedding when I did. But that's the thing... I loved *planning* it.

It kept my mind busy. And it kept the thoughts and emotions at bay because I was working toward something.

But I don't think I was ever excited about the actual day itself, which of course had nothing to do with actually wanting to marry Gunnar. I just don't exactly like getting dressed up. I also don't think I like the idea of having all the attention on me for the day.

In all aspects, I'm much happier with this decision. Something low-key, something sweet and intimate. And we can be married sooner rather than later.

Basically, I can get all the bullshit out of the way now, the applications and whatnot for the license before he gets back, since apparently there is a three-day waiting period before it's valid.

Then when he comes home, we can just sign it somewhere with two witnesses. Honestly... it's all perfect. But then, my mind runs, because I still have to plan where to do it, when, how, and with whom.

Even if it's not going to be big and grand right now, at the very least, I would like it to be special.

From there, I picture the forest. The place where I decided I want the house to go. That stump in the woods. I want to go with Charlotte and Adrian as the witnesses. I want to go early in the morning, when the sunlight is dappled through the trees and there's a magical type of feeling that floats in the chilled air.

My heart flutters in my chest, but is soon interrupted as Charlotte comes to plop down next to me on the couch, where I've been doing all this research and thinking.

She has a big bowl of cereal with her and leans her head against me as she watches my computer screen.

"Whatcha doinnnn'?" she asks in her playful, singsongy tone.

I can't help the small smile that pulls at my lips.

"I'm filling out the application for the marriage license," I murmur.

"Marriage license? I thought you guys weren't getting married for a while?" she asks before she takes a spoonful of cereal into her mouth.

I glance at her, watching the spoon move from the bowl to her lips.

"Gunnar wants to do the legal portion when he gets back," I say.

As I continue my glance, I see her brow furrow and she pulls away. "Already? Is he making you get married sooner?" she asks in an accusatory tone.

I roll my eyes as I lean my head back against the couch. It rolls sideways in her direction, and I stare blankly at her.

"Do you really think I'm going to be doing something I don't want to do?" I ask.

"Fair point. However, he seems to want to move fast," she says with a shrug.

My eyes narrow at her. "Again," I say.

"Mmmm. I just don't want you to do things you don't want to do," she says as she takes another bite of her cereal.

I sigh. "I would honestly like to get it out of the way now. It knocks one thing off my list and makes life easier for me in general," I explain.

Charlotte blinks. "Mmm... that's fair," she murmurs.

My brows rise in a 'duh' expression before I go back to filling out the blank spaces on the online application.

"Then I can shift focus to baby stuff and adding the house. Which will be much more hands-off than if I were going to plan the wedding while dealing with the... other things," I say as I gesture dismissively to the air.

"Mmm, he surely knows how to work you, doesn't he?" Charlotte remarks with a shrug.

My eyes widen for a fraction of a second as my mind dissects that completely differently.

Fuck. This is what I get for falling in love with a horny goon. Now, all my stupid thoughts are as dirty as his.

"That he does," is all I respond with.

"So, if you're just going to get legally married, what all do you have to do? Maybe I can bring it up to Adrian and see what he thinks," Charlotte says as she cuddles in closer to me.

The dogs sit at our feet, curling up with one another as Charlotte comes closer.

"Just fill out an application, three-day waiting period and then you have sixty days to get the 'ceremony' done and turned in, yada yada. Pretty easy, really," I say.

"Hm," she thinks out loud.

"Mhmmm," I hum in response as I type some more things in.

"Mom said she wants to do this gift shopping thing on Monday, just by the way," Charlotte says nonchalantly.

My brow furrows wildly as I look at her, almost dumbfounded at the random way she decided to tell me this.

"Monday? When did she tell you this?" I ask.

"I don't know; it was a text she sent. I saw it when I woke up," she says with a shrug.

I throw my head back with a groan as I begin to speed through the application, trying to get it done so I can start thinking about what I want to get Gunnar.

The thing about him is that he's a simple man.

He has his dog, he has his truck and his hockey. I feel like to him, that's all he could ever ask for. But it'd be our first Christmas together, and he has gotten me far more gifts than I have ever given him.

I know if I asked him what he wanted, he wouldn't even give me an answer. And the idea of my needing to get him something is somewhat nerve-wracking.

Not because I need to get him something, but because the something I need to get him has to rival anything he's ever given me.

Because he bought me fucking land! How the fuck do I top *land*!?

The thought of not being able to provide the same level of love and care to him, as he does for me, makes nausea roil in my stomach, and I slam my laptop shut with a groan.

I lean over on the couch, tugging one of the throw pillows from the armrest to hug to my chest as I sigh.

"Whoa, what the fuck was that all about?" Charlotte asks.

I groan again. "I don't know if I have what it takes to be the woman Gunnar needs," I murmur.

"Oh, shut the hell up," Charlotte says.

I scoff as I look at her. "Excuse you?"

"Stop this. If you sit around and mope about shit that isn't real, you're going to drive yourself insane. Gunnar knows you, he knows how you are, and he accepts you for you, Tiana. I don't know how many ways I need to say it, but Gunnar loves you. Is this because of the gift shit?" she asks.

"Obviously," I murmur in response.

"Well, don't. Gunnar seems like the type that would be happy if you shook your ass in his face," she says.

"I mean..." I murmur.

She has a point.

"Exactly. So stop overthinking because I know you're already going there. You've had one Menty-B this morning, and you're only allowed one a day. You're going to be fine. Now, what are we doing today?" she asks.

Sometimes Charlotte has to pull out tough love for me.

And I hate that it works. I'm not the type that responds well to coddling. Sometimes I need to be manhandled. It's how I was raised, and now it's just the thing that stops me from getting too focused on bullshit.

I groan as I sit up, wrapping my arms around my legs.

"I don't know. What did you want to do?" I ask.

Charlotte grins as she looks at me, and my brow furrows.

"Oh, fuck," I sigh.

Getting the Dawn sisters out of the house is always a mission in and of itself. But we did it.

I had to chug the coffee Gunnar got me, and then made another before we left, but it still doesn't feel like enough.

Granted, I actually really like the thing she chose for today.

Part of me wanted to stay in the house, curl into a ball and do nothing until Gunnar returned. Though, I decided that probably wasn't the best idea and a horrible waste of time.

I hate to admit that I really did like Charlotte's idea a lot more.

So after an hour or so of Charlotte getting ready and arguing about who is going to drive and where we need to stop to get Charlotte an iced coffee, here we are.

A home goods store to get decorations for Christmas.

I love fall, sure. But I love decorating for Christmas so much more. There is a level of pure nostalgia and magic that seems to accompany Christmas.

Even if I am internally freaking out about the idea of getting Gunnar a gift. I *do* get to decorate.

Charlotte, for whatever reason, has decided at her big-ass age she wants to ride in the cart.

I mean, Charlotte is a kid at heart. She always has been. So, this really shouldn't surprise me. Of course, that leaves me pushing the damn thing through this store.

I haven't decorated my place since I've lived in it, mostly because I never have people come over, but I always get to go to my parents and decorate their house. And for the most part, I have fun with it.

But now I have Gunnar, and I think him coming home to a decorated house would be the best way to welcome him.

Though I have to figure out what kind of theme to go with.

It's my place, so technically I have free rein... and with that realization, I immediately get in the Christmas spirit.

Sure, we still have Thanksgiving, but Thanksgiving is just part of Christmas; it doesn't matter.

Charlotte has decided to go with a flannel, cabin-esque route. With woody decorations, buffalo plaid, burlap and woodland animals. I bet Gunnar would like that theme simply because of the sheer number of deer that are a part of that aesthetic.

I, on the other hand, went with a blue and silver type of vibe. Elegant, classy, but also beautiful to look at.

"This is so cute!" Charlotte squeals as I stop in front of a bear statue with a buffalo plaid scarf and rugged, burlap Santa hat. She tugs the little statue into the cart with an *"oof"*, and for the next number of minutes we go through the store.

Part of me really wishes I was doing this with Gunnar, but honestly, I think it would be best if maybe we went and picked out the tree together.

I can get the ornaments and other decorations, and then we can decorate the tree together when he comes back.

And getting to spend a bunch of money is sometimes the best therapy.

By the time we leave, we are towing enormous bags with us to Charlotte's car.

We took hers because we know how we can be when we get to shop together. Plus, I know that none of my cars could hold everything. Charlotte has a mid-sized SUV, so it worked out perfectly.

When we get back to my apartment, Charlotte merely keeps all of her stuff in her vehicle, considering she doesn't need it in my place, which gives us extra hands to carry up all the stuff I bought.

Which is honestly a lot more than I expected it to be.

When we get to my door, we drop the bags by the coffee table in the living room before we herd the dogs into the back room.

As Charlotte gets them situated, I shove the coffee table out of the middle of the living room, against the large window on the back wall, and then go to the kitchen for a trash bag.

Since whenever you buy a bunch of stuff, there is always trash to accompany it.

I move all the bags to the middle of the floor and begin taking everything out.

Christmas lights, ornaments, different little knickknacks, wreaths, candles, and many decorative bits and bobs to put everywhere. I got silvery pine cone decorations, some different, large decorative wreaths and with every piece that I take out of the bag, I feel my joy rise.

As well as my excitement, because I can't wait to decorate the tree with Gunnar. I think he'll have so much fun with that.

He seems to be a kid at heart as well.

Eventually, Charlotte comes from the back room, and she sits on the floor with me, throwing some of the accumulated trash away that I've taken off of the decorations.

For the rest of the day, Charlotte and I decorate my entire apartment.

New throw pillows go on the couch, with a Christmas throw blanket on the corner. I bought a few different-sized decorative trees that are almost a cone shape and I place them in front of the fireplace, as well as a bunch of the tall blue candles throughout the space.

I know Gunnar will not be the happiest not to have the Seattle Stags blanket in the living room now, but I'm sure he'll live.

I step back and smile at Charlotte, looking at our handy work and she throws an arm over my shoulder.

"This was fun," she says.

I glance at her with a playful roll of my eyes as I throw my arm over her shoulders in return.

"It really was. Thanks Char," I say.

CHAPTER THIRTEEN
TIANA

Charlotte and I ordered some pizza and watched a movie after decorating, and then we went our separate ways.

When I get back to my room and shower, I remember that I've basically forgotten about my phone all day, and when I remember it; I scramble for it across my sheets, seeing if I have any texts from Gunnar.

Of course, there are several.

> HUSBAND 🖤
>
> Hey sugar :)

> HUSBAND 🖤
>
> We won the game today! 🐱

> HUSBAND 🖤
>
> Damn nevermind I guess we lost I'm sad cheer me up

> HUSBAND 🖤
>
> Are you even alive

HUSBAND 🖤

Tiana I'm actually getting concerned
now

HUSBAND 🖤
15 MISSED CALLS

"Fuck!" I groan. My phone has been on silent and pushed out of my mind all fucking day.

Quickly, I call back, but it goes straight to voicemail.

Soon, a text comes through.

HUSBAND 🖤

Hey, sorry, Banks is sleeping. Are
you okay??

ME

Yes! I'm so sorry! Charlotte and I
were out and about today and I
wasn't paying attention to my
phone, I'm alive I promise

But yay! I knew you guys would!! 😭

HUSBAND 🖤

Ngl I was scared shitless lmao

U never go that long without
responding

ME

I know I'm sorry

But I miss you lots):

HUSBAND 🖤

I miss you too sugar

I wished you were here to watch the
game today

We played hard af lmao

Also, ur getting your passport fixed
when we get home

> I don't think I can do this again lmao

I shake my head with a scoff. Talking to him, even through text makes me realize just how much I miss my big goon.

Yeah, it's only been a day. But I still haven't had to be separated from Gunnar this long in a while. And fuck...

HUSBAND 🖤

> I'm pretty sure I miss you more 🥺

ME

> Oh yeah? What makes you think that?

It feels like he takes a minute to text back, and I watch the three bubbles pop up several times over.

Soon, a picture comes through.

His dick. And he is hard as a rock.

HUSBAND 🖤

> Pretty sure this is a pretty good indicator on how much I miss you

I feel lust pulse through my whole body. And weirdly enough, I feel like my mouth salivates.

ME

> How in the hell are you so hard?

HUSBAND 🖤

> It's easy when I think about your pussy wrapped around it

I take a deep breath. It's kind of strange, considering we've actually never sexted. And I think this may actually be my first dick pic from him.

Relationship milestones, I guess.

And perhaps I'm rusty in my sexting because all I'm able to respond is;

ME

What would you do if I was there?

HUSBAND 🖤

I think the better question is what
wouldn't I do

I scoff, but I feel my pulse raging in my core. It's unfair that he does this to me when he's away. But I want to see more of him, because if I can't have him on me, at least I can admire him from afar.

ME

Are... you going to stroke it?

HUSBAND 🖤

I wasn't going to. But I'll do anything
for you, sugar

I take a deep breath as I scroll back up to it.

Jesus Christ, I can't believe the man I'm marrying has the biggest dick I've ever seen.

ME

Sound on plz 🔊

I feel like he is taking forever to respond this time. But when he eventually does, it's a video.

My pulse pumps hard through my body as I press on the video, waiting for it to play.

His hand grips tight around his cock, stroking himself up and down. It seems as if he's moved to the bathroom.

Makes sense if he's sharing a room with Adrian.

My lips part as I watch with intent, my thighs rubbing together as heat seems to devour my body.

"Fuck," he groans through the video.

His groans are so tortured, so quiet... but deep and husky as he pants in between his groans.

I can see the tight grip he has on himself, as well as the pre-cum that pools at the tip.

"I wish this was your fucking pussy on me, baby," he pants.

"Oh... fuck," I murmur out loud to myself.

Without thought, I flip over on the bed, opening my legs and letting my hand snake down my body. Soon, they slip straight into my pussy. Finding my clit, I swirl my fingers around it slowly as I watch him stroke himself.

Soon, my phone vibrates again. I exit the video to see his text.

I take a deep breath, because holy fuck, I haven't done this since college. Opening my legs wide, I turn the back camera on and point my phone at my pussy. Until it vibrates again.

My brow furrows, and I bring it up to see what he said.

I roll my eyes with a playful scoff. Positioning the camera to point at my core again, I part it for him, moaning as my middle finger circles my clit.

I whimper, picking up my speed just enough.

"Fuck, I miss your cock," I moan out.

I think about the way he feels, the way I feel empty without him, and my pussy tightens around nothing as I speed up more. Soon, I bring the phone up to my breasts, using my arms to press them together, and my hand leaves my core to pinch my nipples with my wetness.

"I wish you were here to suck them," I pant as I tug at my nipples. My pleasure heightens, my breaths lightening as I stop the video and turn my phone around to look at the screen.

I don't particularly enjoy seeing myself on camera, so I at least make sure the pieces I wanted are in frame before I send it to him.

My heart rate picks up. I don't know why I'm nervous about sending something like this to him. He's had me every way I've ever wanted.

But I *am.*

As I wait for his response, I go to his previous video, trying to finish it.

"God, I need you here to bounce on it. I'd make sure the entire fucking Edmonton team knew the way you sound when you're calling out my name," he groans as his speed picks up.

My fingers go back to my clit, swirling and stroking it in time with his.

"I miss the way your fucking cunt locks me in, baby. I'd give anything to be balls deep in you right now," he adds.

I groan in pleasure at the sound of his voice, so clear, so deep and gruff as his hand works his cock.

Suddenly, the video ends, and I growl in frustration.

Luckily, my phone vibrates again.

HUSBAND 🖤

Holy fuck baby 😳

You have no idea how I'm going to destroy you when I get home

ME

Plz do

I'm aching for it

HUSBAND 🖤

I miss fucking you in the morning baby

Your pussy is the best thing to wake up to

Soon, another video comes through, and I open it.

I hear his groans, and I see the way his hand has sped up on his cock. Sometimes taking longer strokes, or pumping just the head of himself.

My fingers go down to my clit again, watching in tunnel-visioned focus as he groans.

"Fucking hell," he pants. "Your pussy looks so good. But I know it looks better with me in it," he says with an exhausted chuckle as his hand speeds up.

My fingers speed up, my orgasm closing in as I watch him.

"Come with me, baby. I know you're close, come with me," he pants.

And fuck he knows me, because I *am*.

"I'm gonna fucking come... fuck, Tiana," he grits and those last few words, the breathless desperation in the way he calls for me. Moans *my* name.

His groans lighten, his hand moving faster, and soon he growls again, his hand pausing as he comes. White streams pump from him, a low groan sounding through the phone, and I come undone.

I bite down on my lip, stifling my moans as my orgasm slams into me from the side.

My hips buck against my hand, riding out my orgasm with the vision of him coming. His words still playing on the phone.

"Fuck... fuckfuckfuck...," he pants.

I groan because I wish so badly I weren't hearing this through the phone. I want it right in my ear, talking me through every pulse around his cock.

Soon my orgasm slows, and I pant as I relax on the bed. My hand with my phone falls to the side, and I take heaving breaths through the aftermath of it all.

Fucking hell, I need that man.

My phone vibrates again, and I wait a minute to recuperate before I bring it up to my face to read his message.

HUSBAND 🖤

Did you come? I did

I roll my eyes with a laugh.

ME

Lmao yes. I wish it was you though

HUSBAND 🖤

Sweet 😎

ME

Omg I literally just watched you come, why did you tell me you came

HUSBAND 🖤

Idk I had to make sure you knew. I could have come, but you could be fibbing 👀

ME

When have I ever faked an orgasm
with you?

HUSBAND 🖤

HAVE YOU?! 😭

ME

Omg Gunnar, no. You think I can
fake the way my vagina locks
you in?

HUSBAND 🖤

That'd be impressive ngl

ME

Omg did you clean up your mess?

HUSBAND 🖤

Ugh yes. I forgot how messy this
was. I've been coming in you for so
long I forgot

I smile as the clarity of the day comes back to me and my
excitement from earlier comes back ten fold.

ME

Oh, so I wasn't responding earlier
because Charlotte and I went
Christmas shopping 😬

HUSBAND 🖤

Christmas shopping?? Like gifts??

ME

No we got decorations

HUSBAND 🖤

oooo sounds fun. Did you guys
decorate?

ME

Some, but I bought us some stuff to decorate a tree 💀

HUSBAND 🖤

Do you have a tree

ME

No I figured you and I would go pick one and we'd decorate it together (:

HUSBAND 🖤

I like the sound of that. Thanks for waiting for me sugar 🤍

ME

I couldn't decorate our first Christmas tree without you!

HUSBAND 🖤

Silly girl lmao

I have to get to bed, gotta wake up early tomorrow

I just wanted to make sure you were alive since SOMEONE WANTED ME TO FREAK OUT FOR SEVERAL HOURS 🗣️

ME

I'm sorry!!! I'll text you quicker tomorrow I promise 🤍🤍🤍

HUSBAND 🖤

U better or you're going to get it when I get home

ME

Is that a promise??? 👀

HUSBAND 🖤

Try me, see how well I keep my promises

ME

Yes sir

HUSBAND 🖤

Love you baby!

Sleep well please

AND DON'T FORGET TO EAT

ME

I willlllllllllll! I love you most!!

HUSBAND 🖤

You don't but good night, baby!

With a heavy sigh, I clutch my phone to my chest. Being able to get my mind off of Gunnar for the day may have helped in the moment.

But when the night falls, and the darkness closes in, it makes me really miss the quiet evenings together.

The ones where we'd crawl into bed, curled in one another's arms, and he held me as I slept.

The small forehead kisses and back rubs. I miss those especially right about now.

I hate that I have to imagine them. And I hate even more that I won't have them for sleep tonight.

Soon, I get under the blankets, curling them tight around me with a heavy sigh as I wish they were my big dorky goon.

And then, I fall asleep.

CHAPTER FOURTEEN
GUNNAR

Today, thank fuck, there's no game. Which means, at the least, we don't get to stress ourselves over a win. However, that doesn't stop Bubbles from doing some random team bonding exercises.

Which means he has brought us back to the rink, where we will spend the rest of our day doing stupid shit. I mean, we have rink time, so might as well.

And I love hockey. This is a fact.

What I *don't* love, however, is elementary school shit in hockey.

This is the NHL, so why in the hell do we need to go over this shit?

But Bubbles is on a warpath this morning, and he wants to get us back to the basics. While somehow mixing some other shit in with it.

More advanced things to keep us on our toes.

Eventually, there's a lull, and I'm able to crash on the bench beside Banks.

He looks unimpressed and has barely even broken a sweat.

"You talk to Miss Tiana yesterday?" Banks asks as he keeps his eye on Bubbles and Stamen talking to each other on the rink.

"Ah, yeah. She and Charlotte were out buying Christmas stuff," I say.

Not hearing from Tiana for that insane amount of time drove me insane. Only because Tiana usually always responds and with me so far away, of course I was terrified that something had happened to her.

Poor Banks had to hear the end of my fears, but he had assured me they were fine.

He didn't want to bother Charlotte because he likes to give her space when he's away.

That's all good and dandy, but shit, man, I needed to make sure *my* lady was okay.

"Sounds about right. Them girls love their Christmas," he says with a nod.

"Yeah, well, you sure weren't any fuckin' help," I grumble as I tug my chain from my jersey to slide between my lips before I fold my arms against my chest. I take a frustrated breath through the chain as I lean back against the wall with my feet crossed, one over the other, in front of me.

"To be fair, I did that for you. If you go buck-wild when she doesn't return a message for a little bit every time we gotta be sent over yonder, you'll give yourself a damn heart attack. The girls are more than capable of handlin' themselves," he says.

I huff through my chain in response.

"Don't grunt at me, Hayze. You know just as well as I do, you don't stop when your mind gets fixated. So let the women breathe."

"You don't worry about Charlotte when you're gone?" I mumble as I watch my foot. It tips back-and-forth lazily, and I concentrate on the small area on the wall that the tip of my skate scratches.

"Of course I do. But you know just as well as I do that a woman likes her space, and if Miss Tiana is busy, then she's busy. That's simple arithmetic," Banks says. Though he watches Bubbles and Stamen. Rather intently, I might add.

"You know I know how to give that woman space. But this is also my first time away from her like this, give me a break, man," I say with a groan.

"I've seen stud bulls with more patience," Banks grunts in return.

"Yeah, yeah. Cows and all that jazz," I say with a dismissive wave of my hand.

"Mmm," Banks responds. "You lay off the baby talk?"

"Haven't even really talked. But she asked for a video last night, and I didn't mention breeding, so there. Happy now, ya' fuckin' grouch?"

"Thanks for waiting until I was asleep."

"Yeah, well, I didn't have a choice, it was when she finally responded," I mumble.

"Y'all got any plans for Thanksgiving and Christmas?" Banks asks.

And honestly, I hadn't thought about it yet.

I know Tiana asked, but I figured she would end up solving that problem.

"Nah... Not yet," I murmur with a sigh. Soon, my tongue slides back and forth against my chain in thought, and my gaze moves to the ice to where Bubbles and Stamen are talking.

Part of me feels like I should try to plan it myself, and just let her take the reins on the projects she wants to do.

The other part wants to let her do it because Tiana likes control, so if she knows what's going to happen, it'll ease her stress.

But...

My gaze returns to Banks, where he is *still* just staring at Bubbles and Stamen.

"The fuck is your issue? You haven't taken your eyes off them," I say.

"Bastards are cooking up trouble," he mutters.

"Jesus Christ," I say with a sigh and a roll of my eyes.

I send a high-pitched whistle out toward the two of them, who jolt as they look over at us.

Bubbles looks like he's three seconds from choking me, but I nod for him to come over to us, anyway.

He tosses his head back with what appears to be a sigh before he leisurely skates over to us.

"What is it, Hayze?" he asks with a sigh.

"What are you guys doing for Thanksgiving and Christmas?" I ask.

His eyes linger on my lips for a long moment before they go back up to my eyes. "The fuck is on your lip?"

"What? It's my mustache. The team is doing No Nut, No Shave November," I say with a grin.

"Why doesn't he have one?" Bubbles asks as he nods to Banks.

I look over at Banks before I look back at Bubbles with a shrug. "I reckon he can't grow one."

Glancing at Banks, I notice he gives me a side-eyed glare before it tracks back to Bubbles.

Bubbles sighs. "What's your question again?"

"Christmas, Thanksgiving, what's the move?" I ask.

His brow furrows. "We're playin' fuckin' Edmonton tomorrow and you're stuck on that?"

"Banks asked, and I want to take some of the pressure off of Tiana for planning something like that."

Bubbles looks between Banks and me for a moment.

"I can't believe you two fucks are going to be my sons-in-law," he says as he drags his hands over his face.

I glance at Banks, who merely watches Bubbles like some kind of guard dog.

Until his words register for me.

"Sons? Plural?" I ask.

"Banks asked me for Charlotte's hand a few weeks ago. Don't think he's popped the question yet either, so keep your mouth shut about it to Tiana," he says as he points a harsh finger at me.

I give him a mock salute with a nod. "Aye aye, sir."

He rolls his eyes in annoyance. "Christ Almighty," he says with a sigh. "Now what about Thanksgiving and Christmas?" he asks.

"What are you guys doing?"

Bubbles laughs. "Well, since for the first time in a long ass time that both of our girls have someone to spend the holidays with, Tamisha and I are going on a cruise. So, we will be gone for Christmas. We haven't had a vacation with just the two of us in years," he says with a smile.

"Fair. So when do you leave?" I ask.

"Mid-December. So we'll be here for Thanksgiving but not Christmas," he says.

I hum in thought.

I know my family is going to Wisconsin for Christmas, but I'm staying here. They wanted to go see my grandparents, who still live out there.

"What about you?" I ask Banks.

"Miss Lotty and I are goin' back home to Montana for a few weeks. Won't be here for Christmas. Be here for Thanksgiving, though," he says with a nod.

"So everyone is here for Thanksgiving, and only Tiana and I will be here for Christmas," I murmur.

"'Peers so," Banks responds.

"Alright, well... what if Tiana and I did Thanksgiving with

my parents, and then we did a second Thanksgiving at your house, Coach?" I ask.

Bubbles' brow furrows and his upper lip curls in annoyance. "We're just inviting ourselves over now?"

I groan. "Big Papa Coach-in-law, can Tiana, Charlotte, Banks and I come over for Thanksgiving dinner, please?" I ask as I clasp my hands at my chest and give him a big convincing grin.

"Never do that shit again or you're doing suicides on the ice," he grumbles as he skates away.

"Is that a yes?!" I call out as I stand.

I press my hands to the edge of the box, waiting for him to answer.

"Gotta talk to the Missus and I'll get back to you!" he calls back before he spins to stop himself as he gets back to Stamen.

I groan as I sit down on the bench and throw myself back against the wall with a huff.

"You think he'll say yes?" I ask as I tilt my head toward Banks.

"I reckon he'd have to deal with a lashing from Miss Lotty if he said no," Banks says.

"Sweet," I respond with a grin.

Soon the whistle blows and we're sent back to the ice for more torture.

By the time we get back to the hotel, I would sincerely like to chop my legs off.

Walking or even skating right now seems like it would be the worst thing ever. I crash on the bed because I had made it a point to shower before we left the arena.

It's probably just habit, but I also was not trying to shower when I got back to the hotel. I merely wanted to lie down.

But I remember I have a fiancée and scramble into my pocket for my phone.

SUGAR

I hope you have a good day!! I love you

I got your coffee again today! Thank u

Wow so is this payback for yesterday??

I stg if you don't text me back in three seconds I'm not letting you see my boobs for a month

welp, no boobs for you ig

Fuck! Damn Bubbles and his bullshit.
Quickly, I text back.

ME

I'm so sorry sugar):

Ur dad worked us to the fucking bone today

We didnt even have a game today he just wanted to make us suffer

It takes a few minutes, but eventually the bubble that says she's typing pops up.

SUGAR

He gets real intense in Canada

Charlotte has always said as much

ME

Yeah well, he proved it today

SUGAR

Well you only have a few days and
you can come home (:

ME

Trust me I'm counting down
the days

What did you guys do today?

SUGAR

I've been doing courthouse wedding
research stuff

I've applied for the license and I
have an idea for how I want to do it
when you get home

My heart pounds a little harder in my chest at that.
Holy shit, I'm going to have a wife in less than a week or two.
That's insane to think about in the grand scheme of things.
But fuck...

ME

I also have a few ideas of how to do
it when I get home

SUGAR

Omg

ME

I'm kidding

...

not really but I can't wait to see what
you've planned

I know it'll be amazing sugar (:

I smile as I wait for her text, holding my phone to my chest.

I really hope that Bubbles lets us come to their house for Thanksgiving. I know I'll have to tell my parents that we're coming to their place and to have some things for Tiana to eat.

And it'll be our first holiday together. I mean, yeah, of course Halloween counted, but Thanksgiving and Christmas are different beasts entirely...

Christmas.

Wait! FUCK! CHRISTMAS!

I haven't put a single fucking thought into what to get her at all!

Turning over on the bed, I scramble for my backpack on the floor and haul out my laptop.

Opening it, I frantically search through anything I can to find what she may like.

Sure, I could let her buy more books; I could do any number of things.

But this is our first Christmas. I can't be a fucking chump with her.

I groan, and as I do, Banks comes out of the bathroom with a towel around his waist.

"The fucks got your panties in a bunch, dozer?" Banks asks with a furrow to his brow.

I groan as I toss my head back. "I haven't thought at all about what to get Tiana for Christmas," I grumble as I scroll through a bunch of websites.

"You realize you just bought her fuckin' land for a house, right?" Banks asks.

"Yeah, yeah, land shmand. The fuck is she gonna do with that for Christmas?" I ask with a sigh and a wave of my hand before it pauses... because *land*...

Wait.

"How much can your truck tow?" I ask as I glance at him.

His brow rises as he looks at me cautiously. "Enough. Why?"

"I think... I know exactly what I'm going to get my little lady," I say with a grin.

"Christs fuckin' sakes," he says with a sigh as he goes directly to his bed and curls up under the blankets.

A grin twists my face as I sit up in bed to get comfy with my laptop in my lap.

For the rest of the night, I dive headfirst into research.

CHAPTER FIFTEEN

TIANA

There should have been more prep to go into this excursion with my mother and Charlotte today.

Luckily, like clockwork, my coffee showed up at my door this morning. It has given me a small glimmer of happiness in the morning knowing Gunnar set something up like this for me.

But I was silently dreading having to spend the entire day with my mother and Charlotte.

The three Dawn women don't get together that often. Our personalities are all so different, all of them strong-willed, which makes going out together a bit of a chore.

So many opinions, so many thoughts and ideas all being thrown around at once.

You have a law firm mother, a social-media/equipment manager, and a young lawyer... the whole scenario is just ripe for tension.

Not to mention, my mother is a tad feral with gifts.

We have always sort of been on the higher end of privileged

because of my parent's jobs. And that shows in the way my mom likes to give gifts.

So now, Charlotte and I are standing in the lobby of my apartment complex for our mom to grab us.

I think it makes the most sense for my mom to drive us today, simply because she has a massive Suburban, and knowing the three of us, we'll end up stuffing it to the brim.

That's going to happen when you have a bunch of women with deep pockets. I send a text to Gunnar as we wait for my mom to arrive. Especially since he was so scared last time.

It was nice of him to worry. But at the same time, it's a feeling I don't think I'm used to.

For me, it's sometimes out of sight, out of mind. With my phone being out of sight, we were just so focused on all the Christmas decorating. I felt bad when I realized I had scared him, but I also enjoyed that I could let go of my worries for a little bit.

Mostly because I know Gunnar would not want me to be sitting at home moping all day.

So many thoughts... so many feelings.

I sigh as I pull my phone out and go to Gunnar's contact.

Quickly, I type out a message and send it.

ME

Me, my mom and Charlotte are going out shopping today

Try not to worry, I may not respond for a while 😉

I love you!!! Try not to maim my father please! I really like him in my life 😅

It's later in the day for him because of the time difference between Canada and Washington, so I imagine he's busy getting tortured by my dad. With that knowledge, I throw my phone into my backpack and situate it on my back before I press my hands tight around my cup of coffee and bring it to my lips to chew on the edge of the sip hole.

Charlotte finally looks up from her phone as my mom rolls up in front of the complex, and I sigh.

"Shotgun!" Charlotte cries as she punches me in the arm and rushes out the door.

With a groan, I throw my head back and reluctantly follow Charlotte out to the vehicle.

She hops into the front, and I see her lean over the center console to give my mom a hug, and I move myself into the back seat.

To be honest, I don't mind riding in the back because the second row has really nice captain's chairs. So I get my own little space here.

I take my backpack off and place it in the middle, between the two seats, and buckle my seatbelt before I bring my coffee back up to my lips.

"Morning, Tiana," she says as she looks at me in the rearview mirror with a grin.

"Gooood morning," I mumble with a sigh before I sip at my coffee.

"Where are we going first, Mommy?" Charlotte asks.

"Well, there are a few things I know your dad wants. But you guys didn't mention what you guys want to get for your men. Charlotte?" she asks as she pulls out from in front of the complex. The vehicle moves down the road, and I settle into my seat.

"Adrian is apparently building an upgrade onto the stables. I want to get some more stable equipment for him. Or even a new bridle for Chauncey and Cilla. I think he would like new cowboy boots too," she says with a proud nod.

I groan as I place my coffee in the cupholder and lean against the armrest to look out the window.

Of course, she would get the easier man to shop for with all his things and hobbies.

"Ah, yes. The stable upgrade. I remember that," my mom says with a sigh.

My brow furrows as I turn to look toward my mom in confusion. "What do you know about a stable upgrade?" I ask.

"When your darling fiancé was making the contract for your land, Adrian didn't want money for it. Gunnar insisted and offered a thousand per acre. But again, Adrian said no and said he could pay a thousand for the land and fourteen for a stable upgrade," my mom says.

I hum an annoyed groan as I bring my fingers up to rub my temples. "Fourteen grand for a stable upgrade? Seriously? Those were the terms and conditions?" I mumble.

My lawyer brain aches at the thought of all this, and another groan works out of me as my hands move from my temples to run over my face. I should have fully expected this from those two. I mean, after reading the deed, that is. But it's still insane that that is the agreement they came to.

"Hey, they wanted it. So they got it. I know not to come between weird gentlemen's agreements and the like. I'm just the one that writes them down," my mother says as she turns out onto the highway.

"Lord have mercy," I say with a sigh.

"Trust me. I know," my mom responds.

It's small moments like these, where I feel like my mother are on the same wavelength, that make me feel closer to her. Not that we aren't close. We just have a different relationship compared to Charlotte and her. Charlotte can also express herself better than I can. Which is easier for my mom to process, I think.

"What about you? What are you getting Daddy?" Charlotte asks as she leans her elbows on the center console to look at our mom.

"He wanted some more of his figures. He paints these... Warhammer?? Is that what they are? I don't know. He does it after work for hours. Has an entire army of them. So, I plan on getting him more paints, figures, and brushes. Whatever makes him real happy for so long," she says with a shrug.

Again, these women with their men and their hobbies.

Gunnar lives and breathes hockey, and I don't even think he'd care about extra pads. He has literally tons of pads.

I feel like my mood dampens when my mom parks at the first store. Some kind of gaming hobby shop. Which I guess makes sense for whatever the fuck she's getting my dad.

We all climb out and head into the store. My mom goes to talk to the person at the counter for the things she needs, while Charlotte and I listlessly roam the store.

She bends over to look at some of the smaller figures on display, her head tilting as she appraises them.

"Interesting," she says softly.

"You ever seen Dad do this little hobby of his?" I ask as I watch her.

"Not really. To be honest, this is the first I've heard of it. But, ya know, with the new draft picks and age, it seems like the game stresses him out more and more. So this little thing of his makes sense, I guess," Charlotte responds as she continues looking over the figure. "These ones can't piss him off with the wrong plays," she adds with a giggle.

I give her an unimpressed huff before she comes to a stand and continues walking around the store. I follow, looking at the kits on the wall, and at some displays of tiny paints.

My brow furrows, and I sigh in frustration.

"I have no idea what to get Gunnar. All I know is that he loves hockey," I say.

"Go with that. There're tons of hockey things you can get men," she says as she makes small skips around the store.

"Yeah, okay. Just *more* hockey stuff. The fuck kind of hockey stuff would I get him?" I ask.

"Well, I don't think a new stick is in order. We just got new sticks from our supplier. Granted, he wasn't the most thrilled with it. But I mean... they got new sticks," she says with a shrug.

"Okay, well what would *you* get a hockey player who only really likes hockey?" I ask.

She hums in thought as she stops at a fully set up display, her head tilting as she looks over it.

"I'll get back to you on that," she murmurs as she rises to her full height.

"See, you don't even know," I respond with a scoff.

"I do, I'm just really intrigued by this strange hobby," she murmurs.

"Whatever," I grumble in annoyance.

"Girls," my mom calls to us, where she lingers at the entrance of the shop with a large bag in tow.

Charlotte squeals and runs off after our mom, and I follow.

My mom holds the door open for us, and again... I retreat deep into my brain.

"What the fuck do I get a hockey player for Christmas?" I mutter out loud to myself.

As we climb into the vehicle, the question gnaws incessantly at my brain. At my entire *mood*.

I'll feel like the biggest fucking failure if I can't figure out this gift situation.

I know Gunnar is going to go all out. He always does. Even when it isn't a fucking holiday.

As I settle into my seat, I scroll through some options on my phone.

When an idea comes to me... it's lame.

It's *so* lame. It's *so* dumb. But I think the gesture behind it is really... what matters, right?

I sigh as I look through my notifications again.

There were no messages on my screen and none in the notification center, which means Gunnar is still probably getting his ass beat by my dad.

Poor guy.

I'm going to have to give him so many massages when he gets home.

Lucky me.

"Charlotte, where is this place you wanted to go?" my mom asks as she pulls out of the parking lot.

Charlotte leans over the center console to type in the address for the next place she needs us to go.

Which I imagine will be some sort of one-stop shop for all the shit she needs.

In the meantime, I will scrounge for ideas.

Maybe I won't have to get anything while we're out and about today. I can lie to them and say I ordered it on the way there.

Yes. Perfect.

Fake it 'til you make it type of situation.

But as I'm scrolling on my phone... an even more devious idea comes into play.

I glance up at the two of them, who are chatting about something else–I have no idea; I wasn't paying attention–before I look back down at my phone.

Gunnar seems like the adventurous type.

And while I don't really think we need anything for the bedroom... there is more than one way to have fun.

Oh God, is he going to think I don't enjoy him enough if I'm doing this?

No... no, that's preposterous. Gunnar is spontaneous...

He'll enjoy this well-enough.

I search for the thing I'm thinking of, and I come across a few websites.

One has a much nicer webpage than I expected, with many more things that I didn't even really know existed.

Sex swings? Sex chairs?? Oh fuck, what have I done?

This is so incredibly far out of my comfort zone.

My hand comes up to my mouth, nibbling at the edge of my finger for a long while, contemplating whether I should... or *shouldn't.*

But at the end of the day, I too am slightly curious. And this sort of thing has always been a part of us. Exploring curiosities.

With that excuse, I get sucked into my phone, looking through all the different toys and gadgets.

Insane, the amount of things they have just for sex nowadays.

I don't even realize my mom has stopped the car until she speaks to me.

"Tiana?!" her voice breaks through my intense research.

My head shoots up, and wide-eyed, I stare at her.

"Are you coming?" she asks.

"Oh... I uh..." I look back down at my phone, thinking about whether to go in or stay.

Looking at where we are, I notice we've stopped at some kind of down-home tack supply shop, and know there's not a damn thing in there I would need.

I turn to my mom and give her a wide grin. "No, no, it's alright, I'll stay here," I say.

"Are you sure?" she asks with a furrow of her brow.

A blush runs over my cheeks, as I feel like my mother has caught me red-handed.

Technically she has, but I'm a lawyer, and I'm not showing my tells.

"Yes, I'm all good. There's nothing I need in there anyway," I tell her with a confident nod.

"Alright. Well, I'll leave the keys here then. Lock the doors," she says as she and Charlotte climb out of the car.

Luckily my mom leaves the vehicle on, so I lean forward over the center console and lock all the doors.

When I sit back, I take a deep... *deep* breath and add far too many things to my cart for the entire time they're gone.

Crashing into my bed that night is as satisfying as it is annoying.

Annoying because I'm fucking tired. Being out all day is a pain in the ass. Because there were still more places that my mom and sister wanted to go to.

Aside from getting things for them, I decided I would buy some stuff for some of the other men in Gunnar's life, and my dad.

I went with something Formula One themed for my dad, considering that was something we used to watch together.

For Gunnar's dad, I went with a splitting maul since he likes to chop wood so often.

And then I got stuff for his brothers, his mom, which I felt good about.

Still, I did not feel any better about the things I got Gunnar.

Quickly showering, I curl up in bed, tugging on my bonnet and tying it tight around my forehead before laying back and finally checking my messages.

There were a few from Gunnar and I let out a sad sigh as I read it.

HUSBAND 🖤

> Long fucking day sugar

> I'm so sorry

> I hope you had fun shopping with your mom and sister!

> But I'll text you in the morning

> I love you only 4 more days till i'm home

I really wanted to talk to him today... but I guess this is part of reality as a hockey wife.

I know my mom had gone through it way before I was born, when my dad was a hockey player... but I feel like my mom is much stronger than me. She's been in this game a lot longer than I have.

This is my first time loving someone like this, let alone being without them.

I plug my phone in with a heaving sigh before I roll up in the blankets, where the loneliness bears down on me. No big warm goon at my back, holding me close and stroking my belly to sleep.

Not to mention, I don't feel entirely pleased with what I bought today. It was an idea, but that doesn't mean it was the best one. It makes me feel like I don't know fuckall about my man.

I've never been the best at reciprocation. Never been the best at giving others as much as they give me.

But God help me, I want to try so bad for Gunnar. Because he deserves it. He gives me so much love, care and attention every day, and I need him to feel that in return.

The frustrations burn and whirl for what feels like hours until eventually, I fall asleep.

CHAPTER SIXTEEN
TIANA

Charlotte didn't plan on doing anything today, so she accompanied me on some errands I have to run in town.

One of which is going to get the marriage license papers.

We end up taking the Corvette today since it's easier to move around Seattle with it, and she also said she wanted to grab a few more things for the ranch house, which meant we were going to some kind of store afterwards, I'm not even sure.

But my mind works the whole morning as we drive down to the courthouse.

My heart also pounds at today's errands.

Holy *fuck*, I'm going to be a wife... I never thought I would be... probably *ever* in my life.

It was never something I looked forward to; it was never something I really put much thought into. In actuality, I thought I'd be on my own forever.

Maybe have a cat or some kind of furry companion at some point when I got lonely enough.

But then this big goon literally checked his way into my

life, and now I'm going to the courthouse to get wedding papers.

All of it... is *harrowing*.

But also... thrilling.

There is an entirely new chapter of my life that I get to have with someone who truly loves and cares for me in the most complete way.

Someone who damn near lives for me and my happiness.

Fulfilling, I think, is a better word for it.

After so many years of thinking you weren't supposed to belong to someone... there's a hope you get for the rest of your future when you find something you weren't looking for.

A smile paints my face as I think, driving through the streets toward the courthouse.

Until Charlotte interrupts my thoughts.

"What's the smile for?" she asks teasingly.

I glance at her from the corner of my eye before I look back at the road.

"I'm honestly in shock that I'm going to be someone's wife," I say.

"Me too. I definitely thought I would be the one to get married first," she says with a shrug.

My brow furrows as I turn my head to look at her. "Rude, much?" I scoff.

"Yeah, okay, like you didn't think the same thing. Bye," she returns with a wave of her hand.

"I'm literally older, but whatever," I say with a small grin.

"Two minutes, Tiana. You are older by TWO MINUTES. We're TWINS," she says with a cross of her arms.

"Either way, it's still crazy," I respond.

Soon, we park in one of the parking lots beside the courthouse building, since it's not too far from the complex, and I take a deep breath.

I make sure I have all the files and information I need before I look at Charlotte.

She gives me a reassuring smile.

"But I am happy for you, Ti," she says. Her voice softens, and I smile back at her.

"I'm really happy for myself, too," I say.

"And you should be. You deserve to be happy," she responds.

My eyes begin to burn with the emotions running just a little too high for my liking, and I realize I have to get out of this situation. Quickly, I throw the door open to the Corvette, waiting for Charlotte to get out before I lock it.

She skips around the front of the vehicle to wrap her arms around one of mine, and we cross the street to where the courthouse building is.

As we climb the stairs, I try to look at this with heart eyes. Another step forward for Gunnar and me's future.

Usually, the stress and fear of it all would drive me into sheer panic. There's a small part of me that's proud of myself for doing this. Proud of myself for falling in love.

Which seems silly, I think.

But when you have lived your life with the idea that you were unlovable, or that you'd never love someone else...

I think pride is good when you have finally discovered you are capable of those things.

Shaking my head, I fill my lungs with air as we get to the top of the steps and into the building.

Since I'm a lawyer, this is a building I need to come to sometimes; however, I'm not usually going to the marriage division of the building.

Sure, I deal with divorces and pre-nups, but I'm usually doing them from my desk. Or at least signing off on them.

When we make it to where we need to be, I speak to the clerk at the desk, handing in the proper paperwork.

It takes a bit of time for her to print out everything from her end, but when all is said and done, the clerk hands me the license and other papers for the marriage ceremony, and Charlotte and I make our way back out to the Vette.

I can't help looking through all the papers as we make our way through the building and across the street to the parking lot. The entire time, my arm jostles with the way Charlotte holds onto it and skips in glee beside me.

I imagine in the womb, Charlotte was the one that took all the fun and radiant energy, so she usually has enough to express it for the both of us.

So I let her.

Even if I'm not able to express my excitement the same way she can, I am glad that she does. It makes me feel like I'm able to experience it.

When we get into the car, I settle into the driver's seat and take a deep breath as I come up on the one paper I was expecting.

"Gunnar Hayze and Tiana Dawn" written on the license.

"I'm going to be a wife," I murmur softly.

"The best wife!" Charlotte giggles from beside me as she gets in and throws her arms around my shoulders for a hug. But my eyes and hands are still stuck to the paper in awe.

She rocks me back and forth, and I finally turn to smile at her.

"I'm so proud of you, Ti," she finally says with bright tears in her eyes.

I can't help shaking my head playfully before I bring a hand up to her head and pull it to mine in comfort.

"Thanks, Charlotte," I say softly.

Next, Charlotte wanted to get more Christmas decorations, so when we get to the store she wanted, I'm able to sort of enjoy the fact that I've got that part of my life squared away.

There's a pep in my step now as we make our way through a different home goods store.

But as I follow Charlotte around–where she looks for kitchen stuff–we end up passing the baby section, and my heart squeezes.

I release a deep sigh, feeling my mood tank and veer off course almost magnetically.

"Ti!" I hear Charlotte from behind me, but I just keep walking.

I don't know why. But I have a feeling that whatever we did before Gunnar left didn't work. In the process, I can't help but feel a small bit of disappointment. Grabbing one of the onesies on the rack, I look it over with a sigh.

I hear Charlotte's shopping cart as she comes up beside me, and I look at her with a small frown.

"What's wrong?" she asks.

"I think it's going to take longer for me to get pregnant that I expected, and it makes me sad," I say softly.

"Well, yeah. It's not like in the movies. It takes a little bit of time," she says as she throws an arm around my shoulder.

I groan as my head tosses back. "Yes, I know I'm aware. But still, I can't help feeling upset," I say as I lean my head onto her shoulder.

"Well, I know you like to make things. And I know you love to research. So, to stave off your sadness, how about you make like... I don't know... a little baby-making PowerPoint for you and Gunnar?" she asks.

My brow furrows as I look at her, leaning up from her shoulder. "A what?" I ask.

"If you're, like, super serious about this, maybe you should research all the stuff you need to do to get pregnant. And put it in a PowerPoint-type thing to present to Gunnar. Because there is stuff he needs to do as well," Charlotte says with a shrug.

The longer she explains this little idea, the less outrageous it sounds.

I like information; I enjoy knowing things. And when I know as much as I can, there is a level of ease I'm able to have with my situations.

As insane as the idea is, part of it may keep me from being so upset about it.

Looking up data and other things so I won't have to beat myself up so hard over it.

"I hate that that may be a good idea," I mumble with a deep sigh.

"I just know you, Ti," she says with a giggle.

I roll my eyes, and move through the store with her, helping her find the stuff she's looking for.

There was one more thing I needed to do before we went home, but I made sure Charlotte stayed in the Vette while I got it. I told her I needed pads.

But when I get out of the car and into the drugstore, I head straight for the pregnancy tests. I think if we're going to be trying for a baby, it's probably good to have them on hand.

Going to the section with the condoms and pregnancy tests is the strangest feeling. Mostly because I've never had to buy condoms with Gunnar. Which is funny when I think about it, but also... holy shit, I'm buying *pregnancy tests*.

I don't even know which ones are the best... but I recognize the blue and white ones, so I grab a box of those before I head to the front of the store. However, because I don't want Charlotte to ask many questions, I grab her a bag of her favorite candy to distract her.

Quickly paying for my goods, I shove the tests in the pocket of my hoodie before I walk out of the store, only appearing at the car with the bag of candy.

I get in the car with a sigh as I toss the bag of candy into Charlotte's lap.

"They didn't have what I was looking for," I mumble.

Charlotte squeals as she grabs the candy and starts ripping open the bag.

A sly smirk pulls at my lips before I throw the car into gear and drive home.

When we get home, Charlotte helps me bring in the Christmas decorations I bought on this trip to the home goods store.

I couldn't help it when I saw it. There was a lot of cute Christmas stuff they had out on display that matched the look I was going for, and I envisioned exactly where it could go in the apartment, so I bought it.

Little white deer statues, some of those cute Christmas townhouses that people make villages with. It made me think about when Gunnar and I get our house, and we can decorate every year. Over time, we could collect a bunch of the houses, and eventually have a massive village.

So, I bought a few to get us started.

Charlotte and I put up a few more of the things I bought before she retreated to the bedroom to ready herself for bed.

I go back to my room, shower and crawl into bed to relax before I'm able to finally check my phone.

Gunnar had texted me only a few times.

HUSBAND 🖤

> Another big game tomorrow

> I'm sorry we haven't talked more, sugar

> your dad is ruthless

> I have to get to bed though; I love you

> I'll talk to you soon

Part of me is sad that I don't get to talk to him tonight. I wanted to tell him about the marriage license stuff.

But there is also a lot of work I need to do as far as this PowerPoint situation goes, and when I get sucked into these things... well.

So I pull out my computer, and since there's no one to stop me, that's what I do into the wee hours of the night.

I research everything I can about baby-making and compile it into a massive PowerPoint until I pass out with the laptop in my lap.

CHAPTER SEVENTEEN

GUNNAR

Homecoming day. Thank the gods... Thor, Odin, Zeus, Poseidon.

I don't give a shit. Thank all of them for all I care because I get to see my girl today.

The past few days have been a blur of training and games. Having won three of them, and having lost only one, I'll take that. I don't give a shit. I hated this entire week.

Playing in Canada is hit or miss. It really depends on the teams playing. But we had some heavy hitters this time. One of the hardest weeks of my hockey career thus far.

And I don't mind tough work, but I am not the biggest fan of being a rising star with that much hope for our wins on our shoulders.

Because Banks and I have become so close, play so well together, I've been pushed up on the team.

Not to mention, I'm just good at my fucking job, and the coaches seem to like that.

Go figure.

Either way, I damn near burst out of my fucking bed this morning knowing that I got to get on a plane to see Tiana.

It's been a loooooong week, and the entire next week we are fucking around on the ice for some R&R. Which is fine, maybe with some workouts in between; it doesn't matter. I'm just ready to see my girl.

Now the problem lies in what she'll say when she sees my new womb broom. We're playing a dangerous game. I made a very risky play, so let's hope it works out.

As of right now, the plane finally lands, and I breathe a heavy sigh of relief as I turn my head toward Banks.

"You ready to see your lady?" I ask with a grin.

He turns his head to look at me, his eyes flicking down to my mustache before coming back up to my eyes.

"I reckon Miss Tiana will not be happy about that thing on your lip," he murmurs as he turns his gaze back toward the front of the plane.

"You underestimate the hots my lady has for me," I say in response as I throw my hands confidently behind my head.

Though I have a feeling that he may be right. Tiana doesn't like change, so I've made it a point to keep my face out of view in any pictures I took.

After a lot of waiting, we can finally deboard, and I walk with a little pep in my step down the ramp. And as we make our way to the escalator that goes down to the baggage claim, I get even more excited.

Apparently these is a bus coming for us, but we could get picked up if we didn't want to wait.

I surely did not want to wait, so Tiana, and I imagine Charlotte, are going to be waiting for us at the baggage claim.

I'm so glad because I think if I had to wait to board a bus with a bunch of other men who just want to take their sweet fucking time, I'd probably lose my mind.

As we get to the escalator, I look over the number of people waiting at the bottom, and catch those sweet gold and brown curls.

A sigh of relief works through me, along with a rush of pure happiness that causes a grin to pull at my face.

I get restless as I bounce on my step, and when the last person makes it out in front of me, I drop my backpack and crouch just enough for Tiana to run to me with a teary-eyed grin.

She jumps into my arms and wraps her legs tight around me like a little spider-monkey, and I wrap my arms tight around her back.

Her coconut and sea-salt scent overwhelms me, and I take a deep inhale of it before letting an enormous sigh of elation go.

Fuck, *my* Tiana. Always, *my* sweet Tiana.

I let her weight settle in my hands, grasping her curves and dips. I relish in the way she feels held against me.

"I missed you so much," I hear her murmur into my neck.

"Oh, sugar, you have no idea how much I missed you," I say with a soft sigh.

I take a peek behind me to make sure I'm not in the way of anyone coming off the escalator and move from some of the other players coming down so they have more room. All the while, I have a death grip on Tiana.

She presses small kisses all over my neck, and I soak in the feeling of her lips against my skin with a quiet moan.

Of course, my dick hardens almost instantly in my sweatpants, and I have to put her on her feet so it doesn't escalate further. I'd fuck her in this airport if I even brought it up to her.

I wanna at least enjoy *her* for a bit before I bury myself in her. I may be a horny psycho, but I do love spending time with her.

I turn around to grab my backpack, throwing it on my back before I run back over and smile down at her. She looks up at me with a relieved smile, but her brow immediately furrows as her eyes catch my lip.

Her face slackens with boredom as she looks at me. "Gunnar... what the fuck is that?" she sighs.

"What? It's my womb broom," I say with a grin.

"Oh my God, is there a plane leaving that can take you back?" she murmurs as she throws her head back and turns to walk toward the baggage claim.

Banks walks past us, with Charlotte wrapped tight around his torso. He carries a duffle in one hand, a backpack on his back, with one of his hands around her body to hold her in place.

Tiana leads me to the carousel, and I come up beside her to throw my arm around her shoulders, tugging her in close to my side.

"You're shaving it when you get home," she mumbles as she crosses her arms against her chest.

"I can't do that, sugar. The team is doing No-Shave November. Gotta save the prostates and all that," I say as I lean down to purse my lips at her.

She shoves a hand in my face, pushing me away. But I merely kiss harder into her palm.

"That thing is scratchy! What the hell?" she groans as she rips her hand away.

"All the better to feel you with, my love," I say teasingly.

Her eyes narrow at me in a playful challenge before she leans in to my body. Even though she hates the mustache, I know she missed me, and she wraps her arms around my middle.

"Did you have any fun while I was gone?" I ask as I watch the first few bags fall from the baggage drop and onto the carousel.

"I had some fun. But... there are some things I got... it'd be an early Christmas gift," she says as she nervously looks up at me.

My brow arches as I look down at her. "What kind of things?"

She glances at my eyes before she looks at my lips again. "Please shave that thing."

"Can't," I whisper as I lean down to kiss her lips with a big grin.

She reluctantly kisses back, but I grab her face, pulling her in deeper. She stays for only a moment before she pushes away with a playful grimace and goes back to waiting for my bags.

I didn't think I could ever miss another human like this. One where even through the heavy days I thought of her. This trip taught me a few things.

One, I *really* fucking love Tiana. Two, she's everything to me.

And three, goddamn, am I happy to be back with my girl.

What I didn't know was that Charlotte drove her vehicle to come get us, because Banks and Charlotte are going to leave straight from Tiana's apartment to go home. Charlotte basically packed up all her stuff in the SUV before she and Tiana left to come grab us.

Fine by me, I need to spend some alone time with my lady.

Tiana and I stuff ourselves into the back of Charlotte's vehicle. But the entire way home, she presses herself tight against me. Her hands mindlessly stroke up and down my arm, coupled with a death grip, as if I'll leave again.

Which unfortunately I can't really stop, but at least I won't be leaving for a while. Plus, I'm making her get her damn passport fixed, so she doesn't have to be stuck here without me again.

The drive home goes by quickly, and Tiana and I hop out of the car. Since I have to take Tucker out to pee, I tell them to stay here and I'll just grab Waffle when I take him out.

Tiana and I walk into the complex, and I sincerely missed the way it felt to walk through here with her. I hadn't even really thought about small things like this when I was in Toronto. But now that I'm home, I'm so glad to be holding my baby's hand again.

When we get up to the apartment, Tucker is extremely happy to see me. He barks and jumps all over me, and so does Waffle. So I get them both ready to take out, making sure Charlotte didn't miss any of Waffle's things before I take them downstairs.

When I get downstairs to the lobby, I put Waffle in Charlotte's car and say goodbye before I take Tucker out to the park. I spend a little bit more time there playing ball with him and enjoying the cool weather. It's an ugly day, to be honest. Rainy, gloomy, cold. But it doesn't really matter because my girl is waiting for me upstairs.

Tucker and I soon come inside, where I take him to my apartment so I can spend some time with Tiana and shower. But I hadn't had time to really look at the apartment when I came to get Tucker. So when I come back to Tiana's, I'm able to really see what she and Charlotte have done.

There are decorative throw pillows on the couch, with lights and wreath-like garland hanging from the mantle, and she's even started setting up a little village there. The entire apartment even smells of warm cinnamon and holds all the cozy Christmas energy.

I think she switched the light bulbs too because it's a warmer golden glow than what it used to be. It's so inviting that it feels like I should turn on the electric fireplace and sit with her in front of it with a mug of hot chocolate.

There is a place she's cleared in the corner of the living room that is reserved for the tree, I imagine. There are even small lanterns and cone-like decorative trees placed to give a more homey feel.

I wasn't really sure if Tiana was the decorating type. But I guess all it really takes is the holidays.

That works for me. I love Christmas.

As I move around the apartment, I keep my eyes open for Tiana, only to find the shower running when I get to our bedroom.

She's also already in there. Whether it's a little ploy, I'm not entirely sure. But I'm run ragged from this week, so there's no way I'm going to be able to fuck her the way I want to. I just want to give her all of me, and unfortunately, all of me is not on the table tonight.

Moving slowly through the bedroom, I peel off my clothes and throw them into the hamper before I make my way to the bathroom.

Quietly, I move the glass shower door to the side, and she spooks as I slowly step in behind her. She squeaks in surprise as I wrap my arms around her, and I lean my head against the top of hers, taking a deep inhale of the steam.

There is nothing that could have prepared me for the way it feels to have her against me like this. Like everything is right in the world. Hockey doesn't exist. Bills, hell, the world doesn't exist outside of this little space I've taken with her.

Her wet skin against mine is like being set on fire in the most incredible way.

This is also a trial in restraint, because it is an actual battle not to get hard right now. But, fuck, it's so difficult not to when I'm around her.

She leans back against me, letting the hot shower run over

her chest. The water melts our skin together, and I breathe in the feeling of her held against me like this.

No practices, no texts to respond to. Just her.

I lean my head down onto her wet curls, rocking us side to side.

"Can I wash you?" I ask softly as I press soft kisses to her shoulder.

She peeks over her shoulder at me, nodding with a soft smile, and I come closer to press kisses to her neck. Her skin is like velvet against my lips and she has the faint scent of just... *her*. Not even perfumes or body washes. Just the natural scent of her skin. The part of her that unlocks the feral little dog in my head.

But I tamp down my need, regardless.

"I know it's very like me to want to fuck on the first night, but I want to recuperate and make sure I can give you everything when I've gained my energy. I just want to feel you in my space again," I whisper against her skin.

She gives a light confirmatory hum, and I smile while I continue pressing kisses. Soon, I reach over her for her body wash and the loofah hanging on the wall. Shifting my grip on the objects, I squeeze some of the soap onto the loofah before squeezing it a few times, getting the bubbles thick and plentiful.

I put the bottle of soap back before I wrap one arm around her middle and drag the loofah down her front. The suds trail behind where I press the loofah, and she melts into my arm. She tilts sideways, relaxing in my grasp, and she bares her neck for me in the process. I lean down, still holding her in place as I continue running the loofah over her. Softly, I nip and press kisses into her bared neck. I slide my tongue against some of the bites, absorbing as much contact with her as I can.

By this point, my cock is completely hard, and I have to fix my hips so it doesn't bother her. I can't really help it now. But

I'm a man of my word, because as much as I love fucking Tiana... I also just love holding her like this. *Caring* for her like this.

She's my entire world, and sometimes I don't need to fuck her to have her feel like she is.

I love the way she becomes so pliant with me. The way she relaxes in a way I know no one has ever seen from her.

I love... *loving* her.

I love giving her something that no one else can.

Slowly, I run the loofah over her, her curves, her ass, and then I make it to her back. I rub in small circles, seeing if there is any tension in her shoulders from what I imagine is her worrying. Every so often, she makes small hums of approval as I grip her shoulders and knead into the flesh there.

There really isn't much as far as tension. But I take my time touching her.

Soon, I rinse off the loofah before hanging it on the wall, and I slowly turn her around under the water, rinsing all the soap from her body.

Then I get to work on her hair.

With her front held against me, she grabs my hips, pressing her body against me to keep her steady. I hold the back of her neck, letting her tilt her head back and wet the curls some more before I grab some shampoo and work it through her scalp.

Her moans of approval do nothing for my cock as it presses against her stomach. She even seems to be completely ignoring it. Thank fuck, because this is a hard task I've set for myself. But I stay my course, trying to get her hair washed and done so she doesn't have to worry about it.

By the time I finish coiling each strand and getting it bound in one of her hair towels, I carry her to the bed. She's not entirely asleep, but she is *very* relaxed. When I get her nice and comfy in the bed, I run back to the shower to wash my body before jumping out and drying off.

Tugging a pair of boxers from one of my bags she brought into the room, I pull them on and slowly climb into bed with her.

As I do, she cuddles up close to my side, with her arm and leg wrapping around my body. She holds her warm and naked body against mine, and I lean my head down to press kisses to her forehead as my arm comes around her, rubbing her arm softly.

"I really missed this the most, you know," she says as she looks up at me with sleepy eyes and a dazed smile.

"Yeah? How come?" I whisper softly.

"I missed my heater. It was cold without you," she breathes with a sigh.

Her head buries into the crook of my armpit as her hand comes up to trace the lines of the deer antlers tattooed to my chest.

All the while, I lay there, enjoying the feeling of this. Just us in the dark with each other. I listen to the sound of her quiet breathing as it evens out, and she eventually falls asleep. Soon, I also fall asleep; happy that my sugar is held here with me.

CHAPTER EIGHTEEN
TIANA

The next morning is so... *so* fucking nice. Because Gunnar is *here.*

He's in bed *right now.* WITH *ME.*

I missed this more than I even have words for. There is a general level of calm that courses through my blood now, knowing my sweet goon is in bed with me.

He's even got his arm still wrapped around me, and his chest moves up and down in slow, steady breaths.

My eyes run from his chest, up to his face, where I admire it for a long while.

Save the damn mustache.

It's not ugly, to be honest. I've just never been one for a mustache.

Gunnar is also pretty diligent as far as shaving goes. I don't think I've ever seen him with anything more than a shadow. Granted, I don't think it grows quickly, considering the one he has now isn't entirely as fluffy as it should be.

But I do take the time to admire the other parts of him I missed. His powerful jaw, the perfect ridge of his nose. His nicely carved cheekbones, but also the weirdly boyish charm he seems to have. The swoop of his lips, and also the general relaxed nature that seems to take over all of his face as he sleeps.

God, I missed this face.

But as I admire him, another thought comes to mind. The moment he came into the shower last night, and washed me. It was so calming, so relieving. Like being able to breathe well for the first time in a week.

And God, just seeing him on that escalator when we picked them up.

My big goon, so easy to spot amidst all the others. I couldn't help myself when I ran to him, because at that moment, all I wanted was *him*.

Am I slightly disappointed we didn't have sex last night because of how bad I wanted him?

Yeah, a little. But his reasoning makes sense. He had a hard week. So I don't hold any of it against him at all.

This morning, however, it feels like a challenge not to reach down and touch the bulge under the blankets.

He only slept in boxers, and with the size of him, his boxers never do much as far as keeping him... "contained."

So, considering I don't know how exhausted he still is, I merely trace light lines over his tattoo as I wait for him to wake up.

It's nice that I can relax here with him. I don't have to waste brainpower on what to do today. There's no having to keep myself busy, no trying to think about Christmas gifts or this thing and the next.

No, it's just me and Gunnar right now.

And there's so many times I wish I could live in moments like these. The quiet, slow mornings. The ones where it is just us.

I rest quietly against him until eventually my eyes close,

and I listen to the steady thrum of his heartbeat in his chest and the whoosh of air that flows in and out of his lungs.

Until he begins to stir.

Slowly, my eyes open, only to see how much harder his dick has gotten.

I take a deep breath to calm myself as my thighs clench together.

It's been a week without him filling me. And earlier this week, some things I ordered had come in.

But I want this first time back together to be just us because, fuck, I want to see what he does after a week without me.

His muscular arm shifts as he turns over on his side, wrapping around my naked body and tugging me further into him before he makes a sleepy groan.

"Mmmmm, sugar," he mumbles in his sleep.

I can't help the smile that tugs at my lips as I press myself closer and inhale some of that forest-y scent of his that I missed so much. Not to mention, the connection between us is like a live wire. Especially when I feel how hard he is against me.

I felt it last night in the shower, but he had drawn his line in the sand, so I wasn't going to tempt him further.

But right now... *fuck,* I need this man.

His arms wrap tighter around me, and his hand lazily swirls small circles into my back as he presses sleepy kisses onto my forehead.

"Good morning," I whisper as I return his small kisses to the skin of his chest.

"Morning," he responds sleepily.

I glance up, and he opens a tired eye at me before a small half-grin rises on his lips.

"How'd you sleep?" I ask as I continue pressing kisses to him.

"Like a fucking baby," he says with a heavy sigh and a groan.

I give a small giggle, and one of my hands slips past the band of his boxers. His cock is pressed into the waistband, half of it peeking out from the top. Slowly, I glide my fingers over the underside, where he lets out a low hum of approval. Not only is his skin like velvet, he's so hard he fucking throbs. It causes a pulse of lust to course through me.

"Mmmm... naughty girl," he purrs as a gruff chuckle emanates from his chest.

"I missed you, Gunnar," I whisper softly.

Bringing my hands up, I wrap them around his jaw to hold his face in my hands.

His eyes blink sleepily open, and his hand slides down my side, pausing at my hip to grip tight.

I missed this feeling. The feeling of his strength, and the way his body swallows me whole.

But I want to feel *all* of it. All of *him*.

"I missed you so much more, Tiana," he whispers.

I press myself up higher, kissing softly on his lips. Though, this scratchy mustache is something that is going to take some getting used to.

The hand on my hip pulls me closer against him, with the bulge of his cock pressing against my stomach as he kisses me back.

Flutters run rampant in my belly at the heat that climbs between us, and the raging sparks that are set off when we touch. While the low groan he makes sends shivers straight to my core.

I love my soft Gunnar. But I also love my dominating Gunnar.

"Did she miss me? Does she want me?" he rasps into the kiss.

I nod desperately. "So fucking much," I respond.

He deepens the kiss, slowly pressing his body into mine to force me onto my back.

The hand on my hip slides up my body, to my cheek, holding it as he continues to kiss me.

"I hope you know I'm going to take my time. I spent too much time imagining you underneath me. I'd be a fool not to enjoy it when you actually are," he whispers.

"Please," I respond desperately.

I bring my hands to his biceps, feeling the way his muscles flex under my fingertips before I roam higher. I apply the slightest amount of pressure as I move, learning every striation of his strength that sits just under the surface of his skin before wrapping my arms around his shoulders. With just enough strength, I pull him down, letting his weight settle on me. Like gas to a flame, the feeling of his skin meshes with mine, lighting me ablaze. His heart pounds in his chest as he bears his hips down just enough to tease my naked core with the bulge in his boxers.

I make a small whimper where our lips meet, my eyes rolling at the pressure of his hardness finally against me after all these days.

"My perfect girl," he whispers as his free hand roams up and down my body. His calluses, rough as they are, feel like everything I've missed as he touches me. Because it's familiar, it's real, and it's all *mine*.

My hips grind back against his hardness, seeking friction from where his cock presses out of his boxers.

He takes the hand from my face, reaching down to press the band of his boxers off his hips. Slowly, he works them down further and further until he can kick them off behind him.

With his cock free, the hot and heavy weight of him rests on my pussy. I feel him throb against my clit, and I grind harder against it.

"Eager little thing. Just can't help yourself, can you?" he

whispers with a chuckle as he takes soft grinds against me. His cock just barely brushes against the hood of my clit as he does. I make a small groan, hitching my hips to get closer to him.

"I just fucking missed you," I whimper as my eyes find his and they half-lid, begging for more through my gaze.

"Such a good girl. Obedient and desperate..." he says with a grin before he tsks with his tongue. "Just how I like you, huh, baby?" His hand comes down, applying pressure to the top of his cock and grinding back and forth against my clit.

"Oh... oh fuck," I moan as my eyes roll, but he grasps my jaw, keeping me focused.

"Nah, ah, ah. No, not yet. You're gonna look at me. You don't get to look away. You're mine right now. I get all of you," he says with a wolfish grin. His eyes glance down as he leans up just enough.

I get sight of what he sees. His cock, dripping with pre-cum, as he slides between my pussy lips. Not only is he slick from that, he's glistening and already covered with me.

"See that? See what I do to you? You're so fucking wet and I've barely touched you," he rasps.

"It's so good... I-I," I whimper as I look up at him.

"You what, baby? Love my cock? Love the way it feels against your pussy? Say it, use your words," he whispers as he loosens the grip on my jaw.

"I missed seeing you there," I pant softly.

His grin widens, and he leans down to kiss me. "Oh, yeah?" he whispers.

I nod, biting down on my lip as I drown in the feeling of him. My hips swirl and grind where he keeps pressure on his cock, where the ridges and heated hardness of him sends me deep into a sea of scorching relief. I could live under him like this forever just because of how fucking good it all feels. But soon, his cock leaves my center, and I groan in frustration.

With my head tossed back in annoyance, he brings me back

to the present by pressing kisses down my exposed throat. Threading my fingers through his hair, I pull him deeper into my body, letting the heat of his kisses throw me deeper into ecstasy.

As if he's trying to make as much contact with me as possible, his hands roam up and down my sides. He moves like heated sap, branding my body with every place he collides with as he works down further and further. It causes my breath to quicken, and my heart rate speeds up with it.

Kisses linger in the middle of my chest, before they're pressed to my tits. He pauses at each nipple, sliding a tongue over the hardened peaks and eliciting a small moan from me as my fingers tighten in his hair.

As he continues down, his mustache tickles my stomach, and I can't help the giggle that comes out of me when he moves further down, kissing into the skin above my seam.

His hands move with him until his calluses have landed against my thighs, caressing the skin there before they roam freely over my legs. My inner thighs, my shins, my calves. He doesn't leave a single inch of my body untouched, and I feel like every bit of me is vibrating from his touch.

Settling his body between my legs, I lean onto my elbows, looking down at him as I loosen my grip on his hair to hold the back of his head. With his eyes on me, he dips down, his tongue sliding from his mouth to take one long lick up the lips of my pussy.

I watch as his eyes roll, a low groan coming from him before he presses his tongue in deeper.

"Mmmmm... Fuuuuck... Missed your taste," I hear him growl as he presses his mouth deeper. The pressure parts me, and soon his tongue flattens against my clit, sliding up and down against it.

"F-fuck," I pant as my head falls back, and I pull him into me. The feeling is transcendent, and my legs widen to accommodate his large shoulders. Without thought, my hips grind against his face, in time with his languid licks through me.

His moans of pleasure vibrate through my core, adding to the sensation as one of his hands leaves my thighs to press into me. So slow, he takes his time as he works two fingers in and out of me.

"Right here, sugar. Eyes here," he says between his licks.

My head tilts up, my chest heaving as I look down at him.

His hazel eyes watch me like a predator, daring me to look away as he flicks his tongue against my clit faster.

"G-Gunnar... fuck... fuck!" I pant as I fight the sensation of going limp.

"Stay here, eyes right here, baby. Watch me," he says into me. The gruff rumble of his voice spears into me, only heightening the combination of all he does.

I nip my lip, using it as a grounding point as I watch him.

He parts his fingers inside of me and my moans grow louder, my thoughts fleeing as I continue grinding against his tongue.

"Gorgeous fucking pussy. I can't believe I get to come home to this," he murmurs, and the jolt of pleasure that pulses in my blood from the sound of his voice nearly does me in.

Soon, his fingers speed up just enough, the wet sounds filling the room as he continues licking and sucking the slick from me.

"So fucking good..." I hear him. But it's the only thing keeping my head above water as he works faster, his tongue moving quicker and my orgasm creeping up my spine.

My moans turn to pants and groans as I climb higher, ascend faster.

"Gunnar... oh my god, your tongue," I whimper as my fingers tighten in his hair, almost trying to pull him away from how intense all the pleasure is.

He reaches behind his head to grasp my wrist and rip my hand from his scalp, tossing it away.

"Take it; you're gonna fucking take it, Tiana. Don't run from me," he growls as he speeds up.

He keeps going, keeps moving, his speed increasing the closer I get. His dominance only further pushes me over the edge. The pleasure wraps around my throat and breaks me in half with a shrieking moan. My hips writhe; grinding against his face as my upper half falls to the bed with my hands scrambling for purchase against his shoulders while I ride out my orgasm against his face.

When it wanes away, and I'm left a panting mess on the sheets, he kisses back up my body; his hands coming with him. Except for the one he quickly sucks clean. Soon, he reaches my mouth, kissing me deep with me fresh on his tongue.

"Beautiful girl," he whispers against me before he wraps an arm around my waist. Taking me with him, he moves to the headboard, sitting against it and placing me in his lap, facing away from him.

His cock rests right against my pussy, still pulsing from my orgasm, and I relax against him. I get a few breaths in, all the while admiring his dick as his hands glide up and down the sides of my shoulders. Small kisses pepper my neck, and his cock twitches as he waits for me to recuperate.

My inner thighs stretch, trying to accommodate his thighs. But before I have time to think, he grasps under my knees, tugging me up against his body as he opens them wide.

He shifts his hips, and presses me just a bit higher before he grinds under me. The lips of my pussy part against him as he grinds against my clit.

I hear a thunk as his head falls against the headboard and a soft groan. "Fuck," he growls.

My head falls back into the crook of his neck, and he leaves more kisses on the exposed skin.

"My pretty girl... You have no idea how long I've waited for this," he whispers before his hips shift again.

He presses me up more, and his hips down just enough before his cock seats at my entrance, slowly pressing in.

The combination of his moving me and the strength behind his press makes my mind go blank, but his words keep me present.

"Look at how you stretch around me," he whispers as he fills me more and more.

"Fuck... fuck, please, more," I whimper.

"Just wait. Patience, baby," he whispers. His kisses come back to my neck, his tongue lathing against some kisses, and my eyes threaten to roll, to leave the sight of him, but I can't. I just want to watch.

"That's a good girl. Keep your eyes on my cock, sugar. I want you to see the way you make me disappear," he groans.

Every inch fills me more and more, with the pressure in my lower stomach building rapidly.

When enough of him is pressed into me, he shifts his grip, wrapping an arm around my ribcage, to snake up between my breasts and hang loosely at my neck. While the other wraps around my waist, coming to rub small circles into my clit. His skin is sticky and damp from the excitement as his strong chest heaves at my back.

"There she is, look at you. You're so fucking beautiful speared on my cock," he whispers.

More and more, I fall down his length, every bit of him filling me, with small gasps escaping me.

"My sweet girl, you're doing so good for me. Deep breaths, baby," he whispers. With his breath skating across the shell of my ear before he moves down to press kisses into the pulse point beside my throat.

I lift just enough, trying to move on him, but he slowly grinds his hips under me, working in and out of me.

My eyes roll, my head falling back against his shoulder as his arms grip tighter around me.

"That's it, Mama. Give in. Let me take care of you," he whispers with a pant as he continues rolling his hips. He keeps applying pressure and circles to my clit, making me liquid in his arms.

"Gunnar... oh my fucking god," I whimper helplessly.

With my body held against him like this, and his cock situated perfectly for him to use, he plays me like an instrument. His hand on my neck tightens on my pulse points, squeezing and releasing, causing a dizzying effect as his other hand continues on my core.

"I missed these noises... these sounds, the way your pussy fucking grips me. The way you beg," he pants as his hips continue to move.

"You feel so... fucking... *good*," I manage to pant out.

Every part of me touches him; adheres to his skin. My back, my ass, his muscular arms tight around my body.

"Fucking hell, sugar," he pants against my skin as his thrusts speed up under me.

He holds me up just enough to work his hips in and out.

"You're so fucking close again, baby. You gonna come for me? Show me how much you missed this cock?" he pants as he speeds up.

And damn him for knowing my body so well, because I feel myself climbing again.

His hand moves from my neck to grip tight on my tit, squeezing it as he speeds up. His fingers work quicker over my clit as my body tightens against him, only for him to tighten his grip on me as if wrangling a wild animal.

I can't help but admit how fucking good it all feels.

"Good fucking girl, sugar. Give in, come for me. Lock me in that pussy," he grunts as he thrusts up mercilessly into me now.

And with that, I *do.*

My moans pitch to a shriek, my back arching against him, only for his groans to fill my ear while his cock stuffs me to the hilt. My hips meet every bit of him, riding out everything against him, letting it crash over me in wave after wave after wave, drifting on a sea of *him.*

He comes in hard, throbbing pulses, pumping me with all of his release, making me feel so incredibly full.

"There's my girl. Keep going; you have more in you. Ride me out, I'm here, I've got you," he grunts as my hips roll and swirl against him, his fingers still strumming my clit as my orgasm goes and goes and *goes.*

"G-Gunnar," I manage to gasp as the last of it wanes away.

"I've got you, baby. I'm right here, you're safe," he grits through his own orgasm in between the small nips he leaves on my neck.

I collapse, boneless, against him, my chest heaving as I relax against his hot and sweaty body.

His arms loosen from around me, though he still keeps a soft grip on my tit, a thumb sliding back and forth lazily over a nipple as he presses soft kisses into the sticky skin at my neck. His hand slowly slides from my pussy, resting on my hip.

"My pretty girl," he croons tenderly, his lips still pressing soft pecks into my skin. "You did so good for me, baby," he says.

My heart swells, my body satiated as I lay back against him, enjoying the feel of his sturdy strength.

"Fuck, I missed that," I say with a soft pant.

"I'm glad I could live up to your memories," he says.

He relaxes against the headboard, leaning me back with him and stroking a soft hand over my side.

We lay there for a few moments, and I float on that sea of bliss with a hum of content before his voice breaks through my drift.

"I have to go let Tucker out, but I'll be back, sugar. Rest," he says quietly.

I nod sleepily, and slowly, his arms snake from around my body to come under my legs.

I squeak as he lifts me with ease off his softening cock, but as he does, I feel a gush and groan in annoyance as he places me on the bed.

"Shit, sorry. I didn't have time to get rid of it before I came home," he says as he quickly gets up to grab a towel.

"I was gonna shower anyway; it's okay," I say as I get up and stretch wide. I forgot how good morning sex was because I feel like I could fight a bear now.

"Alright, sugar," he says with a warm smile.

As I turn to go to the bathroom, he grips my wrist and I turn around, only for him to tug me into his body. He leans down, giving me one last kiss. Deep, passionate, and so full of love, he lingers there before he pulls away and presses a kiss to my forehead.

"I'll be back," he whispers as he brushes a lock of hair behind my ear.

A blush creeps across my cheeks as I nip my lip with a small nod. He quickly grabs a pair of shorts and a shirt from the duffel bag to throw on before he leaves the room.

With a lovesick sigh of satisfaction, I turn to shower for the day.

CHAPTER NINETEEN
GUNNAR

Damn, that was a good-ass way to wake up.

I really didn't want to initiate anything because I didn't want her to think that I'm just here for her body. That couldn't be further from the truth.

But I'm sure not going to deny her if she wants me. Especially after all this time.

After I leave the bedroom, I go to my apartment to grab Tucker, and when I take him for a walk down the street, I also get Tiana her cup of coffee.

It's a nice little wake-up to fuck my lady and then go out for a walk in this brisk air. It gives me a real clear head and relaxes me.

Tucker and I walk for a while, getting Tiana her coffee, and when I enter the apartment, she's sitting on the couch under one of the seasonal blankets she bought while I was gone.

Though, because her back is against the armrest, she tips her head all the way back to see me, which means when she gives me a smile it's upside down. Then she turns over against the armrest, propping her chin up against her hands as she pins her elbows into the cushion.

Fuck, there is nothing like coming home to a face like hers.

I can't help the smile on my lips as I walk over to her, handing her the cup of coffee with a kiss to her lips before sitting on the couch beside her.

She shifts her body to sit better next to me before leaning against me. Her knees come up to her chest, and she pins her heels into the couch to keep them there as she cradles the cup in her hands.

"Mmmm, thank you so much," she murmurs with contentment as she takes a deep inhale of the steam wafting from the little sip hole.

I really missed quiet mornings like this with her. Banks is great, but he surely isn't what I want to wake up to in the morning.

This, however.

I look down at her, admiring the way her freckles spatter across her nose, her cheekbones. Her long lashes that fan over her cheeks. Not to mention her perfect eyebrows.

I don't think I'd ever really taken to looking at a woman's eyebrows.

But there is nothing about Tiana that I'd overlook.

As I watch her, she takes long, deep sips of her coffee as she relaxes her head on my shoulder.

"Did you have anything you wanted to do today?" I ask as I wrap an arm around her shoulders and tug her in close.

"Mmmm, I just wanted to be here with you. Though, I do have a... presentation of sorts. But I'll wait until later," she says with a smile.

My brow arches. "A presentation? You know you can ask me for anything you want, sugar. It's yours, always," I whisper as I bring a hand up to her chin, tilting her head up for her eyes to meet mine.

They flick down to my mustache before they float back up to my eyes in boredom.

"What do I have to do to get you to shave that thing?" she mumbles.

"It's staying. Anyway. This presentation," I say with a grin.

She groans as her head throws back. Her finger comes up to circle around the sip hole as she stares at it. She's quiet for a long moment, as if she's trying to figure out what to say before she brings the hand back down to cradle the cup and she frustratedly leans her head against me.

"I don't want to give anything away. But it's something I worked really hard on, and I think it'll help whatever is going on in my brain," she grumbles.

My brow furrows as I look down at her. "You can tell me anything, sugar," I whisper as I lean down to press a kiss to her forehead.

I pull away, smiling at her, and her eyes shy away. "I know. I just... I just need to do the presentation," she says with another deep breath.

I watch her eyes for a long moment before I nod. "Alright. Whatever you need, sugar. I've got you."

"But other than the presentation?? No, I don't think I had anything in mind," she says.

Suddenly, she jumps up with a gasp.

My brows furrow wildly at the sudden change when she stumbles from the couch, quickly placing her coffee onto the table before she wraps her robe tight around her body and runs back to our bedroom.

She returns a few minutes later with a stack of papers.

One of my brow arches as I watch her, her fingers flipping through the edges of the papers.

Though I get caught on the way she looks in that fucking robe.

Goddamn it, she's so fucking beautiful.

A dreamy sigh leaves my lips as I adjust on the couch.

Tugging my chain out of my shirt, I pull it into my mouth, grasping it with my tongue before I splay my arms against the back of the couch. Then, my left foot tucks under my right knee, while the foot on the floor bounces as I watch her.

Tiana comes to sit next to me, though she places the papers on the table and fans them out. My brow furrows as I lean forward to get a better look at them, placing my elbows on my knees as I look over them all.

They've got our names on them, and a few say things like...

Marriage. License. Application.

My heart pounds in my chest as I look over them before I look at her, and my teeth grit tighter on my chain.

"I got them all done while you were away, so all that we need to do now is have the 'ceremony'," she says as her fingers punctuate the last bit with air quotes.

My head tilts before I look back down at the papers.

Holy shit, I'm going to have a wife.

Tiana Dawn is going to be *my fucking wife.*

I can't help turning to her, grabbing her face, releasing the chain from my mouth and bringing her in for a deep kiss. She makes a startled noise as she falls back onto the couch and my body hovers over hers.

My hands move to grip her hips, holding her as I kiss her deeper. Our lips and tongue tangling together.

"You're going to be my fucking wife," I say with a panting smile as I pull away. One of my hands moves up to her cheeks, where they brighten with pink as she looks up at me. She nods sheepishly as a small smile tugs at her lips.

"You're going to be my husband," she whispers in response.

I kiss her again before I sit up, bringing her with me.

"So what is it we need to do?" I ask.

Her grin widens, and I feel my face tense with excitement.

"I have a few ideas. We can talk about them tomorrow. But for now, what do you want to get your brothers for Christmas?" she asks.

I groan as I lean back against the couch, pulling my chain back into my mouth. "Do I really need to get those fuck-nuts anything at all?" I mumble.

"Well, yes, they're your brothers," she says.

"Okay, but are you going Charlotte anything?" I ask.

She's silent for a long moment, and I glance at her from the corner of my eye.

"See!" I say through my chain as I point at her.

"Charlotte and I don't give each other gifts! It was a thing we made up a long time ago, so we didn't have to stress ourselves out over making sure we get each other something," she says with a pouty huff as she folds her arms against her chest.

"Well, I need to give my mom something. And my dad. And my grandma... They're going to Wisconsin for Christmas, so we won't be spending it with them," I tell her as I wrap an arm around her shoulders, stroking the opposite one as I lean my head against hers.

She hums in thought as she leans forward to grab her coffee and then snuggles into my side. Her legs come up beside her on the couch, and she gets comfortable next to me.

"My parents are going on a cruise this Christmas. And Charlotte said that she and Adrian are going to Montana. So... I guess it's just us for Christmas," she says softly as she glances up at me.

I glance back at her and give her a small grin. "I love that," I say softly.

"I don't mind it. But my mom said something about possibly doing Thanksgiving at their house? What about your parents?" she asks.

"Well, so... I may have had something to do with all of that," I say with a nervous smile.

Her brow quirks as she looks up at me, and I take a deep breath.

Fuck. I really need to prepare these sorts of things for her better.

"Alright, so, I wanted to ease some of the stress on you as far as the holidays go. Since I don't really know how you get during them, I wanted to take care of some events so you could focus on the things you wanted to focus on," I explain.

Her brow furrows as she watches me, her lips thinning in thought as her eyes dart around my face.

Because her silence fucking scares me, I keep going.

"So, when we were in Canada, I asked your dad if we could spend some Thanksgiving at the Dawn house after we have our Thanksgiving at the Hayze house. We'll trade our gifts then, and after, we'll focus on our December together," I say.

I don't realize that by the end of my words, my heart is beating furiously out of my chest.

Tiana is... a leader, I think, by nature. At least in our day-to-day life. And for me to take the reins on something like this... it's a risk, and a toss-up. Same as the land was.

But I took it anyway because sometimes if you want to know your partner better, you've gotta throw some stuff out into the ether and see what happens.

And boy howdy, part of me is scared that I threw this damn thing *out* into the ether.

I wait for a long while for her response, watching her face.

She seems to be thinking, and I don't think I can fault her for it. But soon she takes a deep breath and relaxes back against me.

"Alright, fine, that works for me," she says as she waves her hand dismissively and sips her coffee again.

Apparently, I was holding my breath because as soon as I know it's okay; I let it go.

She looks up at me with a furrow of her brow before she looks at my chest.

"The hell was that?" she asks.

"I was scared to make an executive decision like that without you," I say as my arm bends to rub the back of my neck nervously.

"Right... well, I appreciate it, because I have my mind on other things right now, so that takes another thing off my plate," she says with a content sigh and a sip of her coffee. "Thank you, my love," she says softly.

My head falls back against the couch, and it tilts to look at her. In triumph, my tongue fiddles with my chain, and she looks at me with a smile before she cuddles deeper into me.

We spend the rest of the day relaxing around the house. Considering all the stuff we want to do, we decide we'd do tomorrow.

We cuddle on the couch for a while, watch a movie, and at a certain point, Tiana falls asleep. So I switch to some of the other hockey games that were on when I was gone.

Eventually, she wakes up with a wide stretch and lies in my lap silently for another long while.

I think after a week of not having me, she's finally able to relax the way she wants to.

I look down at her head in my lap, where she has her hands under her head as she watches the game I currently have on the TV.

I know she woke up a little while ago and has just been relaxing against me.

Soon, I run my hand over her shoulders, over her side, and she turns over, looking up at me with a smile.

"So, this presentation?" I ask as I remember her earlier words.

Her eyes widen for a fraction of a second before she takes a deep breath.

"Okay, so while you were gone... I was worried again about the whole baby thing," she says.

I try not to let the disappointment in myself show on my face, so I merely watch her.

"And I cope better when I have all the information I can and steps to take. So, I put all the information I found into... a presentation," she says shyly.

My brow arches as I look down at her, slowly putting together the words she's trying to say.

"Did you... put together a baby-making presentation?" I ask.

Her cheeks tint a light pink as she nods slowly.

I hate that I've been so obsessed that it's pushed her to this. But if this little method of hers will help her feel better, then I'll indulge, because at least it's something that might mitigate her worries.

I'm also always interested in hearing her talk. I enjoy watching the gears in her head turn.

She's magnificent to watch.

Soon, she flips over against me before she scurries from the couch. Running off to the bedroom, she returns a few moments later with her laptop and some sort of... small remote in her hand.

My brow furrows as I pull my chain into my mouth, sliding my tongue across the links before my arms extend over the back of the couch, getting comfy.

"Alexa, lights down," she calls into the room.

The lights dim to almost nothing, considering night fell and now the only proper light is the streetlights shining up from the street, some floors down, and the light from the TV.

She places her computer on the coffee table, clicking around a few things before she grabs the TV remote and changes the input. Now, instead of the hockey game, there is a mirrored image of her laptop on the screen.

Of course, she hasn't changed from this morning, so she's still in that small, thin silky robe she always wears.

Not complaining, I love it.

But if she's going to give me some kind of course on baby-making, I reckon I'll end the night giving her one.

My attention goes back to her as she takes a deep breath and grabs her little remote.

"Okay, so... this is my presentation on baby-making," she says.

Without thinking, I clap, whistling through my chain.

"Woooo! Yeah!! Baby-making, let's go!" I say encouragingly.

"I'm deleting it," she murmurs as she bends over to slam her laptop shut.

But I'm quicker and snatch it from the table before she touches it.

"Nope. Proceed, Madam," I say with a grin as I hold the laptop at my side.

Her eyes narrow at me in a glare, with her arms crossing against her chest. I merely give a little roll of my hand for her to continue with a sly little grin.

She stomps her foot in protest as her head tosses back with a groan.

"Can you at least put my computer back on the table?" she grumbles.

"Only if you promise to show me your presentation. In full," I say with a devious grin against my chain.

"Yes, fine, I promise," she huffs.

I nod triumphantly as I put the computer on the table and wave my hands over it with a flourish.

She lets a heavy sigh go before I lean back again to watch her.

The cover is a blue and pink situation, with big bubble letters on the front and some kind of... emoji thing of the two kissing faces.

It's cute, I'll give her that.

She takes a deep breath as she clicks her little remote, and it moves to the next slide.

"What is baby-making?" she asks as she traces the same words on the screen with the laser pointer on the remote.

My brow rises, enjoying this little thing she's put together, and I raise my hand.

Tiana sighs with a groan as she reluctantly points at me. "What?"

"P in V, you and me," I say with a nod.

"Oh my fucking god, Gunnar," she groans.

"Sorry! I'm sorry! Okay, keep going," I say with a nod.

She glares at me before she goes back to her presentation.

"Is making a baby as easy as it seems? No, apparently, it is not," she says.

The slide itself has a few bullet points she points at with her remote.

"Factors include," she says as she points to the first bullet point.

"Female reproductive health," she says before she moves on to the next bullet point.

"Male reproductive health," she adds, then moves on.

"Timing. Timing. Timing," she says. She clicks the button on the remote, and it goes to the next slide.

"Female reproductive health. That's my job — sleep, eating iron-rich foods, prenatals, yada yada, female stuff. Staying stress free," she says as she glares at me with the last one.

"Hey, I think I do a pretty good job of that one!" I say in response.

"Mmmm.... Sometimes," she mumbles before she goes to the next slide.

"Male reproductive health," she says. "This means *you* need to take care of yourself," she says as she points to me.

The laser shows up on my chest, and I look down at it before it moves to my dick.

My brow rises before I look up at her. "And what exactly does that entail?" I ask.

"Wellllll," she says as she goes to the next slide.

"Healthy diet," she says as she points to the first bullet.

"Done," I respond.

Her brow furrows, and she points to the next one.

"Exercise," she says, though her brows jump because well. That one is already out of the way.

"Uh huh," I say with an encouraging nod.

"And you have to make sure you don't overheat..." She groans in annoyance. "Your balls..." she mumbles.

I nod again, though a tad more enthusiastically because I know she hates saying it, even if I love hearing it.

"And you can't restrict them too much; it's bad for sperm health," she adds as she points to me again.

"Well, that's not really something I can do," I say with a nervous grin.

She sighs. "Yes, I'm aware, but I don't know, maybe go boxer-less at home," she says.

My brow arches and I nod. "Roger that, Big Mama," I say.

She sighs before she goes to the next slide.

"Ovulation," she starts.

I nod vigorously because yes, please.

"This is part of timing, because there is a two-to-three-day window where I can get pregnant. But, they recommend having... as much sex as possible," she says.

"As much as possible?" I ask with a grin.

A tint washes over her cheeks as she nods, her gaze connecting with me. "As much as possible."

My grin widens. "Noted."

She clears her throat. "Anyway... I also have to be more... on top of my... body signs, I guess, for ovulating," she says with a deep breath.

"How do *you* know when you're ovulating?" I ask as I lean back against the couch.

"There are signs... don't worry, I'll let you know," she says with a dismissive wave of her hand.

I put my hands up in surrender as I clench my chain with my teeth.

She takes a deep breath before she points back to the screen, and the slide goes to the next one.

This one, however, *really* catches my attention.

It's specifically on the most exciting part.

"Deep," she says as she points to the first bullet point.

A pulse runs through me, straight to my cock. With the thought of her under me, with me bulging through her stomach, flashes through my mind.

"Mhm... got it," I murmur.

"Frequently," she says.

Day... night. During work, after work.

"Yup..." I mumble as my attention goes from the slide to her.

She clears her throat again as I see the blush increase on her cheeks. But my dick only gets harder.

"Some of the best positions... are doggy, and missionary. And," she says, though this time it's quieter as the slide turns. "I have to orgasm," she says with a quirk of her brow.

My grin widens, peering straight into her soul. But fuck... all I can see is her bent over in front of me, her ass rippling as I ram into her... the way her eyes turn white as I bury myself deep inside her from above.

"Can... do," I respond with a grin as I look her up and down with a heated gaze.

"Every. Time," she adds.

"Roger that," I say as I look her up and down. "Big Mama," I finish.

She presses the button on her remote, and the presentation ends.

I watch her for a long moment, my eyes starting at her feet, trailing up her bared legs, smooth and shiny from the light outside of the window.

Soon, my gaze moves up, taking in her hips... her tight waist. The way her nipples have hardened against that thin robe.

I'm harder than stone now, and I can't help myself when I lean back against the couch, gripping the base of my cock through my sweatpants. I wrap the fabric around its length as it lies against my thigh, taunting her with it.

"I'll give you a fuckin' lesson on baby-making," I say with a grin.

Her eyes widen, and she tugs her lower lip between her teeth with a shy nod. "Please..." she breathes.

"Perfect," I say in a low purr as I come to a stand.

She stands perfectly still as I approach her. My eyes stuck to her like a predator has just caught its prey.

Fuck, my submissive Tiana has come out to play, and I've *missed* her.

I stand in front of her, bringing a hand up to her chin and pressing her gaze up to mine.

She beats her eyelashes up at me, her mouth turning in a grin as she bites harder into her lip.

"Who is she tonight? What does she want?" I whisper.

"Yours... she's all yours... she wants you," she returns desperately.

"Terrific," I whisper as I lean down. My mouth captures hers, tongue coming to tease her lips, beckoning hers, and she complies with a small moan of approval as her arms go around my neck.

Our tongues twist and twirl around one another as my hand moves from her chin to her tit. Sliding a thumb back and forth over her hardened nipple, I linger there, winding her up.

Small whimpers bleed between us, and I take the moment to pinch it.

"Fuck," she pants, and I grin against our kiss. I press my hands down her hips, pulling her up into my arms to carry her to the bedroom.

All the while, I kiss deeper, with my cock damn near bursting in my sweatpants. When I enter our room, I kick the door closed behind me. The entire space has darkened into nothing but the shine of the moon from the window.

I take her straight to the bed, placing her on it before I lean up and quickly rid myself of my clothes.

Tossing my shirt to the side, as well as my sweatpants, I watch as she presses herself up to the pillows, opening her legs wide for me.

Even though her robe is still tied in the middle, the bottom portion barely covers the lower half. The panels at the top fall open enough to see the patch of skin on her chest between her tits.

Getting between her legs, I take my cock in hand, pumping it slowly as I look down at her, *admire* her.

Even if she gave me the presentation... and I presented this to her as that chance.

It's not about that.

It's about loving her. No matter what, no matter *how*.

I lean down, kissing her again, slowly, deeply, our tongues dancing and our lips tangling against one another. Her hands come to my shoulders, her nails slowly scraping against my muscles as I hover over her.

"You're so fucking beautiful, Tiana. You know that, right?" I whisper against her lips.

She nods softly. Her hips lift enough for her to grind against the underside of my cock.

"Fuck," I growl as I feel her hot, wet cunt. She's still dripping from where I finished in her this morning.

"I need you," she whispers.

I give a small, breathless chuckle as I press my hips down just enough for her to feel how hard I am.

"I know, baby... I just wanna... enjoy this, for a second," I respond.

I bring a hand up, tugging at the end of the sash around her middle, loosening it enough for it to fall from her. Soon, the fabric panels of her robe slide to either side of her body, baring all of her for me.

I lower my body to hers, feeling the way her tits press against my bare chest, the way her skin feels against mine.

The warmth, the softness, the rabid pulsing of her heart through her chest.

I bring a hand to my cock, slowly gliding it through her wetness, lingering at her clit, where she responds with a soft moan. Her body arches into mine before I press myself down to her entrance, teasing her with shallow presses.

She makes a small gasp, and I steal it, capturing it from her as I look into her eyes.

"There she is. There's my good girl," I whisper.

I work in and out of her slowly, shallow at first, letting her feel me the same way I want to feel her.

"My gorgeous fucking girl," I pant as I work deeper with every thrust.

"F-fuck... fuck," she gasps.

"So... fucking perfect," I say as I capture her mouth again.

She moans into our lips, my thrusts moving slowly in and out until I'm moving balls deep in her.

My groans dance with her moans, the temperature of her skin against mine climbing the longer I move in her.

One hand stays on her hip, gripping tight and holding her in place as the other comes to slide a thumb over her nipple.

Soon, I lean down, taking the nipple into my mouth, moaning against it as I continue moving. I keep a slow, steady pace. But on every downward stroke, I grind into her clit, making her climb with me.

My tongue lathes against her nipple, tugging or sucking it into my mouth as I feel up and down her body with my other hand.

Her nails claw into my shoulders, moving across them to my scalp, where she tugs at my hair.

"Oh... my god," she pants desperately. All the while, her body tightens and grinds under me.

"I've got you, baby," I murmur against her tit.

Because, God fucking help me, I *do*.

Every fucking touch against her is fire in my blood, every fucking thrust into her is like lightning through my soul because there is nothing in this world that will ever compare to Tiana fucking Dawn.

My girl. My woman. God, *my* woman.

I take one last lick over her nipple before I come back up to her lips, kissing softly.

I lean up, taking her knees in my hands and opening her wide.

"God, fucking look at you," I whisper almost to myself.

Her hands come up, squeezing her breasts, and pinching her nipples, her hips swirling as I thrust into her.

But at the sight of her, I speed up. My instincts take over, and I bury every stroke deeper than the last, watching as her tits bounce, her head presses back, and my cock bulges through her stomach.

Her pussy flutters around my length, and I take that as my chance to move a hand to her clit, rubbing over it.

"That's it, baby, climb. Take it," I grunt as my thrusts speed up, but I keep the depth.

"Gunnar... fuck it's so fucking much," she whimpers as her legs try to clamp shut.

I lean down, forcing my body between them to keep them open as I cage in her head with my arms, coming face to face with her.

I kiss her deeply again, grinding against her clit as I keep my rhythm.

"Deep, right? You need me deep? And an orgasm... remember? You need to come, baby," I pant into our kisses.

"Yes, I'm... fuck, yes, it's so fucking good, please," she moans into our lips, her arms desperately wrapping around me as she lets go of my mouth.

My lips drift to her neck, pressing kisses there as I grind in deep, hard, hitting as far into her as I can.

She lets out gasps of pleasure, whimpers as she climbs. Her pussy spasms around my cock. The muscles shivering as she gets closer and closer.

"Come for me, baby. You're right there, come for me. Come around my cock," I murmur against her skin.

"F-F... I'm g-... Fuck!" All at once, her pussy clenches and she lets out a scream as her back bows, her body tightens and she gasps and moans in pleasure.

Her orgasm triggers mine, and I groan with her as it hits me, my cock pulsing and twitching hard, pumping cum deep inside her.

"Fuck," I grit as her pussy clamps down, holding me in

place. I groan as she lengthens my orgasm, my cock throbbing the longer she comes.

Her hips grind against me as her orgasm runs and runs. Her moans and whimpers keep going until her body loosens–pussy included–and she relaxes against the bed, pressing depleted kisses into my shoulder as her nails still grip into the flesh at my back.

I keep myself there on top of her, kissing softly against her collarbone and chest. I keep my cock inside of her as well, because truthfully, I just don't really want to move.

It's rare that I take the soft and slow route with her. Even if I sped up at the end.

By nature, I'm... kind of just an animal. But she's been worried about this instance because of me.

And even if I still want to have a baby with her, and want to make that family, she needs to know it's not just that.

Above all, it's always her first. She's not just a vessel or a carrier. She wouldn't just be a mother. She's Tiana. She'd be my wife. My partner.

My love, and no matter what, I never want her to forget that before all of those other things.

She'll always be my love, and she's always be *her*. And that's why she is my love. Because she is *her*.

I take a moment to feel her damp and warm skin on mine. The sound of her heart as it comes back to a calmed pace, the way her chest moves in a more fluid rhythm. All the while, her hands slowly stroke through my hair, scratching at my scalp and my shoulders.

It's calming, especially after fucking her.

And I reckon she may be feeling the same, because we lie there for a long while in silence. The two of us enjoy the dark together, the quiet, and the way the night slowly swallows us whole.

CHAPTER TWENTY

TIANA

I was terrified of showing Gunnar the presentation. Mostly because the idea is honestly so fucking ridiculous. Who the fuck gives their *almost-husband* a Power-Point presentation on baby-making?

Me, apparently.

Either way, the night had been nice, calming.

I was shocked at the way he took his time and the lack of the aggressive and dominant Gunnar. But it was... sweet.

By the end, I felt loved. Cherished. I felt *so* important.

I know I'm important to him, and I know he loves me.

But to feel it... to experience the breadth of his love from the way he touches me.

I don't think there is anything like it on this planet.

So when we get up this morning, I damn near bounce around the apartment. In a way that makes me want to throw my arms out and breathe in the fall air.

But there are more pressing matters to attend to.

With the presentation out of the way, I would like to focus on the other important things.

Our "wedding."

Or, I suppose, the lack thereof, at this point.

Luckily, there isn't really anything we need to do.

And I really don't want to make it a big deal, so I have an idea... but I need to make sure that Gunnar is okay with it.

So I've brought us to the living room, where I placed all the papers out on the table, and have him sit on the couch beside me.

He has a satisfied smile on his face as he leans his head back against the couch, his fingers slowly running up and down my spine as he looks at me. Of course, his chain lies loosely on his jaw, and his tongue wraps the surrounding chain around it before he messes with it some more.

"A few things," I say as I turn to him.

"Shoot," he says with a smile.

"A prenup?" I ask.

"Don't need one," he responds.

My brow furrows. "Why?"

"If there is anything I did where I deserved to have you walk away from me, then you deserve everything anyway," he says with a shrug.

My eyes widen, and my heart hammers in my chest.

I've seen a lot of prenups. Heard a lot of reasons for the prenups.

Not once in my career have I ever heard *that*.

I nod sheepishly and clear my throat.

"Right... um..." I take a deep breath. "Finances?" I ask.

He tilts his head in thought before getting up and moving toward the bedroom.

My brow furrows as I watch him, and he returns a few moments later with a pair of jeans.

My confusion deepens, and he comes to sit on the couch again. Rifling through the pockets for something, he pulls out what looks like a small metal card holder.

He tosses it onto the coffee table with a metallic clang before he puts the pants on the floor in front of him and puts his arms back on the couch.

"What is this?" I ask.

"My wallet. I've asked my accountant to put your name on everything already," he says.

My brow furrows wildly. "You what?!" I squawk.

"What? What's mine is yours, baby," he says with a grin as he grits down on the chain to show all his pretty teeth.

"What about my accounts?" I ask.

"Do with them what you want, but you've got access to all of mine," he says with a shrug.

How in the fuck am I marrying this man? What did I do to deserve this? I don't even know *if* I deserve all of *this*!

I groan because how does he have all of this squared away already?

"Okay... um..." I take another deep breath, rifling through all the things we need to go over in my head.

But his voice breaks through my moment of panic.

"Look at me, baby," he says, and I glance at him from the corner of my eye.

I see him grin as he shakes his head. Taking my chin in his fingers, he turns my head to him.

"I said... eyes *here*," he says, and I nip at my lip with a small nod as I finally connect my eyes with his.

"I told you, from the very first moment I met you, I'd be so *fucking* good to you and that I keep all my promises," he says softly.

I nod slowly, watching his eyes.

"And I intend to make very good on those promises. There is nothing in this world you don't deserve... there's nothing of *mine* you don't deserve, and I'd give you everything the world offered if it meant your happiness, sugar. No prenups, full access to my accounts, anything you want, and the love and care you deserve. Forever. That's my vow," he whispers.

I gulp, nodding softly.

"You... are... so... fucking good to me, Gunnar Hayze," I whisper with a small smile.

He grins, the points of his canines peeking from under his lips. "I always... *always* told you I would be, Tiana Dawn," he whispers in return.

He leans in to press a soft and tender kiss to my lips before he pulls away, watching my lips as he rubs a thumb over my chin.

His eyes flick back to mine before he leans back on the couch, splaying his arms over the back, and nods to the papers on the table.

I take a deep breath, recovering from the insane amount of love this man constantly gives me before I refocus on the task at hand.

"So, basically, we need two witnesses, and then, this paper... thing, I guess. And then... someone who is ordained to officiate weddings," I say with a sigh.

Which leaves one piece of the puzzle missing.

"My lawyer is ordained," Gunnar replies casually.

My brow furrows as I look at him.

"He what?" I ask.

"Yeah, I guess he has a lot of clients that do shit like this. So he got ordained to make the process easier for them," he says with a shrug.

"Okay... so... uh... can... he do it?" I ask.

"Yeah, I reckon so," he says with a smile as he continues lazily moving his fingers up and down my spine.

"Uhm... Okay... Alright. Well, this is what I had in mind," I say as I turn toward him on the couch.

"Shoot," he says.

"The land. Where we'll put our house, that way we can go

back out there, spend a pleasant weekend," I say with a daydreamy smile.

"Of course," he says as his hand comes to rest on my thigh.

His touch sends flutters through my belly and a blush through my cheeks, but I keep going.

"I want to go into the forest. At the stump. I want to do it there. Next weekend," I say, though my tone gets increasingly more excited, and I lean closer to him as my smile grows.

He watches me, his eyes half-lidded, and nods slowly. "Whatever you want, sugar. It's yours. It's always yours," he says softly.

My smile widens, and I lean in to throw my arms around his neck.

He wraps his arms around my back, burying his face in the crook of my neck and pressing loving kisses against it as he rubs my back up and down.

"I love you so fucking much, Tiana... You don't even understand," he whispers against my skin.

I pull away, taking his face in my hands to look him in the eyes.

It gets easier to connect with him this way.

My fierce protector, my wonderful almost-husband...

"How did I ever get so lucky?" I ask in a soft whisper as I stroke his cheek.

"I ask myself the same thing every day," he responds with a lovesick grin.

His hands go to my hips, and I feel his thumbs slide back and forth against them as he admires me, his head tilting to lean on the couch as his eyes melt at the sight of me.

But that goddamn mustache...

"Please... *please* shave that thing," I ask with a playful grin.

"No can do, sugar," he says in response before he leans in to rub it against my face and I squeal as he crushes me into the couch.

CHAPTER TWENTY-ONE
TIANA

I feel insatiable. In a way, I don't think I've ever felt.

According to my app–and some other telltale signs–I have a feeling I'm ovulating or coming up on it, and I feel like I'm losing my fucking mind because there is only *one* thought.

When he came home from Canada, I was convinced my "appetite" was because he had just come home, and we had to make up for lost time.

But there is no *fucking* way I can work today.

My *thoughts!*

The only thing I can focus on is all the dirty things Gunnar has said to me in the midst of our trysts.

"Such a good fucking girl."

"You take my cock so well, sugar."

"That's it. Come for me."

I have been zoning out on this contract for what feels like hours until, frustratedly; I slam my laptop shut with a groan.

My thighs are hot. My pulse is running wild. All I fucking want right now is *Gunnar*.

Without thinking, I grab my phone from my tote. I scroll through a few of the pages before I reach my period app.

There isn't very much information I've been able to put in. I started tracking my cycle after my first period. The one right before Halloween.

That was about two weeks ago...

I look through the months, and my app 'predicts' that I should ovulate...

Now?!

Sure, great timing with him getting home, so for the next few days I imagine I'll be sore.

But, fuck, could these moods wait until we got home?!

"Fuck... is this what ovulating feels like? This is torture," I murmur to myself as I lock my phone.

I feel like a cat in heat. I want Gunnar's body, his smell. I want him filling me, fucking me until I'm screaming. I *need* the weight of his body on mine.

Hell, all I want to be is a hole.

And I want it *now*.

The research said nothing about having to go through ovulation when you work with your fucking partner.

I growl as I contemplate the absolutely insane thing I'm considering.

I really shouldn't... like I really... *really* shouldn't. It's the middle of the day! He's AT practice! He's on the ice as I speak!

But we're trying to have a baby. I would be remiss to ignore signs from my body saying, *"Oh hey bitch! I'm ready!"*

I take a look around my office... thinking... weighing the options. He fucked me here before he left. But I need more than that. I need... *fuck;* I need *him*!

I say 'fuck it' and swipe everything off my desk and onto my office chair with a cacophony of flittering papers and metal stationery items. Inhaling a deep breath, I make my way out to the rink.

The tapping of my heels does nothing to distract me from my inane mission. They echo through the back tunnel hallways as I stay on my projected course.

I take a steeling breath, telling myself this is necessary, if not fucking insane.

As I walk down the main tunnel to the rink, the players are paused on the ice as Russel emphasizes whatever the fuck my dad is saying. I don't even fucking know. I don't need to.

Charlotte turns to see me coming down the tunnels. Probably because she knows what my heels sound like at this point and she tilts her head with a smile.

"Hi Ti! What brings you down here?" She asks.

"I need Gunnar," I murmur mindlessly as I look over the rink.

I'd love to talk more, but my plan does not include Charlotte.

"For what?" I hear her ask.

"Urgent... need," I murmur again. My eyes gaze over all the men until I spot the massive behemoth I came looking for.

That bright white "HAYZE" embroidered right above that fucking "33."

For whatever reason, at the sight of him in his gear, the size of a fucking monster, my heart picks up and heat rushes through my body.

I want that body towering over me, and I want it *now*.

"Need?" I hear Charlotte ask in confusion.

"I think I'm ovulating," I whisper as I keep my gaze on Gunnar.

Fuck, he's so hot. He's so fucking big and strong. And his face.

"You *think*?" she asks in surprise.

"I've had an IUD for so long, I have no idea what ovulating feels like anymore. Well, I think I feel it now," I say as I take a deep breath.

I wait for him to turn around and look at me so I can give him some sort of nonverbal cue.

"Do you feel like if you saw a hand flex you'd bark?" Charlotte asks.

I look at her incredulously, my brow furrowing as my lips curl in confusion. "Why would I-" I pause as a vision comes through my head.

Gunnar's hand pulling on a doorknob, or grabbing something from me. The tendons at the top of his hand taut with the flex of his fingers.

I feel like my insides rage at the thought of not seeing it here in front of me now.

"Fuck," I breathe.

"Ah, yeah. Ovulation. Have fun. They have a few more hours left," Charlotte says.

I turn to her, gripping her shoulders. "Charlotte, you don't understand. I can't wait a few hours. I'm going to howl soon," I beg as I shake her.

Her brow rises with a grin. "Welcome to real hormones, sister."

"Oh, fuck you," I grumble as I push her away.

The boys finally break off, and I take a deep breath of relief as Gunnar turns. His head tilts with a small smile as he catches sight of me.

I nod for him to come to me, and he gives me a quizzical look.

I groan as I toss my head back in annoyance.

Fucking men and their inability to understand.

"*Office. Now,*" I mouth.

His brow furrows as he shrugs.

God fucking damnit.

"*OFFICE. NOW,*" I mouth slower.

His furrow deepens as he watches me. "*Right now?*" he mouths back.

I nod furiously before I look around to make sure no one is watching me.

I see him shrug in acceptance before he comes toward the wall.

When I see him coming my way, I turn around and book it down the tunnel.

My heels click rapidly as I run to my office, making sure the desk is cleared off, and the door is closed.

Taking deep breaths to steady my urge, I pace, waiting for him to come.

It takes a few minutes, but eventually, my office door opens. But on his skates, Gunnar is fucking enormous as he ducks even further down to get inside. I have to really crane my neck back to look at him. And the submissive little demon inside of me screams in glee.

No helmet, no gloves, just *him* in his gear and skates.

Slowly, his head tilts as he looks at me curiously and shuts the door behind him.

"What did you need, sugar?" he asks.

He is completely perplexed.

Honestly, I probably would be too if I were him.

But I admire him for a long moment. The damp sweatiness of his hair, the pink flush of exertion on his cheeks and the way he already looks absolutely worn out.

"I need you to fuck me. Now," I say with a breathless pant as I come up to him. I jump in an attempt to get my arms around his neck, but I fail with a groan of frustration.

I reach up to his face, tugging him down to kiss me.

His surprise is muffled in the kiss, and he slowly brings his hands up to my hips, holding them as he kisses me back.

"Right now, sugar? I'm in full fucking gear. And I'm sweaty," he says as he pulls away.

He adjusts his feet on the carpet, which I'm incredibly thankful for in this moment.

"Don't care. Need. Now," I pant into his lips as I pull him into me.

He grips my hands, trying to slow me down, and I glare at him with an annoyed groan.

"What in the seven hells has gotten into you?" he asks as he appraises me.

"I... I think I'm ovulating, and I can't fucking work. Can't focus," I murmur.

He looks back toward the office door, pulling the shutters down over the window before he locks the door.

"Do you know how hard it is to get my dick out of this?" he asks as he turns back to me. He looks over the bottom half of himself, as if he's trying to figure out how the fuck he's going to do this.

But I don't know how hard it is to remove this stuff. And I don't *care*.

"Better get them off quick before your dick gets stuck," I say as I continue trying to get his attention.

"Christ, sugar," he murmurs before he grasps tight onto my hips, pulling me up.

My legs instinctively wrap around his waist, and he moves toward my desk. I press passionate kisses all over his neck, his face, wanting to get every bit of him I can as I grind up and down his body. The rigidity of his pads actually helps some of the ache as I grind.

He's damp with sweat, but even now I don't care. Most men's sweat would be a turnoff. Most, if not all, man sweat, is.

But fuck... Gunnar's natural smell, especially right now for whatever fucking reason. I could drown in it. I've experienced nothing like it before. I want to devour him whole.

"What did you do to your desk?" he asks as he pauses in front of it.

"Couldn't focus," I pant against his skin.

Gunnar sets me down on the desk, and I lean back,

opening my legs for him. With the action, my skirt rolls up, bunching around my hips, and I feel the cool air of the arena hit my molten core. It's a slight reprieve, considering I've been on fire for hours.

Gunnar groans as he rubs a hand through his hair. "Fucking hell," he murmurs in surprise. "You're soaked, babe," he says. Though it's with a tortured breathlessness.

He pulls his jersey up, clasping it in his teeth to bare his warmup shirt underneath as he works to undo the laces and buckles on his hockey pants. He pushes them down quickly, as much as he can with his shin pads on. The cup in his jock shorts is already pressed taut before he pushes it down enough to release his cock.

He releases a hearty groan as he does, his hand coming to stroke himself as he looks down at my open legs.

The pressure of it all is too much. I need touch; I need *something*, so I press my fingers down, in-between my legs to swirl my fingers around my clit. I moan out, and quickly his free hand comes over my mouth.

"Baby, you know I love those moans. But if your dad comes looking for me and finds me balls deep inside of you on your desk, I may crash the fuck out," he says with a breathless chuckle as he continues stroking his cock.

He groans low again before he releases my face and presses the hand into the desk to steady himself.

He moves a bit differently on his skates as he shoves himself in between my legs, and because of all his fucking gear, I can't even get my knees around him. I just have to pin my heels into a portion of his gear I find at his back. His eyes are focused on where he slowly presses the head of his cock into me.

The glorious stretch is everything I needed, and more than what I wanted. I bite down on my lip as my head tilts against the desk, registering the feel of him.

"Fuck," he groans again under his breath.

He advances more, letting me settle around his girth with every inch he adds.

"You're doing so fucking good for me, baby. Keep those noises down," he whispers as he leans in. As he lets go of his cock, he presses both hands against the desk, hovering above me. He leans in, capturing me with a kiss as he slowly moves in and out of me.

My soft whimpers and moans are caught between our lips, and I grind my hips as he slowly thrusts in and out.

I wrap my arms around the upper portion of his shoulders, pulling him deeper into my body. Though I can't feel the normal closeness I usually would when he's naked, I love the pressure of his weight on me.

"Tiana, babe... *fuck,* this is insane," he whispers as he watches where he enters me.

"I know," I pant back.

"Naughty thing begging for my cock during work?" he asks with a tsk of his tongue and a grin.

My heart swells at that, and I kiss him deeper, my tongue roaming the inside of his mouth for a long moment as he thrusts.

His pace picks up, one of his hands coming to stroke between us, strumming against my clit.

"I love your pussy, sugar, but if I'm gone too long, they're going to come looking for me. I need you to come with me," he pants softly as he moves his kisses to my neck. "I'm so fucking close, come with me," he pleads.

I nod desperately, the pleasure climbing with every bit of stimulation he adds, not to mention the urgency of it all. His depth, his speed, the way he rubs my clit. All of it begs me to fall apart for him.

I writhe more, feeling myself climb that summit, and he picks up more, slamming into me so hard I feel the desk inch away from us with every thrust.

"Fuck, I'm gonna fucking come, come for me, baby. Lock me in that cunt, let me pump you full," he pants.

And I do. I bite hard on my lip, stifling every ounce of my noise as my orgasm falls over me in a downpour of pleasure. It washes over me in waves, over and over. And soon he fills me with his own release, a low growl coming from his chest as he pumps me full of heat.

"Goddammit," he grits as my pussy locks him in, taking him for all that he has.

He braces both hands on the desk, his back heaving with his breaths as he lets my orgasm ride as long as it goes.

"There you go, baby... keep... going..." he grits lowly.

My hips move and work, riding the wave for as long as my body will let me, until eventually, it finally wanes away, and he's able to pull out.

Leaning in, he presses soft kisses to the inside of my neck, licking the small sheen of sweat collected there.

"Such a naughty girl, sugar. You needed me to stretch you that bad, huh?" he asks with a teasing grin.

"I was so fucking horny, I'm sorry," I admit as I take deep breaths to settle myself.

"No need to apologize. I'd do it again if you asked," he says.

Slowly, he pulls out, watching his cum follow him, and he grins as he quickly presses it back in with his fingers.

I make a small yelp, and he chuckles as he pulls his fingers out.

"Might wanna keep your hips elevated for a bit; there was a lot," he says. He tugs his jock shorts up and shoves his cock back into them before he replaces his hockey pants and redoes the buckles and laces on them.

I take a deep breath, feeling at least a small bit of reprieve from the feral horniness gripping my brain.

"Thanks," I say as I shift my hips on the desk, throwing my legs over the back of my office chair.

I don't even wanna get up right now. I just wanna relax.

"Well, I gotta get back, sugar. I'll see you after pracky," he says as he leans down to press a kiss to my lips.

"You don't say fuckall to anyone about this, goon!" I call as he heads for the door.

"No promises that Banks won't know!" he calls back as he ducks out of the office and closes the door behind him.

As he leaves and I relax against my desk... there is a small thing that gnaws at my mind as I regain some mental clarity.

But...

I'm sure it's nothing.

CHAPTER TWENTY-TWO
GUNNAR

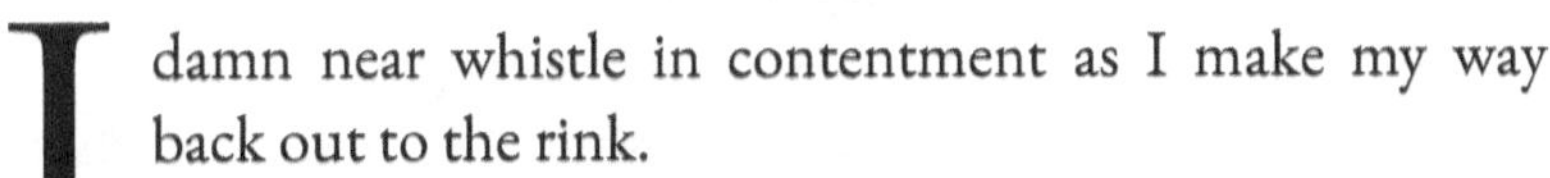

I damn near whistle in contentment as I make my way back out to the rink.

It's a pretty calm week, considering it's the week before Thanksgiving and Bubbles didn't wanna bust our balls too hard since he did that last week.

So when I return, Banks is sitting in the box with Charlotte, watching the rest of the players fuck about on the ice.

I collapse on the bench beside him, taking the bottle of water from his hand and spraying it in my mouth before I hand it to Charlotte.

"Be a doll and fill this up for me," I say with a grin.

Her brow furrows as she takes the bottle and looks down at me. "Hello?"

"Hi! Anyway, I gotta talk to your man. Men shit, shoo," I say as I brush her away.

"Talk nice to my lady or I'll stuff my stick down your throat," Banks says in a low growl as he glares at me.

My brow arches as my eyes dart to his crotch before they go

back up to his eyes. "The carbon fiber stick or the fleshy meat one?"

"Hayze," Banks grits in warning.

"Fine, fine, I'm sorry," I say as I turn to look up at Charlotte. "Please, Miss Lady Dawn, canst thou fetch thyself some water for mines poor soul? I am parched beyond reproach," I say.

Her brow furrows again, and she rolls her eyes as rips the bottle from my hand and walks off.

I turn back in my seat and pull my chain from my jersey, putting it in my mouth with a grin.

"Anyway. Got a few things I need to ask about," I say as I cross my arms against my chest.

Banks looks at me from the corner of his eye as he leans forward on his stick. "Where the fuck did you go?" he asks.

My brow arches with a cunning side grin. "Gentlemen don't kiss and tell," I say with a wink as my tongue slides purposefully against my chain.

"During practice?" he asks with an arch of his brow.

I nod once before I throw my hands behind my head and wag my feet in front of me.

"What's this thing you need now?" he asks as he goes back to watching the ice.

"Gonna buy Tiana a fifth wheel for Christmas," I say with a grin.

His brow furrows at me. "First land, now a camper? The fuck for?"

"Well, remember when I asked about your truck a few weeks back?"

He nods with a confused arch of his brow.

"Miss Tiana and I got some business to attend to, and I reckon you don't want me to break that bed in your house. So for your ears, and your headboards, a fifth wheel would be good to keep on your property. Not to mention, Tiana will wanna be closer when work gets underway on it," I explain.

Banks watches me for a long moment. His eyes narrow at me before he turns back to the ice.

"What was that look for?" I ask as my forehead scrunches in question.

"Nothin'," he mumbles.

I sit up and knock into his shoulder. "The fuck do you mean 'nothin'? Spill, hick," I say.

He glances at me for another long moment before he looks back at the ice. "You remember in college? When you couldn't keep a girl for longer than a second?" he asks.

"Didn't wanna keep 'em. What's your point?"

"It's interestin', I reckon," he says with a shrug.

"What is?"

"The lengths you go to for Miss Tiana's happiness," he adds.

My brow furrows. "Why wouldn't I?" I ask.

"Not sayin' you shouldn't. You're a good man. But I've known Miss Tiana for a while. Know how she moves, how she works. It's impressive you've read all her books in such a short amount of time," he says.

"Get to the point," I say.

"She's a good woman, who works hard for us... protects us. Always has. Always fought for us in the best way she knows how. I think it's her roundabout way of showin' us she cares. I'm just glad that Miss Tiana found someone to care for her. Especially knowin' how she is. She's skittish. Always been on her own. Certainly didn't think the wild goon would woo Miss Tiana," he says with a shake of his head and a small smile.

"Real peculiar, that one. But if we ever wanted someone for her... it was someone that took care of her. She does a lot for the team. Deals with a lot of our shit. We talk about it sometimes... but we're glad someone is carin' for Miss Tiana the same way she's been carin' for the team. Especially since I know the way you ride, Hayze," he says with a sly grin.

I didn't know the team cared this much about Tiana...

"There were some property skirmishes that happened with Crowder a few years back," Banks adds as he nods to Crowder on the ice.

He pretends to play goalie with Robinson's helmet. That does *not* fit him in the slightest.

"She fought tooth and nail to get those papers done. And Leroy, he had some stuff with family a bit ago. Some nasty will issues... she went to bat hard for him then," he says.

My heart squeezes, thinking about all the things she's done behind the scenes.

"Scott over there... he had some kind of sponsorship... commercial, something or other. They wanted to offer him less than what Miss Tiana thought he was worth. She wasn't having that, made sure he got paid the right amount for it," he says as he nods to Scott, who skates back and forth across the ice.

Dumb as rocks, that one. But he's a beaut in the physical sense. I reckon that's what the commercial was for.

"She steps up to the puck for every single one of us, every time. She makes sure our contracts don't fuck us... makes sure we get what we're worth, and even when a few of us got traded, she made sure they got what they needed... secured their contracts, gave them information to make sure whoever got them in the future didn't fuck them," Banks adds.

"I didn't know she did that much for you guys," I murmur.

"And you won't. You won't hear it from Miss Tiana, and she never, *ever* asks for thanks. She asks only for space. So it's all we've ever given her. But all *we've* ever wanted for Miss Tiana was someone to love her. Gotta be honest, we were scared at first when you caught wind of her. You're a wild one. So we tried to steer you away, if only for Miss Tiana's safety. But we're glad it worked out," he says.

The playfulness fades for just a moment as I see the way this team cares for Tiana.

She never talks about what she does for them. Hell, the team doesn't say much other than the warnings they gave me in the beginning. She tries to leave work at work, mostly. But I knew from the beginning, they all knew how Tiana worked, even if no one went for her.

I wondered, maybe for a second, how they all knew so much about her when she didn't do stuff with them.

But it's *this*.

This thing she cares so much about, that she does every day, and the way she operates in her day to day.

And Banks is right; she doesn't know how to express her feelings. It's taken her some time to actually tell me how she feels, even though I know how much she loves me.

I can't imagine what she doesn't say to the team. To know all that she does for them, even if I don't get to see it.

It only makes me love her that much more. Even if it's unconventional, or different, it's so uniquely Tiana the way she shows her care.

I glance at Banks. "Well... what's that thing they say? When you know, you know?" I say with a smile.

"I reckon you know, don't 'cha?" he asks.

My smile widens, and I nod. "Sure do, bud," I respond.

"I'll help you with this fifth-wheel thing. Just wanted to let you know you're doin' a good job," he says.

I wrap an arm around his shoulders and bring him into my chest to rub a knuckle into his head before he shoves out of my grasp and gives me an annoyed smile.

When practice ends, I head to the locker room to shower before I go to Tiana's office, only to find her desk back to normal and she's curled up in her office chair fast asleep.

I can't help the smile that tugs at my lips knowing the things I know now. But I won't mention them.

If she hasn't told me, then it wasn't within her threshold to share.

But it explains why she's always tired. With all she does for everyone, moving in silence, thinking on behalf of everyone else to make sure they get the life they're entitled to... it makes sense why she's so tired now. Even if her gears spin around a different way, if she moves a bit differently.

It doesn't matter.

That's my girl, always.

I approach her desk slowly, kneeling beside her and softly nudging her shoulder.

"Sugar... hey," I whisper softly.

She jolts in her seat, looking around with sleepy eyes before she looks at me in dazed confusion.

"What time is it?" she murmurs as she looks toward her computer.

"Day's done, sugar. Time to go home," I say with a smile.

"Thank God," she says with a sigh.

I watch her for a long moment, sitting with the knowledge I know before I lean in to wrap a hand around her cheek.

She looks at me quizzically before I lean in to kiss her softly. Slow, deep. But enough to show her what I feel.

She tenses for a moment, confused before she slowly kisses back, and I pull away to press a curl behind her ear.

"Love you, baby," I say with a smile.

Her head tilts before a nervous smile rises on her lips. "I love you too?" she says confusedly.

"Let's get you home, yeah?" I say.

She nods, but I can tell she really doesn't understand a lick of anything right now. Not with being awoken from a random sleep and the things I'm doing.

But... it's fine.

At least through it all, she knows she's loved.

CHAPTER TWENTY-THREE
TIANA

The next day, at work, after I finish some things I need to do for the day, I go out to the rink to talk to my dad and Charlotte about this Thanksgiving situation.

I know Gunnar said it was going to happen, but I would like to talk more to everyone else... since everyone else is *here*.

I feel like some of my hormones have waned some... maybe not entirely, but enough to think clearly.

But... there is an itch at the back of my head. One that seems to fester the longer I sit with it.

We even had sex when we got back home last night because as soon as I got up from my nap at work, I was ready to go again.

He was thrilled to oblige. But something has been missing... something that I've noticed the past few sessions, and it buries a little deeper into my head.

But... I push it away, because for now, I'm going to focus on Thanksgiving.

As I walk out to the rink, I listen to the sounds of skates and yelling on the ice as I walk down the tunnel.

Adrian, Gunnar and Charlotte are all sitting in the box, talking, while everyone else sort of just...

I don't even think they're doing anything.

"What's going on?" I ask with a furrowed brow as I come up beside the box.

A smile pulls at Gunnar's lips as he wraps an arm around my waist and pulls me into him.

I stumble slightly on my heels as he does, running my fingers through his hair as I lean down to kiss his forehead.

"Hey baby," he murmurs softly before he rests his head against me. I stroke through his damp hair as I take a better look out to the rink.

"What's happening?" I ask again.

"Bubbles is taking it easy on us. So this week has been a bit of a fuckabout just because we have rink time. We basically suit up and do some warm-ups, and the rest is fend for yourself," Gunnar says with a shrug.

"Hm," I murmur in response. "Where's Dad? I wanted to ask about Thanksgiving," I say as I look over the rink.

He's pretty easy to catch, considering he's bald, stout in the middle but still a tall guy.

"He and Russel have been talking about next week. They're gonna go harder on workouts before Thanksgiving because he doesn't want 'em to get fat and lazy. So they'll be in the gym next week," Charlotte says.

"Right," I mumble. "Dad!" I call out to the ice.

He turns around, his brow furrowing as he looks for the source.

When he sees me, he skates up the box, looking at the four of us here. He sighs in annoyance.

"I can't believe I have to deal with all of you at once," he grumbles.

"Hey?" I mumble.

"Not you two. You two are fine. But add in the goon and the fuckin' stallion here. We saw how your little trial went," he says with a sigh.

"I don't know what you expected. Work in hockey, have a hockey daughter and a sports lawyer and then you're shocked they get with hockey players," I say with a shrug.

"Yeah, yeah. My fault. Anyway. What did you need?" he asks with a dismissive wave of his hand before he presses them to his hips.

"Thanksgiving," I say.

"Ahhh... Yeah... Thanksgiving," he says as he glares at Gunnar.

Gunnar glances up from where he rests his head against my stomach and gives my dad a big grin.

"It's a good idea, Bubs. You know it is," Gunnar says with a confident nod.

My dad rolls his eyes. "If I weren't scared of the wrath of three terrifying women, you'd be wrong," he murmurs.

I smile at that.

"Mom said Black Friday, since Gunnar said somethin' about you and him being at his parent's house for Thanksgiving," my dad says.

"Mmmm..." I hum before I look down at Gunnar. "Do your parents know we're coming?" I ask.

"Yes, ma'am," he says with a nod against me. He doesn't even look up at me, he merely nuzzles into my stomach like it's some sort of warm blanket.

My brow arches as I watch him. "Do they know what I can't have?" I ask.

"Yes, ma'am," he says.

"Do I need to bring anything?"

"Only if you want."

I think for a moment.

"Can they make mac and cheese?"

"Mmmm... Nah. Can you?"

"Her best dish," my dad says with a smile.

A shy tint creeps across my cheeks as I glance at my dad and then back at Gunnar.

"Works for me," he says.

"So, it's all agreed?" my dad asks.

I nod and glance at the three others, who nod in unison.

"Good. I'm leaving," my dad says before he skates off.

"Are you bringing anything to Mom and Dad's?" I ask as I look at Charlotte.

Her eyes float to the top of her head in thought. "I'm not sure yet. But I'm not bringing mac and cheese," she says with a shrug.

"So I've gotta make two pans?" I ask.

She nods. "I'll probably bring an apple pie or somethin'," she says.

"Fine," I mumble. But all this planning reminds me I have to tell Adrian and Charlotte about their roles in our "wedding."

I grip a handful of Gunnar's hair and tug his head back harshly for him to look at me. "Have you mentioned the ceremony thing to them?" I ask.

He bites down on his lip, his eyes half-lidded as he looks up at me with a submissive grin.

"Be careful, sugar. I like it rough," he purrs.

I roll my eyes. "Answer the question, goon," I say.

"I have not. You're welcome to punish me for it though," he says. His eyes pin to mine, and I see the lust swirling in them.

I gulp because I can't do this here today. I press his face back into my stomach, wrapping my hands around his head as if I'm guarding his sight from something. Though it's mostly to keep his horny mouth shut so I can talk to Adrian and Charlotte.

"So, this weekend, we're having the ceremony at the ranch," I say as I look between Adrian and Charlotte.

Adrian has been leaning over on his hockey stick, watching the people on the ice for a long while, while Charlotte has sat on the higher portion of the wall, kicking her feet and volleying her gaze between us.

Though now, this has caught Adrian's attention, and he glances at me from the corner of his eye.

"Ceremony?" Charlotte asks with a tilt of her head.

I nod. "It's just the four of us, and Gunnar's lawyer. Apparently he is ordained, and you two will be the witnesses. I wanna go out to the stump in the forest. The two of you will watch, the lawyer will speak and then we'll sign papers, bing, bang, boom. Married. Hurray," I say unenthusiastically.

A high-pitched squeal is heard before rapid clapping, and I clap my hands over my ears as I wait for it to subside.

Charlotte kicks her feet furiously against the wall in excitement. "Yes, yes, yes!! I love that idea!" she squeals.

A small smile turns up at the corner of my lips. "Good. We'll be coming out on Friday," I say with a smile as my hands slowly lower from my ears.

"Perfect! You can see what I've done with the house with the stuff I bought!" she says with glee.

"Can't wait," I say. "Could you come over after work on Thursday and braid my hair? I don't wanna straighten it for this weekend."

"Of course!" she says.

Gunnar's head shoots up. "You guys will be busy?" he asks as he looks up at me.

He props his chin on my stomach to gaze at me, and my brow arches as I look down at him.

My eyes narrow suspiciously at him. "The fuck do you have brewing, goon?" I ask.

"Nothiiiiiing. I have something to do for my family, is all," he says with a wide, unconvincing grin.

I roll my eyes. "Gunnar," I groan.

"Whaaaat?! It's Christmas, sugar!" he says with puppy dog eyes and a pouty lip.

"I swear on everything holy, Gunnar," I warn.

"You can't stop me. Anyway, Thursday you said, Charlotte? Perfect," he says with a nod.

I sigh before I pat his head, stuffing his head into my stomach again.

"What are y'all doing after work?" Banks asks.

My eyes widen, because I know *exactly* what we're doing.

"Stuff," I murmur.

"Mmm," Banks grunts in annoyance.

"Banks! Hayze! Come here!" my dad calls to us.

Gunnar's head shoots up to look toward the rink before he looks at me.

"Sorry, sugar, duty calls. See you after pracky," Gunnar says as he comes to a stand. He leans down to kiss me before he reaches for his gloves on the bench, his stick against the wall, and his helmet.

With that, he jumps over the wall to the rink and skates off, with Adrian right behind him.

I let out a soft sigh as I watch.

"Anything you want me to have for the day of?" I hear Charlotte ask from behind me.

I glance at her with a smile. "Can I have some steaks?" I ask.

"Anything for you, Ti," she says with a nod.

"Thanks, Char," I say before I turn to the tunnel and make my way back to my office.

CHAPTER TWENTY-FOUR

GUNNAR

"**F**uck," I grunt as I crash into our bedroom door.

Tiana grips my body tight as she kisses all over me. She's devouring me like I'm some kind of meal she's been waiting to have all damn day. Which is insane because she was rather quiet on the way home.

However, as soon as we came in the front door of her apartment, she had jumped me, and now I'm stumbling to get into our bedroom.

I know she said she was ovulating when we were in the office, but that was two days ago.

I've gotta admit, the amount of sex we've been having is a nice perk to all of this. I just had no idea Tiana could be this insatiable.

As I stumble toward the bed, her heels fall from her feet and onto the floor with a loud clatter. Her legs have cinched around my waist, and my hands scramble around her body, working to get her suit jacket off. The entire time, our lips and tongues collide in a symphony of grunts and moans.

I'm throbbing in my sweatpants, and it doesn't help that

I've had to go without boxers recently. I don't think that has helped Tiana's appetite at all because you can damn near see the veins on my cock through the fabric.

She hitches herself down enough to grind against me. Her skirt bunches up around her hips, baring her core, and I feel the hot pulse of her against me.

"Fuck, you're so hard," she pants as she looks down between us.

I give a breathless chuckle as I move her to the bed, leaning down to set her on it.

When I lean up to remove my shirt, she spreads her legs wide, her fingers running through her center. With a devious arch of my brow, I watch the way her fingers swirl against her clit and open her up.

"Goddamn," I say with a grin. Her pussy is soaked, and she grinds against her own hand, as if she can't wait for me.

I lean in to kiss her, bracing one hand against the bed as I use the other to press my pants down, kicking them off behind me before I bring that hand up to run through her center.

Molten, I think, is the best way to describe her.

Hot as sin and *so* fucking wet. My lips widen against hers, my fingers slipping into her with ease.

"Jesus, you're on fire, baby. How badly did you need me today?" I ask with a grin against her lips.

"So... *so* bad... I've thought about you all day," she pants.

"Take your shirt off, baby," I rasp into her lips as I keep pressing my fingers in and out of her, the heel of my hand rubbing up and down against her clit, working her up further.

Her hands scramble around her front, unbuttoning all the buttons on her blouse before she sits up to shrug out of it. Her hands reach back, unclasping her bra, and I take the moment to remove my fingers.

Because I don't think I can have this mustache without her taking a nice ride on it.

Crawling onto the bed, I lay all the way down, and she looks back at me in confusion.

Grinning, I wrap my hand around my cock, pumping it as I pant.

"Come here," I rasp.

Her brow scrunches and she stands, unzipping her skirt and pressing it off of her hips before she climbs onto the bed with me.

My free hand grabs at her hip and I pull her toward me, where she lets out a small squeal. Then, releasing my cock, I shift my grip just enough to get my hands under the crease where her ass and thighs meet, bench pressing her until she's hovering right above my face.

She looks down at me through her legs in sheer confusion, and I merely grin.

"Time for a ride, sugar," I say as I lower her down.

"Gunnar, what are you-"

Before she has time to think, my tongue comes from my mouth, colliding with her core, and she lets out a moan of surprise.

"Oh... fuck," she pants out.

I bring her down further, until her knees are on either side of my head, and she hovers her cunt above my mouth.

My hands rest on the tops of her thighs, stroking softly as I lap at her pussy, flicking my tongue against her clit before running over the length of her.

She continues hovering, her hips moving just enough to get me where she needs me, but that's not enough for me.

My hands slide up her thighs, caressing the skin there before I get to her hips, gripping them tight.

"I said, fucking *sit* on my face," I growl as I tug her hips down, forcing her to plant her pussy on my lips.

Her moans and gasps get louder, and her hips instinctively grind deeper against me.

"That's it, *more*," I groan. My hands grip tighter on her frame, with my cock throbbing so hard that it twitches in time with my heartbeat as her wetness covers my face. I lick and devour every bit of her, my tongue working over her clit and entrance.

Her moans stretch through the room as I feel her body tighten and writhe against me. Just as she approaches the edge, I grab under her thighs, bench pressing her up from my face with a feral grin.

Her hands scramble for purchase, finding my hair as she squeals from the movements, and I sit up with her.

Even if she's facing me, I place her on the bed in front of me before I grip her hip and twist her onto her stomach.

She makes another small noise of surprise as I do, and I lean over her, a hand braced into the bed while the other wraps around her throat.

"What do you need from me, sugar? Tell me," I rasp.

But my cock throbs so hard from licking her I need friction, something, *anything*, and I let my cock rest between her ass cheeks, grinding against it for reprieve.

"Fuck," I growl as I feel her soft skin against me.

"Hard... dominant... control me, *please*," she pants.

Her head pulls back, baring more of her neck to me, and I lean down to nip into the skin.

"Perfect," I rasp against her.

I drag the hand from her throat, over her shoulder, her back, her waist, her hip, before I lay a swat on her ass cheek.

It ripples from my hit, and I grip a palmful of one of her cheeks before swatting it again.

"Perfect fucking slut," I growl as I climb over her.

I lock her legs between mine, fisting my cock and stroking it as I admire her body.

The small dimples at the bottom of her spine are accentuated by the perfect curvature of her ass. I don't overlook the tension in her muscles as her upper back expands with every anticipated inhale.

Releasing my cock, I pull her thighs apart enough to bare her pussy for me, and with a hitch of my hips, I seat myself at her entrance.

When I've gotten the head into her, I grip one of her hips before I thread my fingers into the hair at the nape of her neck. Roughly pressing her head forward to get a good handful of her curls before I tighten my grip and I pull her head back with a hard tug.

She makes a soft grunt of approval, her breaths coming quicker as I rock a quarter of my length in and out of her, quick enough to work her up, but just shallow enough to drive her crazy.

"Your fucking pussy is so... tight, sugar. Christ," I growl as I look down to where she takes me.

"You're so fucking *big*," she pants back.

A wolfish grin tugs at my lips, and my head tilts as I watch my cock disappear. Slowly, I press more and more of myself into her, watching the way she stretches around my girth. Her moans are tortured, turning into whimpers until I lean over her and tilt her head to the side with a rough tug to bare the side of her neck for me.

"That feel good, you naughty thing? You like me throwing you around like the dirty little fuck toy you are? You like the way I use you for *my* pleasure?" I pant with a low growl against her skin.

"Yes... *fuck*, I'm your fuck toy. I'm yours, all *yours*," she pants desperately.

I tsk my tongue, punching forward in one hard thrust, filling her with every inch of me, holding myself in with a rough groan as she tightens around every inch of me. It throws me into a sea of bliss, and I can barely fucking breathe with the way she pulls me under.

I come back to the present, watching the way her mouth gapes, and small gasps leave her as I tug her neck further to the side.

"You take me so fucking well... Why's that, Tiana? What's the answer?" I pant as I twitch my cock against her walls and press gentle kisses to her pulse point.

Her heart beat rages against my lips and I can't help the grin as I feel it in her pussy.

"B-B... Be-ca-ca," she gasps, her eyes open and locked on me, though misty with pleasure that slowly consumes her the longer I stay bottomed out.

"Ahhhhaha, there's a good girl. Keeping her eyes on me. Such a fast learner," I say teasingly with a small kiss to her lips before I pull out enough for reprieve.

A moan works through her, her eyes rolling in her skull before I punch forward again and she cries out, her head trying to work against my grip.

"But she's not using her words..." I say with a grin. "Why can you take me so well, Tiana? Tell me, baby, I wanna hear the reason," I taunt breathlessly.

"B-... B-... Y-Yours... it's..." she keeps trying to work the words out, but I hold myself in, flexing and twitching my cock inside of her to keep her mind aloft.

"Say it again, baby. You're so close, so fucking close, but I can't *quite* understand you," I tease before I pull out and punch forward again with a rough groan of pleasure.

"*Fuck*, you feel so good," I pant quickly, almost to myself as my head tilts back, before I look back down at her.

She bites down on her lip, quick breaths pulsing out of the side of her lips as she locks her eyes on me.

"Yours... it's yours. Made... for... you. Made. For. You," she whimpers, her form twisting like a heel-spun dog, shrinking with a pleasured obedience.

"There's a good girl. Such a good fucking girl... takes me so well because," I pull out, thrusting in one more time before I position myself perfectly for a ride.

I pick up a pace, grunting with every deep thrust, and her moans answering each of them. Her ass slaps back against me as I release the grip I have on her hair to hold the back of her neck and press her into the bed.

"This."

thrust

"Fucking."

thrust

"Pussy."

thrust

"Was."

thrust

"Made."

thrust

"For."

thrust

"Me," I growl with every word, filling her with every fucking inch on every downward stroke.

Her pleasured sounds muffle against the comforter, and her back arches to take me with every one.

"That's it. There she is. Arch it for me, baby," I grit as I watch her hips tilt and her ass ripple as I take every ounce of her pleasure for myself.

I pound into her a few more times before I release her neck and pull out. Sitting up, I grip her hips and twist her onto her back.

She makes a startled "oof!" and I take her legs, throwing them over my shoulders as I press myself back in.

Her head tilts back, her eyes rolling as her hands scramble along my sides. Seeking my skin, her pretty nails bite into the flesh, sending delicious shoots of pain through me the harder she digs.

"G-Gunnar... fuck... It's... fuck," she whimpers and gasps. I bend her legs all the way to her ears, my hands braced into the bed as I thrust into her.

I bring a hand up, gripping her cheeks, forcing her gaze to me

I whistle, patting her cheek before I grip them again to get her eyes back on me.

"Eyes here, come on, open 'em," I pant as I keep my pace.

Her eyelids flutter open, and her eyes circle before they land on me, where her pupils dilate and constrict to bring her focus back to my gaze.

"There she is. There's my good girl. Where are you?" I ask.

"C-close... so... so fucking close," she pants. But her eyelids close half-way, fighting hard to keep her sight on me in a hypnotized trance.

"Yes, you are, pretty girl... so close, I can feel it. But I wanna play a game," I whisper with a feral grin.

"G-game? What?" she responds, though in a daze.

"You're not coming until I let you. I want you to beg for your release, *plead* for your orgasm. I want you *screaming*," I growl.

"Fuck," she whimpers as her eyes roll back.

"That's it. Feel that?" I pant as I press her chin up with my nose, baring the column of her throat for me as I move slowly, purposefully, grinding against her clit on every downward stroke.

"G-Gunnar... pl-please," she gasps.

"Feel how easily you take me? How wet you are? You're throbbing, baby," I pant against her skin. Soon, I drag my tongue up her throat, the same time my free hand comes to center, rubbing circles into her clit.

Her moans turn to gasps as I work her higher and higher.

"Pl-pleas... fuck... pl-please... come... I-I-" Her words are chopped apart with sharp breaths as she holds back, her pussy tightening hard around me and I tilt her head back down, gazing into her eyes.

"Words, baby. Use your words," I remind her. She tightens so much that I have to slow down or I'll fucking finish before she does.

"Come... Please let me come, *pleasepleaseplease*, it's so much I can't," she whimpers. Her eyes are glassy with desperation, her body cowering under me as she forces her eyes on me.

Shifting my grip on her chin, I slip two of my fingers into her mouth.

"Suck," I growl.

Her eyes stay on me, obedient and docile, as her lips close around my fingers and she swirls her tongue around them.

"Good girl, baby. Show me how you use that tongue," I pant.

She opens her mouth, dragging her tongue along the bottom of my fingers, and I part them against it before pulling them out and gripping at her throat again.

"You wanna come?" I whisper as I press small kisses into her parted lips, her gasps sucking the air from each one.

"Y-yes, come. Please. So bad," she pleads in a breathless whisper.

I grin, speeding up my pace on her clit as I pound my thrusts deep. Her back arches as her nails sink into the skin at my sides, bringing about the most delicious pain as she tightens around my cock more and more.

"Come with me, baby. I'm so close, come with me," I pant into her lips.

She nods mindlessly against my grip, her gaze on me like a lost soul looking for solace.

"Gorgeous girl. So beautiful when your thoughts are gone... wiped clean, aren't they?" I say with a breathless chuckle.

"G-gone... very gone," she repeats.

I grin, looking down at where I pound into her. She's drenched every bit of me. Her slick runs down her ass and covers my balls.

I grin as I look back at her. "Gorgeous sight, that," I say before I speed up, pounding into her faster, her pleasure climbing as her moans turn to gasps and her pussy tightens and pulses around me.

"Fu-fuck! C-come. I-I'm g-"

I groan as her words hit their mark and her pussy clenches around me; her back bows as it hits her, and she shrieks. Like a raging bull, her body writhes as she rides through her orgasm around me.

I growl, my thrusts halting when she swallows me and locks me in, as I come with her. My cock twitches and pulses rigid pumps of cum into her, and I can feel how deep I am. Removing my hand, I bear my hips down into her clit and grind up and down against it, working her through it.

"Almost there, baby. Wring it out. You're doing so fucking good, ride me out," I say before I release my grip on her throat and move it to her jaw, kissing her deep.

Her body continues to writhe and buck as her orgasm goes, until she slumps into a boneless heap onto the sheets, her chest heaving.

I take the lull to pull her legs from my shoulders and hang them loosely around my waist.

I sit up, panting and reaching over to grab my shirt from the bed and wipe my face with it before throwing it to the floor. All the while, I admire her shimmering body and the way she glistens with sweat. A grin rises on my face before I bring my hands to the center of her chest, dragging them soothingly over her body to bring her back to earth.

As my cock softens, I pull out, pressing my knees back so I'm in a plank, and slowly lower myself down onto her body to press soft kisses into her sternum. Even as she continues to relax, her heart thrums in her chest.

Her hand comes up to my head, running her fingers through my hair as she breathes.

"Was I too rough?" I ask quietly as I keep pressing soft kisses into her skin, rubbing my hands down her sides.

"No... no, no. Perfect. Always perfect," she says with a breathless smile.

"You did so well, baby. You're such a good girl for me," I say as I come to lie beside her, hanging my arm around her middle and kissing into her neck.

She presses her body closer to mine, making a noise of satisfaction as we lay there.

"Thanks for that... I was struggling all day. But I needed more than what we could do in the office," she says with a sigh of satisfaction.

"I don't blame you. It's hot fucking you in your office, but sometimes I wanna do... well... that," I say with a chuckle.

Slowly, my finger traces a circle around her belly button, and I lean my head against her shoulder as we relax together.

She looks behind me, where the headboard is, and reaches over me for a pillow before she hands it to me.

I grin as I take it, and she lifts her hips for me to shove it under, elevating her.

"When do you want to tell our parents we're married?" she asks.

I watch my finger, where it circles her belly button, thinking.

"Well, it's happening next weekend, right?" I respond.

"Mmm," she confirms.

"Thanksgiving is the week after... so, I reckon we tell them during Thanksgiving," I say with a shrug.

"Do you think they'll be okay with that?" she asks.

"They don't really have much of a choice. My parents don't really bat an eye at the crazy things I do anymore. Plus, you know they love you. I don't think they'll be upset there's no wedding right now," I say as I look up at her with a small smile.

The entire time, she's run her fingers through my hair, sometimes twirling a lock of it around a finger.

"Will your parents be upset there's no wedding right now?" I ask.

She watches where she curls my hair around her finger. "I don't think so. I think if I were Charlotte, they might think differently. But... I'm glad we aren't having a wedding right now. I like that I just get to be Mrs. Hayze without all the fluff and pomp," she says with a smile.

"Are you sure?" I ask.

Because I know she had been so focused on the planning... but the more I've learned, I know that her obsession was with the planning aspect, and not actually the wedding.

"Yeah... I'm glad that I can spare the bandwidth for the house and the baby stuff," she says reassuringly.

My head turns, and I look back down to where I trace her belly button.

"Me too, sugar," I say softly.

I've tried keeping the baby and breeding talk to a minimum, because I feel like that seems to be the best course of action for her. There was too much pressure I was putting on her... something that I have never wanted for her. And I don't want her to worry.

So, I change the subject.

"I think the loggers are going to get to the property in the next few weeks," I say.

"Really? Already?" she asks.

"Well, it's fall. Typically, that's the best time they want to do it, and it's going to take a few months. I know they are moving some trees, so when we go out there next week we can spend some time looking over it all, making sure they know what trees they can and can't remove," I tell her.

Her hands continue moving through my hair, but they move in a pattern, almost as if she's in thought.

"What are they going to do with the wood?" she asks.

"Banks said he wants some of it. Depending on the quality, we could build with it. Like your parents, they have their cabin house. But it's up to you, sugar. I want you to build it exactly how you want," I tell her as I turn my head back to see her.

Her eyes meet mine, and she smiles thoughtfully, even if her smile doesn't reach her eyes.

Peculiar.

"When do I get to do that?" she asks as she gives me a teasing grin.

I return her teasing grin before kissing her shoulder.

"As soon as we get the trees out, you can start looking at house stuff. We need to know what kind we want so at least they can get the foundation done right," I say.

Her smile widens, and she nips down on her lip in glee. "Sounds perfect," she says quietly.

"It does," I say with a grin before I lean up, capturing her with a kiss.

CHAPTER TWENTY-FIVE
GUNNAR

Change of plans.

If I want to have the fifth wheel for Tiana by this weekend—which I technically don't, but I just got far too excited—I need to have her distracted, and there isn't much happening today.

So I called in a bit of help to set my little plan in motion.

"What is it you need from me again?" Charlotte asks with an arch to her brow as she crosses her arms against her chest.

For whatever reason, she's challenging me today, and I can't for the life of me understand why Little Miss *Eager* is now Little Miss *Defiant*.

But she picked the wrong time to do it because I am on a time *crunch*!

"Whatever you do, do *not* let that woman out of her fucking cave," I say as I point towards Tiana's office.

I usually see Tiana before I come out onto the ice, which means I'm completely geared up to make this entire plan believable.

But Banks–the lucky bastard–he merely gets to meet me here at the rink, dressed in his normal cowboy get up.

"How often does Tiana actually come out here?" she asks.

My brow scrunches wildly at the audacity, because what?

"A lot more since we started dating, and you know that. What are you on about?" I ask.

"Fair, okay. That's *fair*. But what do I do if she wants to come out and see you?" she asks.

I groan as I think for a moment. "How long does it take to braid Tiana's hair?" I ask.

Now, *she* thinks.

"It takes a bit. The girl has a lot of hair," she says.

"Okay, so here's what I'm going to need you to do. Start talking about the house, persuade her to look at floor plans, structures, whatever it is, and braid her hair or some shit. I don't give a shit what you do. I just neeeeeeed her in that damn office for the whole day, because this is going to take, *all damn day*," I plead.

I try to tone down my urgency, but with the games she's playing with me, it only brings it up higher.

"Caaaaan you do that for me, Charlotte? I will get you absolutely anything you want for Christmas, but I need her in that office today, and possibly tomorrow if I don't get this thing squared away." My hands come up in a mock prayer as I damn near get on my knees for her to listen. *Move. URGENCY, ANYTHING, CHARLOTTE, FUCK.*

"What is it you guys are doing?" she asks.

"Hayze is buyin' Miss Tiana a fifth wheel," Banks says from behind me. I look back to see him staring out at the rink with his hands in his pockets.

"A fifth wheel? You don't even have a truck," she says.

"Well, I *do* have a truck. Just not one that can tow the type of fifth wheel I'm looking at," I tell her.

"Right. But why a fifth wheel?"

I groan as I press the heels of my hands into my eyes. It's like she's trying to hold me up.

"Charlotte, I swear to God, I don't know what I've done for you to hold me up right now, but for the sake of appeasement, I'll tell you," I groan as I bring my hands down.

Her brow furrows and she rolls her hand for me to continue.

"I want to give us a place to stay when we're out there, and I know that when construction gets underway, Tiana is going to want to be out there more often," I explain.

"Oh, what, so my place isn't good enough?" She scoffs as she presses her hands to her hips.

"Miss Lotty," Banks scolds from behind me.

"But babe, he-"

Banks holds up a hand, stopping her.

"Don't go gettin' your panties in a bunch. You know how your sister is, and you know how *they* are. It's a solid idea, them folks aside. They can be out there and closer to their homestead," Banks says.

Charlotte rolls her eyes as she crosses her arms again. "Fine. But I want..." She pauses as she thinks. "I want you to shave your lip," she says as she points at my face.

"Not happening, next option," I murmur quickly.

Why does everyone hate this damn thing? I quite like it. It's really hockey-like.

She stomps her foot with a pouty huff and a whine as her head rolls back. She sighs as she brings a hand up to her chin, thinking again. "I want three weeks with Tucker," she finishes with a triumphant nod.

My brow furrows. "My dog? What for?"

"Waffle weally misses him," she says as she presses out her lower lip in a pout.

I groan as I toss my head back. "Yes, okay, fine, three weeks with the boy. Is that all?" I ask.

"That's it. Go do whatever you need; I'll keep Tiana busy. I just wanted to fuck with you; you were all twisted, and it was funny," she says with a giggle.

"Jesus Christ," I huff as I make my way out of the tunnel.

Charlotte runs ahead of me, making her way to Tiana's office.

Thank God.

The woman is a godsend, if not a little crazy.

I damn near stumble with the speed I come out of the locker room, only to see Banks waiting for me.

The man has always been at peace with... anything, to be fair. I almost never see him on his phone. And if he's waiting–like he is now–he just... *stands* there.

Even now. He's got his arms across his chest, his foot propped against the wall and his head tilted back as he looks up at the overhead lights.

"The fuck are you doing?" I ask.

"Nothin'. You ready?" he asks with a sigh.

My brow furrows. "You all right?"

"Yeah. Not real excited to go home," he says as we walk toward the exit of the arena.

"Why not? Don't you love home?" I ask as we press the doors open and out into the crisp air.

It's a rainy, ugly day. But it's fall in Washington; that's just a default here.

"A lot. But there's a horse back home that I grew up on... couldn't bring him here because he was gettin' old, and I reckon it'll be the last time I see him," he explains.

"Damn... I'm sorry, man. That's heavy," I say as we get to his truck and climb in.

"Sall right. Circle of life. He was a good horse. Just glad I get to say goodbye," he says as he starts the truck and pulls out of the parking lot.

I know Banks loves his horses. Even in college, most of the time he ever really talked to his family was to check in on the horses he had back home, so I imagine he's doing pretty rough.

But... it has me thinking about grief... about the last time I saw my grandpa.

He was really sick at the time. And we knew he had little time left, but he still tried to do everything he could until the end.

He always watched my games from his hospital bed.

As the visions of that day play through my head, I become quiet, staring out the window. The world on the other side blurs, showing me that memory in 4K.

The heaviness of it all weighs on me, because as happy as I am for Banks that he gets to say goodbye to his horse, I'm reminded of how sad I was not to be able to say goodbye to Pa.

Funny enough–because life is a cruel mistress sometimes–I had a game the night he passed.

I remember checking on him before the game. I still went to see him before all my games, to see what knowledge he might have for me about that team. I even considered not attending that game, because he was doing worse than usual. But Pa told me he'd be alright; that I'd get to talk to him after the game.

He knew I couldn't miss these games... that I was being watched by The Stags. And playing D1 here in Washington; I had big eyes on me. He knew how badly I wanted to get to the pros, so he always made me go to the games.

Pa wouldn't let me miss any of them, just to watch him wither away. Even if I wanted to.

But he insisted.

The fiery trail of a tear falls down my cheek as I continue gazing out the window and take a deep breath.

I didn't get to talk to Pa after that game, unfortunately.

I still remember that game. It was a real good win. One I fought hard for. And looking back, I think I knew I wouldn't be able to talk to him after that game. It made me angry, and I left it all on the rink that night.

And when I looked up at Dad in the stands... I just knew. Mom wasn't there with him, and if Mom was in the stands, Pa was okay.

But Mom never came.

I still remember the look on my dad's face when he shook his head, but he still clapped when we won.

As soon as I could, I got off the ice. No one could stop me then. I threw my gear in my cubby, didn't even do it properly.

Dad met me at the exit. And...

I shake my head, clearing my throat as that day fades away, and I focus on the world moving outside the window as I sniffle away the rest of the tears that threatened to escape.

Soon, a thick, strong hand grips tight on my shoulder, rocking me.

"I know, bud. I know," Banks says gently.

I nod, letting one last tear roll down my cheek before I wipe it away and smile at him.

"So," I clear my throat. "My mom will meet us at the lot. I want a woman's opinion," I say to change the subject.

Banks glances at me from the corner of his eye before he pats my shoulder once and replaces it on the steering wheel.

"How big are you looking at?" he asks.

"Big. I don't want her to feel cramped, but I want it to be nice, since I imagine we'll be living in it eventually," I say with a shrug.

"Mmm," he grunts.

"You know anything about fifth wheels?"

"I know about big-ass horse trailers. Same difference," he says. "What's your plan after the house is built?" he asks.

"Dunno. Might sell it, might keep it and get a truck, take us camping. I'm not worried about that part. I just wanna make sure Tiana is comfortable out there for the time being."

Eventually, after a silent ride, we make it to the RV lot.

Lines of massive campers take residence on the lot. There are some Class A's that look bigger than the tour buses that take us to closer away games and to the airport. There are some toy-haulers, some tow-behind campers that are just as big.

But during my research, I had decided to go a more... luxurious route.

I don't want my girl roughin' it for that long.

Maybe for short periods of time if we're actually trying to, but I can't have Tiana doing that all the time. Aside from my just wanting her to be comfortable, I can not imagine Tiana being happy with that kind of arrangement. Especially if we won't have an apartment to go back to at some point.

I did some research when she would go to sleep. There were some things I knew she would want, but I needed to ask my mom.

We used to have a fifth wheel growing up. It came in handy for some longer tournaments when we had to go out of state. But we got rid of it when we all outgrew it.

I miss those times, and if you get a nice enough one, living in them isn't bad.

So my mom knows what to look for.

As we roll up to the RV lot, I find my mom's Subaru in the parking lot, and she's already gotten out, looking at some of the fifth wheels nearby.

Banks parks beside her car, and we get out.

When my mom spots me, she squeals with excitement and runs up to hug me.

"Gunnar! It's so good to see you," she says as she squeezes me.

I hug her back. Before she pulls away to look up at my face, and her brow furrows.

"Hey Mom," I say with a smile.

"Why on earth do you have that thing on your lip?" she asks.

"What? You don't like it?" I ask with a grin.

"It's... something. What does Tiana think about it?"

"Hates it," I add.

"Mmm... well," she murmurs as she trails off. Mostly because Banks has joined us and has now caught her attention. "Adrian!" she says cheerfully.

He tips his cowboy hat as he approaches. Of course, his boot heels clack against the wet pavement.

"Mrs. Hayze," he says.

"You want to buy Tiana a fifth wheel?" my mom confirms.

"Yeah, so remember I told you I bought the land to build our house on?" I ask.

She nods. "Yes, of course."

"So, Tiana is really peculiar about specifics, and I think once everything gets underway, she's going to want to be closer to the land. And I don't wanna take up space in Banks' house. Plus, if he's not there, we can go out there when he's gone, and he doesn't have to worry about us because we'll be all set up," I explain.

My mom smiles. "I think that is a wonderful idea," she says.

"I thought so too," I respond.

"Well, let's go! I haven't seen what they've been building nowadays. You remember how much fun we had in ours!" my mom says as she wraps her arms around mine.

"I know. I was thinking about it on the way here," I say with a smile.

"But how are you going to move it around?" she asks.

"Well, Banks will get it out to his property, since I don't need to do more than that right now," I tell her.

"Mmm, mhm, makes sense," she says with a nod.

As we approach the building, a man in a branded windbreaker comes out. With slicked-back hair and a picture-perfect smile, he's got that... classic salesman look to him.

"Hey there, how can I-" he stops as he gets closer.

His eyes widening. "Holy fucking shit... Fuck! I mean. Shit, I'm so sorry. It's the Stallion and the Bull-Dozer? In real life?" he asks.

I give him a small smile before I glance at Banks, who steps forward, pressing his hand out.

"Howdy. Good to meet you...?" Banks says as he turns up the charm. The man grasps his hand almost greedily, and Banks gives it a hard squeeze and a shake.

Banks doesn't always enjoy meeting fans, only because he doesn't enjoy the idea that he's technically famous. But he knows who he is; he knows what he is to Seattle and the professional hockey scene, and he always knows how to rock a play. So he plays the game as he always does.

"Uh, Roger. God, the pleasure is all mine. What are you guys doing out here?" Roger asks.

"Well, The Dozer here is lookin' for a big fifth wheel for his lady, and we're hoping you can help him out," Banks says as he grabs me by the shoulder.

"I'd love to help you guys out! Is this your lady here?" Roger asks as he gestures to Gunnar's mom.

She laughs as she pats Gunnar's chest. "'Fraid not. This is just my son," she says proudly.

"Well, you raised an insane unit, ma'am," he says as he presses his hand out to her.

She takes it and shakes it, pressing her other hand on top. "Thank you so much," she says.

"Alright, so. Fifth wheel, you said? What's your budget? What're your non-negotiables? What are we lookin' for?" Roger asks with a grin as he claps his hands together, rubbing them.

From there... we get to work.

I bought my girl a fucking fifth wheel. And just in time to get back to the rink.

Had to leave it at the dealership, so we'll have to borrow Charlotte's time tomorrow. And I also had to make a few calls to my accountant when he was upset at me for spending money on a depreciating asset like this, yada yada. Don't care.

I bought my girl a fifth wheel, and it's *perfect*.

I got the biggest one on the lot, because, *duh*. But I can't wait to show it to her.

How does Tiana feel about fifth wheels? To be fair, I have no idea.

But it's not about the fifth wheel itself; it's about the reason behind it. And I know Tiana is a girl of logic, so I know she'll end up loving this.

I signed the papers, and before we left, they installed a trailer hitch into Banks' truck so we could make the drive out to his homestead tomorrow, and we'll figure out how to get it done.

With time to spare, we make it back to the rink just before practice ends, and I quickly shower to make it seem like I had just finished. Banks stays in his truck because if Tiana sees him in his normal clothes, she'll know something is afoot.

She's smart in that way.

When I make it to Tiana's office, Charlotte is digging through a file cabinet inside Tiana's office.

My brow furrows as I look over the scene because it seems as if a fucking paper bomb went off in here.

There are binders *everywhere*. They're open, papers in page protectors, pages without page protectors. On the floor, on the cabinet, on Tiana's desk. They're just fucking... *everywhere.*

My eyes widen, and they lock onto Tiana, who has two long braids going from the top of her head, along either side and down her back.

I've never seen her in braids, but I think they might be one of my favorite looks on her.

"You look amazing, babe," I say with a smile.

She gives me a mocking smile as her eyes point desperately at Charlotte, begging me to help her.

I clear my throat, trying to get Charlotte's attention.

"Uh... Charlotte?" I ask.

Charlotte perks up, looking over at me like a deer in headlights.

"Gunnar! Is practice over?" she asks.

"Yeahhh... what is going on here?" I ask cautiously.

"Oh, Tiana didn't want to go through her old files in her cabinets after I finished her hair. So I got bored and did this," she says with a grin.

"Yes... she's been... helping me," Tiana grits through a fake grin.

Uh oh.

"Alright, Charlotte... well... uh... we're going to go now..." I say as I approach Tiana's desk.

Tiana stands quickly, throwing all her things in her tote before she shoves it at me and rounds her desk, pushing me out with her.

"Don't worry, Ti! I'll have this cleaned up before I leave!" Charlotte calls.

"You BETTER!" Tiana yells back, pausing in the hallway to do so.

I freeze in place, watching the scene unfold.

I don't know why Tiana didn't stop her. Maybe she was too focused on something else.

But what I do know is that Tiana is... *nottttttt* well with the way Charlotte is moving her things around.

"You all right?" I ask cautiously.

"Yup, get me home. *Now*," she murmurs.

"Roger that, Big Mama," I say as I wrap an arm around her shoulders and speed the fuck up.

Tiana has a few moods. This is not one I see often. But I have seen it.

If there is something I put back in the fridge or pantry wrong after we get groceries, or if I move something of hers in the apartment.

Yeah, *nooooo* bueno. She doesn't like those things.

I've had to learn exactly how she likes things, and she's very particular about *her* things.

Especially her books. I am *not* allowed to touch those unless she asks.

I made that mistake once. I shall not make it again.

But at least I got the fifth wheel squared away. So I have enough of a good mood to share between the both of us.

CHAPTER TWENTY-SIX

TIANA

Thankfully, Charlotte cleaned up my damn office before I went into work on Thursday. But she still stuck around and re-braided my hair. It was strange how adamant she was about staying in my office these past two days. I had almost begged her to leave, but she would change the subject, or ask about something else.

I don't know if maybe she was going through something and she just needed my company, but *I* needed her gone.

Aside from that, she told me to make sure I wore my bonnet, but if it was messed up by today–Friday–to have her redo it.

Luckily, when we get to the ranch, my hair is perfectly fine.

I'm actually excited to get out here. I love coming out to the ranch, especially now that we have land here and I can daydream about the place our house will be.

I would love to have a balcony, so I can sit out on it and have coffee in the morning sun with a good book.

When we get to Adrian and Charlotte's place, there's a lofty exuberance that pulses through me. As if I'm walking on air. There are only a few nerves. I'm still processing the fact that I'll be a wife at all. But Gunnar is here, and I feel like I can let some of those nerves go because he *is* here.

I get to marry my goon this weekend.

And I'm so fucking thankful for it... for *him*.

However, today we're relaxing, settling in before we finish the marriage process tomorrow.

As Gunnar parks the BMW in the grass beside Adrian's truck, he opens the door to let out a rowdy Tucker, who is extremely excited to see Waffle.

I look around for the little ball of orange fluff, to find her hauling ass from the stables, straight for us. Her barks echo through the small valley as she races for Tucker.

He meets her halfway, and the two of them do a little dance with each other before they circle and run off into the field beyond the stables.

I climb out of the car, stretching wide after the drive here and embracing the day.

Work was basically cut short, so we got to get out here before the sun went down. Even if there isn't much to see. It's rather gloomy, but at least it's not nighttime.

Gunnar crawls out of the passenger seat, throwing his upper body over the top of the BMW with a sigh.

"Sugar, I would love to have a nice sleep," he says as he tilts his head to look up at me.

I smile as I lean over the top of the car to ruffle his hair.

"If I don't see what Charlotte has done with the house, she'll have a coronary," I tell him.

He groans, flopping over onto his back to fling his arms out like a teenage boy having a meltdown.

"Make it quiiiiiick, please!" he groans.

I shake my head with a roll of my eyes as I close the driver's side door and go to the trunk to grab our bags.

When thinking about what I wanted to wear for our ceremony... honestly, I'm not a dressing up girl.

I dress up only for work because, well... I have to be taken seriously.

However, I will not be riding an ATV in a nice dress out to the middle of the forest. So, I made sure I packed the first jersey that Gunnar ever got me, and some nice bell-bottom jeans, and one of my hoodies.

It's unconventional; getting married in something so casual. But at the end of the day, it's not about the pomp and the fluff... it's about coming together and becoming one.

I don't think the other things should matter. At least not right now.

Gunnar pushes off the BMW and comes to the trunk to take the bags from me before he leads the way up to the porch of the ranch house.

Outside the door is where Charlotte put the little bear statue she bought a few weeks ago. As well as a Christmas-y welcome mat in front of the door.

I smile as I look up at the door, where a big wreath sits on the front, and Gunnar opens it, leading the way in.

He drops the bags by the front door, hurrying through the house to find... someone. I already know Adrian and Charlotte are out at the stables, but I at least want to get the stuff inside before we venture out.

My brow furrows as I look to where he dropped the bags.

"Gunnar? Why did you just drop these here? Take them to the room," I say as I follow him.

"No can do, looking for something," he murmurs loud enough for me to hear as he continues walking around the house. I continue following him, taking in some things Charlotte has already done. They've already got their tree set up and decorated, with rugged burlap and plaid ribbon, as well as some other wooden Christmas ornaments.

Their fireplace mantel has the stockings hung up already. One for Charlotte, Adrian, and Waffle, who has a tiny stocking with a little paw on it.

There is some of the piney garland we had bought that she lined the mantel with. As well as massive red and green glass ornaments and some other tall, white candles interspersed between them.

She had also bought some Christmas throw pillows, and those are sitting on the couch. As we round through the living room, to the back hallway, my brow furrows, and Gunnar exits from the back door.

"Gunnar, what the hell are you doing?!" I ask with a groan.

When he makes it onto the back patio, he presses his hands to his hips, looking out across the field at the back of the house.

There's a henhouse off to the right, positioned some way behind the stables, and I see there's a small carport as well. That's where Adrian keeps the ATVs.

I hear a ruckus coming from the stable, mostly neighing and the sound of scraping. And apparently, so does Gunnar because when I come out onto the patio, he closes the door behind me and damn near runs out to the stables.

I groan as I tip my head back because I wore my Uggs out here. I really only use the cowboy boots Charlotte has here, and I haven't had the chance to put them on yet.

I run after him, wondering what the hell his issue is when we round the front of the stables.

"Can we do it now?!" Gunnar asks excitedly as he finally finds Adrian.

He's mucking out the stables, tossing the soiled hay into a wheelbarrow, while Charlotte rubs the snout of the small white horse that's in the other stable across from Chauncey.

"Calm *your* horses, Hayze. I'm almost done," Adrian huffs.

Charlotte squeals as she catches sight of me, and runs

toward me to throw her arms around my neck in a crushing hug.

"Ti! You're here!" she giggles.

"I am. I like what you did with the inside. At least what little of it I saw," I say.

"Oh, thank you! I had so much fun. I wish you had been here to do some of it with me, but at least I got to help you at your house. So I guess it's not so bad," she says with a grin.

I give her a small smile in response. "Do you think there are any trees here we could take at some point? I totally forgot you guys have some pines out here," I say as I look around.

"Ohhh! Yes, of course! Down on your guys' property, there are some off to the right. When we go down there, I'll show you," she says with a nod.

"Thanks, Char," I respond softly.

My attention returns to the zooming Gunnar. Who has gone as far as grabbing a pitchfork to help Adrian muck out the stable as fast as he can.

Adrian merely shakes his head with a sigh as he continues moving at his normal pace.

"What in the hell is wrong with you, Gunnar?!" I shout as I throw my hands out.

"Important MATTERS, SUGAR! JUST TRUST ME!" he calls back as he continues moving.

I sigh as I pinch the meat between my brows.

"Lord help me," I sigh.

"Well, while they're finishing up, let's get the ATVs going. Adrian already tacked up Chauncey, so he's just gotta ride him out," Charlotte says as she threads her fingers through mine.

"Alright, fine," I say with a sigh.

Leaving the stables, Charlotte leads me to the house, where she grabs four sets of keys before tossing me two of them.

I find the fourth set to be strange. But I don't question it; it's not my house.

I take the moment to change out of my Uggs for the pair of cowboy boots I use and follow Charlotte out of the house.

We leave from the back of the house, avoiding Gunnar's insanity to make our way to the ATVs in the carport.

I reach into my pants pocket, grabbing the squishy earbuds and stuffing them in my ears before Charlotte has the chance to start the engines.

One by one, Charlotte and I move the ATVs to the front of the stables. When they're all in the front, I sit on my ATV as Charlotte grabs the helmets.

When she returns, Gunnar is holding a helmet of his own with one of the biggest grins on his face, while Adrian rides Chauncey out of the stable with a few clicks and whistles, getting ahead of us.

Charlotte presses her helmet to her head and climbs onto her ATV, revving the engine a few times before Gunnar does the same, looking to me with a nod.

Tucker and Waffle go mad running around Chauncey and Adrian, before Adrian kicks into Chauncey's side and he bolts, off through the field and toward the tree line out north.

Charlotte moves after, then me, with Gunnar taking up the rear, and I'm reminded how happy I am to have land out here.

I love the feeling of this. It's so nice getting out in nature, where the rest of the world is just an arm's length away. Close enough to be comfortable, far enough to have peace and quiet. I take a deep breath of air as I stand up on my ATV, following Charlotte and Adrian down the path we usually take.

It seems as if Adrian and Charlotte have been quite busy out here. The path has become much more refined since the last time we were here, and it even seems... bigger? Wider? It's surprising since it's only been a few weeks and it already feels so different.

It just means we're a few steps closer to getting the house

started, or at the very least the loggers in to get stuff out of the way.

Eventually, after a bit of riding, and much less maneuvering than we usually have to do, we make it to the ridge above our land. Chauncey and Adrian take up the far left, with Charlotte beside him, me beside her, and Gunnar beside me.

But there is something... down there? Next to the lake.

My brow furrows as I squint to look at it.

I've forgone my glasses over the past number of weeks and traded them for contacts. But with the ride out here, they feel like they've dried some, and I have to blink a few times to get a better look at whatever is by the lake.

As my contacts moisten and I'm able to focus, I realize it's a fucking camper? And it's *enormous.*

Who the fuck would bring a camper out here? And on *our* property? This is trespassing. I can get someone down here in three seconds flat if there are people trespassing here.

Gunnar continues down the ridge on his ATV, and my head volleys between him and the land before I follow him. I pump the brakes on the way down the ridge face as he rides out to the camper.

The grasses are dying with the cold, leaving a carpet of dark brown reeds below us. It's also damp and soft; as it's been rainy and muggy out here. Still, Tucker follows us.

I cut the engine of my ATV and climb off, not even bothering to take my helmet off as I approach the massive thing.

Gunnar shuts his ATV off as well, and apparently so has Charlotte, because it's completely silent now. Save for the birds chirping in the forest beyond the lake.

I quickly walk around the camper, surveying the surrounding ground. I can see the tire tracks in the mushy grass from where it was brought in. And it looks like fresh tracks, if I were to take a guess. It doesn't seem like this thing has been here long.

I take a few steps back, moving toward the ATVs to look over this thing again.

It's... huge. It's almost a house. It's incredibly long, and very *new*. Honestly, it doesn't even look as if it's been used.

It looks straight off the showroom floor.

I turn around to look at Gunnar, who has taken his helmet off and placed it on the ATV. But there's... a smile on his face, with his thick mustache only accentuating his glee. An anticipatory one, and I put... all the damn pieces together.

His eagerness to get out here, the reason he ran through the damn house looking for Adrian and Charlotte like his ass was on fire.

I remove my helmet, grasping the open face as I hang it beside me, and I lean my head back with a groan before I bring my free hand up to pinch the meat between my brow. My eyes clench shut, and I take a frustrated breath.

"It's ours, isn't it?" I sigh.

"Yup," I hear him respond.

"And you had Adrian put it on the land," I add.

"Yup," he says.

"Yeah..." My hand falls from my face before I bring it up to my hip and turn around to look at the thing.

Slowly, I turn to look at him, half of my face scrunching, as if the sun is in my eyes.

"Why'd you get a fifth wheel?" I ask with a sigh.

"Well, I figured you would want to be closer to the land when stuff gets underway. And if Charlotte and Banks aren't here and you wanna come spend time out here, we have our own space until the house is ready. Plus, I can fuck you as loud as I want out here," he says with a grin as he throws his hands out, gesturing to the land.

I sigh, my head tossing back again.

This big goon... goddamnit, he knows me so well.

I don't know if I would have ever asked for a fucking fifth

wheel in my life. We don't have a truck big enough to tow this thing. But he's so entirely right. This *is* really nice if we wanna come out here.

It's a simple start to *our* space, without giving up our commitments for good, and without having to possibly live with Charlotte and Adrian.

I take a look at the camper again before looking back at him, where he has a massive grin on his face as he stuffs his hands in his pockets and rocks back on his heels.

"I made sure to get the biggest one," he says proudly.

I take another deep breath, moving over to the ATV and placing my helmet on it before I extend a hand out, gesturing for him to lead the way.

"Are you upset?" he asks as he turns around with a small frown.

I sigh softly. "No, Gunnar, I'm not mad. I am just struggling sometimes with someone who..." I pause, realizing I'm about to say something like this out loud. Because it means I'm facing something that constantly sits on the back burner.

"Someone who just does everything they can to make my life... easier... better," I say as I give him a nervous smile.

His frown softens, and he comes up to me, wrapping a hand around my cheek before he leans down to press a kiss to my lips.

"Sugar... you know what I've always said," he says.

I look up at him through my lashes, the corner of my mouth tilting in a reluctant smile. "You always told me you would," I whisper.

"Atta girl," he says before he wraps a hand around the back of my head and pulls me toward his lips. Pressing a kiss to my forehead, he lets go of his grip to stroke a thumb over my cheek as he gazes at me with a smile.

"Come on. It's really nice in there!" he says as he takes my hand and leads me to it.

He pulls the keys out of his pocket, and my brow furrows. They're the same keys Charlotte had. But she must have given them to him in the stables.

With his height, he's able to reach up and unlock the door, tugging on the handle and pulling it open.

The steps unfold from under the camper, extending out to the ground and providing an easy way to get up.

He steps to the side, gesturing to the door, and I smirk playfully as I pass him.

"Ladies first," he says with a grin, and I roll my eyes as I grab the handle beside the open frame, climbing up the stairs and poking my head in.

Walking in is the kitchen sink, and a small island, with a surprisingly nice light fixture above the residential, stainless steel stove *and* refrigerator directly behind it.

All the appliances are residential and stainless steel.

My brow furrows as I look around. This thing is incredible.

You could *actually* live in something like this if you wanted to.

To the left of the door is a small area. I imagine where one of the slide-outs is, because it has a small table and chairs right in front of the front window. And beside that area, in a small depression, is an entire living room with what seems to be wood laminate floors. There are massive leather couches on either side of the living room, and a large cabinet with a glass front below a large window at the end of the trailer.

"Check this out," he says.

He comes in, moving toward the living room to walk down the recessed steps, to the large window at the end. Leaning over to one of the side cabinets, he presses a button on the wall.

Whirring starts up, and an electric fireplace turns on in the glass front of the large wooden cabinet, as an entire fucking TV rises from the wooden platform, blocking the massive window.

My jaw drops, gaping as I watch what looks to be a seventy-inch flat screen just... *move*?!

"Pretty cool, right?" he asks with a grin.

I nod mindlessly, trying to wrap my head around all of this, before he turns around, leading me toward the other end of the camper. There's a small, hatch cover on the wall beside the steps, and he opens it.

"These are the slide-out controls, other buttons and things," he says before he closes the door.

I nod mindlessly, watching in rapt confusion as he opens a door beside the hatch.

"Bathroom," he says with a smile before he leads me up the steps.

It's a bedroom, with what looks to be a king bed, though Gunnar has to kneel in this area because the man is fucking huge.

On the far wall, there are big glass mirrors on the sliding doors.

"My mom helped me out, and she made sure I got a unit with these," he says.

My brow arches as he shuffles to the glass doors on his knees, opening them.

"Hookups for a washer and dryer," he says with an enormous grin as he sits back on his heels.

My jaw drops. And I can fucking do laundry here?

"Gunnar..." I murmur.

"I know it's a huge decision. But I wanted to make sure you had a good place to be when we get closer to construction. And it's early to do this, but I figured since you like coming out here, and it's Christmas, I don't think there was a better time to do this a-"

I cut him off, getting up close to him and grasping his face, kissing him deeply.

He makes a startled noise, his hands coming to my hips as he kisses back, humming a soft noise of approval between us.

I pull away, holding his face and volleying my gaze between his eyes in shock.

Because he just... *keeps* surprising me.

His gaze holds a hint of question in them, but hope as well.

"I... absolutely love this," I say slowly.

"Oh thank God," he says with a relieved breath. "I was terrified. I didn't know what you were going to think of this," he says as his lips pull into a nervous smile.

"Yeah, I mean... it's a really bizarre gift, I think, for anyone. But... your entire reasoning is incredibly sound. I'd be dumb not to appreciate it," I respond as I look around the bedroom.

"You know how I am, sugar. I just want you to have a place where you're comfortable," he says quietly.

A happy frown thins my lips as I tilt my head, pressing back some of his hair before I hold his chin in my hands.

"This is one of the sweetest gifts ever, Gunnar," I say. A sigh of happiness creeps out of me as I look at him.

"Sweet," he says with a grin.

I roll my eyes as I shake my head playfully before taking in the bedroom again.

Though my eyes catch on the mirrors... the ones that seem to sit perfectly beside the entire bed.

"Those mirrors didn't have anything to do with your decision in this one, did they?" I ask as I nod to the mirrors.

He lazily glances over his shoulder at them before he looks back at me. His eyes dart to my lips before darting back up to my eyes, and he pulls his lower lip into his teeth.

"They may have had... a bit of influence," he says in a low purr, his hand tightening where it holds my hip.

I glance behind me, waiting a second to see if I hear anything. It seems silent for a long moment, but I look back at him.

"Stay here," I whisper, and as if he understands, he nods.

"Can do," he says breathlessly.

I bounce down the steps and press my hands to either side of the door frame, looking out to the ridge.

Charlotte and Adrian are talking to each other, with Waffle propped against the handlebars of Charlotte's ATV, barking out at Tucker. As if the good boy is indebted to Gunnar, he merely sits at the bottom of the steps, looking back at the ridge as he whimpers.

"Psst! Go back to Waffle!" I whisper at Tucker, shooing him away. Tucker looks back at me with a bark before he takes off for the ridge.

As Waffle's barks increase, Adrian and Charlotte look toward me, and I wave.

"Go away!!" I yell out at them. Charlotte seems to clap eagerly before she starts her ATV, and Adrian merely shakes his head.

When I see Tucker is up on the ridge, and the five of them have disappeared back toward the ranch house, I lean out, grasping the handle of the door and pulling it closed before I lock it and turn to Gunnar with a grin.

His grin seems to understand exactly what mine is saying.

CHAPTER TWENTY-EIGHT
GUNNAR

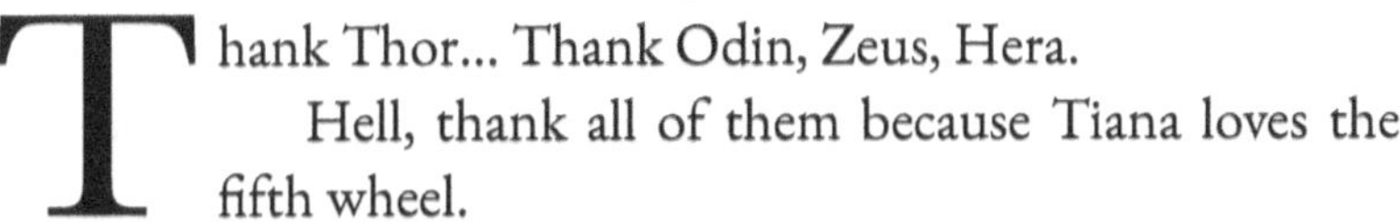

Thank Thor... Thank Odin, Zeus, Hera.

Hell, thank all of them because Tiana loves the fifth wheel.

So much so that I think I'm about to be greatly rewarded for it.

I *love* being a good boy. If I had a fucking tail it'd be wagging right now, I just know it.

And I surely feel like one when Tiana looks me up and down with a heated gaze from the front door. Her teeth nip into her lower lip, and before I have a chance to think about what she may be thinking, she runs toward me, wrapping her arms around my neck and latching her lips to mine.

A startled *"oof"* makes its way out of me as I catch her, wrapping my arms tight around her to kiss her back. My arm threads tight around her back as my other comes to grab the back of her head, pressing her deeper into my embrace.

Because this area is a tad... smaller. I have to move around this area of the camper on my knees. But I have no qualms about it. I'm closer to Tiana's face this way.

I sit back on my heels and her legs wrap around my waist. Already, her hips grinding against the hardening cock in my jeans.

In the few days before today, her "appetite" had decreased. Enough for her to not jump my bones every chance she had. But we've still been having sex constantly. Because... well... duh.

Fine by me.

"Are you going to fuck me in front of the mirrors?" she asks with a pant into our kiss as she continues her grind.

"I'd be a fool not to," I respond with a grin.

She tugs my lower lip between her teeth as I weave my hands from her back and head. With a slow, thoughtful slide of my hands, they move down her sides; all the way down her body until I'm gripping her ass tight. I press onto my knees and shuffle to the bed and to place her on it.

Releasing our kiss, I look down at her with a grin and a breathless pant before I tug off her boots, and peel the bell bottom portion of her jeans from her.

No fucking panties.

I grin up at her as I toss the jeans to the side. With her hands pinned into the bed behind her, she props herself up so she can look down at me. Leaning in, I press tender kisses into the bare skin above her seam, but she giggles as my mustache tickles her. My hands move up and down the inside of her thighs, caressing the soft skin there as I move my kisses to the inner crease of her thighs. I want to wind her up, so I delay going straight to her pussy.

"When are you shaving that thing?" she pants with a grin.

"Never," I respond.

She groans in annoyance as her head tosses back and her hand threads through my hair, tugging me into her pussy to shut me up.

I've always loved a woman who can lead.

My tongue hungrily falls from my mouth, dragging up

from her entrance to her clit, lingering there to swirl my tongue lazily around it.

She's louder here, I can tell already, because her moans fill the bedroom as I lap at her. Her hand tightens in my hair, gripping it for reprieve as I devour her.

My hand leaves one of her thighs to press my fingers into her slick entrance. Her pussy squeezes around my fingers at the same time her hips buck against my face.

I glance up, watching her, and her gaze has already come back to me, her head tilting as she watches me lick her clean.

I pull away just enough, my thumb replacing my tongue as I press my fingers in and out of her.

"You like watching me eat your pussy, baby?" I pant with a grin before using my tongue again, moving my thumb away.

"So... so fucking much," she pants. She loses herself in the sight of me. The way I obediently look up at her from between her legs, with lust-hazed eyes.

I flick my tongue faster, up and down her clit, and her eyes roll. Her hand grips tighter on my scalp, pulling me in further, and her hips move in time with my tongue. I add another finger, her moans getting louder in this confined space.

"Ohhhh fuuuuuck Gunnar... fuck!" she moans out as I feel her climb higher and higher.

"There you go, baby," I growl against her.

And while I rarely hold back in general, I reallllly feel like I can let go here.

I keep my fingers on her core, coming up from her pussy to kiss her deep. Her arms wrap around my shoulders as she kisses me back and grinds against my hand.

Soon, I remove my hand from her pussy, pulling from our kiss to quickly suck them clean before I tug her hoodie from her body. When I get it off, she reaches for the hem of my hoodie, pulling it off of me with rushed, urgent breaths. As if she can't bear not having her skin pressed against mine.

It's cooler inside the fifth wheel, considering there's no AC or heat, so it's just the same temperature as outside, if not a few degrees warmer. But the air hits my skin, causing the heat radiating from me to pulse in time with the pulsing in my cock.

I stand in the small space, though the ceiling bends my head and shoulders, and I let out a chuckle as I reach down to undo my jeans, kicking off my Timbs in the process.

As I get my jeans down enough for my cock to spring out–considering I can't really wear boxers anymore–her hands go straight for it. The pressure is so mind-numbing as she strokes me up and down, all the while she slinks from the bed to get on her knees before me.

A groan works out of me as warm, wet heat surrounds the head of my cock. I'd know that mouth anywhere, but I still love seeing who it belongs to.

"Fuuuuck," I pant as I look down. Her glassy, docile eyes glance up at me through her long lashes, her spine serpentining under her as she sinks lower, dragging her tongue from the seam of my balls to the tip of me.

Her delicate hands wrap around my cock, one over the other, while her tongue swirls around the head of my cock.

"Eager little slut," I growl with a wolfish grin.

I try to toss my head back, but it's too fucking cramped in here, so I slowly pull away, wrapping a hand around my cock before I nod to the end of the bed.

"There," I say with a pant. "I wanna watch you over there."

She nips at her lip, nodding as she backs up on her knees, giving me room to move to the end of the bed. Sitting down, I place my feet on the floor and prop myself up on my elbows. I glance at the closet doors, leaning over to close one of them so that I can see the arch of her back in the mirror.

My cock is so hard it stands completely up for her, and she rests her elbows on my thighs as she wraps her hands around me, dragging her tongue from my balls all the way to the tip.

"What a good girl, getting my cock nice and wet to stretch you with," I pant as I watch her. She wraps her lips around the head of me, before sucking and pressing it deeper into her mouth. But the entire time... her eyes are right *on me*.

Almost daring me to look away.

"I thought you weren't a fan of eye contact," I tease with a tortured pant.

She pulls her mouth off of me, a grin pulling at her lips as she drags her tongue along the underside of me as she strokes me eagerly. "I enjoy watching what I do to you," she says with a grin before she takes me back into her mouth.

My eyes roll, my hand coming up to wrap around the back of her head. My own head lolls back at the way she sucks me.

She takes me deeper, with another groan working out of me as her tongue slides along the underside of me.

"Fuuuucking hell, Mama," I groan, and my head moves to the side, watching her in the mirror.

I didn't think it was possible, but it almost feels like my cock gets harder as I get sight of her arched back and the way her ass shines from some of the light from the window. The way her body moves as she swallows my cock.

God, just her fucking side profile. She's a fucking beauty, this one.

"Sugar, I love your mouth on me, but I need to fuck you. Now," I growl as I slide my hand from the back of her neck to her chin, gently pressing her off me.

It throbs without the feeling of her mouth and is slick with her saliva, and a look of awareness comes over her face as I grab under her armpits and put her on the bed.

Though I bring her to the other side, lying her down so she's across the bed on her stomach, facing the mirrors.

As I climb over her, I see the stark difference in our sizes. Getting behind her, I see how much broader my shoulders are compared to hers; the way my body engulfs her. It only makes me hornier as I realize how well she handles me and my cock.

A grin rises on my face and I gently grip her bra clasp from the middle of her back, releasing it and pressing small kisses into the exposed skin as it springs from her ribcage.

She gazes in the mirror, her eyes moving around it, taking in the entire scene.

I continue my work, letting her admire it all, as I clasp her legs together between mine. Pressing my hands between her thighs, I open them enough to press into her. I like this position because I love being able to control her, but she also feels good as fuck here.

When I seat myself at her entrance, I groan, feeling her stretch around me and her eyes roll the further I press into her. Bracing myself against the bed with one hand, I wrap the other around her jaw, squeezing her cheeks together and forcing her gaze on the mirror.

"Watch closely, sugar. I want you to see what you look like when I fuck the thoughts out of that pretty head of yours," I pant as I punch forward, filling all of her in one stroke.

She screams out, her neck craning back as her hips arch into me. I tug down once, bringing her gaze back to the mirror, making her watch.

My thrusts start, slamming hard and deep, filling her with every one. I grunt and growl as I ram into her, my eyes locked onto the way her ass ripples back against me before I look up to the mirror, watching her fall deeper into her pleasure.

"Look at you... God, fucking *look* at you," I growl. My hand tightens on her cheeks, keeping her gaze on the mirror. "Taking every thrust from this thick cock like you were made for it..." I say as I keep pace.

Her eyes linger on my shoulders, the wide breadth of them compared to hers. Until her eyes meet mine in the mirror, and I make a point to thrust in, hold myself there and twitch against her walls to watch her come apart.

"Look at my pretty girl. You're so beautiful," I growl with a grin.

Soon, I feel the need to see a different angle, so I pull out. Tossing her legs sideways, with her head toward the pillows, I've moved us so we're parallel to the mirror. I get behind her, taking a grasp at her neck to pull her onto all fours before I press down into the middle of her back, forcing her head into the bed.

Her back arches, her ass rounding as her head turns against the mattress, looking into the mirror as I slip myself in again. I prop a leg beside her, gaining the leverage I need as I grip her hips. As she watches me take her, her pussy tightens around me and my head tilts back with a low growl of satisfaction.

"Fuck, you're such an obedient little whore," I grit as I look down at where my cock comes out of her, shiny and covered in her slick.

She rocks back against me, and I can see the way her eyes have moved to my abs in the mirror before they go to my cock, watching the way she fucks me and her eyes roll again.

"Good girl, sugar. Thatta girl. Own that cock," I pant as I look back down between us.

She continues rocking back against me, using me, until I hold her hips in place for her to stop, and I start up my own thrusts.

I switch between pulling her back onto me and thrusting into her, reaching a hand down to rub into her clit as I keep moving. All the while, her mouth parts, her eyes roll, until she buries her face into the bed, her moans muffled in the brand new bedding, and her fingers gripping tight into the fabric.

"Fuck, fuckfuckfuckfuck," she whimpers, and I feel the way her pussy tightens, climbing that edge, and I pull out again.

I twist her hips, getting her on her back before I tug her legs, bringing her toward me. Her butt lifts, placing her at an angle as I wrap her legs around my waist and press myself back in.

I sit back on my feet, her angled butt on my thighs as I press slowly into her and then lean over, pressing a hand into the bed and the other around her throat.

"You're gonna come for me, aren't you? I feel how tight that cunt is for me," I say as I latch back onto her lips. I kiss sloppily over hers, and her arms come around my shoulders, with her nails pinning into my muscles.

I grunt as I rock into her, picking up pace and burying deep into her.

"The best fucking pussy I'll ever have," I growl as my thrusts move faster, slamming into her and rocking the camper. Soon, my growls turn to grunts, and my orgasm barrels through me like a shoulder check, and I burst into her with a deep groan.

Mine triggers hers, and she screams out, her back arching into my body as her sounds consume the air in the space, and she grinds her nails into my skin.

My hand tightens on her hip, holding her there as I continue pumping cum into her, groans working through my chest as my head tosses back, letting her pussy spasm and clench around me.

"There she is, there's my good girl," I grit.

Slowly, her orgasm slows, and I feel her loosen around my cock. The camper fills with the sounds of our heavy breathing, and my hands release her hip and throat to run over her stomach slowly.

I take one of her legs from my hip, lifting it to duck under it so I can roll her to the side while keeping my cock held in her. Slowly, I press kisses into her shoulder as I stroke a hand up and down her side.

"You bought this for us," she pants softly.

"I did," I say with a breath of satisfaction quietly in response.

"I can't believe you bought me a camper," she says with a soft chuckle.

"It was a thought I had early on. After I bought the land. I don't think you were going to stay at Charlotte's place all the time. I think you would have gotten sick of it quickly," I say between my kisses to her skin.

"You're probably right." She giggles and wiggles her butt back up against me.

My cock has softened, but I still feel her around me, which makes it hard not to get hard again. But if it does... oh well.

"I have no idea how my gifts are going to top this," she says with a sigh.

My brow furrows as I sit up on my elbow, bringing my hand to her chin to turn her face to me.

"Sugar, you know you don't have to get me anything, right?" I ask.

"Yeah, yeah. Shut up. I'm getting you something else. But I also bought some other things... they are not going to live up to this though. I usually am good at giving gifts, but..." she sighs softly as her gaze falls away.

"Baby... you're all the gift I need. I promise. There's not even anything I can think of that I want. I have everything I want right here," I tell her with a smile.

She looks up at me with a playful roll of her eyes. "Mhm... sure," she says.

I shake my head as I press more kisses to her shoulder again.

"Oh, and, uh... Tucker is going to be staying out here with Charlotte until they go to Montana," I say.

Her brow furrows in confusion as she looks at me. "What for?"

"Well..." I say with a sigh before I shake my head with a

chuckle. "In order to get this fifth wheel thing done in time, I had to ply Charlotte with something to keep you in your office over the past two days," I say with a nervous smile.

Her eyes gaze off, as if putting everything together again. "So, THAT'S why she wouldn't get out of my office! I was wondering why she was so glued to me those few days. I was going insane with her touching all my things," she says with a groan.

"Yeah, that's my bad. I'm sorry, sugar. I had no idea she was going to go crazy on your files like that. I would have done something different," I say in response.

"Mmmm," she hums as she glares at me. "She cleaned out my file cabinets. Which I guess was nice, but the process was not fun," she mumbles.

I laugh and bring my hand back down to her waist, holding her tight to me.

"Can you believe you're going to be Mrs. Hayze tomorrow?" I ask with a grin.

Her body temperature goes up in response, and I see her cheeks tint as well.

"What if I didn't wanna take your last name?? Hmm? What then?" she teases.

"You can do whatever you want, sugar. But I'm still going to call you Mrs. Hayze when you're riding my cock," I say.

Her eyes roll playfully, and she makes a confirmatory *"hmph."*

"That's what I thought," I whisper against her skin.

"So... what do we do now?" she asks.

"Well, if you want, we can just hang out here for a bit. I'll go get some food at Charlotte and Adrian's. Or we can go back to the ranch house, hang out with them, and then come out here... honestly the possibilities are endless," I say as I gesture out to the room.

Her smile is playful as she listens to me, but soon her mind runs again; I can see it. She's weighing my options.

"Go get some food from Charlotte and Adrian's. I'm going to stay here and explore for a little bit. Maybe even rest. Go grab our stuff, and we'll spend the night out here before we have them come down here tomorrow for the ceremony portion," she says.

I kiss her shoulder before I rub a hand over her stomach. "Copy that, Big Mama," I say.

Bringing a hand to her hip, I hold her in place as I pull myself out.

I move to the edge of the bed, getting onto my knees to grab my clothes from around the floor before I move to the stairs and go down them to move around better.

I pull on my jeans and hoodie before I look back up at Tiana, who cuddles into the blankets, situating herself on the pillows with a satisfactory hum.

With that, I finish getting dressed and head out of the camper and up to the ranch house.

CHAPTER TWENTY-EIGHT
TIANA

The man bought me a fucking camper.

A camper... A *CAMPER*????

I'm *still* in shock.

But even as I hear his ATV start up and fade into silence... something else comes to the forefront of my mind.

He did it again.

Or I guess. He *didn't* do it again.

The past few times, he hasn't done it. It's been eating and burrowing deeper into my brain, and I've been trying to ignore it. But he hasn't mentioned anything about his breeding kink. He hasn't told me he's going to fill me, that I'm going to be such a *"pretty Mommy"*, nothing!

I tried to write it off as something else in the beginning. That maybe he had just returned from Canada and was trying to focus on me.

But as time has gone on, he hasn't said it... *at all*.

It causes a dark, ugly pit to form in my stomach.

One filled with *fear*.

Obviously, he loves me; he wants to be with me.

But why would he stop mentioning that? It's something we talk about; something we've talked *at length* about.

And yet it's just... poof. *Gone.* As if it hadn't even existed to begin with.

Aside from the fact that I miss him talking about it, it makes me nervous.

Did *I* do something wrong? Did I make him not want to have kids anymore?

I shake my head, pushing the thought away, because the longer I think about it, the more nauseous I get. It's silly to even assume such a thing... Right?

Of course, he loves me. Of course, he wants a family with me.

Why would he do all of this if he didn't?

But with the time he's going to be gone getting the food and our things, I know that my mind will run all on its own.

I get up, making sure the door to the camper is locked before I move back to the bed, curling up under the blankets and wrapping myself in them.

One thing about these sheets is they're actually really nice. They don't feel strange or intrusive on my skin.

Not sure if that's just what's stock for these units, or if Gunnar went out and bought some. But I don't really care; I need to sleep, because if I keep thinking about all these things that make me feel icky... I won't be able to really enjoy my time with Gunnar like I would like to.

We're getting married tomorrow... I just need to push it out of my thoughts. There is no reason to think about stuff like this right now, because in all honestly, I'm probably just overthinking.

So, that's what I do.

I cuddle up in the blankets, and I let the silence take me deep into sleep.

The entire night that Gunnar and I spent together was perfect. Calm, quiet and full of sweet cuddles.

We talked about the house, and we even went out before the night ended so that we could get a better idea of exactly what we wanted and where to put it.

We talked about what to do when the loggers come out, and I pointed out some trees I knew for sure I wanted them to get rid of.

Until we retreated into the camper and had *more* sex.

It was nice because we had the entire space to ourselves.

He moved and contorted me in any and every way he wanted me. It's impressive sometimes how he comes as much as he does. But he is a hockey player, and he is massive. He also... has some larger balls so maybe it takes longer to empty him?? I don't know; that's a stupid throwaway thought.

But... again, no breeding talk. There were times it somewhat took me out of the moment not to hear certain pieces I would expect him to mention it. But nope...

Nothing.

I decide not to focus on it. Especially not right now, considering I'm about to marry the damn man and don't want my nerves to ruin our day.

Even as I stand here and look in the mirror, I push the uncertainty away as I take a deep breath.

Gunnar is outside, waiting for us, and Charlotte came down here earlier this morning to make sure my hair looked nice. She even tried to bring me some dresses. But I declined.

There is no way I want to wear a dress out here.

A smile spreads across her face, one that holds so much

pride, even if I'm basically just in a hoodie and jersey, and some jeans.

"You have no idea how happy I am for you, Tiana," she says gently.

I smile sheepishly back at her, trying to understand why.

"Thanks, Charlotte," I return quietly.

"No, Tiana..." she holds my shoulders as she takes a deep breath and her eyes mist over with tears, but not in the normal way it does for Charlotte.

This time, it looks as if she's got so much happiness behind her tears.

"We have *always* wanted someone for you... *always*. Because you deserve love. You are always fending for everybody else... and all we have ever wanted was someone to fend for you. For you to care enough about your happiness to realize you deserve it. And I am so, so glad you found it. Gunnar is a great man, and I'm so happy for you. Seriously," she says with a soft smile. A tear runs down her cheek as she looks at me.

And while this isn't a normal ceremony... my parents aren't here. His aren't here.

The emotions appear to be all the same.

I didn't know how much everyone was rooting for me to find someone for myself. I never even really rooted for it for myself. I felt as if I was doing fine on my own. I've never really understood the reason people would want happiness for me.

But at least I know have people in my life that care about my well-being.

"Thank you, Charlotte... he really is a great man," I say softly.

She nods, wiping away a tear from her face with a deep sigh.

"Do you have the papers?" she asks.

I nod, turning around to face the bed, where I've spread the papers out on the mattress. I look over them. Some are grouped in paper clips for each person, because one paper needs to go to Gunnar's lawyer, and the rest, I hand to Charlotte.

She takes them, holding them to her chest as a massive grin spreads across her face.

"Congratulations again, Ti," she says sweetly.

I wrap my arms around her in a hug, and with one of her hands still holding the papers to her chest, she wraps the other around me.

Soon, there are barks sounding outside, along with the sound of galloping and an ATV.

I pull away to take a deep breath, and Charlotte gives me a nod of confidence before we take the few steps down to the door of the camper.

As I reach to open it, someone beats me to it, and I come face to face with Gunnar.

We apparently had the same idea.

Hoodie, jersey, and jeans.

A smile rises on my face at the simplicity of it all.

"Hey," I say with a soft breath.

He's silent for a moment as he looks over me, and his mustache stretches as the smile on his face widens.

"You ready, sugar?" he asks softly.

I nod, and he extends a hand out to me.

Taking it, the rough calluses of his palm scrape against mine, and I linger there, letting the weight of his security settle on me.

It's familiar, safe, and strong.

Just like him.

He tugs me just enough for my upper body to fall out of the camper, and I make a squeal of surprise as I fall into his arms and he cradles me against his chest.

I settle in his grasp, shaking my head of the fall before I look up at him.

He smiles down at me, lingering on my eyes for a long moment.

"You're the most beautiful woman I'll ever know, Tiana," he says quietly, though there's a calm severity in his words.

"You're the kindest man I'll ever know, Gunnar," I respond.

"Sweet," he whispers before he leans in to press a small kiss to my lips.

I shake my head playfully before I hear a noise of fear from behind us.

Luckily, Gunnar turns us around, where I see Philip getting off of Adrian's horse.

My brow furrows as I watch the scene. Adrian seems to be the only one who took this seriously. He wears one of the nicest shirts I've ever seen him wear, and a pair of *very* pressed Wrangler jeans. He even has a cleaner cowboy hat today. Probably one of his special hats.

"You look good, Adrian," I say.

Philip is someone I worked with once upon a time.

I picked him because, while nervous, he's very good at his job. And I'll be damned if I handed Gunnar off to someone incompetent. He's one of the few people I don't have to correct with contracts, and he seems to do things just how I like them. He also seems to go out on a limb for his clients.

Case in point... riding a house out to the middle of fuckass nowhere to marry us.

But I still check in with him and make sure he's not letting my man get the short end of things.

"Thank you, Miss Tiana. It's a special day," Adrian says, and I swear I see a genuine smile on his face.

"Okay lovebirds! Gunnar and the rest of us talked. Adrian is going to walk you through the woods, while Gunnar, Philip and I wait by the stump!" Charlotte says as she climbs out of the camper.

My brow furrows as I press my legs against Gunnar's grip for him to release me, and plant myself on the ground.

I come around Gunnar's back to look at Charlotte as she turns around on the steps to close the door before she continues down. Though she jumps off the last one.

"What are you talking about?" I ask.

"Well, we want it to be kind of sweet. So Adrian is going to 'walk' you down the 'aisle'. If you're okay with that, of course," Charlotte says with air quotes before placing her hands on her hips.

I look back at Adrian, who gives a slow nod in confirmation.

"Uhhh... Alright. I guess," I say as I look up at Gunnar.

"It'll be great, sugar. I promise," he says with a smile.

And God damn his smile, even with the mustache. It's beginning to grow on me, and I can't help admiring it now. I give a nervous smile in response as I nod with a calming sigh. Then, I turn around to Philip.

"Thanks for doing this for us, Philip. I had no idea you were ordained," I say kindly as I hand the papers out to him.

"Ah, yes, Miss Dawn. The pleasure is all mine. I usually get paired with the 'rookies' and they have a tendency to do well... this," he says with a nervous grin as he takes the papers from me, scanning over them as he speaks.

"Something I think I should do. But most of my work is in contracts," I say with a wink.

"Right. Well, we will see you out at the stump. Congratulations Miss Dawn," he says again with a soft bow before Charlotte, Gunnar, Philip, and Tucker all start walking around the camper to get to the tree line beyond it.

Gunnar turns around to send an air kiss to me before he walks forward. I watch as Waffle stays, her tongue out as she pants, watching them all walk away. My gaze stays on her as she watches them, before I look up at Adrian.

Stoic as ever, he has his hands in his pockets as he watches them. But soon, his attention turns to the land, surveying it before he looks down at Waffle.

"Why is Waffle staying here with us?" I ask.

"Well, Hayze said he was gonna send Tucker to get us when they're ready. And he seems to have a better time findin' us when we got Waffle nearby. So, she's walkin' with us," he says.

"Ah, alright," I murmur absently as I look back out toward where they left.

The camper basically blocks the entire treeline, so I'm only able to look over the camper from the outside, now that I have a chance.

"You know, Miss Tiana," Adrian says, scaring me with the low timbre of his voice.

I look up at him, though he continues to look off over the lake.

"I know Miss Lotty must have said somethin' to ya already. But I do have to put my own hat in the ring. Because I told Gunnar some things as well," he starts.

My brow furrows, wondering where this is going.

"Ever since you came to the team, we've seen men come and go for you. The team, that is. We watched you get mistreated... watched them walk away. And we watched you take it all in stride. You never cried, never shed a tear, and life never stopped for ya," he continues.

I think back to those times, trying to see everything from their point of view. And I imagine they are right, but those men never meant much to me to shed any tears over them.

"We knew how you were. You wouldn't listen to reason from us, and we knew that. But we wanted to protect you. Because you always protected us in a way no one else could or did. So when we got wind of Gunnar gettin' in your space... we tried to get in the way. At least a bit. We didn't know how that would go, and I knew Gunnar better than the rest of 'em. And well," he says with a sigh as he shrugs his shoulders.

"We didn't want you hurt, and I surely didn't want a friend of mine hurtin' you. Because you ain't deserve another beatin' to the heart. Even if it didn't look like it was. We were tired of seein' our lawyer not get the care she deserved. But... Gunnar, I think, is the best man that could have been given to you. And us, the team, we're real happy for y'all. We're happy you got someone to show you the care you show everyone else. Goes to bat for you, protects you... we're glad someone loves you," he says.

Tears burn in my eyes, and I nod slowly, sniffling quietly.

"Thank you, Adrian," I say. Though I don't realize it almost comes out in a whisper.

"You're like a sister to me, Miss Tiana. And I know I'm not real good at showin' it. I reckon you don't mind that much. But I've always hated the way you were treated by those men. It's why we tried to show up on Valentine's Day. It's why we bug you... so at least you know you got some people in your corner. Because you're always in ours. Day or night, we can always trust Miss Tiana to get it done," he says as he finally looks to me with a smile.

I nod. Because I have no words to say. I've always just done my job, and I'll be damned if someone gives my clients less than what they deserve. That's just what I do.

It's never been a big deal for me. But that's why I'm a lawyer. Aside from watching my mom do it, I enjoy fighting people to get others what they deserve.

It's amazing I've never done it for myself.

"Congratulations, Miss Tiana. You deserve every bit of this day. And all the love you get in the future," he says softly, low and serious.

I nod again, sniffling the tears from my nose. "I appreciate that," I say.

His lip quirks to the side, and he holds his arms out to me in a hug.

I look at him, reluctantly considering, before I come close and he wraps his arms around me in a big hug. He pats me hard on the back.

"I'll make sure he never does you wrong. Promise," he says.

I nod against him before I pull away and wipe a few more tears from my eyes with a deep breath.

"You guys just wanna see me cry," I say with a teary chuckle as I wipe the tears from my waterline, sniffing one last time before I blow the sadness away.

"Maybe a little. But, you needed to know," he says.

"Thank you," I say softly.

Soon, barks sound from the forest, and Waffle barks back in response.

Tucker runs up to us, and Waffle runs up to him, where they wiggle and lick all over each other.

"I reckon that's our cue," Adrian says with a nod.

With that, I turn, leading the way to the dogs, through the forest.

Taking a deep breath, I lump over logs and other fallen forest debris, with my heart racing the closer we get to the stump.

I can't believe... after all this time. I'm going to be a wife...

But I'm so glad that I get to. Because Gunnar is everything I've ever needed in life.

And I couldn't ever find anyone better to love me.

I hear the dogs running up behind me before they take the lead toward Gunnar and the rest of them.

Adrian continues behind me, and as we pass the stream, I know we're getting close.

I feel the air in my lungs pulse in and out in shallow bursts, trying to spot the three bodies in the forest.

When I spot the big lovable goon first.

I can't help the nervous smile that pulls at my lips as he catches sight of me. While the smile that pulls at his lips is warm, with a restrained excitement.

His eyes glow, and I can tell this moment means just as much to him as it does to me. I pause, waiting for Adrian to catch up, and when he does, he offers me his arm, and I smile up at him.

"Are you ready, Miss Dawn?" he asks.

I smile up at him, blinking a few times. "Is anyone truly ever?"

He pauses, watching me for a moment before he speaks, "Guess we'll find out."

My lip quirks shyly, and I nod.

Soon, he walks us through the trees.

I chose the stump because of the small clearing. Circular in shape, there is room to move around, with a wall of trees surrounding it.

So when we breach the treeline, it's a straight shot to where they all stand.

I peek at Charlotte, who wipes happy tears from her cheeks from where she stands behind Gunnar.

Adrian leads, taking steps toward Gunnar and Philip. All the while, the nerves fizz through my blood, my veins, and my heart seems to pound like war drums in my ears.

But... all of it fades away when I get to Gunnar, who smiles down at me, extending his hands out for me to grasp. He holds them tight as I step up onto the stump, and for once, I become eye level with him.

Keeping my eyes on him, the world fades away, and all I can see is his face and the feel his calluses grip into my skin.

"You're going to be my wife," he says quietly, almost in disbelief.

"You're going to be my husband," I return with a nervous smile.

His smile widens. "Fuck yeah," he says with a proud nod.

I shake my head with a playful quirk of my lips before Philip clears his throat.

"Friends, hockey players... and Tiana," Philip starts with a small smile toward me.

I nod with a smile in return.

"We are gathered here today to witness the coming together of Gunnar Hayze and Tiana Dawn in holy matrimony," he starts.

I lock eyes with Gunnar, who looks at me with all the love and brightness one could ever hold for someone.

"Marriage is a trial, a test, and a reward, all at once. Today, we witness the reward of these two individuals. Two people who have grown and seen each other. Learned and cared for each other. Individuals, so different in their own ways, share one similarity. Their love and devotion to each other," Philip says.

"Gunnar, repeat after me," Philip says as he turns to him.

Gunnar keeps his eyes on me, only giving a small nod to Philip.

"I, Gunnar Hayze, take you, Tiana Dawn, forsaking all others, to have and to hold, through better or worse... in sickness and in health... for richer or poorer... for as long as we both shall live, till death do us part," Philip starts, reading over the paper in his hands.

"I, Gunnar Hayze, take you, Tiana Dawn," Gunnar repeats, his eyes volleying between mine. "Forsaking all others, to have and to hold, through better or worse, in sickness and in health, for richer or poorer, for as long as we both shall live... till death do us part," he says quietly.

His eyes sparkle as he tries to keep the tears he holds to a minimum.

"Now Tiana, repeat after me," Philip says.

"I, Tiana Dawn, take you, Gunnar Hayze, forsaking all

others, to have and to hold, through better or worse, in sickness and in health, for richer or poorer, for as long as we both shall line, till death do us part," Philip says again.

And as I look into Gunnar's eyes, I repeat every word. With Gunnar, every so often, nodding encouragingly.

"Do you have any vows? The two of you?" Philip asks.

My heart pounds nervously because... I *don't*.

But I feel that right now is the best time to speak from the heart.

"I do," Gunnar says as he nods to Philip.

"Go ahead," Philip says, gesturing to us.

Gunnar tightens his grip on my hands, tugging just enough.

"Tiana Dawn... never in my life had I become so enamored with a stranger before I met you. But from the moment I laid eyes on you, I needed you. I needed you more than air, and I didn't even know why. You captured me with a mere glance, and it hadn't even been your intention. But I would let you capture me over and over again for the rest of my life if it meant I'd be by your side. Never have I met someone so steadfast in their mentality, so willing to protect their carefully crafted peace, but embraced the parts of life that were chaos. Someone so independent, beautiful and willing to open her eyes and arms to the unfamiliar, when their life revolves around familiarity," Gunnar says.

Tears stream from my eyes, cooling rapidly in the fall air surrounding us.

But even the chill of fall does nothing to cool the warmth between us.

"I have never wanted something so badly in my life. Not hockey, not the pros, *nothing*, has ever topped the way it feels to have you in my life. To love and care for you has been one of the greatest honors I will ever have. And I am so lucky that I,

Gunnar Hayze, get to love you for the rest of my life," he finishes.

I sniffle, nodding softly as I listen.

It's not the first time he's said stuff like this to me.

But... it hits the same way every single time, because... someone loves *me*. Someone loves me through my faults, through my intricacies... and they love me *because* of my intricacies.

"Tiana?" Philip says.

I'm pulled from my trance of gazing into Gunnar's hazel eyes, looking over at Philip.

"Your vows?" he says.

"Oh... yes," I say before I clear my throat and take a deep breath.

My hands clench tight around Gunnar's, and his thumb comes to the top of mine, rubbing softly.

"You've got this, baby. I'm right here," he whispers with a small, encouraging nod.

"Gunnar Hayze... for most of my life, I've encountered men that didn't know what it meant to be a real man. That took and took, but didn't know what it meant to give. Until I met you, I thought that's how all men were. That it was just the default... But you showed me what a real man does. The way someone is supposed to be loved and cared for. Not only romantically, but for the people in their lives. I am so lucky to be marrying someone who is so kind, so thoughtful, in every facet of their life. Their family, their friends, their job. Someone who knows how to treat people, someone so disciplined, but so eager to embrace differences they'd never seen..." I shake my head, my voice cracking as I look down to where our hands grip tight to one another.

"Thank you, Gunnar Hayze... for showing me what love is. Because I don't think I would have experienced it without you. Thank you for loving me, because loving you is the greatest thing I'll ever experience," I finish, the tears streaming down my cheeks, converging under my chin to run along my throat, and down into my hoodie and my chest.

Gunnar smiles, tilting his head sympathetically as he brings his hands up to my face, wiping the tears from my cheeks with his thumbs.

"Good job, sugar. You did a good job," he whispers softly as he leans in to press his forehead to mine with a soft sigh. His hands guard some of my tears from the rest of them until they stop flowing, and when they do, he presses a kiss to my forehead before pulling away. He strokes a thumb over a cheek one last time before he reaches down to grasp my hands.

We look to Philip, and nod in unison.

"Do you, Tiana Dawn? Take Gunnar Hayze to be your lawfully wedded husband?"

Looking back up at Gunnar, I smile, nodding. "I do," I whisper.

"Do you, Gunnar Hayze, take Tiana Dawn, to be your lawfully wedded wife?"

"Fuck yes," Gunnar says with a wide grin.

Charlotte scoffs, and I can't help the laugh that bubbles out of me.

"Then by the power vested in me by the State of Washington, I now pronounce you husband and wife. You may now kiss the bride," Philip says as he steps back.

Gunnar's grin widens, with my heart hammering wildly in my chest as he tugs my hands toward him. Releasing them, he wraps an arm around my back, bending me against him as his other hand comes to my face.

He captures my lips, and my hands come up to his face, grabbing his cheeks.

Our lips tangle, our tongues dance, and our hearts beat in unison against our chests.

Adrian whistles and claps from behind us, Tucker and

Waffle bark in excitement, and Charlotte squeals with excitement as we pull away.

Gunnar's thumb rubs over my cheek.

"I love you so fucking much, Mrs. Hayze," he says with a grin.

"I love *you* so much more, Mr. Hayze."

CHAPTER TWENTY-NINE
GUNNAR

As much as Tiana and I wanted to stay and chat, I needed to have my wife to myself.

Fuck... *my wife.*

Tiana Dawn... is Tiana *Hayze.*

I think... I'm not entirely sure she's taking my last name... I'm about... ninety-nine percent sure...

Doesn't matter, I'm calling her Mrs. Hayze as I stretch her pussy tonight.

I carry her out of those damn woods, not even waiting for everyone else. I already told Charlotte and Banks what to expect. Plus, Banks knows me.

With a quickness, I say goodbye to Tucker, because he's going to be staying at the ranch for the next three weeks, and before I came out to the woods, I had already packed the bags in the car.

And within the hour, I'm able to get Tiana and me back to the apartment.

She wanted to shower first... so now, here we are. My hands

around her jaw while the hot water melts our skin together as I kiss her deep and grind my hard cock against her stomach.

She said on the way here that she had something she wanted to show me. Part of her gift. So she's calling the shots... at least for now, because there's no way I'm not dominating her tonight. I don't think I can control myself.

Her hands run over my wet chest, with her nails clawing into my skin as she restrains herself from going too far here.

"Go get in the bed," she pants into my lips.

"Yes, Mrs. Hayze," I whisper as I nip into her lower lip, tugging softly.

A blush rises on her cheeks, and we finish washing our bodies off before I quickly grab a towel to hop out of the shower.

I run to the bed, jumping on it and pressing my hands behind my head as I watch her come out of the bathroom to run into the closet.

My brow furrows as I watch her, because I wonder if she got another cute little outfit for me.

Soon, with her towel still wrapped around her, she comes to the bed with a shopping bag.

She sets it on the bed and sits in front of it with a nervous grin.

"I don't know how lame this is as far as gifts go... but I thought we could... try some things," she says with a nervous bite to her lip.

"I don't think anything you can get me is lame, baby," I say with a grin.

My cock lies against my stomach, though it twitches every so often as I watch her.

She pulls the first thing out, laying it on the bed.

"Nipple clamps," I say with a grin as I glance back up at her.

"Yes," she says before she takes a deep breath to steady herself. She pulls the next thing out.

"Cock ring, with... a bunny?" I say.

She nods.

And the last thing she pulls out is... what looks to be a bunch of straps.

My head tilts as I look over it, grabbing some straps and pulling it up.

Her eyes go down to my lap, lingering on my cock before she looks nervously at me.

"What is this thing?" I ask curiously.

"It's... a swing," she says.

My brows jump. "A swing, huh?" I say with a grin. "Where do I put it?"

Her teeth tighten on her lip and she glances up.

Somehow, because apparently I missed it, there is a well-placed hook secured into the ceiling.

"Right above the bed, sugar? Naughty, naughty girl," I say with a tsk as I come up onto my knees.

I look around the straps, finding the thick, metal carabiner before standing up to attach it to the hook. As I move the straps around, I have my attention absconded from me when a warm mouth and hands wrap around my cock.

"Oh... fuuuuck," I groan as I look down at her.

Her towel has fallen from her body, and her back arches so perfectly that I can see down her spine, to her plump ass. My eyebrow quirks with delight as I watch her swirl her tongue around the head of me, my other hand coming to cradle the back of her head as she slides her tongue along the underside.

My head tosses back, my breaths coming in and out in tortured bursts, until she takes me deeper, her tongue gliding along my shaft until I feel the back of her throat.

I tighten my fingers at the back of her neck, since her hair is still in her braided ponytails, and shift my hips forward.

My head tilts down, watching as her gaze stays on me, her eyes watering as shallow gags pulse against her throat.

"There she is. Gag on it," I grit. I press her head harder, forcing her to take me deeper.

Tears drip from the corners of her eyes, the same way the drool slips from the corner of her mouth, and I can't help the grin on my lips.

"My pretty wife is so good at choking on my cock, isn't she?" I say with a breathless chuckle.

And even now, she nods against my cock, gagging one last time before I grip tighter on the back of her neck and pull her off.

She takes a breath, wiping the saliva from the corner of her mouth before she bites her lower lip.

Coming down onto my knees, I stroke a thumb along her jaw, grinning at her, and my cock twitches again, damn near aching. Then, I look over this strappy contraption, wondering how I would like to have her...

But, fuck, there's nothing better than looking into her eyes while she takes me.

I glance at her before looking over the thing again.

"Sit in it, face me, feet in the stirrups," I say with a grin.

Looking over the straps and pieces, she tries to figure out where she should go, so I hold it open for her.

She climbs on, her butt sitting on the middle panel that's the thickest before she grabs onto the straps and leans back into the higher panel for her back.

When she looks up at me, wide-eyed, I hold one stirrup for her foot, and she brings it up, placing it delicately in before I do the same for the other.

And just like that, she's at the perfect height for me to see her tits, watch her take me, and for her to watch too.

Fucking *stellar* gift. I love this thing.

"Beautiful thing you are," I say with a grin. Gripping the

back of her neck, I hold her in place as I reach a hand down to grip the base of my cock, running it through her pussy lips. She's already wet and pulsing for me.

"You have no idea how I'm about to ruin this pretty cunt, sugar," I say as I latch onto her lips.

She moans into me, her hips grinding against the underside of my cock as I let it go, letting it rest against her clit.

"There you go, baby, use me," I whisper into her lips as I reach down for the nipple clamps.

When I feel the chain that attaches them together, I bring them up and take hold of one of the red rubber-tipped clamps. I run the tongs slowly over her areola, around her nipple before I slowly glide over the hard peak.

"Fuck," she whimpers into my lips.

Her hips continue to grind, and I piston my hips, working with her.

"Keep going, work yourself up. You need to be soaked for what I'm going to do to you," I rasp.

I press the clamp open, placing her nipple between the small tongs and slowly letting it close, getting her used to the tightness.

"Fuck... fuck!" she gasps as her head tosses back.

"Is it too tight?" I ask as I lean in to press gentle kisses to her neck.

"No... no. Perfect, it's perfect," she says with a pant.

"Good," I say as I do the same to the other nipple.

She growls as it attaches to her nipple, her breaths coming out harder before I use a hand to grip the shaft of my cock and position myself at her entrance.

I press in just enough to feel her tightness, and as I do, my head rolls back, letting myself descend into her.

With her basically dangling in the air, she moves on her own, and the movements I can't anticipate, which makes all of this so much better.

"What does it feel like?" I rasp against her skin as I bring my hands to her hips, holding and gripping her, swinging her slowly back and forth against me.

Her hands slip into the free cuffs above her head, where she presses her hands into them and grips tight at the straps.

"Good... fuck me, it's so good," she pants.

"Fuck you? Alright," I say with a grin as I punch forward at the same time I pull her toward me, filling her with every inch.

She cries out, her eyes rolling into her head as it tilts back.

"No, nah ah ah, eyes open, sugar. You're going to look me in the eyes when I fuck the soul from you," I grit as I pull her onto my cock.

Her body folds, her hands gripping tight at the straps as she reluctantly brings her head up and opens her eyes, her lip clenched in her teeth as she attempts to focus on me.

I pick up my pace, rocking her on me, burying deep inside her.

"Fuck, there she is; there's my pretty girl," I growl.

Her eyes connect with mine, glassy, full of pleasure and lost to the feeling of me.

One of my hands leaves her hips, coming to grasp tight around her throat, while the other holds her in place.

I piston my hips, hard and deep. I wanna take all of her I can; I wanna feel her strangle every fucking inch of my cock because, holy fuck, I've got myself in my wife.

Her moans change as her pleasure climbs. Gasps, whimpers, pleas. Every single one of them hot and tortured.

"I can't believe my pretty wife takes a cock like this. Such a good fucking girl, aren't you, Mrs. Hayze?" I say as I latch onto her lips.

She whimpers into our kiss with a mindless nod of agreement, her hips grinding and meeting me with my thrusts.

"That's my good girl. You're doing so fucking good for me, baby. Whose pussy is this?" I pant.

"Yours, yours, fuck it's yours, it's all yours," she whimpers back.

I pull away, pressing my forehead into hers, keeping pace in her.

"Whose cock is this? Who's filling this pretty pussy?" I pant as I glance down to where her stomach bulges in and out from where I fuck her. The room fills with the sound of me pounding into her, skin slapping against wet skin and her moans.

I bring my hand from her throat, pressing into the bulge and making her moan out again. Her back bows as her head tosses back, and I nip into her exposed throat.

She growls from the way I mess with her before she calls out, "M-mine! It's my cock."

"Who is filling this pussy, Tiana? Who has his cock buried to the balls inside of you, right now?" I grit.

"H-husband. M-My husband, you," she moans desperately.

"Fuck yes, it is," I say with a devilish chuckle.

I open one clamp from her nipple, removing it before I suck that nipple into my mouth to suction hard on it.

"Perfect fucking tits," I growl against her skin.

But I need to hold her in place, so I pull out, and her body lies limp against the straps as she catches her breath. I love making her boneless like this.

Slowly, I pull her feet from the stirrups, and tug her out of the swing to place her on the bed. Moving the swing to the side, I get onto my feet, detaching the swing and throwing it to the floor.

I look down at where Tiana lies. Her arm over her face as she breathes deeply, and her legs are spread, with her pussy plump and dripping.

But I'm absolutely feral for the fact that she's my fucking

wife, so I grip under her knees and open her more. Shoving my face between her legs, I bury my tongue in her pussy.

She gasps, her hands scrambling to my head as her moans grow louder, consuming the air in the room.

"She's so fucking wet," I growl. "Tastes so fucking good," I pant as I lap all the slickness from her.

My tongue flicks fast over her clit, my arms wrapping around her upper thighs and tugging her so she's upside down.

I sit back on my heels, devouring her like a man starved, and she responds with screams and moans before I put her back on the bed. Soon, I throw her feet over my shoulders and press myself in.

Slow, because this position is deep as shit.

I kiss sloppily over her lips, my hands gripping her face as I press in and out of her slowly.

"G-Gunnar... Fuck... Mr.-" she groans, her head tilting back as she writhes back against my length. "Mr. Hayze, you're so deep," she pants.

"Because she takes me so fucking deep every time," I say back. I move one of my hands down, seeking her clit. "Fuck, you're throbbing," I pant as I glance down.

"So... so close. So fucking close," she pants.

"I know, baby, I can feel it," I say with a grin.

I calculate my thrusts, hitting deep, slow every time, with my speed on her clit kept high.

"F-fuck! C-coming, fuck, I'm com-" She ends with a screech and her pussy tightens around me, triggering my orgasm, and I growl as I come with her.

"Fuck, take it. Take it all; let me fill this pussy. Make me drip out of you, baby. I wanna see myself running down your fucking thighs," I growl.

She grinds and writhes against me, and as she does, I struggle to move my hand up to her other tit, releasing the clamp on her nipple before I let her legs down to rest on my hips. With my cock held balls deep, I feel her thighs tighten against my hips at the same time her pussy tightens around my cock, and the sensation is maddening.

I growl as she continues riding her wave, her hips bucking and her moans slowly dying until her body relaxes into a heap on the bed.

She pants hard, her body twitching every so often as she continues coming down.

I grin as I look down at her, licking the sweat from my mustache as I run a hand down the center of her chest.

"My first time fucking you as my wife," I say with a chuckle as I lean down to press kisses into her skin.

"Mmmm," she responds softly, peeking out from under her arm to look at me.

"The swing was a great gift, sugar. And the nipple clamps. We didn't get to the cock ring, but I'm sure I'll get good use out of it," I say as I drag out of her.

I watch because I love knowing how much I've pumped into her, and it gushes out to run down her ass. With a wolfish grin, I get beside her in the bed.

She makes a soft noise, and I sigh softly as I wrap a hand around her stomach, pressing kisses to her shoulder.

"I love you, Mrs. Hayze," I whisper.

She takes a minute to respond, but when she does, it's soft.

"I love you too, Mr. Hayze."

CHAPTER THIRTY

TIANA

The weekend went to shit.

Aside from the fact that for the rest of this week I have to cook; I also started my fucking period.

It was a disappointment to see red this morning when I woke up. *I* damn near saw *red*.

After everything we'd done, it. Didn't. *Work.*

Not to mention, with Gunnar not talking the same way in bed.

I feel like things are pressing in on me, and I'm... *irritated*. But so much so that I feel like I'm shutting down. I don't want to talk to anyone; I don't want to do *anything*, and part of me wishes I didn't have to participate in Thanksgiving this year. It all feels like too much to interact with humans at this point.

But I have to. There isn't really much of a choice, and that's the shitty part about being a wife, or an adult in general.

Luckily, there's no work or games this week. But Gunnar and Adrian had to go to the arena to do some workouts since my dad doesn't want them getting lazy over Thanksgiving.

Which means Charlotte is coming to help me cook. Or at the least to keep me company. I don't relish people helping me cook. If they touch anything in my carefully laid plans and the steps that I have predetermined in my head, all hell will break loose. Though Charlotte is well aware of her role in my cooking.

Don't touch fuckall.

But maybe she can help calm my nerves some.

I've been getting all the things out of my fridge and cupboards when Charlotte knocks once on my door before walking in.

"Ti!" she says as she spots me in the kitchen.

She shrugs off her winter coat and hangs it on a hook by the door before coming to give me a big hug. All the while, Waffle and Tucker run inside after her. Though Tucker scurries around the apartment, sniffing the floor to see if he can find Gunnar. He goes to the couch, to the bedrooms and down the halls. He goes as far as whimpering when he can't find Gunnar, and I have to call him over to me.

Tucker perks up when I call his name and trots over to me, panting and wagging his tail.

Kneeling down, I scratch his head and ears with a sigh. "I'm sorry, buddy. Gunnar's not here. But I'll make sure Charlotte stays long enough for you to see him," I tell him.

I don't know if he understands me, but he ends up going to find Waffle, and the two go to the guest bedroom.

My brow furrows as I come to a stand, and I go to the kitchen with a sigh.

I wash my hands a bit more aggressively than I need to before turning around and looking over all my ingredients to make sure I didn't miss or forget anything.

Earlier this morning, I had a grocery delivery of all the cheeses and other ingredients I needed to make mac and cheese.

And since I have to make two enormous pans, I get to work shredding it all.

Charlotte goes around the kitchen island to sit in one of the chairs that hide under the breakfast bar. She pulls it out and sits down with a deep breath as she places her purse in the chair beside her.

It's silent for a few moments as she watches me shred the first block of cheese, before her voice breaks through my concentration.

"What's your issue?" she asks

I've barely said two words to her, and of course she knows something is wrong.

"Mmm..." I hum in annoyance.

"Spill," she says again as she folds her arms against the counter, watching me.

I glance up at her, and she gives an accusatory raise of her eyebrows. All the while, she twists her hips back and forth in the chair.

"Just started my period is all," I murmur.

"Mmmm," she says. Though her face doesn't change.

"What?"

"That's really unfortunate, and I'm sorry. Because I know it's something you guys want... but that's not it," she says as her eyes narrow on me.

Damn twin brains.

I groan as I tilt my head back and finish shredding the block of cheese I'm working on. When it's all gone, I lift the grater from the flexible cutting board to dump it into one of the large bowls. Unwrapping another block, I shred this one a bit more aggressively as I think about how to say this.

"Spill, Tiana," she says again.

"I'm working on it," I grit as I keep shredding.

I focus on the movement of the grating until the words work through my brain.

"I'm scared that Gunnar doesn't want me," I murmur.

I glance up to gauge her reaction, and her face scrunches almost in disbelief.

"Shut the fuck up," she says with a sigh and a roll of her eyes.

"Hello?" I scoff.

"You always do this, Ti. One thing goes wrong, and you overthink. The man just married you. He bought you a fifth wheel; he bought you fucking *land*. What in the world could make you think he doesn't want you?" she asks.

I roll my eyes. She wouldn't understand. Her brain works perfectly fine.

"When we would have sex... there were things he would say, pertaining to... ya know. The breeding kink stuff, getting me pregnant, yada yada," I say.

"Uh huh?"

"And he hasn't said ANYTHING pertaining to it basically since he came back from Canada," I say with a sigh.

"And?"

"What do you mean 'and'? Obviously something's wrong," I say as I finish that block of cheese, dump the pile and then move on to the next one.

"So he stops doing *one* thing. Maybe Canada made him get all weird in his head, I don't know. But do not stew over this, please. The man is literally so in love with you," Charlotte says with a sigh.

"Too late, I've been stewing for weeks already," I say. "And my period is not helping," I add with a sigh.

"That part does suck. And I know why you're sad about it. But the other thing, no. You need to remember that this is literally your husband now. Do you think he would marry you if he didn't want you?" she asks.

"I don't know! Why would he stop saying those things?!

Aside from the fact I'm freaking out internally, I miss it," I say as I throw the wrapper away and move on to the next block.

"Girl, I do not know. But it's literally a drop in the bucket compared to everything else he's ever done for you," she says as she leans back in her chair, folding her arms across her chest.

"And if the entire bucket now had a drop of bleach in it, are you still drinking it?" I ask.

Charlotte scoffs. "This isn't fair. You're a fucking lawyer!" she says as she throws her hands up.

"Regardless. I can't stop that *one little thing* from just eating into everything," I say.

One by one, I keep going through the cheeses. And while I hoped the movement of this activity would be enough to keep my mind from even entertaining the idea.

It isn't.

But I can't... *fucking help it...*

It's not fair that I overthink this. I *know* he loves me. I am well aware, and I love the fuck out of him. But the idea of Gunnar not wanting to be in my life...

I shake my head of the thought, looking up at Charlotte, who has been scrolling through her phone.

"So, are you excited to go to Montana?" I ask to change the subject.

"Yes! I get to meet Adrian's sisters. And I think it'll be fun. But he's really upset about going," she says with a sigh.

My brow furrows as I look at her.

"He's got an old horse back home that he doesn't think he'll see again," she says.

"That's unfortunate... I'm sorry, Char," I say.

"I'm just trying to be there for him. You know how much the man loves his horses. But Adrian, you know... stoic and what have you."

"Mmm," I hum in confirmation.

She looks around the living room behind her, taking in all the different decorations.

"When are you guys going to get the tree?" she asks.

I look behind her at all the decorations, remembering we *do* need to find a tree.

"Well, I think we'll be going back out there again. I don't know. I got Gunnar another gift, and I would like to take him out to the land to use it," I say.

It came to me recently, and I actually feel a bit more confident about this one than the sex toys.

I had been able to talk to Adrian, and he helped me out. The gifts came in recently, so I'm going to give them to him at the gift exchange we're doing at his parent's house.

Even if he enjoyed the sex toys, it seems lame to me that was all I could come up with for him. But I'm eager to see his reaction to this gift.

Charlotte and I talk for a while as I make the mac and cheese, and at some point, she helps me when things get too messy. She cleans up the dishes as I use them, which is so nice because I can't stand doing dishes.

Charlotte never minds doing dishes, but they are the one thing I feel as if I need to be bribed to do.

Gunnar is the one who usually does the dishes after dinner.

Eventually, Gunnar and Adrian come back to the apartment, and Gunnar spends some time with Tucker before Charlotte and Adrian leave.

After they leave, I'm immediately worn out. I go over all the gifts I got for Gunnar's family, considering I couldn't show up to Thanksgiving with none.

And luckily, I could wrap Gunnar's gifts before he got home, so they're just stacked in the corner where a tree would be.

I shower quickly and go to lie in bed, cuddling up under the blankets.

The energy was strange when Gunnar came home. Not because of him, but I knew it was because of me. I just... I don't know what to do about the entire... not talking about breeding thing. I don't want to bring it up and make him think he's not doing what he's supposed to. He is a good man, and he doesn't deserve to feel like he's doing less than he is, because that couldn't be further from the truth.

I find it to be on me, and that I shouldn't bother him with things that I'm putting on myself. So when I get into bed, I'm reading quietly, and soon, Gunnar joins me.

He curls up in bed beside me, wrapping an arm around my stomach as he presses soft kisses to my shoulder.

"Your dad is a very mean man, sugar," he says playfully as he looks up at me.

My brow quirks and I close my book as I look at him with a small smile.

"What'd he do this time?" I ask.

"He made us work really hard and called us fatasses. So he made us do a lot of... fast-twitch muscle bullshit in the gym for reaction times. It was really lame," he says with a sigh.

I shake my head playfully before I place my book on the nightstand and lean over to turn off my lamp.

"You alright, sugar?" he asks softly.

I know that I'm withdrawing... but I don't know how not to.

So, I try to show him everything is alright. At least as much as I know how to.

I lean in, giving his forehead a small kiss before I ruffle his wet hair from his shower.

"Yeah, just exhausted from my period and making all that food," I say softly.

"Ahhh, yeah. That's the worst. I'm sorry, sugar. I know that's gotta be a pain," he says softly.

I roll over in bed, giving him my back, and he presses

himself against me, kissing into my shoulder as he relaxes behind me.

His arm wraps tight around me, and as I hear his snoring... I really can't help the confusing thoughts swirling in my head as I fall asleep.

CHAPTER THIRTY-ONE
GUNNAR

"Ahhhh! Tiana! It's so good to see you again!" my mother says as she wraps her arms around Tiana in a big hug.

I smile, trying to hold on to all the gifts Tiana got for my family. While Tiana holds the pans of mac and cheese.

"Mom, be careful. She's got the goods, let her go," I say with a playful shake of my head.

"Oh! Let me take that. Here, come in, come in!" my mom says as she ushers us in, taking the pans of mac and cheese from Tiana.

She brought both because we're heading straight to her parents tomorrow, and she didn't wanna run back to the apartment to grab the second pan.

Tiana gives her a nervous smile as she kicks off her Uggs in the entryway, and I do the same, before my mother leads us deeper into the house.

Tiana and my mom branch off to go to the kitchen, while Gretz, Brooks, and my dad sit in the big, formal living room, with an older game playing on the TV.

"GUNS AND ROSESSS!" Gretz calls out as he turns around on the couch to look at us.

I shake my head and chuckle as I walk toward the Christmas tree set up in the living room. My mom always goes all out for Christmas when she decorates. She has all these small houses for villages; it's almost as if she covers every square inch she can in Christmas, so she's always taken it seriously. I place all the gifts we brought under the tree before I crash on the couch on the far wall with a deep breath.

I tug my chain from my hoodie and loop it on my tongue before splaying my arms over the couch and crossing a foot over my knee to watch the game they're watching.

It's the Bruins against the Maple Leafs. Solid.

A few moments later, Tiana and my mom come to the living room, and Tiana gives me a soft smile before she sits down next to me.

I wrap my arm around her shoulders, clenching the chain in my teeth so I can press a kiss to her forehead as I rub her shoulder.

"All good?" I ask quietly as I look down at her.

She nods. "Yeah, your mom said your dad is still cooking the turkey, so the mac and cheese has some time to bake before we eat," she says.

"Perfect," I whisper with a grin.

I take her chin in my fingers, release the chain in my teeth and lean in to give her a kiss.

Though, I think it makes her even more nervous because a blush rolls across her cheeks and she merely gives me a small kiss back before she cuddles into my side.

"So! What's new?! What have you guys been up to?" my mom asks as she goes to sit beside Brooks, who has been intently watching the game as he snacks on a massive bowl of some kind of chip. I don't even know, but he's locked *in*.

I glance down at Tiana, who meets my gaze with a small nod and a deep breath as I smile.

"We got married! Tiana is now Mrs. Hayze," I say with a proud grin as I rub her opposite shoulder.

The room, aside from the TV, goes quiet, and they all meet us with wide stares. Well... except for Brooks. He ends up choking on his chips, and as my mom beats him in the back, trying to get it out, Gretz and my dad just continue to stare.

"You what?" Gretz asks in shock.

"We got married. Legal whatsit. Just something out on our land," I say.

"Already? What if we wanted to come? Gunnar," my mom says with a frown.

"Listen, I know, I know. Let me explain," I say.

I glance down at Tiana, gauging her response, only to find her frozen. Her lips have sucked into her mouth, and she merely stares wide-eyed at everyone.

"Go on," my mom says.

"We were trying to prioritize everything in our life. You know I bought the fifth wheel because we're going to be building a house. And we have some... other things that need to be done. So we pushed the actual wedding out, and just got the legal part out of the way. So we willll have a wedding at some point, just not right now," I explain.

My mom's brow furrows before her gaze fixes on Tiana.

"Is he making you do this?" she asks.

"Mom!?" I scoff.

"Shut your trap, Gunnar. You know how you can get," she says sternly as she points a finger at me.

I roll my eyes, sitting back against the couch as I bring my chain back up to my mouth, hooking it on my tongue before I grab my ankle that sits across my knee.

"Is he moving too fast for you, Tiana?" she asks again.

Tiana is wide-eyed for a long moment before she takes a

breath. "No, no. He actually made things a lot easier for me. I move fast in life usually. It's part of my job. But there were so many things going on at once, he helped relieve some of the pressure surrounding everything. I'm glad I get to be Mrs. Hayze sooner rather than later," she says with a smile as she leans into me.

"Good... good. I know he can be a bit... aggressive in his approach. So, I just want to make sure he's not throwing you into something too quickly," my mom responds with a kind smile.

"Nothing like that, no," Tiana reassures.

"Gooners gonna goon!" Gretz shouts as he wraps his hands around his mouth to amplify his voice.

"On fucking Thanksgiving!" my mom grits as she whacks Gretz in the back of the head.

"What?!" Gretz says as he guards himself. But considering Gretz is beside Brooks, and my mom is on the other side of Brooks; Brooks knows the deal and leans forward for my mom to reach him easier.

"Knock your shit off, Gretz. I'll send you to your damn room," she says again, with a pointed finger, and he puts his hands up in surrender.

"Okay, okay! I'm sorry!" Gretz groans as he curls up into the corner of the couch. I shake my head with a scoff before I turn my attention to my dad.

"So, Wisco, huh?" I ask.

"Yep, gotta go see Grandma and Grandpa," he grunts.

"Reckon so, eh?" I say in response as I look back at the TV.

"You hear I'm going to UDub Madison next year?" Gretz says with a grin as he throws his hands behind his head.

"Transferring? The fuck is that gonna do for you? Why not go to Michigan? Better stats," I ask.

"The fuck I look like danglin' out in Michigan when I

could shack up in Madison and play for a team I do like? Bigger school, better hockey, better bitches," he says with a nod.

"Gretzky Jean–[Zh-awn]–Hayze. I *will* choke you," my mom says low and serious.

"REALLY GOOD HOCKEY. I'M GOING BECAUSE REALLY GOOD HOCKEY," Gretz reiterates quickly.

"That's strike two. Get your shit together," she grits as she points a finger at him.

"Fine, okay!" Gretz says. "But that's another reason we're going. I wanted to meet the coach up there," he says with a nod.

"You don't know him already? Haven't you played against Madison?" I ask. All the while, my fingers mindlessly stroke Tiana's shoulder.

"Sure have. But the fuck I'm gonna do? Have a chat with the dude while the boys are danglin'? Fuckin' sight adjustment on the scope, bud, that's bad optics," he says with a shake of his head.

"Mmmm," I hum in agreement.

"What about you, Brooks?" I ask.

Brooks keeps his eyes on the TV, still snacking on his chips. "Really just want more UDub merch," he says with a nod.

"Right," I say with a sigh and a shake of my head.

The three of us have always been so vastly different. Because I spent more time with Pa, I had to live up to the older brother role. He always said I had to be the one who was strong, steadfast, to help my mom when I needed to and just be *good*. That was his general rule of thumb.

Just be a good man.

Gretz, being the middle child he is, is all of that and more. I like to think I'm pretty feral. But Gretz... he makes me look tame. He's always been wild and out there. I'm not sure if maybe it's an attention thing, or if that's just simply how he is.

And while he's pretty good at hockey, there's a lot of discipline he lacks since he didn't get as many lessons from Pa as I did.

Brooks, he's always been quiet, to himself. I think he enjoys hockey, and he does it because we do it. But I really don't see Brooks going to the pros. Not because he's not good. He is actually solid with a stick. I just think he doesn't have the same eagerness for it as Gretz and I. I know he enjoys watching it. But who knows? Brooks is a bit of an enigma, to be fair.

I've always just tried to be the hard-won big brother that I've needed to be, because Lord knows Gretz needs it at least.

A loud clap pulls me from my thoughts, and a series of groans sound off in the room as the TV turns off and my mother stands. She has a look of pure glee on her face as she looks between everyone, but everyone else couldn't be more upset.

"Hey!" the three of them groan in unison. My dad included.

"Hush! It's gift time!" my mom says as she goes to sit by the tree.

"Tiana did all the gift buying. I'm getting yours when you get back, Mom," I say with a nod.

In actuality, I've been so focused on Tiana, the marriage, and her gift that I hadn't gotten her anything yet. But I bought my Grandmas' something, and it's already on its way to Wisconsin now.

"Oh, don't worry about it. The truck is the best gift I'll ever have," she says with a shoo of her hand.

"Gretz, come help me, please," my mom says as she waves Gretz over to be gift passer.

Gretz groans as he presses up from the couch, swinging his arms lazily back and forth as his head tosses back in annoyance.

He approaches my mom, pressing his hands out to receive the first gift, before my mom slaps him in the ankles.

"Ow!?" Gretz says as he jumps.

"Manners, damn you!" she grits through her teeth.

He groans again before she hands him a gift, and he looks over it for a name.

"Uhhhh, okay, Brooks, this is for you," he says as he brings a wrapped box over to Brooks.

He seems to light up at this and puts his bowl of chips on the table before rubbing his hands together like the greedy little fly he is.

He hands the box to Brooks, and he takes it, ripping the paper off and lifting the lid on the box. Inside is a Seattle Stags jersey, but it's signed by every member of the team.

"No way!" Brooks says as he holds up the jersey in front of him, looking over it. "This is so cool! Thank you guys, so much!" he says as he holds the jersey to his chest with a grin.

I glance down at Tiana, who gives a shy smile as the blush on her cheeks deepens.

My mom picks up the gift, an envelope, and hands it to Gretz for him to look over.

"Oh, this is mine, tits," he says as he places it to the side, offering his hands for another gift.

He looks over it again, and my mom hands him another on top of it.

He juggles the two, looking for the names.

"Gunnar... annnnnd Tiana," he says as he looks at them with a furrow of his brow.

Me?

I am also confused now.

He hands the boxes to us, and I remove my hand from around Tiana's shoulders to unwrap the paper, but underneath is...

"Who the fuck got me Shadow Supremes?" I ask as I look around.

Everyone shrugs, and I glance down at Tiana, who looks guilty, as much as she looks smitten with her idea.

"Baby, you got me these? These are fucking insane," I say as I look over them.

I like my skates worn in, so I really didn't care to get new ones. I get some from the league all the time.

But...

She bought me fourteen hundred-dollar skates.

She unwraps her box and shows me the top of hers. It's another pair of skates, my brow furrowing in even more confusion. Though hers aren't nearly high tier as mine, which, I mean, if she's just learning to skate, that tracks.

"I bought us skates so we could go ice skating together. I want to learn so we can go to more rinks," she says with a nervous smile.

Scratch that. She bought me fourteen hundred-dollar skates to fuck around in.

Holy shit, my fucking wife.

I press the box beside me, wrapping my hands around her cheeks to bring her in for a kiss.

She leans in, kissing softly back before I pull away.

"You got me fucking Shadows..." I whisper before I bring the box back into my lap.

I pick up one skate, moving it around and seeing what else has been done to them.

Wouldn't you fuckin' know?

My number, "33" and "Check 'Em," are on the tongue.

Which means she not only bought me top of the line skates, she bought me *customized,* top of the line skates.

"How did you know which ones to get?" I ask.

"Adrian is a very eager accomplice," she says with a wink.

I lean in to her ear, gripping tight on the one skate in my hand, so as not to allude anything to anyone else.

"You are so fucking lucky you're on your period right now,

or I'd take you downstairs and fuck the shit out of you," I whisper before pressing a small kiss to the side of her neck.

Tiana, however, can keep a very good poker face when push comes to shove.

Maybe she expected this sort of reaction; I have no idea.

But this is the best gift I've gotten in a long time.

Next, my mom grabs a large gift bag, looking it over before she hands it to Gretz.

"Dad, this is yours," he says as he hands it to him.

My dad sits up in his recliner, placing the gift bag on the floor in front of him.

He pulls some of the holiday-themed tissue paper out from the top, and then, an orange handle.

My brow furrows as I look over it, my head tilting.

"Splitting maul," he says with a ghost of a smile on his face. "Thanks, Tiana, I needed a new one," he says with a nod.

"You're welcome," Tiana says with a nervous smile.

That's about the best reaction I could get out of my dad, so at least I know Tiana did well.

My mom has a small box, and she tilts her head as she looks over it. She unwraps it and pulls the lid off the top of it. As she looks inside, she presses a hand over her mouth, and her eyes glisten as she pulls out a silver bracelet.

"A Pandora bracelet?" she asks softly as she looks up at Tiana with a watery smile.

Tiana nods. "Did you look at the charms?" she asks with a small point at the bracelet.

My mom looks down at the bracelet, moving some charms around.

As my mom finishes her look about, she gets up quickly, coming over to hug Tiana tight.

"You're the best first daughter I could ever ask for," I hear my mom whisper to Tiana.

Tiana squeezes her back with a smile. "Thank you for raising such an amazing man," Tiana responds.

My mom pulls away, holding the bracelet as she wipes tears from her eyes with a small chuckle.

"Ahh, you just like to see me cry," my mom jokes.

"Can I see it?" I ask.

My mom crouches in front of me, showing me some charms on the bracelet.

There's a hockey one that goes around the band, as well as a dual heart charm that says, "Mother and Daughter".

"Aw, babe. That's sweet of you," I say with a smile as I look over at her.

Her blush deepens, and she gives me a smile. "I thought it was really cute," she says.

"You really are," I say with a grin as I lean in to kiss her.

My mom rushes over to the tree and pulls out a small card before she brings it back to Tiana.

"We all got this for you, Tiana," my mom says as she offers the card to Tiana.

Tiana smiles sheepishly as she takes it. "Aww, you guys didn't have to get me anything," she says sweetly.

"Oh hush! Open it!" my mom says cheerfully as she flaps her hand in dismissal.

Tiana bites her lower lip nervously as she slowly opens the envelope and pulls the card out, reading it before she makes a small gasp.

"No, you're kidding," Tiana says softly.

"Yes! I know you said you have a lot of books, so I thought this would be perfect for you guys," my mom says with a smile.

"Can I see?" I ask. Tiana hands me the card before she hugs my mom in thanks.

I scan over the card, reading my mom's handwriting;

Thank you so much for taking care of my son and
fixing the truck. I hope this helps when it comes time
to build your house!
I hear their bookcases are all the rage right now!
Merry Christmas!
Love your soon-to-be-mom!
Mrs. Claire and The Hayze's

It's a gift card for IKEA. A very *hefty* gift-card at that.

"This is for bookshelves?" I ask as I look up at my mom.

"Or whatever you need for your home, I don't know! I wanted Tiana to have a place to put her books!" my mom says cheerfully with a clap of her hands.

"I love this. I don't have any bookshelves in my apartment, so this is wonderful, thank you so much," Tiana says sincerely.

"Oh, anything for you, Tiana," my mom says with a smile.

Gretz interrupts our sweet moment.

"Holy shit. You're fucking kidding me," he says.

My brow furrows as I look over at him to see him holding an envelope.

"Your wife got me a fifteen hundred dollar gift card for Bauer?" Gretz says as he looks up at us.

He looks at Tiana with a gaping jaw.

"Can I kiss your feet?" he asks.

My face contorts with a grimace as I watch him.

Tiana makes a nervous laugh. "Uh... I'd appreciate if you didn't," she says softly.

"That's fair. Can I kiss your husband then?" he asks.

Tiana looks at me with a wide-eyed look of confusion before she turns back to Gretz.

"I think you'd have to ask him," she says.

Gretz looks at me with a grin. "Whadd'ya say, Guns and

Roses?" he asks as he holds his arms out in a wide hug and a waggle of his eyebrows.

"I'd rather shit in my hands and clap," I groan as I rub a hand over my face.

"Rude. But thank you, Tiana. This is really nice, honestly," Gretz says with a genuine smile.

I give him a small smile in return before I grip Tiana's shoulder tighter.

"Good job, baby," I whisper as I press a kiss to her forehead.

After we opened gifts and talked for a while, my dad had gotten up to check the turkey, to find it done.

From there, we all moved to the kitchen to help grab the food and set up the dining room table before we all sit down to eat.

Tiana watches everyone dig in, her eyes roaming over everything, trying to figure out where she can jump in. There's turkey, of course. Stuffing, mashed potatoes, Tiana's mac and cheese, buttered rolls, cranberry sauce, green bean casserole.

"What all do you want, sugar?" I ask as I take her plate from in front of her.

I can tell she's nervous because she's silent for a bit as her gaze blanks out on the food.

"Turkey, mac and cheese, potatoes and bread, please," she says softly.

I nod, loading up her plate with the things she wants before I get to the turkey.

"White or dark meat?"

"Dark," she says with a small nod.

I pick some of the thigh meat from the turkey plate to put on her plate before I place it in front of her, where she bites down on her lower lip in delight.

Tiana doesn't eat too terribly much. Something I've tried to get her to change. And it's the only thing I have ever tried to change about her. Only because I eat constantly, and anything. I rarely see Tiana eat, and part of it makes me nervous, because how can someone eat so little? But most of the time, she says she's not hungry. She doesn't like having to think about food sometimes, is what she's told me.

I don't entirely understand that. But I try to accommodate where I can.

Sometimes she gets into these modes where she just eats the same thing for days. It'll be the only thing I see her put in her mouth.

Well... aside from my dick.

Either way, I usually have to make sure there's enough of that in the house, or she just won't eat.

It's been a struggle, and I don't know how someone can go without eating for as long as she does. But that's just how she is. It's something I've had to learn with her.

Tiana looks over the food for a long moment before she picks up her utensils, digging in slowly, as I make my plate.

"Thank you so much for making the mac and cheese, Tiana. I've never been too good at making it, but I love eating it!" my mom says as she takes a bite of her food.

"This shit slaps, Tiana. What'd you put in it?" Gretz asks.

Tiana's cheeks brighten up again, and she smiles shyly. "There's cheddar, gouda, and some other things. I've been making it for many years. I'm always the 'mac and cheese bringer' for family dinners and stuff," she says.

I take a bite, and my eyes roll as I taste it.

Holy shit, it's the best mac and cheese I've ever had in my life.

"Damn babe. I didn't know you could make this. Why don't you ever make it for me?" I ask.

She glances at me with a small smirk on her lips. "It makes a lot at once and takes a while. But if you want me to make it more often, I can," she says as she peels apart her bread to press into her mouth.

"Please, sugar," I say as I lean my head into her.

She brings a hand up to pat my cheek before she goes back to her food. "If you buy the stuff, I'll make it whenever you want."

"Fuuuuck yes, I love you," I say with a grin before I kiss her cheek and continue eating.

"So, when the fuck are you shaving that thing on your lip?" Gretz asks as he points his fork at me.

"Hey man, I'm trying to save the prostates," I say before taking a bite of my turkey.

"I've been asking him to shave it since he got back from Canada," Tiana mumbles as she shakes her head.

"Looks like you got into a fight with the caterpillar and the thing won," Gretz says before he shakes his head and goes back to his food.

"Aw, I think it looks cute. It was strange at first, but I love it now!" my mom says with a smile.

"That's it, I'm shaving it," I grumble.

"Nooo! Keep it," my mom begs playfully.

"Cute? It's a mustache," I groan.

"You hear Gunnar and Tiana are already trying to have kids?" Gretz says slyly.

Fucking hell.

"Already? Grandbabies?!" my mom says with a look of hope glittering in her eyes.

I rub my hands over my face.

God, not here. I don't want more pressure on Tiana.

"Eventually. I said that last time, Gretz," I say with a sigh.

I look over at Tiana, who seems to dig into her turkey with a bit more force as Gretz talks.

"Last time?" my mom asks as she looks between me and Gretz.

"Yeah, remember? Gunnar said you wouldn't hit Tiana because she's the one making your grandkids," Brooks says matter-of-factly.

"Hm. I must have missed it. But I wouldn't hit Tiana anyway, because she has MANNERS, unlike the rest of you fuckin' hooligans," my mom says with a huff.

"You raised us!" Gretz says as he throws his arms out.

"So did hockey, and I blame that," my mom says with a solid nod.

"I think I'd concur," Tiana says playfully.

My mom winks at Tiana and I see Tiana give her a smile in response.

Eventually, we finish eating, and after a lot of talking, Tiana retreats to the basement, where my old room is. However, I stay on the main floor, in the living room with my brothers, and my mom and dad go upstairs to get in bed. I actually went and showered with her before I changed into some sweatpants to come watch some games with Gretz and Brooks.

Tiana and I decided to stay the night here since we'd be closer to her parents. Tiana didn't want to have to go home and then drive back out to her parents when we're going there for another Thanksgiving tomorrow.

With a deep breath, I crash onto the couch as I ruffle my hand through my wet hair. I lean back against the armrest and prop my feet up in front of me before throwing my hands behind my head.

"Beer?" Gretz asks as he comes from the kitchen with a bottle for me and him.

I lean my head back to see him. "I'll have a beer," I say as I take the beer he offers.

I knock the bottle back as I turn my attention to the game on the TV.

Penguins and the Oilers.

Another solid match.

"How's married life?" Gretz asks as he tips his beer up for a swig.

"Real nice to have the same lady for the rest of my life, I'll tell you that," I say before taking another sip.

Brooks is locked into the game, with the same bowl, though this time it's filled with popcorn. He sits next to Gretz, his legs crossed as he leans all the way over, with his eyes fixed on the TV.

Brooks really loves watching hockey. Honestly, I think he enjoys watching it a lot more than he enjoys playing it.

Gretz sighs as he runs a hand through his hair and leans his head back against the couch. I turn to look at him, where he has his beer propped on his knee, though the other leg seems to bounce nervously.

"If I go to UDub... I do have a problem though," he says before he takes a deep swig of his beer.

"Yeah?" I ask.

Penguins get the biscuit past the Oilers goalie, and I send a whistle out.

"Shocking," I say sarcastically with a shake of my head and another tip back of my bottle.

"Yeah, uh..." Gretz groans before he takes another sip, almost stalling as his foot continues to bounce beside him. "Willow's goin' to UDub."

This piques my interest, and I turn sideways on the couch to get a better look at him.

One thing Gretz and I have in common... or I suppose had, is our love for women.

I just have a bit more respect for them.

Gretz is a playboy. Always has been.

But Willow Teagues... that's one girl that's always had Gretz' heart.

"Teagster, huh? Pretty nasty debacle you got there, eh, bud?" I say with a shake of my head.

"She's got a boyfriend now too," he says with a sigh.

"Sucks to suck. Reckon you'll be fine though. Big school, you probably won't see her," I say with a shrug.

"She's playin' girl hockey at Madison," Brooks responds.

I tsk, shaking my head again. "Real tough play. Better watch the puck."

"Yeah, yeah. I know," he says as his eyes zone out on the game. His head shakes, and he takes another sip of his beer.

"What was your deal with the baby shit earlier?" Gretz asks.

I groan, running a hand through my hair. "I think I went a little too fast for Tiana and the baby-making shit, so I'm laying off the talk so I don't put more pressure on her," I explain.

"Damn, you want a baby that bad?" Gretz asks.

"I want a baby with *Tiana*. Not just a baby. There's a difference," I say as I tip my beer at him to punctuate my statement.

"You do understand you met her... maybe two months ago, right?"

"Yeah, yeah. But she's never even looked at another hockey player before she met me, and now she's my wife. I reckon she likes me enough," I say with a shrug.

"Still. Already?"

I look back at him with a furrowed brow. "Why are you so

concerned about what I do with my dick all of a sudden?” I ask.

“What if she doesn’t want a baby?” he asks.

“Well she got her IUD removed, and she gave me a presentation on how to make a baby, so. I think all of those are pretty solid indicators.”

His mouth gapes, his brow furrowing as his head tilts. “A what?”

“Exactly. I was too much, too fast, and I just kinda... I don’t know. I felt like I was doing too much because she kept getting disappointed that she was getting her period,” I say with another sip.

“Ahhh... yeah, I reckon that is your fault, huh?” Gretz says with a shrug.

“Between you and Banks... you fuckin’ shits,” I grumble.

“Hey man, you’re a goon in every sense of the word. On and off the ice,” he adds.

I roll my eyes as I sit up on the couch. “Whatever, fucko.”

The three of us end up sitting in silence, watching the game, with only a few words spoken about the plays, until I finish my beer and stand to hand it to Gretz.

“Hittin’ the hay. Night dipshit,” I say as I walk past Gretz, ruffling his hair, and I make my way down the steps to the basement.

My old room is as perfect as I left it.

All over the walls I have my old jerseys. It’s also big enough that I’ve got a shooting pad for fucking around with pucks when I had the chance, or was just bored.

One corner has a few stacks of history books. Because once upon a time, I read. But hockey took precedence, and I ended up leaving my books behind.

Luckily, I also have a massive bed, so when I get downstairs, Tiana is curled up under the blankets with her bonnet on and her back rising and falling slowly.

I come downstairs quietly, getting into the blankets behind her and wrapping an arm around her waist and pulling her in close.

To me, this was the perfect Thanksgiving. And I'm glad it went so well.

With that, and the feeling of a good day, I fall asleep with my wife in my arms.

CHAPTER THIRTY-TWO
TIANA

I would like to go home. I don't even want to go to my parents' house today.

I am so worn out from yesterday's festivities that I almost cancelled coming to see my family. But since they're leaving, I had to see them.

Not to mention, I imagine Gunnar wants to see and talk to Adrian. Especially since I know it'll more than likely be a rough time for him.

But along with that... I am having the hardest time with the way Gunnar talked about the baby thing yesterday at Thanksgiving.

Did the rest of Thanksgiving go great? Yeah, overall, it was a great time. I had fun; the food was good, everybody liked the gifts I got them, and I got a really nice gift I wasn't even expecting. It was a calm, family-like Thanksgiving.

But, with me being at the tail end of my period, I couldn't stop focusing on the fact Gunnar basically brushed off the entire grandchild thing. I didn't say anything because I don't think it was my place to speak. It's his family, so he calls the shots with what he wants to say, but that didn't stop me from worrying and overthinking it all.

I feel like the longer I go without talking to him about it, the angstier I get. That dumb worm just digs deeper into my brain.

But I can't bring it up. He'll think that I think less of him, or that his efforts are for nothing.

There's also the what-ifs of it all.

What if he gets irritated with how much reassurance he's given me already? What if he just gets mad or feels like I don't appreciate the other things he does for me, and I just focus on this one thing instead?

I hate the way this entire thing is making me feel because it *stresses* me out. I don't feel like Charlotte has been much of a help because her advice is, "Just stop thinking about it."

Cool! Great! Sure wish I could fucking do that. Thanks Char.

There have even been nightmares, where Gunnar walks away because of what I said, or even what I didn't say, and I just become bitter and resentful.

This entire week has felt like it's crushing me with the weight of the holidays, the hypothetical idea of not having Gunnar, even if none of that is even remotely close to being on the table. It swirls so violently in my head that it even dampens my mood as we drive to my parent's house this morning.

I tell Gunnar that I'm tired from socializing. That I'm just worn out, and he seems to take that as enough.

Which makes sense. But I just...

My mind is a jumble of fear, nerves, and confusion.

When we get to my parent's house, we knock, and my dad opens the door.

I give him a small, warm smile as he does, but he tips his head back with a sigh.

"Fuck," he groans.

"Wow, be a little bit more excited to see us, why don't you?" I grumble as I lead Gunnar in.

Gunnar carries the pan of mac and cheese, since my family said no gifts this year. I had brought both pans with me yesterday and just kept the other one in their fridge since Gunnar's family was gracious enough to let me use it.

"Sorry. It's not you, Tiana. I just can't believe I'm spending even more time with these fuck-nuts during the holidays," my dad grumbles.

Gunnar shifts the pan of mac and cheese to one of his arms so he can offer a hand out to my dad for him to shake it.

"Good to meet you sir, I'm Gunnar," Gunnar says with a wide grin.

"If you don't get your ass in the damn house," my dad grits as he shoves Gunnar's shoulder.

Gunnar snickers as he walks toward the kitchen. I take off my long puffer jacket and hang it on one hook by the door before I kick off my boots.

The house is delightfully warm from the fireplace in the living room, and it already smells of more Thanksgiving foods. Stuffing, the ham hocks in my mom's collard greens, the cinnamon from her yams. And *so* much butter.

"How's it going?" I ask as I turn to my dad.

"Ah, it's alright. Good to see you, Tiana," he says with a small smile as he wraps an arm around my shoulder in a side hug.

He leans over, pressing a kiss to the top of my head before he squeezes me. I wrap an arm around his back, squeezing him back.

"Good to see you too," I say.

I really don't get to spend as much time with my dad as Charlotte does. Mostly because, obviously, Charlotte works closer with him.

But it's always nice to spend time with him and my mom outside of the rink.

"Are Charlotte and Adrian here?" I ask as I walk further in, looking around.

"Yeah, they're in the backyard with the dogs. I'm grilling the turkey, so I'm going out there. Your mom is in the kitchen."

"Great," I mumble as I walk to the kitchen.

As I get to the kitchen, I look out the window to see Adrian in the back with Charlotte, and the dogs. Gunnar left the pan of mac and cheese on the counter because he went out to see Adrian.

Gunnar crouches to say "Hi" to Tucker, who jumps and licks all over him before Gunnar grabs a tennis ball on the ground and chucks it. Tucker bolts, with Waffle hot on his heels, and Gunnar presses his hands in his pockets as he turns to Adrian.

Soon, Charlotte hugs Gunnar before she comes up the steps, onto the elevated deck and comes inside.

"Hey Ti!" Charlotte says with a smile as she wraps her arms around me in a hug.

I pat her back softly, a small smile pulling at my lips. "Hey Char, how's it going?"

"Pretty good. We leave for Montana in a few weeks, so we'll come drop Tucker off before we leave," she says with a grin.

"No Waffle?" I ask as I sit down on a stool at the kitchen island.

My mom is putting her candied yams in the oven before she moves back to the stove to mix her collard greens.

I personally do not like collard greens; I don't like the texture.

But I enjoy the yams. So I'm excited to have those.

"Waffle is coming with us to Montana," Charlotte says with a happy nod.

"Mmm, well that's good," I mumble as I get lost watching my mom make the collard greens.

"Tiana... you better not," Charlotte murmurs.

"What?!" I groan. Because I already know she's about to start.

"What's wrong with you?" my mom asks as she looks between Charlotte and me with a confused furrow of her brow.

I groan again, crossing my arms against my chest. I am already overthinking it, but Charlotte knows I don't like talking about it; so she's going to bring it up.

"Tell her," Charlotte says.

I roll my eyes, refusing to speak.

"Tiana is up and arms about some shit with Gunnar that is so far out of reach that it's not even funny," Charlotte says with some gestures of her hands as she shakes her head.

"Like what?" my mom asks.

"Well, I can't get into specifics. Because, gross. But he was doing something, and now he's not, and now I'm in my head about it," I mumble.

"Mmm," my mom says.

"I told her, Momma," Charlotte says.

My mom sucks her teeth. "That's on you, Ti. You know what you've gotta do," my mom says with a shrug.

"I don't want to do it," I grumble in annoyance.

"And why not? You are a grown-ass woman, who has more than enough voice to stand up for her clients, but not for herself? Miss me with that, I raised you better," my mom says as she points her collard green spoon at me before she goes back to mixing them.

"Mmmmmhm," Charlotte hums in agreement.

"This is why I don't tell you guys anything," I murmur as I glance away.

"You're being dramatic, Ti. And you know you are. You're

going to run yourself ragged, and you know that. So why is it you want to stay in the same lane when you can switch gears and win the fuckin' race? Be better, because I know you know how to be," Charlotte says.

"It'll blow over. I'm just overthinking. Leave me alone," I grumble.

I glance up to see them glance at each other before they both "Mmm" in unison.

"Anyway... you said you and Dad are going on a cruise? Where are you guys going again?" I ask, trying with all my might to change the subject, because I'm over talking about this.

"Bahamas. Far away from this rainy, dreary ass weather," my mom says.

"When do you guys leave?" I ask as I find a napkin on the counter and start peeling the plies apart.

"In two weeks," my mom says.

"Are there any clients I'm going to have to take over?" I ask.

"Nope. Just finish up whatever you're working on, and then you're free until New Year's. There are other attorneys looking for pickups during the holidays," she says.

"Thank God," I murmur.

"Mmm, you're tellin' me," my mom says with a sigh. "These football players are runnin' me left, right and upside down. I don't know what kind of water they're putting in the bottles for them. But they've got barely a brain left in 'em," she adds with a shake of her head.

"That's why I didn't go to football," I say. Reaching over the counter, I nab a fork to snag a stray yam piece from my mom's pot before blowing on it and popping it into my mouth.

"Count yourself lucky. I don't remember the hockey players giving me as much trouble."

"You still got some hockey players; what are you talking about?" I ask with a furrow of my brow.

"I do. But not as many as football and basketball. Too many basketball and football teams here."

"I know that's right," Charlotte says with a nod. "We need more hockey teams."

"You would say that," I say.

"What are you guys going to do while you're stuck here?" Charlotte asks me.

"Well, I know for sure we're going back out to the land. We've gotta grab a tree. And I bought Gunnar and me skates so, maybe if the lake is frozen enough, we can skate there," I say with a warm smile.

Even though I am irritated with being overstimulated, the holidays, baby-making and Gunnar's change in tone, I want to focus on Christmas things. I don't want it to sap the joy from my first Christmas with Gunnar.

I have next week to work, and then the rest of December is for me and Gunnar.

"Ohhhh! Did Gunnar tell you? The loggers get out there the second week of December," Charlotte says with a grin.

My eyes widen. "Oh my God, they do? No, he didn't. I think with everything going on, it slipped his mind. I know he mentioned they're out there in the next few weeks, but I didn't know if he had a date for sure," I say.

That seems to help my mood some, because if we're breaking ground on land, I can shift my focus. I can think about the house and the stuff I want to do for it.

There's a small pulse of happiness that rushes through me, and I'm so excited to actually think about something that I know for sure Gunnar wants.

Yeah... see! That's what I'll do.

He doesn't want a baby right now, fine, whatever.

But I know for sure he wants the house. So, I'm going to throw everything I have into that until he's ready.

Everything is going to be fine.

Soon, Adrian, Gunnar and my dad all come in from the back door, where the dogs run in, going wild.

Adrian whistles, leading the dogs to a room further into the house, while Gunnar comes up to me, wrapping a hand around the back of my head to bring it to his lips, pressing a kiss to my forehead.

He smells of the cold outside, and I have to admit I love it.

Gunnar leans in as if he's going to kiss my neck, but he whispers instead, "He's going to do it over their vacation."

He pulls away to watch me, and my brow furrows, my eyes widening in question. I feel my brow arch, looking for confirmation.

Gunnar merely leans his elbow against the counter in front of me, nodding slowly as he purses his lips into duck lips.

"Shit," I say softly.

"Yup."

"Why didn't you tell me the loggers were going to be out on the land in December?" I ask louder now.

"Ah, fuck, Banks did tell me that. I'm sorry, baby. There's been a lot going on. Did you wanna go when they're there?" he asks as he brings a hand up to my cheek.

"If we could, please?" I ask with a soft smile.

"Whatever you want, sugar," he says with a smile in return before he leans in, kissing me on the lips.

He snags the fork from my hand, leaning over to grab a bit of collard greens from my mom's pot and stuff it in his mouth.

"I didn't know you liked collard greens," my mom says as she watches him.

"I like anything with some flavor. Why do you think I'm with your daughter?" he asks with a click of his tongue and a wink.

I groan as I press the heels of my hands into my eyes.

"Lord have mercy," my mom says as she rolls her eyes.

"I kid. I'll eat pretty much anything," Gunnar says as he reaches into the collard green pot for more.

My mom slaps his hand with the spoon, and he yelps as he flings his hand back.

"Out of my pot, goon," my mom grumbles before she keeps stirring the greens.

"Can confirm. Disgusting at times, actually," Adrian says with a sigh as he comes from the back room where he was setting up the dogs.

"Tucker being good for you?" I ask. Gunnar comes up behind me on the stool, wrapping his arms around me and resting his chin on the top of my head.

"Real good boy, that dog. I reckon he'd be a good duck hunter if he had training," Adrian says as he comes to stand beside Charlotte.

He runs his hand up and down her back, lighting hanging his hand around the back of her neck before she tilts her head back and he kisses her.

"Greens, Mrs. Dawn?" Adrian asks as he nods to the pot.

"Yes, and Tiana brought her mac and cheese," my mom says as she nods to me.

"Sounds like good eatin' to me," he says with a small smile.

Suddenly, Charlotte gasps, and the group of us freezes where we are. Even my mom, who looks at Charlotte like she's about to slap her.

"Ti!!! Did you tell them?!?" Charlotte asks.

My brow furrows as I look at her. Because I have no fucking idea what she's talking about.

She nods down at my hand, and I look to see the ring on my finger.

Oh, fuck. I got married.

"Where's Dad?" I ask as I look around.

"DADDY! GET IN HERE!!" Charlotte yells.

I groan with a clap over my ears. "Charlotte!" I growl.

She shrinks with a nervous scrunch on her face. "Fuck, sorry, Ti," she says.

I shake the shriek from my head before I take a deep breath, waiting for my dad to come back.

"What is it?" my dad sighs as he comes from the living room.

"Tell them, Ti!" Charlotte says with a giggle and a rapid clap of her hands.

I look up at Gunnar, and he gives me a nod of pride.

"Gunnar and I got married," I say as I look to my mom and dad.

My dad merely sighs as he walks back out onto the porch.

"Already? No wedding?" my mom asks.

"No. We just... went out to the land and did the legal stuff," I say.

"Mmm..." she says in thought. "Well, congrats. I was not trying to deal with a wedding right now," my mom says.

"And honestly, I'm glad we aren't having one either right now," I say with a sigh.

"What is it with you people and not wanting to do weddings?!" Charlotte groans.

"Too many people," my mom and I say in unison.

"You guys are lame. You don't care about the dresses and the dancing and music and fun!?" Charlotte says as she jumps around Adrian, trying to goad him into dancing with her. He merely holds his hand out for her, letting her spin under him.

"I actually do not, no," I say.

"Gunnar, what about you?! You didn't wanna have a big, beautiful wedding?" Charlotte groans.

"Well, I was actually the one who offered the idea of skipping the wedding, anyway. We had a lot of things coming up, and we decided this was the best route for us," Gunnar says confidently. His powerful hands come to my shoulders, and his thumbs slowly knead into the muscles, where I sink into the feeling of it. Because for whatever reason, I hold an enormous amount of tension there right now.

"I'm going to have the biggest, most beautiful wedding on the planet," Charlotte squeals excitedly as she spins under Adrian again.

And if Gunnar hadn't told me earlier, I may have missed it, but there is a lovesick look on Adrian's face as he watches Charlotte spin.

"I reckon you will, Miss Lotty," Adrian says softly.

After a lot of talking in the kitchen, and waiting for the food to be ready, we're able to sit and eat.

But by the time we finish eating, I do not want to stick around any longer. I love my family; I love spending time with my family, but I am so fucking tired, I can't be around humans any longer. I need to hide in a hole.

I feel as if I've overextended my ability to socialize. Luckily, my parents know when I've had too much and they know when I need to go somewhere else, so leaving was easier than one would have imagined.

I think having to go to Gunnar's family yesterday may have burned my battery out faster than it usually would if it was just one family dinner.

Before we left, I helped my mom and sister clean up the kitchen while the men talked more hockey off in my dad's office.

Gunnar has somehow become Adrian's right hand on the

team. Along with their ability to work together, Gunnar is just a really good player, and that has put him above the rest.

As soon as we finish cleaning, I quickly say our goodbyes and damn near shove Gunnar out of the house.

He wanted to stay longer, but I just couldn't anymore. I didn't even want to drive; I was so tired.

When we get back home, I quickly shower, not even waiting for Gunnar, and shove myself into bed.

But along with showering, I realize my period has ended, and I'm... worried all over again.

Because... do we keep trying? Do I just go through life as normal and wait for his cue?

That's not what I want to do, because his reasoning before was sound as far as having a kid so soon. And I shouldn't have to wait for a man's cue to do *anything*.

Just because I love Gunnar doesn't suddenly mean he's the ready whistle for everything in my life. I've never waited for a man's cue in the past, and I won't do it now. I know Gunnar knows that, too.

And unfortunately, those swirling thoughts and doubts are the only things that get me to bed that night.

CHAPTER THIRTY-THREE
GUNNAR

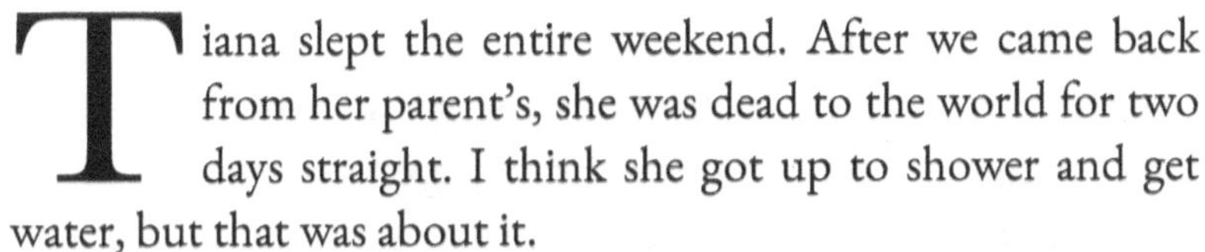

Tiana slept the entire weekend. After we came back from her parent's, she was dead to the world for two days straight. I think she got up to shower and get water, but that was about it.

I'm slowly learning her limits as far as socializing. She didn't seem so bad, but I think she saves it for when she has a safe place to crash. I could tell she was touchy at her parent's house. Something was bothering her. And when she ended up sleeping the entire weekend away, I thought maybe she'd be back to normal on Monday when we go into the arena.

But this morning, it was the same, if not worse.

She's been off in a way I don't think I've ever seen from her. Iffy.

Angry, even.

I tried to talk to her about it on our way to the arena. But she had said it was nothing.

So after work, I want to get to the bottom of it.

Tiana is utterly silent our entire way home, having almost a scowl on her face. She's never this mad, and I can tell there's something on her mind.

As we walk up to the apartment, she tries to walk ahead of me, but I keep pace beside her.

"Are you okay, sugar?" I ask softly.

She glances at me before her gaze turns back to her strides toward the apartment.

"Yes, work is... work," she mumbles.

But there is something that does not sound right about that.

I don't ask anything else as we get to the apartment, where she opens the door and starts shedding her suit jacket, putting it on a hanger by the door.

"I'm going to shower," she murmurs.

But I grab her wrist, holding her in place.

"Tiana," I say low and serious.

She turns around, with a tone of shock in her eyes as she looks from my hand on her wrist to my eyes.

"What is wrong?" I ask in the same tone, though slower now.

"Nothing is wrong, Gunnar," she responds, and it's terse, short.

"Don't lie to me, Tiana. I know you better than that," I say as I pin my gaze into hers.

Shockingly, her gaze locks on mine, challenging me with fire.

She snatches her wrist away. "Fine. You want to know what's wrong? Do you even fucking want me anymore?" she asks.

My brow furrows wildly as I look at her. "What in the world are you talking about? Of course, I want you. I just married you," I say.

I'm confused about where any of this is coming from.

"You haven't said *anything* when we're having sex about

putting a baby in me. You used to say those things to me all the time. Made me feel like *I* was the one that you were supposed to be doing this with. It's been going on for a while, and I just ignored it. But it's *gotten* to me, and I can't fucking handle the idea that you may not want to be with me anymore," she says. Her eyes pinch as she glares at me, anger twisting at her brow, with her chest moving in quick bursts.

Fuck...

"Say something!" she shouts as she throws her arms out.

"Tiana, I-" I sigh softly as I run a hand through my hair.

God... fucking... dammit.

"Do you not want me anymore, Gunnar? Is that it? Did I finally do something that was too much? That wasn't enough?" she asks.

Oh... Tiana-baby...

I know she's experienced this feeling in the past. But from my understanding, it never mattered before. But, fuck me... it matters more than ever to her right now, and it's all my fault.

I watch her for a long moment. I take in the way her eyes blaze with anger, the way her chest moves and her teeth grit.

I think carefully over my words, because she's vulnerable right now, and I don't want to make it worse. Especially when my reason for it all was merely to take pressure off her.

But... as always, I'm learning with Tiana. Because that's all I've ever wanted to do with her.

My hesitancy is only because of my failure, and my heart fractures bit by bit as I watch her. This is my fault, and I always promised I would never put her in a position to feel like this.

"Since the beginning, you always said you wanted this, and then we get married and suddenly, it's gone?" she says as she paces in the living room in front of me.

I stay silent, letting her use her voice, because if she's using it, I want her to *keep* using it. Especially if I'm doing something wrong.

"I put all this work and effort into this thing you said you wanted, and *I* want it too, but now it feels like you don't! How am I supposed to think everything is okay when I see this one consistent thing fall apart in front of me? I thought it would all be different and that you could accept me because that's what you said, right? You accept me!? So, why are you pulling away now?!" She stops in her pacing, facing me.

Her eyes tear up. The emerald that rings her pupils is bright and dripping with pain... *fear.*

"God, even after the fucking presentation. It just stopped! I don't fucking get it! I don't even understand!" she says as she clenches her hands into fists, pressing them over her eyes.

She groans in frustration before she throws her fists at her sides, glaring at me as she stands her ground, because even if she's mad, I can tell she feels like a cowering animal. She's scared her future is going to hang in the balance, just like it did for her in the past.

I slowly press my hands into my pockets, coming up to her and gazing down at her. The corner of my lips tilts up, though apologetically, and I bring a hand up to her curls, wrapping it around my finger before I press it behind her ear.

"Sugar..." I say with a soft sigh.

She doesn't say anything; she merely stares, her nostrils flaring as she huffs out her exhales.

And the flames in her eyes... they're rabid... I've never really seen her angry, but right now, I'm glad that she is.

I'd never want her to take mistreatment, even from me. So I'm glad that she's standing up to me. It means she's found her voice and her worth.

And she deserves to have those.

"I do want a baby with you. I *only* want a family with *you.* But... before I left for Canada, you were worried about being able to get pregnant for us, and I felt bad. I moved too fast... I moved at *my* pace, and I learned you don't work that way. I drove you to a place of fear. I made you feel you would lose me if you couldn't give us this thing we wanted. And I... am so sorry that I-"

"You didn't-"

"No. Stop. I'm talking. Let me finish," I say with a sigh as I put a hand up. "I've let you down. I promised I would never put you in a position to fear your place with me. But I backed away from the breeding talk in bed and baby talk in general, because I didn't want you to feel you had to be that to be loved by me. I know I told you that... but you need *action*. You need to see that I love you for *you*, so I toned it down. It was hard, because I love doing it. But I couldn't keep making you feel that way," I say. I take a deep breath, hoping that she understands what I'm saying.

Tears roll down her cheeks as she looks up at me, and her face is frozen, trying to process everything.

"Why didn't you tell me, then?" she asks quietly.

"I... I don't know. I'm still learning how to do things with you. And if I need to be more direct with my words and what I'm going to do from now on, I will," I say in response.

Her lips tighten, her eyes volleying between mine.

But I keep going, getting my thoughts and feelings out as well. "I did what a goon does... I forced myself in from the beginning. I bull-dozed it with my eagerness. I put pressure on you that you didn't deserve," I say as I bring a hand up to her cheek. I hold it, and soon her lip quivers as more tears fall.

"There's not been a second that has gone by where I didn't want anything that we have. There's not a moment when I wanted anything else than what we have. And I'm so sorry that I made you think otherwise. Whether we're in a box under a bridge, in a mansion in Calabasas, or living in a fucking canoe in the middle of the lake. We could have absolutely nothing, we could have everything, and I will still love you as fiercely as I always have. You have been my priority from the moment I met you, and that will never, ever change. No matter our circumstances."

The tears continue to run, and she sniffles sharply as she watches me. Her eyes continue to volley back and forth against mine as she continues her process.

"If you want me to start doing it again, I will. I stopped only because I felt like I was hurting you. And I could never live with myself if I knew I had caused you pain. I could never put more on you than you could handle. And I know you can handle a lot. But I could see what *my* impatience was doing to you. That was never, ever my intention."

The tears continue streaming down her face, inhaling sharply before she wraps her arms tight around my waist, burying her face into my stomach. Sobs are muffled in my shirt, and I can feel the way her back trembles as she lets them go. I hug her tight, rocking our hips side to side in comfort as I run a hand up and down her back.

I let her work them out, because if she noticed this when I came back from Canada, she's been thinking about this for a while and she's said nothing.

I can't imagine how much she's been holding back.

Slowly, I move us toward the couch to sit down. Then, I pull her onto my lap, where she clutches my body as she continues to cry.

"I was so scared," I hear her murmur between her tears.

"I'm sorry, sugar..." I say softly.

Fuck... she really thought I didn't want her...

She pulls away, her eyes puffy and her nose running as she takes sharp inhales of air, her eyes gazing off at what looks to be my shoulder.

"I... it'd been in my head... for *weeks,* and I tried to push it away. I tried not to let it get to me. I tried *so hard* not to over analyze everything. I tried to see all the other things you do, because you do *so* much for me and us... it felt unfair to put that on you... but I was scared. Fuck, I was so scared, I just couldn't stop the what-ifs... the vision of you not in my life..." Her voice breaks again as she stops herself, more tears breaking.

"Hey, hey, look at me, sugar," I whisper as I wrap my hands around her face.

Reluctantly, her eyes slide to me, and she huffs in breaths to calm down, her eyelids droopy as she looks at me.

"I will never not be in your life. The only way you're getting rid of me is if you ask me to leave. And even then, I'm lingering to make sure you're taken care of, always. I always promised you that," I whisper.

She nods softly, sniffling again, and I take a moment to wipe her tears away with my thumbs.

"Does this mean you'll start saying you're going to put a baby in me again?" she asks softly.

I can't help the playful grin that tugs at my cheeks. "Is that what you want?" I ask.

She nods softly as she sucks her lower lip into her mouth.

"I really miss it," she whispers.

"I really missed it too, baby," I respond as my smile softens. "But I need to know that you understand I'll always be here. Baby or no baby. Marriage or no marriage. I will always be here. No matter what," I tell her.

She nods again, slowly, before taking a deep breath. "Even if we aren't married?" she asks in a teary, playful sniffle.

"Even then. I'd be the best friend you'd ever have," I joke back with a smile.

She rolls her eyes before leaning back into me. Her arms come up to wrap tightly around my neck. Like a spider monkey, she clings to me. With her legs wrapped around my hips, and her body pressed tight to mine.

"I'm sorry I thought that at all... You don't deserve that," she murmurs softly.

"You're learning, sugar. I know it's hard, coming out of a

life you knew so well. But I promise the one I'm taking you to is so much better. I'll always make sure of that," I say as I kiss her softly on her shoulder.

She leans back, her hands wrapping around my jaw as she smiles at me.

Her head tilts, her eyes warming as she admires me. "You are too good to me, Mr. Hayze," she says with one last sniffle.

I smile at her, my hands resting on her hips as I look at the bright relief in her eyes. The way her fear has dripped away, and she only has a sense of joyous relief in them now.

"I always told you I would be, Mrs. Hayze," I whisper back.

CHAPTER THIRTY-FOUR
TIANA

I feel like the weight of the world has been lifted off my shoulders. With the ability I have to breathe, the only thing left is me and the love of my life.

Thank God, because I couldn't take it anymore... I had been stewing at work over it all *fucking* day.

It was eating at me... To ask, not to ask. To let it go, or pick it *and* his movements apart, trying to solve the problem on my own. When in reality, I don't have to do that anymore.

I think part of what made me so angry was that I hadn't done this in the past with any of my exes. They were never worth the mental anguish. Hell, I don't think there were any I had ever seen a future with.

But to feel as if Gunnar was pulling away–even if he wasn't–made me feel backed into a corner. With the worst part being that I backed *myself* into a corner. I saw things that weren't there, and I misinterpreted things. Over-thought; when all he had been trying to do was not put pressure on me.

I feel stupid for even thinking that about him, but I also don't feel like he's ever tried to pressure me; he's always tried to go at my pace. Even if he said he was going at his, I still don't interpret the way the baby stuff has gone as his fault.

I think it's just a natural sort of response to things like this as a woman.

But if he feels as if he pressured me, then I can't take those thoughts from him. And if he felt bad about it all, I'm not going to invalidate the way he may feel about what role he played in it all, even if I don't see it that way.

Either way, I have to break out of the woods on my own to fight this sort of fear and mentality.

Over and over, he told me he's not going anywhere. He's not leaving... and for some reason, my brain wants to preserve a happiness that isn't going away.

And that's hard, unlearning things at my big age to embrace something new.

Maybe not scary, because the new is much better than what you *knew*.

But definitely hard... and at the very least, Gunnar deserves someone who isn't insecure about her worth. So, as I look into his apologetic hazel eyes, I try to hold on to the words he said.

That he'll be here, no matter what.

I pull those words in close, forcing them into my chest, and taking them to heart. He doesn't deserve to have his love undermined. He's done so much to make sure it hasn't been.

"I love you, Gunnar," I whisper softly.

"God, I love you so much, Tiana," he responds.

Wrapping a thick hand around my jaw, he threads his fingers through the hair at the nape of my neck, gripping a handful of my curls and pulling me in for a kiss.

My hands wrap around his cheeks, and our lips meet in a collision of relief and heated passion. Pulling him in deeper, my tongue presses from my lips, seeking his, with all the love he deserves. And soon, I feel a hardness beneath me.

My body heats almost immediately, but I stay my course. Our heads tilt against one another's, feeling each other's cues.

A low hum of arousal emanates from his chest as the hand on my hip pushes just once against it, asking me to grind.

I comply, my hips sliding back and forth over his hardening cock. With my skirt bunching up around my hips and him going without boxers more often, I feel him throb beneath me, and soon, small whimpers escape me at the feel of him.

"Fuck yes," he growls as he moves his hips in time with mine.

With my suit jacket already off, my blouse and lacy bra are the only things standing between him and my breasts.

The hand in my hair loosens before moving down my shoulder. His fingertips graze my collarbone before he loosely hangs his hand on my neck. Soon, he swipes the back of his fingers down my chest, where sparks skitter across my skin, and he grips the top button of my blouse.

He flicks the button open, then the next... then the next, until they've all been released, and then presses one panel open.

As if we're one body, my arm snakes from the sleeve as he continues kissing me, though his tongue has teased and swirled around my own as he slowly rolls his hips against me.

When my arm lifts out of the fabric, he slides his hand back along my ribcage, seeking the clasp for my bra and unclipping it before it springs off me. That same hand slides down my back, gripping my hip before the other moves up my body, pressing the other sleeve off, but with the band of my bra this time.

Soon, the other hand comes back up, running a thumb over a sensitive, hardened nipple, and I hum in approval.

"You have no idea how badly I've missed telling you that I'm going to fuck a baby into that perfect cunt, sugar," he pants into our lips.

"I've missed it so fucking much," I pant back. The tension

between us climbs higher and higher as I feel my core heat and dampen against him.

"What do you want from me?" he rasps as he tangles his hand back into the hair at the nape of my neck.

"Anything. Everything. I don't care, I want *you*," I pant desperately.

His mouth widens in a grin against my lips.

"Perfect," he growls before he wraps an arm around my back, springing up from the couch.

I squeak from the sudden movements, and quickly he carries us to the bedroom, with my bra and shirt falling to the floor.

I tilt my head back as my arms wrap around his neck, where my fingers grip the controlled tension in his shoulder muscles. His tongue glides along my throat as we get to the room, and he lays me on the bed. Leaning up, he pulls off his shirt, pushes down his sweatpants and kicks them off before he rips off my skirt.

Like a man on a mission, he moves with an unheard-of urgency as he tosses my legs onto the bed and shoves me up into the pillows.

Soon, he's above me, and his stag pendant taps me in the chin as he hovers. His mouth meets mine as his cock rests on my soaked center, with the underside of it gliding against my clit in a maddening tease.

"My pretty girl..." he pants into my lips as his hand plants next to my head, bracing himself against the bed.

I grind against his cock, feeling the rigid heat tease my core.

"There you go, use me," he groans as a hand comes up to squeeze one of my tits, though harder, as if he tries to stop himself.

"Your tits are going to get so fucking big... I won't be able to keep my mouth off of them," he rasps into my mouth.

"Fuck... I can't fucking wait," I whimper against his lips.

He pulls his hips back, and I feel the head of his cock glide through my pussy, grazing my clit before he seats himself at my entrance. My eyes roll as he presses forward, just enough for the fill to make me see stars.

The hand on my tit comes to wrap around my cheek, his thumb slowly stroking over my cheek.

"Ohhhh, fuck," he pants into my lips, stealing the gasps from me. "So good... fuck you stretch so well around me, baby."

He presses inch by inch in slowly, and my legs instinctively come up to wrap around his hips, pulling him in deeper. His groans get louder as my hips swirl and roll against him.

"There's a good girl, Mama. It's all yours, take it," he pants into my lips as he slowly works with my grinds.

Our bodies move with precision against each other, like we know who is going to move when and how. It's a connection I've never felt before. Something that takes me from this plane of reality entirely, and moves me through the clouds.

"You're doing so well, baby. You take such good care of my cock," he breathes through our kiss.

"Fuck, it's so much," I pant as he sits himself balls deep in me.

"I know it is, baby. You're so tight," he whispers as his thrusts start up.

Slow at first, he moves in and out of me, as if he wants to memorize every inch of my pussy. He groans and growls as his lips move down my chin, and he nudges my head up to nibble at my neck. The hand on my cheek shifts, grabbing the side of my head to hold me in place, as the other grips tight on my hip.

"You know how gentle I have to be when you start showing?" he asks with a breathless chuckle. "I'm going to have to be so gentle with you when you're growing my kid, sugar," he pants against my skin before kissing into it.

I whimper in response, my arms wrapping around his

shoulders to get him closer to my body so I can feel the way his skin adheres to mine. The flood of his piney scent against me, all the pieces of him that make me so desperately head over heels for him.

"You feel so fucking good. I love the way you squeeze my cock," he says as leaves my neck to kiss my lips again.

More whimpers leave me at his voice, his praise, and more moans blend between our lips as my hips swirl and grind with him.

His forehead presses to mine, his hips moving slowly, sensually.

"Tiana," he pants.

He shifts his grip again, holding my cheek as he slows down more and more.

"Eyes here, look at me," he whispers.

I come to the present, my eyes fluttering open to see his.

"I need to say this now, baby," he adds before he presses his lips to mine softly.

It's so fucking hard to concentrate when he moves in me like this. Filling and stretching, with the pressure building in my lower stomach.

"You are my *sun*. My *moon*. My *stars*. You are my whole fucking universe," he pants. Every so often he presses a kiss to my lips, his hips still pistoning in and out of me so... *so* slowly. "Every move I make, every thought I have, every decision I make revolves around you." He pauses his words to roll his thrusts in and out, keeping me aloft.

"F-fuck... Gunnar, fuck it's so good," I whimper as I look deep into his eyes. A submissive cower contorts my face, pleading for more movement but he shakes his head with a pant.

He stops entirely, holding himself in. "No, baby, listen. I need you to listen... focus," he pants as he holds my face. "If this is what I have to do to get you to understand, then I'll do it. I'll climb Mount Everest. I'll sail every one of the seven seas for the rest of my life, and sprint over miles of broken glass for as long as I fucking live, just so you can go to sleep knowing you are safe with me. *You* are my everything," he says.

He continues to hold himself balls deep inside me, and my eyes roll, my hips grinding for more friction against my clit.

"You've shown me worlds I never knew. Things I never thought I'd know. I want to be the woman you deserve. I want to give you the love you give me... and I'm sorry I'm so difficult to be with... to love..." I pause, my movements halting to focus on the rest of my words as I bring my hands up to hold his face.

"This is so hard, you feel so good," I whimper as I look in his eyes.

"You're alright, sugar. I've got you," he whispers as he pulls out just enough to slowly press back in.

My moan rings through the room, my fingers flexing against his cheeks.

"B-but I'm so lucky to have you in my life. You're my beach, m-my shore. You're the calm in m-my storm... oh fuck," I pant as he flexes his cock inside of me. "Y-you bring sunlight to a winter day, and fire to the cold... I love you more than I even have words for," I whisper, trying to take calculated breaths to steady myself.

"Tiana... it has never been difficult to love you. Not for one second," he returns.

I try to hold my tears back, sniffling as his mouth latches to mine, kissing softly at first, before his hand grips tighter on my jaw and his thrusts start up again. Though they're slow, deliberate, he presses all the way to the hilt with every thrust.

"My perfect girl," he pants against my lips. "You're going to be a beautiful mother... I can't wait to see you swell," he says.

"Please... please... I want it so bad..." I whisper as I lose myself to the feeling of him.

His lips move down my jaw, kissing and licking at my throat again.

He uses the hand on my jaw to tilt my head back, licking over the column of my throat as his other hand moves to my clit, rubbing quickly over it.

The pleasure climbs, the world spinning and my breaths fleeting as he thrusts deep into me with every stroke, applying just the right amount of pressure to my clit.

"Deep... deep," he tells himself with a pant as his hips continue to piston. He leans up, the hand on my jaw moving to my hip as the other keeps pace on my clit.

My body writhes, the pleasure climbing the longer he moves.

"Remember, you've gotta come for me, sugar. I'm trying to put a fucking baby in you, you've gotta come for me," he pants into my lips.

The pressure in my lower belly twists and tightens. More and more, it grasps me by my throat, only leaving me with the ability to gasp with pleasure as my eyes roll.

He presses himself completely in, grinding against my clit, and I come undone. My screams echo through the room as my back bows, and I feel him grow harder before he spills into me. Jets of heat filling me, pressing against him and my walls, and the feeling is mind-numbing.

"Thatta girl. Keep taking, baby, I've got you, you're doing so good," Gunnar pants as he presses kisses to my neck, his cock held in me as he continues orgasming with me.

When it slows, and it feels as if it's seeping away, I wrap my arms tight around his shoulders, bringing his body to mine, relishing in the feel of his damp skin against me.

I don't know why I ever thought this man didn't want me. The way he fucks me should be evidence enough.

I press kisses against the front of his shoulder, sliding my tongue across it as my hunger ramps up again. My hands roam his hot and sweaty back, gliding my nails over his skin.

I grind against where he's still hard in me, loving the way he feels against my walls.

"Fuck..." I pant softly. "I may need more in a few minutes," I add.

He leans up, looking at me with a furrow of his brow.

"More?" he asks with a breathless grin.

I nod sheepishly with a bite of my lip.

Now that I don't have the same mental block I was having... I don't want to stop.

And for the rest of the night, we *don't*.

CHAPTER THIRTY-FIVE

GUNNAR

Ever since Tiana and I had our minor blowup, we've been having sex almost non-stop.

Since Thanksgiving is over, we've had a little bit of time off from the rink and work, so we've spent basically all of that time having sex.

However, now we're back at the land, staying in our fifth wheel. Banks and Charlotte haven't left for Montana yet, so Tucker is up at the ranch house with them and Waffle. Mostly because he would rather hang out with Waffle than us. He's been a tad more clingy around her than usual.

Maybe it's because he knows they're leaving soon, who knows. But luckily for Tiana and me, Banks has a generator, so we can use everything in the camper.

Granted, water is limited, so we have to go back up to the ranch house to shower and whatnot at night. But it's nice to say "Hi" to them at least once a day. But essentially, we've holed ourselves up out here and have been having a small honeymoon of sorts.

One day I'm going to take her on a real honeymoon. Wherever the fuck she wants, I don't care. She can plan it to her heart's content for as long as she wants. I just want to treat her to all the things she wants.

And considering we've basically been on a... 'baby-making-cation' here, Tiana brought something else for me to try. Aside from our skates–because she really wants to go out and skate on our lake–it's another gift she got me we haven't had the chance to use.

I digress. Anyway...

I stare down at this new contraption, almost in fear, along with my hard dick that's in my hand.

With me propped up on my knees on the camper bed, I glance down at Tiana, who sits back on her heels in front of me on the bed, completely naked. But I look between her, my cock, and the cock ring she got me.

"I don't know if this thing will fit," I say as I move it around in my hand.

"I mean, it's silicone. It's made to stretch," she says with a shrug.

"Yeah, no, I get that part. But..." I say as I look over it.

I am... *thick*. Very thick. And uh... I do not think this thing will stretch around it and not absolutely choke my cock.

"Do you need help?" she asks.

I look at the toy and my dick again, trying to work out the best way to do this.

It has a bunny on the top of it that vibrates, which would be nice to use because I could just fuck her and have my hands free to play with her tits or something... But I would be a liar to say I wasn't scared of this thing.

The longer I look at it, the more my best course of action forms in my head.

"Alright, so... stretch it open as much as you can, and I'll... put my dick in it," I mumble.

"We don't have to do it if you don't want to," she responds.

"No, no. It's not that," I say as I hand her the cock ring. "I'm scared it's gonna choke my hog, but I'll be fine. I'm a tough guy," I tell her as I give her a grin.

She rolls her eyes with a small smirk as she stretches the main ring as much as she can. Slowly... oh, so very slowly, I position my cock in it and shift my hips forward, sliding through it.

So far, it's going... fine? My cock is moving through it fine, but as she gets lower, she runs out of stretch.

It also has a separate ring for my balls. Which I know those won't fit through that damn thing. But I reckon Tiana is going to try anyway.

When she gets it to the base, she lets it compress carefully around me.

"Okay... okay this is f- YOW!" I squeal as it catches on one of my hairs. "FUCK," I grit as I try to fix the ring from waxing my bush.

She wants me to shave my mustache but doesn't want me to get rid of my bush because she thinks completely shaved down looks weird. That's fair. I don't really mind.

However, right now, I very much *do* mind because holy *fuck* this shit hurts. Even worse, this thing is squeezing the life out of my dick.

"Ti..." I grit as my face twists in pain.

She looks up at me with an apologetic grimace as her eyes volley between my face and my dick.

"Hurts... very tight... help," is all I'm able to say from the pain.

Tiana almost always has her nails done, so her trying to get her fingers under the ring is... even worse.

I toss my head back, taking a deep breath through the pain.

"Alright, stop, stop, stop. That's not gonna work," I groan before I look back down.

Her hands spring back, holding them up in surrender as she looks between me and the ring.

I, however, have my eyes on my dick, damn near panicking as I try to figure out the easiest way to get this damn thing off.

"I could call Charlotte and ask for some sci-"

"NOPE. NO SHARP THINGS NEAR MY WIENER PLEASE," I blurt.

"Right, okay. No cuts. Got it," she says.

I look over it again, groaning as I feel my dick get so hard it only adds to the pain of it all. Granted, I think that's the point, but, fuck *me*, it is *literally* choking my hog.

"Grab the bottom ring and pull down. I'm going to get my fingers in the space between it, and then... I don't fucking know, we'll workshop it when we get there," I grit.

She nods slowly, coming to grab the ball ring and slowly stretch it down. I hold my cock in place, growling as I watch a smallllll area of space open up enough for me to get my finger in.

Quickly, I slip my finger into the space. "Hold my dick."

She wraps her hands around me, holding it in place as I use both of my hands to slip fingers into the space and slowly work it off of me.

Eventually, I get to an area where it's not as thick and rip the damn thing off. It flies across the room, knocking into one of the mirrored closet doors with a bang.

"FUCK," I groan as I press my hands over my dick and balls, falling over to curl into fetal position. I groan in pain, and soon, a soft hand rubs over my shoulder.

"Are you okay?" she asks softly.

"Tiana, baby. I literally love you so much. You're the light of my universe... but I would very much like to karate chop you in the throat right now," I groan.

"That's fair. Do you think we should have used lube?" she asks.

My face contorts as I look up at her. Almost like that scene in Thor: Ragnarok. A grimace? I don't know; there's a meme of it somewhere. Either way, I know my face has turned into that as I look up at her.

"Is..." I groan as the pain keeps riding through me. "Why didn't you... mention that before this?"

"I... forgot," she says with another apologetic grimace.

"Mmmm... mhm... baby, we can't have sex now," I groan as my head folds back into my body.

"That's okay. I understand," she says.

I groan as the pain keeps going, my stomach twisting with nausea. "Love you," I murmur.

"Sorry," she whispers softly.

"Nope... all good... allllll good," I say.

After a bit of time trying to recuperate from having my wiener pinched, I finally feel good enough to try out these new skates with Tiana. Once I got completely soft, most of the pain went away and we could move on to the real reason we came out here.

As I've tried to push the nausea and pain away, Tiana has been down in the living room area of the fifth wheel, getting herself dressed. So, when I come down the stairs to see her, she smiles at me.

"Your bits better?" she asks with a nervous smile.

"Yes, they're better. It's not your fault, babe, I promise," I say with a soft sigh as I come up to sit beside her on the couch. I tug her head toward me with a grip on the back and bring it to my lips to press a kiss to her forehead. Focusing on her skates, I make sure her laces are looking good enough before I reach for my box and open it.

I swear it sings when I lift the lid, because I'm still in shock that she bought these for me. They're some of the best skates on the market right now. There is a chance that Banks fucked with her and told her that these were the best to make her spend more money. But she also had them customized. Which, in and of itself, is more money that she needed to spend.

I decided I was going to wear my hoodie and jersey combo with some jeans, and because I knew we were coming out here to skate, I definitely brought a stick and my mitts.

I may have also had to make a pit stop on the way out here for pucks because I don't really have any in the apartment.

Tiana presses her foot out, lacing up her skates and making sure they're tight.

I'm so well-attuned to putting on my skates I could put them on blindfolded, so as I put my skates on, I keep watching to make sure she's not over tightening her laces.

These things feel nice as hell, and I notice it as I finish putting them both on and stand on the blade guard.

There's no fucking way I'm taking these to the arena. I'll destroy these in a few games.

Eventually, Tiana gets her skates tied, and on wobbly ankles, she stands.

I let out a soft chuckle as I offer her a hand to keep her steady, and she gives me a nervous smile as she looks up at me.

"I really wanna be able to do this with you more," she says softly.

"You really don't have to sugar. I appreciate you trying to learn, but if it's something you aren't interested in, I understand," I respond.

"Shut up, I'm going to learn," she says with a playful huff.

She tries to step ahead of me, but I stop her, getting in

front so I can get down the camper steps first. I'm also very glad she hasn't taken her guards off yet, because she'd be toast on this floor.

When we get to the door, I open it, and grab my stick and mitts against the wall to throw them to the ground outside. Then, I reach down and grab the stack of pucks and stuff them in my hoodie pocket.

I take a few steps down the small stairs to the grass before I come around the side and offer her my hand.

She has a death grip on my hand as she grabs it, and very, *very* carefully, she takes wobbly steps down the camper stairs until she's on the grass.

As I wait for her, there are shouts and noises of blades going behind the camper.

That is another reason we're out here.

The loggers are taking down some trees, and Tiana wanted to be here to see them.

She plants her feet hard in the grass, and I watch her for a long moment, watching her get her bearings.

"You all good?" I ask.

She seems zoned out on the ground as I drag my arm away to see if she can handle herself. She stands there like a newborn giraffe for a bit, and I lean over to grab my stick and mitts.

"Okay, stay here. I'm going to check the lake real quick. But if you can move before then, do that," I say as I clasp my stick under my armpit and shove my mitts on.

She looks up at me with a furrow on her brow and a gape to her jaw. "Seriously?" she scoffs.

"Alright, Mrs. Hayze. Do you want to walk all the way over to the damn lake to find it unskateable and then have to wobble all the way back over here?" I ask as I turn to her.

She pouts as she glances away. "No," she murmurs.

"Didn't think so. Stay here," I tell her.

I take a few test steps to see how the ground feels, but it feels fine to me, so I go up on the toe of my blade and high-knee my way over to the water.

As I get to the higher grasses on the edge, I reach my stick out to slap at the ice. My brow furrows with my assessment, trying to see deeper into the water. Sounds solid enough.

I lean down to take off my blade guards and stuff them in my jean pockets before jumping from the grass onto the ice, seeing how it feels. I even take a few test jumps on it.

Feels solid.

This lake isn't very deep, and the temperature has dropped well below freezing for it to freeze entirely.

I take a few long strides across the lake and back again before skidding to a stop and looking toward the treeline. There are logging trucks parked out to the east of our camper, and men have been moving back and forth from them all morning. I see a group of men in the forest, yelling and shouting at each other as some chainsaws whir and buzz deeper in the woods.

I think Banks said something about them starting in deeper and opening it up more towards the lake. So they probably won't be down this way until we end up leaving here.

Either way, Tiana said something about wanting to take a tree from the ones they cut down. I reckon that's probably a good idea. I brought my truck out here with us just for that.

I look back over at Tiana, who is nice and cozy in her big hoodie, and goddamnit, she looks so cute.

I whistle to get her attention, and she looks up at me in confusion.

"Ice is good!" I tell her before I dump the pucks from my hoodie pocket and onto the ice.

As they clatter onto the ice, I hit one back and forth as I wait for her.

"Gunnar! I need hellllp!" she groans as she tries to come over to me.

"Gotta work up those ankles, sugar! Better get on them toes!" I call out to her as I keep messing with the puck.

Eventually, Tiana makes it over to me, and I take the moment to put down my stick and mitts so that I can help her over the taller grasses beside the lake.

She makes small squeaks and chirrups as she grips tight on my hands to pull the blade guards off her skates before she steps over the grass, onto the ice. She holds them tight in one hand, and I take them for her to shove with mine so she can use both of her hands.

My brow furrows as I look at her with a tilt of my head, because I don't think I've ever heard her make those kinds of noises before.

"What was that?" I ask.

She looks up at me with wide-eyes, her hands tightening on me, as if I've caught her in the act of... something, I don't even know.

"What was what?" she asks.

"Those noises. Why'd you make those?"

A pink tint rises on her cheeks as she steadies herself on the ice. "They're just noises I make. I like the way they feel in my throat," she says.

My head tilts more, looking curiously at her. "How they feel in your throat?"

"Sometimes sounds feel nice when I make them, and they help... make my brain not so loud," she says.

"Interesting," I murmur in thought with a smile.

My peculiar little sugar.

She nods sheepishly before she looks down at her feet.

Her feet slide back and forth on the ice, as if trying to see how it feels. All the while, still holding onto my hands before she looks up at me with a grin.

"This feels a lot better when I'm not in a pencil skirt and in your massive skates," she says as she slowly gets the hang of the ice under her skates.

"And you know what? I reckon that's probably a fair assessment," I respond with a grin.

I hold on to her hands, letting her move her feet under her, and she keeps her eyes down on her skates, trying to understand the movement.

"How does it feel?" I ask.

She looks up at me with a smile, nervous, but also excited in a way.

"Much better," she says with a small breath of relief.

"Do you think you'd be able to do it on your own?" I ask.

"I... don't know," she murmurs.

I slowly loosen my grip on her hands, letting her try to figure it out on her own, and slowly, she loosens her grip on me, trying to push each of her feet out to propel her forward, until I'm able to let go of her.

"See! Look at you go!" I say as I clap.

She looks up at me with a nervous smirk and continues pushing both of her feet to glide toward me, her arms swinging back and forth to get a bit more speed under her. Soon, she gets a little more adventurous and starts moving in another direction around the exterior of the small pond, and I spin in my spot to watch her.

I feel the warmth of my grin as I see her try this thing for me. It's warm enough to ward off the cold.

For her to want to try this for me after never wanting to skate before, I think, is one of the greatest gifts she could have given me. Especially since she had never tried it and was so closely integrated into the hockey world.

There is not much that I really enjoy other than hockey... and sex.

I'm a pretty simple guy. So, this is everything and more to me.

And for the rest of that afternoon, Tiana and I skate on the lake, where I weave the puck in and out of her legs, and by the end, her cheeks are rosy, pink and she has the biggest smile on her face.

CHAPTER THIRTY-SIX

TIANA

fter the week we spent at the fifth wheel, I was reallll ready to go home.

Charlotte and Adrian had also left, and I really just wanted to be back in my bed.

Especially since toward the end, when the loggers had brought some trees out by the lake, there was a Douglas fir they had thrown right on the outskirts, and I took the chance to ask the loggers for it.

They wanted to know what we wanted to do with the wood anyway, and I told them to keep it for now, until we figure out our house.

But I wanted *that* tree.

And after a pit stop on the way home to grab a stand for the tree, and a few calls to some hockey players, we were able to get the tree into the house and into the tree stand.

Now, my entire apartment has a nostalgic scent of fresh Christmas spirit. Along with stray pine needles everywhere.

It took some yelling at a bunch of massive men, but as I stand back looking at this damn near picture perfect tree, I realize it was all worth it. It's full, tall and in amazing condition, especially since the loggers had somewhat thrown it around.

Most of all, it's *beautiful*.

As I stand back admiring the thing, large, muscular arms wrap around the top of my shoulders, before lips press against my cheek.

Though something is missing.

As I turn to look at Gunnar, I realize he's shaved his mustache.

"You shaved it?" I ask a tad sadder than I should have.

He looks at me in confusion. "Babe, for a month and a half you've asked me to."

"Well, yeah, but I got used to it! You didn't warn me," I grumble.

He groans before he steps back and slaps me on the ass. I make a small yelp as I turn around to glare at him. But he's already walking away.

"Naughty thing, sugar!" he calls as he moves to one of the back rooms.

I told him on our way back to the house that the ornaments I bought were in a room, and now that we've finally gotten the tree up and positioned, I imagine he's going to grab the things to make it pretty.

I move to the tree, going through some branches and fluffing it up, when I hear shopping bags behind me.

With a titter of glee, I turn around to see Gunnar with all the bags. My hands squeeze and flex together at the idea that Gunnar and I get to have our very first Christmas together. I look around for my phone, finding it on the couch so I can connect it to the sound bar attached to my TV.

Soon, the room fills with the sound of old Christmas music, and I grin as I look toward Gunnar, who starts setting down the bags on the coffee table and floor.

A warm smile paints his face as I walk up to him, throw my arms around his neck and smile up at him.

"Even though everyone else is gone for the holidays, I'm really glad that I get to spend every second with you," he whispers.

I smile, nipping down on my lip. "I wouldn't ask for anything else," I respond.

He leans down, kissing me softly as he runs his hands up and down the small of my back.

I return it, with my hands running through the long bit of hair at the bottom of his flow before I pull away.

"You're an absolute fuckin' beauty," I whisper.

"God, I know you are, sugar," he says with a heated grin.

I giggle before pressing one last kiss to his lips and pulling away to go through the bags of ornaments.

Kneeling down, I pull out boxes of the bright and shiny baubles, looking over them with excitement.

"Went a little crazy on the ornaments, did we?" he asks as he pulls some more boxes of ornaments out of the shopping bags on the coffee table.

"I wanted us to have something to decorate together!" I say as I pull some rolls of silver ribbon out.

"I know, and I really love that you want to," he says as he opens the boxes to pull the ornaments out.

Since we don't have any kids or rambunctious animals right now, I splurged on really delicate ornaments.

One by one, he places some ornaments up as I move some boxes onto the coffee table.

Once I get all the boxes out, I turn around, looking at what he's done so far. And... God, I love him. But I have to resist the urge to scream, because there is a very specific vision I have in mind for these ornaments... and unfortunately, Gunnar is not...

"Gunnar... love," I grit softly through a nervous grin.

He pauses with the next ornament he was going to hang to tilt his head at me with a questioning smile.

"I need you to hand me the ornaments, because I love you... so much. I love you," I breathe as I come up to him, wrapping my hands around his cheeks, pulling his gaze to mine.

"But?" he asks as his grin widens.

"But if I have to watch you put these ornaments on outside of the preconceived vision I have carefully crafted in my psyche, I may have a mental breakdown," I say sweetly.

"Roger that, Big Mama," he says with a smile and small nod.

"I love you," I whisper again.

"I know, baby. I love you too," he says as he leans down and kisses me again.

He hands me the ornament, and I take a deep breath.

There was a small part of me that was afraid of being... controlling in that way. Because in the grand scheme of things, it's so small. A normal person would brush it away; it's just ornaments.

But I have spent a lot of time imagining what this tree would look like... and maybe in the past, I wouldn't have cared about saying it. I was going to do the thing I wanted to do anyway.

The thing is... Gunnar has helped me find my voice. And while I know the impact of my voice, and the worth in me and my words, I just get scared to use it with him because I don't want to lose him.

After the last talk we had though, there is confidence I'm gaining in being able to use my voice with him, and having the security that I won't lose him over it.

There is happiness in that. Freedom, even. Because I find myself to be steadfast in my boundaries and the way I do things, they've just had to retreat some because I've realized my past and what it could mean for my future.

The fact is, I want to have a future with Gunnar, and if my past was any indication of how I am and the reasons those men left, I had to realize that those things could push him away. And I didn't want that. I felt myself dealing with insecurities I didn't know were insecurities until I realized I wanted that future with him.

But that's not at all what it means for my future with Gunnar...

Gunnar is *here*. He loves me, how I am, when everyone else didn't.

I smile at him, holding on tighter to the security and safety I have with him, even in this small moment, and soon he hands me another ornament.

"Okay, but what are some other things you guys did?" I ask as I hang up the stockings on the electric fireplace mantel.

Of course, I had to go with some of the heavy stag-looking stocking holders.

One thing about Christmas is the number of stag decorations that just seem to exist and come out of the woodwork. I had to buy more of it to go with the decor because... I knew it would have to be incorporated into the aesthetic somehow.

I got a white corded sweater-like stocking for myself, while for Gunnar... it was pretty easy to know what he wanted.

Growing up in a family that is heavily incorporated into a large, professional hockey team, you sort of know the amount of merchandise that just fucking... exists.

So, Gunnar got a Seattle Stags stocking.

Shocking.

"Yeah, so. My family used to do this thing where my parents would hide a pickle in the tree, and whoever found it first would get a special gift," he says as he cleans up some of the mess left behind from the ornaments, along with the stray pine needles.

My brow furrows as I look over at him with a grimace.

"A pickle?" I ask, damn-near in disgust.

I don't like pickles. And I *especially* dislike pickles on my Christmas tree.

"No, no, okay, so. It's actually an ornament. They just hide it in the tree. We always had a lot of fun doing it," he says with a reminiscent smile.

I smile with him, relaxing a bit because there was no fucking way I was going to be putting a pickle in my tree.

"Okay, that sounds like something we could do," I say with a smile.

Soon, exhaustion seems to grip me.

But it is bone-deep exhaustion. The holidays are usually tiring, but I am much more worn out now.

I crash onto the couch with a big breath of relief as I look over at the tree.

It looks exactly how I pictured it in my head. With the pretty white lights, the blue, and silver ornaments. The silver ribbon I've weaved around the top and sides goes perfectly with the rest of the winter-inspired aesthetic I've tried to achieve.

It's everything I could have dreamed of.

After a few minutes, Gunnar comes to sit next to me, offering me a mug. I look inside it to find hot chocolate with an insane amount of tiny marshmallows in it, and I squeal with glee as I take it from him.

He has one for himself too, and soon, his arm comes

around my shoulder to pull me close as he takes a loud slurp of his hot chocolate.

I look up at him with a playful smirk before he licks his lips clean and leans over, pressing a kiss to my forehead.

I take a long sip of my hot chocolate, letting the old-timey Christmas music play before I lean my head against him, admiring the tree.

"It turned out beautifully," I say softly before taking another sip.

"It sure did," he says. It's so soft, so sweet, and I look up at him to notice he's not looking at the tree.

His eyes lower, and he admires me in a way that is so utterly Gunnar.

"You're so good to me, Gunnar Hayze," I whisper as I bring a hand up to his jaw, rubbing a thumb over his cheek before I kiss him softly.

He sighs contentedly into our kiss. Reaching forward, I hear a small *tink* against the coffee table before the weight of his hand settles on my stomach and he tilts his head, deepening it.

"You know what I'm going to say," he whispers when he pulls away. The hand around my shoulder wraps tighter around me, bringing me closer to rub a thumb over my cheek.

I smile, my grin widening as I nip my lip.

"You always told me you would be," I whisper.

"Bingo, Mrs. Hayze," he says.

CHAPTER THIRTY-SEVEN

TIANA

The past week and some change has been so nice, relaxing. Gunnar and I have just been enjoying time with each other. No one has needed us, no work, no commitments, just time with my husband.

Sometimes, Gunnar and I will go out into Seattle, to some of the smaller bookshops in the area. We even went to IKEA a few times so I could scope out some of the stuff I want to get for our house. I may have also bought a bookshelf or two for Gunnar to put together. Which has only resulted in Gunnar treating me to even more books.

But we don't spend much time out during the day, because after only so long, I am exhausted. And not just worn out, I am *dead*-tired.

Tired is my default. I'm just always sleepy. But this is different. Usually if I lay down for a nap, it's because I'm trying to take a nap. Lately, if I sit on the couch for more than a few minutes, I've passed out entirely, and I'll sleep for hours.

Aside from that... I feel like I can barely *think*.

Even now as I try to look for the gingerbread house kits I bought, I can't fucking remember where I put them!

I could have sworn I put them in the spare bedroom, where I had put the other Christmas decorations.

But I can't fucking find them! I don't even understand, and I feel as if I've torn the apartment apart looking for them.

After a long and frustrating search, I come out of the spare bedroom, after I'd torn it apart, just to find Gunnar at the kitchen island with the two gingerbread house kits.

My brow furrows wildly as I look at him.

"Where the fuck did you find those?! I've been looking everywhere for them," I groan as I come to sit beside him at the island.

"They were in the pantry. You told me yesterday that you had put them in the pantry and not to forget," he says through his chain as he opens the box for his gingerbread house.

As I settle into my chair, I look over my box for a long moment, trying to remember the instance...

But it doesn't ring the slightest bell.

"I did?" I ask softly.

"Yep. You had moved them from the bedroom last week and put them in the pantry. And then yesterday you told me we were doing the gingerbread houses today and not to forget that they were in the pantry," he says as he pulls all his little things out.

My forehead creases as I look down at the counter, trying with all my might to fucking remember any of that.

"I guess I forgot," I murmur softly as I open my gingerbread house.

"So, here's the thing. We used to have gingerbread house building competitions growing up, and I won every year, so you have some intense competition," he says with a grin through his grit chain in his teeth as he kneads his icing pouch with his hands.

I push the memory issue away with a smile and a shake of my head. "It's not a competition. We're just going a cute little couple thing," I say as I shove into his shoulder with my own.

"Well, mine is still going to be better," he says with a grin before pressing his chain into his mouth like a horse's bit and sticking his tongue out at me.

I shake my head again as I unwrap my gingerbread. Only to find it smells... weird...?

"Does this smell strange to you?" I ask Gunnar as I hold up my gingerbread pieces to him.

His brow furrows, and he looks at me before he leans in to sniff it.

"Smells like gingerbread to me," he says with a shrug.

I sniff it again, and I can't help but feel like it smells extremely strong. Like it's been made entirely out of ginger instead of cinnamon or nutmeg.

Placing the gingerbread pieces down, I pick up my icing pouch, massaging it to warm it up as I look over all the pieces.

I think about how I want to make my house look. Charlotte and I used to always make gingerbread houses growing up, so it's one of my favorite Christmas activities, aside from decorating and baking cookies. I've always loved that part too.

Glancing over at Gunnar, I see his tongue mess and slide against his chain as he does a preliminary build of his gingerbread house. Then, he constructs the walls, squeezing the icing onto the little ridges before he tips it over and holds the pieces in place for it to harden before he continues.

He seems to be extremely focused, and I can't help but think how funny it is that this massive man has such a passion for building gingerbread houses.

"What was the best gift you received growing up?" I ask as I glue some of my gingerbread walls together.

Gunnar concentrates on his piping for his side walls, his

head tilting as he looks at it from all angles. But he still answers, "My chain."

My brow furrows as I look at him. "Your chain?"

"Yeah. My grandpa got it for me. It's always been a good-luck charm of sorts for me. And after he passed, well... it was just another way for me to remember where I came from. A kid danglin' on random, snow-weighted lakes to playing in the pros for my favorite team," he says as he looks over at me with a small smile.

The answer seems to come easily to him. As if it hadn't even been a second thought.

"I really would get books, or planners, because that's all I ever asked for," I murmur softly.

But his answer lingers with me.

"But... not a new stick? Top of the line skates? Nothing like that?" I ask as I let go of the walls I was holding to pipe a new line of icing for the next wall.

"Nope. Just my chain. Pa had one similar. I always thought it looked cool. And he wore it all the time. Eventually, he got me my own. And I've had the same one ever since," he says as he smiles over at me.

A small smile rises on my face.

For someone so... difficult or complex as far as my needs are concerned, it's interesting how I fell in love with someone that enjoys the small, simple things in life.

He loves hockey; he loves family, and he loves his dog. And that's really all he ever needs.

It's sweet. It's admirable. Especially with as much emphasis the world has on material things and their reliance for happiness.

He doesn't play professional hockey because he wants to be big and famous. He just wants to play the game he loves with a bigger challenge.

He doesn't idolize the team he plays for because they're professional. He loves them because his grandpa loved them.

And he loves his grandpa because, in his eyes, his grandpa gave him everything he could have ever wanted.

"You're pretty easy to please, aren't you?" I ask softly as I let go of the second wall after the icing dries.

"Yup. Don't need much. Hockey, my dog, and you," he says with a smile. Though his focus is still intently homed in on his building.

My smile widens at that.

"Peculiar thing you are, Gunnar Hayze," I say playfully.

"You'd know, wouldn't you, Tiana Hayze?" he shoots back with a sly glance and a grin.

Gunnar and I have been building these houses for a while. At least the houses were built a bit ago, and we've just been decorating them.

Though, something is niggling in my brain. When I've tried the icing from time to time in the middle of this process, it tastes... *horrible*.

I've looked at the expiration date several times over, and it's not even close to expiring.

My mind works repeatedly, trying to understand why everything has felt so strange.

When I get up to go pee, the thought lingers in the back of my head.

I grab my phone, looking up some things I've felt not just today but the past few days.

My boobs have been sore, and I have been overly

exhausted. Noticeably so. The gingerbread house smell and taste... the memory loss.

Most of the things I look up on my phone all say the same thing...

Pregnant... pregnant... *pregnant.*

I think back to the pregnancy tests that Charlotte and I had bought one day on our shopping excursion.

"This is dumb. There's no way I'm pregnant," I murmur to myself as I crouch to grab the tests from under the sink.

I grab the box hesitantly because if I am...

I shake my head, rising to a stand and pulling one test out, unwrapping the foil wrapper.

I look down at the test with a deep breath, because all at once, the nerves rise in me.

I've never taken a pregnancy test before. All the other times I was hoping not to get my period, it hit. I didn't need to take any.

But now, there's just something off about how I feel.

Maybe even a small voice in my head telling me not to brush it off.

Soon, I sit on the toilet, uncapping the test before doing my business.

I cap it, placing it upside down on the counter and then washing my hands.

All the while, I pace back and forth, nibbling at my fingers as the thoughts run through my head.

How do I tell Gunnar? Holy fuck, I'll be pregnant. I'll have a fucking baby in me.

Jesus Christ. On Christmas?!

The man surely is good at keeping his damn promises, if that is the case.

The longer I pace, the more hesitant I get to look at it. My heart pounds in my chest, and part of me feels like I can't breathe, until I decide I can't wait any longer, and look at it.

Taking it into my hands, I flip it, and it feels as if the world goes black around me.

"Holy... fuck," I breathe.

CHAPTER THIRTY-EIGHT
CHRISTMAS

Christmas Eve

Tiana

It's been three days since I took that test... and my nerves have been on a rampant war path. All the symptoms I've been feeling make sense, and I try to stay on alert to notice anything else that's been different. There's some nausea here and there. Even as Gunnar and I mix this cookie dough.

It's been so hard to keep it from Gunnar. Even though I just spent the last two months stressing out over a perfect Christmas gift... I'm finally able to give him literally the only gift he really asked for.

I have to keep my calm as I continue making this dough.

Gunnar is a sugar cookie guy, shockingly enough. And I like chocolate chip, and he was very adamant about making sure that Santa had cookies for tonight. Which is admirable as it is funny.

But I suppose if we are going to have kids, we're going to have to get used to the idea sooner rather than later.

"Can I decorate them when they're done?" Gunnar asks through his chain as he turns his head to look at me and continues rolling out the sugar cookie dough.

A warm smile paints my cheeks because there is so much about this big man that continues not only to surprise me, but brings me joy I've never experienced before.

He's a silly goon. Dumb at times and simple. But he's also complex, respectful, self-reflective...

There are so many sides to him, and depending on what light shines on him that day, shows me which side I get to see.

That's something I appreciate about him, because I feel like everyone else gets different sides of him.

But I'm the only one that gets *every* side. I get to see him for all that he is.

His dominant, rough side. His playful, goofy side. His sweet and compassionate side.

I even get the smaller, sensitive pieces other people don't get to see.

And that is so fulfilling, because it means he feels as safe to be himself with me, just as much as I can be with him.

All I've really ever wanted to do was reciprocate the love he gives me.

The men in the past were one-note. They had little personality. Or if they did, it was to put on a mask and pretend to be things they weren't.

For Gunnar... he just *is*. He's himself. And he's told me that's why he loves me, but I can see now how that is a wonderful thing to love.

With the knowledge I have, and the future we have together, I can't help but imagine the other sides of him I'll get to see. The caring, generous father. The attentive and loving husband...

I reach for the chocolate chips on the counter, pouring them into the dough and mixing as I glance over to see him pressing the cookie cutter into the cookie dough.

He chose a reindeer cutter. Because... of course he would.

When he told me we were making cookies, we had to go get some of the stuff to make them, and he only wanted the reindeer cutter.

Slowly, he makes all the little presses into the dough before it's filled, and he removes the excess. Then, very carefully, he places the cut-out cookies on a pan before he moves on to cutting more cookies.

I continue making my dough, and then eventually roll it into balls.

In between waiting for the cookies to bake and decorating them, we go back and forth between some of our favorite Christmas movies. And for the rest of Christmas Eve, that's exactly what we do. Granted, we have some extra... "sessions." Mostly because there is an excitement I have to hide that I think can only be masked with sex.

And when the dark creeps in, with the night coming to a close, and our final movie finishing, Gunnar looks at me with a smile. He leans his head against mine as he rubs my opposite shoulder softly.

"Ready for bed, sugar? Santa is gonna be here soon," he says.

I smile up at him because I am actually fucking exhausted. Between sex and movies, I think I slept through most of the movies.

"I'm going to clean up some before I get to bed," I say softly.

"Okay, I'm gonna go shower," he says.

I nod, and he kisses me softly on the lips. When he gets up, he double-checks his plate of cookies and milk he left out for Santa before scurrying off to the bedroom.

I sit on the couch for just a few moments, waiting for the sound of the shower before I get up and run toward one of the back rooms.

When he was sleeping, I had to scour my damn apartment to find where I had hidden that fucking onesie, because of course I'd forgotten where the fuck it was.

I even had to call Charlotte at some point and ask her where it was. I had to tell her, mostly because it's hard to get anything past Charlotte.

But luckily, she knew where it was, and I could find it.

So carefully, ever so carefully, I take the test, wrapping it in the onesie I bought with Gunnar before slipping it into his stocking.

As I walk toward the bedroom, I spot the plate of cookies.

Looking around with a small smile, I walk over to them and take a bite from one of his reindeer cookies before drinking at least half of the milk.

And from there, I move to the bedroom to get into the shower with him.

Christmas Day
Gunnar

It's Christmas morning, and I get to wake up with my arms wrapped around my wife.

I've decided this may be the best gift I've ever received.

I want to let her sleep, but I *reallllly* want to go out to the living room and see the tree.

Even if I know there won't be gifts, because we've already

gotten our gift giving out of the way, I don't care. There's nothing like Christmas morning.

Burying my face in her neck, I kiss her skin softly, inhaling her beachy scent before I nudge her. Though it's with my cock because it's already hard, I might as well use it.

Tiana groans softly, pulling away from me to bury her face in the pillow as she turns over onto her stomach.

That usually gives me the go ahead and I climb on top of her.

Tiana and I usually sleep naked, so when I get behind her, her back arches, and I take a handful of her ass, spreading her apart far enough to slip myself into her pussy. Looking down, I see the way she stretches around me, and I hear the way she moans into her pillow.

But, fuck me, not only is she wet, she's insanely warm.

She usually is, but this almost feels like she's got a furnace in her.

And somehow... tighter, plumper? I don't even know how that's possible, but I lean down, grinding into her as I kiss her cheek.

Fuck me, I shouldn't have done this. She feels incredible.

My hips almost move of their own accord. "Sugar, if you don't get up now, I won't be able to stop," I pant into her neck.

I let out a deep groan as I bottom out, and she lets out a gasp.

"I'll finish you off later, but we have matters to attend to, baby," I say with a grin.

"Gunnar," she groans as she shifts and rocks back against me, almost asking for more.

But I know the little she-devil's tricks. She just doesn't wanna get up yet. That would usually work on me if it weren't Christmas morning.

I pull out, caging in her legs with mine before I send a swat over her ass.

"Let's goooooooo," I say with a chuckle.

She glares at me over her shoulder with narrowed eyes, and I jump off the bed to grab my sweatpants and tug them on.

I look around the room for her robe, and when I find it, I toss it at her.

"LET'S MOOOOOOVE, SUGAR," I say again as I move back to the bed and jump up and down on it. Though on my knees. I imagine if I stood on this thing and jumped I'd fucking destroy it.

"Okay, okay!" she groans playfully as her hand deftly searches for the robe on the bed.

When she feels the fabric, she sits up in bed, yawning and stretching wide before she tugs it over her shoulders.

As she sits up, I notice how fucking gorgeous her tits look, and while it causes my dick to jump, I have to stay focused.

She steps out of bed, wrapping the robe tighter around her before she ties the sash and moves to the bathroom to remove her bonnet and brush her teeth. I brush my teeth with her before we move out to the living room.

And while I expected nothing to happen to my cookies, I realize there is a bite taken out of one deer.

My brow furrows, and I look back at Tiana with a small grin.

"It looks like Santa came this year," I say slyly.

Her smile warms, and she nods. "He surely did," she says softly.

I look toward the living room, where the sun is bright through the windows, with not a cloud in the sky. The sun beams beautifully into the space, where it hits the high points of the silver and blue ornaments Tiana chose.

It gives it the most ethereal look; though, the longer I gaze around the room, I notice there is something in my stocking.

I don't remember it being there before we went to bed.

"Wait," Tiana says as she hurries to the couch. "Grab it,

and then come sit with me," she says as she pats the spot next to her. But there is excitement in her eyes.

I can't imagine what else she may have gotten me, but I move to the stocking and grab the roll of what appears to be fabric and come sit with her.

She smiles at me, biting down on her lip as she watches me. I smile back, wrapping a hand around her jaw before I lean in to kiss her.

"Merry Christmas, baby," I whisper.

"Merry Christmas, Mr. Hayze," she says in response. "Now open it!" she says excitedly as she flaps her hands at me.

"Okay, okay!" I say with a laugh.

I hold the fabric up, and it unrolls, though something falls out of it. A blur of white, yet my eyes stay on the fabric.

It's the Seattle Stags jersey onesie we bought weeks ago.

My head tilts and I place the onesie down to smile at her, before I catch sight of the thing that fell out.

I feel my brow furrow and my forehead crease as I pick it up...

Turning it over, my eyes scan over the thing. And over... and over... *and over.*

Before I look up to Tiana, who has happy, bright tears in her eyes and the biggest smile.

I look back down at the stick before looking back up at her.

"Really?" I whisper in disbelief.

She nods excitedly; the few escaped tears rolling down her cheeks.

Holy shit.

I'm going to be a fucking dad.

I'LL SEE YOU LATER

What had originally started as an experiment, became a healing and learning journey. And while this journey is not over, it *is* paused.

After this book, Checked and With Child was supposed to come out.

But at the time of writing this, I am struggling mentally. I love Tiana and Gunnar. I love their story and their life, but I am not a hockey romance author.

I've always said, "I'm a Tiana and Gunnar author." On top of that, I have been exclusively working on these books for the past four to six months. I don't even know anymore, I've lost count. If you know me and how I work, I am consistently working on several books and genres at once because that is just how my brain works.

I had barred myself from one of my favorite projects and was looking at it through a glass wall. I itched and gnawed at the wall, trying to just get small tastes of it here and there, because I knew if I had some of the work on Tantalia and the fantasy worlds I had built in the mix, Gunnar and Tiana's story would never get told.

I had never just worked on one couple for this long, on such a short leash that I had given myself.

With contemporary and romances like these, I have to pull back on my language immensely. My roots are in poetry. I am more satisfied with cadences like that of Edgar Allen Poe, and write easier when more emotionally charged prose is used.

I can't do that with these two without sacrificing structural character integrity, so not only was I not able to touch something I loved very much, I was barred from alot of the writing I thrive in.

In essence, I was choking myself for the sake of a schedule I had made.

It was a torture chamber of my own design.

This is not me saying I hate this couple, or this story at all. They're fun and a good palette cleanser, but I've realized I have to take these contemporary books in small doses. I had burnt myself out immensely working on just one story, and not dabbling in my other works. I cycle through several books at a time, because my mind changes constantly, and being able to work on multiple books helps my brain stay flexible and fresh.

I haven't been able to do that since June/July, and that was torture for me.

That being said, I can't work on Checked and With Child right now. The thoughts, the scenes, none of it is flowing the way I need it to, and if I can't write in a flow state, then there's no point. I don't want to give you something just because I have to. I want to give you something good, that I feel good about.

And right now, I do not feel good about it.

So, I will be taking my Gunnar and Tiana hiatus early. The next book I'll be moving to, is something called, "His Heart to Steal."

It's a dark romance ft. an MMC that's giving Ghost from Call of Duty, who is hired to kill a Female version of Robin Hood in Las Vegas.

From there, I'm hopping into my fantasy worlds.

I'm sorry to anyone I may have disappointed, and I'm sorry that my mind changes so much. But I'm trying to learn my work flow a bit better, and unfortunately, there were lessons learned here.

With that being said, for Gunnar and Tiana, we must say "See you later" for now. Because it's not goodbye, we will come back to them one day.

But it is see you later.

Thank you guys always for the love and support and I appreciate you guys being here 💀

For my dark romance girls, I'll see you in Las Vegas.

For my fantasy babes, I'll see you in Tantalia.

Your Favorite Four Raccoons in a Trench Coat;

Over and out,

Aurora Steinhart

WHAT'S NEXT
FOR AURORA?
UPCOMING PROJECTS

Early 2026; ***"His Heart to Steal"***; *a dark romance where the MMC is inspired by Ghost from COD and is hired to kill a Female Robin Hood in the city of Las Vegas.*

Spring 2026: **Taken by Fate;** *the second installment in "A Gown of Leather and Bone" dark romantic fantasy series*

Late Fall 2026: **Sweet Dreams-Book One in the Twilight Lexicon Series;** *a separate fantasy series adjacent to the series, "A Gown of Leather and Bone" ft. Aurora's <u>first morally gray shadow daddy.</u>*

I'll see you in the next one.

. . .

X OXO
　　Your Four Favorite Raccoons in a Trench Coat,
Aurora Steinhart

ACKNOWLEDGMENTS

Wooooo look at that! We're at Book 3!

I can't believe the impact this couple has had on me and the people who have indulged in it.

This entire series of stories for Gunnar and Tiana have been some good fun so far.

And of course, I have to always thank the reader. For *my* readers, specifically.

I am not a big author by any means. I don't have a massive reader base.

But, I do have a very strong, dedicated reader base, and that alone is everything and more to me. I write to connect with souls.

Yes, it's horny, it's a bit chaotic. But there is always something I want you to take home with you when you finish reading a book of mine. A life lesson, a feeling, something. And that is what I am in the business of.

Connecting with souls, connecting with *you*.

Because no matter how many readers I have, no matter how many books I've sold, if I'm not able to connect with my readers, and thank them and recognize them just for being here, then what was the point?

So, this first thanks and acknowledgment is to *you*, the reader.

For being here, for making it this far. For interacting with me, with my content, with my stories. For being part of *my* story. Because without you, there is no Aurora Steinhart. She's just a name.

But you give Aurora a purpose, and a reason. So thank you.

Secondly, I want to thank Ana. She is always there for me, always pushing me. Or also telling me to slow down, because we all know I have zero chill and work constantly. But she is always there, always cheering me on, she's always there for me. And I am so appreciative of her and everything she does for me. Truly a wonderful best friend. Also, check out her books because she writes as well! Author AM Fernandez!

Third, I want to thank Talia. We haven't known each other long. But we have become extremely close in the time we have spent together. She is essentially my sister from another Mister, because we have the same level of unhinged chaos, and I appreciate her and everything she does. Whether that's reading my books, entertaining my dumbass, or just keeping me company. Another amazing human being! She also writes books! Author Talia Everhart!

Fourth, my wonderful artist friend Liv! The art in this book and what you may have seen on my page has been drawn by her! She is an absolutely spectacular personality; she is sweet; she is kind, and she is so funny. I love that me and her have gotten so close because she adds so much more light to my day, and life is a bit easier and carefree with her in it. She's an artist, so make sure you go check her out!

Fifth, AAron! If you don't know by now, you need to, but AAron is my number one cheerleader always! She has been mentioned in my acknowledgements in every book except for Elevated Ambitions because I hadn't known her quite yet when I was writing it. But! This woman deserves the fucking world and more because she is constantly helping others, she is always there for the people in her life. She's an incredible reader. She just absolutely blazes through books and when I see her one day, (because I fucking will AAron! I

WILL MEET YOU!) the hug we are going to have will have TEARS, it will have so much squeezing, and I will forever thank her for being in my life, and for being such a huge part of my journey as an author. Thank you so fucking much AAron for being here. Your presence is everything and more to me.

Sixth, to my sweet and wonderful local PA Nea. This girl has been apart of my author journey since the beginning. I credit meeting her to actually having my books in Barnes and Noble in our area, because I really don't think if I hadn't met her and brought my book to her that day, they wouldn't be there. Our meetings and her support have always been so sweet, so warm. Our dates at Chili's are some of the best, because I love our debriefs. I love walking around Barneys with you forever, and just having time with you. I'm so blessed and lucky to have met you and have you in my life. I LOVE YOU NAYNAY!

Seventh, to Cappa-Tiara! (Tia) Tia has been a good friend of mine for a while, but toward the end of writing Merry Checkmas, she decided to try out PAing, and I reached out to her, because I am still working on letting go of control of everything I do. We decided to take this learning journey together, and in the time she's joined me, I have already been able to breathe a bit easier. We seem to get each other on an interesting energy wave length, and our love for Sleep Token has only brought us closer together, and I can't wait to see where this journey takes us. I'm so thankful to have her here, to have her by my side and to just know someone like Tia. I love you!

And to Jasmine! If you didn't know, Jasmine's dog, Waffle, is the real life inspiration for book Waffle. I love talking to her, and I love when she sends me pictures of that sweet boy. He instantly makes my day brighter, and so does talking to Jasmine. She's a wonderful, sweet soul, and she is usually one of the first people to finish my books when ARCs go out. It's impressive actually. But! Everybody go say thank you to Jasmine for letting us have book Waffle!

Writing a book, is a lot. But when you have such an incredible and amazing support system it makes things so much easier. When you have readers that love your work, and when you have people cheering at your back all the time, it makes the dream a bit easier to see.

I can't even begin to explain how grateful I am for all these people.

And as always, thank *you*.

Thank you for being here. Thank you for indulging the chaos, and thank you for reading this.

Your Four Favorite Raccoons in a Trench Coat,
    Aurora Steinhart

ABOUT THE AUTHOR

While Aurora is merely an alias, the face behind the name has enjoyed writing and reading for as long as she can remember.

An army wife and a lifelong Alaskan, she has spent her life baking, cooking, and reading. Her lifelong passions.

Being an army wife means keeping busy with hobbies, which has resulted in a menagerie of different pastimes.

She has tried her hand at drawing, makeup, reading, weightlifting, CrossFit, cross-stitch, diamond art, video games, content creation (TikTok, YouTube, Twitch), and now being an author. Her motivation changing day by day as she gets struck by whatever idea sucked her in.

When she's not writing, she's spending time with her husband, 2 kids, 3 cats, and a dog.

instagram.com/author.aurorasteinhart
threads.com/@author.aurorasteinhart
tiktok.com/@author_aurora_steinhart

For more updates and sneak
peeks
be sure to scan the QR code
for links to my socials!